Sam Llewellyn worked as an editor and fine art dealer until he decided that life was too short. Since then, his novels, published in twelve languages, have earned him a reputation as one of the world's master storytellers and writers of maritime thrillers: many of his books are founded in personal experience. While researching them he has chased pirates in the South China Sea, raced big-money multihulls in France, and run away from cocaine dealers in Spain.

As well as writing novels, Llewellyn has published half-a-dozen children's books, and worked as a journalist for British and American newspapers such as London's *The Times* and *The Daily Telegraph*. He is a keen and knowledgeable gardener, with added interests in ornithology and history. He has also sailed yachts – several of which he built himself – all over the world. He now lives with his wife, award-winning children's writer and novelist Karen Wallace, and their two sons in a medieval house in the Welsh border country.

SAM LLEWELLYN

DEADEYE

HOUSE OF
STRATUS

This edition published in 2000 by House of Stratus, an imprint of Stratus Holdings plc, 24c Old Burlington Street, London, W1X 1RL, UK.

www.houseofstratus.com

Typeset, printed and bound by House of Stratus.

A catalogue record for this book is available from the British Library.

ISBN 0-7551-0005-0

To Barend Wolf

Chapter One

There was fog that night. An evil, brownish fog that pressed hard on the backs of the big waves that slid under the boat. They had come all the way from America, those waves. They had squeezed between the granite fortifications of the Hebrides, shrunk and reformed in the westerly breeze. Now, nothing was going to stop them except the stone shores of Scotland, seven miles down to starboard.

At least, I hoped it was seven miles. It is hard to be clear about things when your eyes are aching because it is four o'clock on Wednesday morning and you have been awake since Monday, and there is no hope of getting your head down for at least another five hours. The fog seemed to have leaked into my head, somehow. The compass card was a blur of eerie green light, and it seemed to be swinging too hard. I eased the wheel, correcting, feeling *Green Dolphin* heel as the rudders bit the water and the mainsail dug its leading edge into the breeze. I took a deep breath of fog, and admitted to myself that I was lost.

As slowly and deliberately as a drunk I put my thumb out and pushed the autopilot button. The motor ticked, and the compass steadied. I crossed the cockpit on legs so tired they were hardly there, and heaved myself painfully through the cabin hatch.

The chart table was on the starboard side. I held my eyes open with my fingers and thumbs and tried to focus on the passage chart, Imray C65, West Coast of Scotland. There were confident

1

crosses backing up the Decca fixes off the end of the long peninsula of the Mull of Kintyre, and in the narrow sound between Islay and Jura. As they passed the bottom of Mull, round the back end of Tiree and in towards the jut of the Ardnamurchan peninsula, they began to look wavery, like four-legged grey spiders. I had come the stupid way, the long way round. Night had fallen somewhere between the Dubh Artach and Skerryvore lighthouses as *Dolphin* hammered into a brisk northwesterly. People had told me that there is very little real darkness in Scotland in July. I had spent a lot of tonight wishing they were aboard, rolling in a forty-five-foot ultralight-displacement cutter through a night so thick you could shovel it.

The liquid crystal figures on the screen of the Navstar glowed green at me. The Signal Lock light shone red and steady. I took the figures down and plotted my position on the chart. It looked fine; just off the northeast tip of Coil, heading in for the mainland and the summer holidays. But there were big rocks out there in the dark, and rocks can twist Decca beams like spaghetti.

I was going to be sick.

I edged out of the navigator's seat, stumbling as a big wave came under. The nausea rolled up to the back of my throat. The cabin had a cloying, new smell, polyester resin and varnished sycamore veneer. It would be all right on deck, in the air. It was always bad below. I thought about checking my position by RDF. The nausea beat it hands down.

I staggered into the cockpit, clipped on, and sucked fog. The autopilot ticked busily to itself, the ghostly mainsail towered into the black, and the waves crunched against the sharp nose, slid under the flat sections by the keel and away from the transom. I took deep breaths. The nausea faded. In its place came a sort of optimism. It would get light, and the fog would lift, and I would get a good visual fix on some of the big landmarks which litter this part of Scotland.

The pressure of the wind on my face flickered, as if something had passed between me and its source.

Suddenly there was sweat on my body under the jerseys. There should be nothing upwind until Barra, thirty miles away. I ran aft, knocked off the autopilot, spun the wheel to starboard. The nose paid off, the deck tilting under my feet, waves roaring under the lee side as the boat picked up speed. I let out the mainsheet and ducked for the locker with the Dymo label that said FLARES. My numb fingers tore at the plastic envelope.

The wind was on the stern now. Everything had gone quiet, as it does when you bear away. But the smell of the air had changed. Before, it had smelled of salt and water. Now, it smelled of coal smoke.

I ripped the plug out of the flare's base, held it away from me, struck it on the cap. It fizzled, then lit, and the night became dazzling white, and I could see the great white wing of the mainsail, and the cabin top, and the arrowhead of the bow stretching forward over the black water and into the pearly walls of the fog.

The night bellowed, a long, grief-stricken wail. I felt a new nausea, the kind you get when fear shrinks your stomach to the size of a walnut.

Foghorn.

The sound seemed to come from everywhere at once. My head jerked round. The flare was hot in my hand as I held it aloft. It spluttered and died. My own foghorn was below. There was no time to get it. Groping for the next flare, I strained my eyes into the blood-coloured glare that was all that remained of my night vision.

Nothing.

Ahead and to port the night thickened and became solid, turned into a high black wall with a ripple of water at its foot and the loom of a dark sail above. My mouth was open. I was yelling, a small, thin sound. Everything was happening with the horrible suddenness of a dream.

As *Green Dolphin*'s nose turned away I had time to see that the wall had a bow and a stern. A man in oilskins was standing by the rail. The side lifted on its wake. There was a gigantic bang as we hit, and a sliding crash of things carrying away below. The flare slid out of my sweat-slick palm and arced into the black water. The deck's lurch flung me all the way across the cockpit. I hit my head on the locker with a bang that made it roar. *No lights*, I was thinking. *No lights*.

I rolled up on to my hands and knees, head ringing like a gong. I did not know where I was.

A huge wave lifted the deck under my shoulder. The fog turned red, a red that had nothing to do with the after-glare of the flare. I saw the man in oilskins lurch as the wave hit. He grabbed at a shroud, missed, folded up like a penknife and fell awkwardly over the side, in between the two boats.

His mouth opened as his head went down, a black O. His head hit *Green Dolphin*'s side with a heavy bang. He went into the water with a big, muffled splash.

It was the splash that woke me up. I scrambled for the horseshoe lifebuoy in its clips on the pushpit, wrenched it out and flung it into the water where the man had fallen. The other boat had sheered off. The sun rose on its deck: a searchlight. It lit black sea, and the yellow reflective tape on the lifebuoy. My brain was working horribly slowly. A blue–white light exploded in the fog. The strobe on the horseshoe. In its flash, I caught a glimpse of something like a whale, billowing. An oilskin. There was no head.

My mouth was dry, my head roaring like an engine. The man in the oilskin was floating face down. Unconscious. He was going to die, unless someone went in after him. The other boat had sheered away, become a hazy nimbus of light in the fog. I pulled the scramble net out of the emergency locker, and looped the sling of the man-overboard line around my waist. The engine started first touch. We were drifting away from the wink of the strobe. I spun the wheel. The nose came round, head to wind. The strobe approached the port side. I pulled the engine into neutral, kicked the scramble net over the side and jumped.

The water hit me like a sheet of icy metal. For a moment I thought my head was going to come off. When I came up the strobe was high in front of me, on the crest of a wave. Between me and it, the black hump of the oilskin winked, reflecting the lights. It all sank in, then. *You bloody idiot*, screamed a voice in my head. *You're overboard, in the middle of nowhere, in fog. You're going to die.* I leaned forward in the water, and kicked.

He was close. My hands hit smooth oilskin. It dented; trapped air bubbled out. The air had been keeping him afloat. Salt stung my mouth as I opened it to swear. The oilskin slid under my hands. I grabbed desperately, found the collar. My other hand tangled in seaweedy hair. *Got you*, I thought. *Got you*. More air bubbled out of the oilskins. The weight came on my arms. We were sinking.

I kicked with my feet. But the other man was a dead weight, dragging me down. Panic started to pummel my ribcage. *Let go!* shouted the voices in my head. I had heard the voices before. It did not make them any easier to ignore, but I ignored them anyway. The hand on the collar let go. The other stayed tangled in the hair. *Finished*, I thought. *We're gone*.

But the hand that had left the collar had moved on its own, following rules laid down long ago, in a different sea. It groped at my chest. There was a roar, a stiffening under the arms as the CO_2 bottle blasted gas into my lifejacket. My head broke the surface. I bobbed in the glow of *Dolphin*'s navigation lights, kicking, pulling the man's head up on to my shoulder. He coughed. I heard him gasp, and breathe.

The line under my armpits tightened. I heaved the man into the bight of the sling with me, and began to haul in, hand over hand, down to *Green Dolphin*'s glistening white hull.

The man seemed confused, swearing and kicking. His boots were tearing at my legs. I did not have the energy to kick back, because I was one hundred per cent occupied with the screaming muscles in my arms, and the rip of the line at my water-softened hands.

A hundred years later, we were alongside my boat, and I was clinging to the scramble netting. I said, 'I'll go up. We'll put you on a winch. Hang on.'

5

The man grunted, his face a dark lump against the white of the boat's side. The breath tore at my lungs as I went up. The deck thumped dry and solid underfoot. Shuddering with cold, I battered down the sails, unhitched the mainsheet and shoved the boom over the side, so the block on the end of the sheet hung down like the hook of a crane. I was afraid I was going to have to go over the side again. But the man in the water knew what to do. I waited till he had tied a bight of the scramble net on to the shackle at the sheet's end. Then I put the sheet on a big winch, and wound.

The net turned into a bag as its outside edge lifted. The man was caught inside like a snarled whale. He thudded on to the cockpit floor and lay there, streaming water.

I was at the end. I lay on the cockpit seat, groped for a flare, ripped away the tape. The fog turned a brilliant blood-red. Somewhere in the night, the foghorn bellowed again. I did not care. I could hardly hear it over the roaring in my ears.

There was a noise chipping away at the edges of my mind. Someone was shouting. I looked up. The fog had faded back to grey. There was a starboard light heaving up there in the fog, dazzlingly green. Green enough to fill my head with broken glass; wine bottle glass. I could see wine bottles. The shouting made them jingle in my head.

'Arright?' roared the voice. 'Are you *arriiiight*?'

I did not know. But I shouted: 'Got him! I got him!' Then I remembered the boat, and through the confusion I felt a new kind of fear. I pulled the flashlight from its clips with fingers that felt like bananas and shone it forward.

Green Dolphin's side decks run up to port and starboard of the cabin with the elegant curve of cavalry sabres. Now there was something wrong with the curve of the port-hand one. It was bent at its outer edge. I crawled forward, swearing weakly. My fingers found splinters.

Over the toe rail and on the fat curve of the hull-deck joint there were more splinters. When I tried to get my head through the lifelines to look, a bag of something disgusting rolled in my skull.

The nausea came back. This time there was no beating it. I was sick.

Over on the other boat, the searchlight came on again. I could see my hands, white and fungoid with wet, the jagged black shadows of the splinters on the white hull. Stove in, I thought. Stove in. First trip out in his expensive new toy, and Harry Frazer the smoothest solicitor west of Reading breaks the thing.

'I'm giving you a line,' roared the voice from the other boat. 'Coming alongside. Fenders.'

I crawled aft, hung fenders over the port side. The fog was brilliant with light, and my head ached savagely. The side of the other boat bore down, black and shining, draped with the round eyes of old motor tyres. Ropes snaked across. My mind ground like a gearbox full of sand. If he got a line aboard, he could claim salvage. His line was already aboard. I was too weak to care. 'Your fault,' I said.

'Arright,' he said.

He came down on deck, trussed *Green Dolphin* alongside, boosted the man in oilskins on to the other boat, turned and pulled me up with a strong hand.

I fell over a high bulwark on to a wooden deck. There was a door, in a deckhouse. The door opened. I stumbled in.

Chapter Two

It was hot, with a smell of burning coal. Everything was made of wood, varnish gleaming in the small lights of the engine and the Decca. Coke stove, I thought. That had been the smell in the fog.

The voice said, 'What about my bloody paint?'

I opened my mouth to tell him that if he was blundering about in the middle of the night without lights, his paint was his own problem, and what did he propose to do about my boat, which he had smashed like an eggshell, and his crew, whom he had nearly drowned. It should have been a considerable speech, but it missed a connection in the head, and came out as a grunt. The thud of the diesel picked up to a rumble. Against the pale deckhouse windows the skipper looked big and solid. Little green figures winked on the Decca, and a depth sounder whirred. There was no radar. If there had been radar, he would not have hit me.

'Bastard of a night,' said the skipper. His voice was soft, not broad enough for a fisherman's. It sounded as if he had thought better of complaining about his paint. He said, 'Thank you for picking up Hector. Wind blew me off. Thought I'd lost him.'

Hector must have been the man in the oilskins. I did not answer. I was thinking about *Green Dolphin*, jerkily, as if in a bad dream. I knew I should get him to agree about salvage. But my eyes would not focus, and my mouth tasted foul, and my mind would not do what I asked it to. I said, 'You weren't showing any lights.'

He said, 'Wasn't I?'

I said, 'We should sign a salvage form.'

He laughed. 'Arright,' he said. 'But only because you pulled out Hector.' He reached into the bookshelf above the chart table, pulled down a copy of Reed's *Almanac*, and tore out the draft agreement. 'I'm claiming zero pounds,' he said, and signed. 'Happy?'

I folded the flimsy paper and shoved it in the inside pocket of my shirt. 'Thanks,' I said. I felt dazed and remote, too sick to ask where we were going.

'This bastard fog,' he said. He sounded exasperated, weary. 'We'll take you back to the house.'

I wondered what house. But my mind kept slipping. Dodging the salvage claim was one thing. But we had spent a year putting *Green Dolphin* together, Charlie Agutter and I. What if a shroud plate came loose, and the mast came down? What if she sank alongside?

'Where have you come from?' said the skipper.

'Isle of Man,' I said.

I had sailed up to the Isle of Man from Pulteney in Devonshire, three-handed, with Charlie Agutter and Scotto Scott. *Green Dolphin* was brand new, straight out of Neville Spearman's yard in Pulteney. Charlie Agutter had designed her, and I had put up the money, with the usual boat owner's confusion of motive over whether I was doing it for fun or investment. She was forty-five feet of short-handed cruiser racer, with electrically pumped water ballast, ten feet of hydraulically lifted keel with a big lead bulb on the end, a fully battened mainsail and three roller foresails. She should have been a hairy brute of a boat. But Charlie had made her sweet tempered and solid, as easy to sail as a fat old cruiser, but alarmingly quick when you wanted her to be. We were bringing her up North to show her off to some people, with a view to raising enough interest to start a production run.

But her good manners had made me over-confident.

Charlie and Scotto had gone home from Ramsey because *Green Dolphin* had been behaving very nicely, and I reckoned she would be no trouble to single hand. Anywhere else in the world, that might have been true. Here on the West Coast of Scotland, matters had not unfolded according to plan.

I had done very little single handing before. I had meant to anchor up at night. But I had put off finding an anchorage and got myself caught out. It had not taken long for me to realise I had bitten off more than I could chew, but by that time, it had been too late; I was in the black night, wishing I was in my office in Bristol with the complacent hum of Orchard Street coming through the window. And now the whole scheme looked like being stillborn.

'Single hander, eh?' said the helmsman. He was a big man, emanating a faint smell of whisky.

'That's right.'

The dark silhouette of his head shook slowly against the red and green reflections in the wheelhouse windows. 'Hard man,' he said. There was an edge of exasperation in his voice.

My head thumped. The thirty wakeful hours piled on top of me in a suffocating heap. I sat down on the chart-table seat and drank the cup of tea I was given. Then I must have gone to sleep.

I had a dream; not the usual dream, but bad enough.

I was in the Lampedusa in the King's Road. I was twelve years old. As usual, my sister Vi was at the head of the table. She had an actor on one side, and a film director on the other, and she was telling a story with big battings of her Venus Flytrap eyelashes. Outside, the King's Road was made of water, not tarmac. There was a man in an oilskin out there, drowning, roaring for help. I wanted to go after him, but Vi kept nailing me with little beckoning movements of her long red fingernails. Next to me, Davina Leyland was explaining patiently that it was silly to rescue drowning people when her divorce needed handling. And the whole table, the whole fatuous bunch of them, was nodding and wagging fingers –

I woke up. I was in a plank bunk in a beautifully varnished slot of a cabin, lit by a polished brass porthole with a faded chintz curtain. We were in calm water, and the engine was running smooth and fast.

I stumbled up the companionway and through the wheelhouse into the cold morning air, and looked through my headache at the big white spearhead of *Green Dolphin*'s deck.

The mast was still up. There was an ugly crushed area three feet down the port side with a hole in the middle. But it looked like a repair job, not a rebuild. Could have been worse. Lucky Frazer. The sweat of relief began to flow and I was able to look around me.

The boat I was on could have come straight off a seaside postcard of the 1930's. She was about sixty-five feet long, with a high, straight stem and a round stern. She had a stubby mainmast, a mizzen, and a squat wheelhouse aft. Forward, where the cabin top would have been if she were a yacht, there was a big hatch cover. Her wooden sides were tarry black, and her pine deck bore palimpsests of fish scales and blood. She was a fine specimen of a beaten-up, overworked, indestructible sailing trawler.

Just at the moment, she was trailing a deep vee of wake down the glassy waters of a bay. On the shore of the bay, green slopes of mountain leaped from stony beaches towards a sky blue as a baby's eyes. The reflections of the mountains were brilliant green in the water.

Ahead, the bay narrowed and turned a corner. There was still fog down there, trapped in the folds of the hills. Waist deep in it stood more mountains, their bases cloaked in mist so their jagged ridges floated free, like peaks in a Chinese painting.

The man at the wheel was tall, dressed despite the morning chill in a once-white T-shirt and filthy blue dungarees. He had a broken nose, kinked reddish hair that looked as if he had not brushed it for a month, a beard, and pale-blue eyes that would have looked mad if they had not looked amused.

The high nose of the old wooden boat had moved round a dogleg bend. A small sea loch lay ahead, a sheet of water four hundred yards long and two hundred wide. Strands of mist lay across the water between us and the shingle of a river mouth at the far end; the tide was high. The man with the beard shoved the wheel hard over, avoiding the glassy patches of hidden rocks.

'Loch Beag,' he said. 'Best shelter anywhere.' He pulled back the throttles. The engine died to a dull chug, so the sound of the wake on the mussel-black fringes of the loch was a powerful roar. Ahead and to port, a wood of grey–green eucalyptus climbed the slopes of the mountain. From the trees rose steep Victorian gables; along the high-water mark, where the green turf became a beach of big pebbles, there was a shed and a solid looking granite quay.

We were nosing up to a red-mottled can buoy. The bearded man padded forward, hauled the mooring pennant aboard and made fast. Then he came back aft, and said abruptly, 'I'm very glad you jumped in after Hector.' He paused, looking at me sideways. 'What's your boat made of?'

'Wood and epoxy core,' I said. 'Glass inside and out.'

'You'll not get that fixed this side of Oban,' he said. 'But I've got the stuff here. It's a fairish step out.' He pointed a thick finger inland. 'Twenty-one miles of single track road that way. By sea, most of a day to Arisaig, if you call that a place, and another bit on to Mallaig. So we'd be glad if you'd stay.'

He had a strange, blunt way of speaking, as if he was not used to the social niceties. I had spent enough time in Orchard Street to find it disconcerting when a complete stranger so obviously meant what he said.

'We'll be glad of the company,' he said. 'Fiona and I.'

Last time I had accepted an invitation from someone I did not know had been for a weekend in Somerset with a lady member of the Bristol Stock Exchange whom I had separated from her adulterous husband. The lady stockbroker had crept into my room on the midnight and proposed the oldest method of securing a discount on my bill. She had been very angry when I had told her in the nicest possible way that I had an office and a sick sister to support, and that cash, in full, was the preferred means of settlement.

This time, things were different. I had no car, and a hole in the boat, and a headache so bad that it was a relief not to have to do any thinking for myself.

So I said, 'Thank you. That would be good,' and stuck out my hand. He looked like the kind of person who would attach value to a handshake. 'Harry Frazer,' I said.

It was like shaking hands with a mole wrench. 'Ewan Buchan,' he said. 'Let's get some breakfast.'

Chapter Three

The quay smelled of peat and wet pine needles. Doggedly, I followed Ewan's huge shoulders along a wet track past a line of roofless cottages, through a gate in a deer-fence and down a tunnel through a thicket of rhododendrons.

The track became a path. The path led across a rushy lawn and up to the front of the house we had seen from the loch. I squinted at the slate-hung gables with eyeballs that felt as if they were full of hot lead.

When I had gone to be a lawyer, old Arthur Somers had sent me to hang around outside a lot of addresses, and I had quickly found out that you can tell a great deal about people by their houses. This one was odd. The windows in the left-hand gable were peeling, and the frames looked as if they would not last long. In the right-hand gable, the windows looked neat and freshly-painted. There was a flower bed on the right of the door, with a big fuchsia bush and some herbs, and no weeds. On the left of the door, couch grass and ground elder swarmed among a pile of rope-pattern edging tiles.

Ewan kicked the door open with a crash. There was a pine-panelled hall, with a stag's head on the wall and a Bukhara carpet reduced by salt and wear to a tan-coloured road map.

'Take your coat off,' he said.

The door of the hall opened, and a woman came in.

'Fiona,' said Ewan.

'Would you mind not kicking the door down?' she said. Her voice was sharp, West Coast American.

'We've got an injury,' said Ewan.

The woman looked at me. She had dark hair cut in a severe pageboy, a wind-brown face with high cheekbones and a saddle of freckles across the nose. She was wearing jeans and a jersey made of a lot of different-coloured wools that were soothing to my aching eyes. The accountant in my head totted up the jersey and the haircut, and found that they added up to considerable money. 'Oh?' she said, in the tone of voice of someone presented with a stray dog.

'I got a bang on the head,' I said suddenly. Nothing was coming out right. I was feeling very weak, and there was a nasty, clammy sweat on my temples.

'We had a wee collision,' said Buchan. 'Hector fell overboard. Mr Frazer jumped in and pulled him out of the water.'

She said, 'Where?' She sounded interested now.

He said, 'North of Ardnamurchan.'

Her eyes were greyish-green. She looked at me hard, for maybe ten seconds. If anyone else had looked at me like that, it would have felt hostile. With her, it was as if she was trying to lever the lid off my mind and look in. She said, 'That was kind of you.' Her face broke into a smile. Broke is the only word for it: the smile transformed her. It lit up her face, and gathered you in, and made you one of the gang. She said, 'Sit down.'

I sat.

She prodded my head with fingers that felt firm and certain of what they were doing. I said, 'Are you a nurse?'

'I'm a knitter,' she replied, off-hand. 'Don't talk.'

I needed no encouragement. She found the lump behind my left ear. It hurt. Despite the smile, I felt ill-at-ease. In my world, strangers who found people injured called the doctor. 'You'll live,' she said. Her voice was impersonal but good-humoured. 'Breakfast's ready.'

We went into a pine-panelled dining-room with windows overlooking the loch. Ewan told Fiona what had happened. They behaved to each other easily, like a long-married couple. But there were no rings on Fiona's hands. I felt out of place; a recipient of charity, through no fault of my own. It was an injury to the pride.

'So,' said Fiona, when she had dealt me out eggs and bacon. 'What were you doing, sailing around by yourself in the middle of the night?'

I chewed at a bit of bacon that I discovered I did not want. 'I was bringing my boat up to see a friend,' I said.

Ewan said, 'Who was that?' I was surprised to see his eyes narrow above the reddish beard, not particularly friendly.

'Prosper Duplessis. He lives just up the coast.'

'The one who has the parties,' said Fiona. I nodded. That was what people usually noticed about Prosper. The bacon was disagreeing with me. I wanted to go to bed.

Fiona said, 'So what do you do for a living?'

I said, 'I'm a lawyer.'

'What kind of lawyer?' said Fiona. She was looking out of the window at the ripple made by a seal's head on the glassy water of the loch. I had stopped being a hero; polite conversation was being made.

'I deal with people's divorces,' I said.

She watched me, nodding, as if her suspicions were being confirmed. I felt an urge to justify myself, but I also felt sick. I got up and lurched out of the front door, and was sick, in a rhododendron bush. Fiona followed me out. 'You're concussed,' she said. Her voice had softened again. The stray dog was ill. I stood bent over the wet grass and felt that I was not appearing at my best. 'You'd better go to bed.' She led me up some stairs and into a faded bedroom that smelled of old carpet. I lay down on the iron bed and told her I was all right, and that I wanted to have a look at the damage on the boat. Halfway through the sentence, I went out like a light.

Next time I woke, my mind was working. My Rolex said eleven o'clock. There was a holiday to be had out there, and I had worked long and hard in a sweaty office to earn it. In the bathroom, I found a razor and a shaving brush. My face is longish, and thinnish, and it seldom looks the picture of radiant health. This morning it was worse than usual: pale, with bags under the eyes and a heavy stubble. The eyes themselves were dark and sunken. The general effect was of a minor Spanish brigand. I improved it slightly with the razor, then went downstairs. Fiona was in a big, dank kitchen hung with drab skeins of wool.

She said, 'I hear you broke your boat.'

I shrugged.

'Hector'll do the work.' She paused. Again, the eyes were sharp and direct. 'Have a little breakfast. Then you can call your friends.'

I opened my mouth to tell her I was off as soon as I could get Prosper to come and collect me. Then I thought about *Green Dolphin*, and the repairs. At Neville Spearman's in New Pulteney, there had been heated sheds and trained laminators and Charlie Agutter prowling the yard with his eyes peeled. Up here, there would be neither. The holiday spirit weakened. Repairs were going to be a problem.

This time, the egg stayed down. Afterwards, I rang Prosper.

' 'Arry,' he said. His family came from Martinique. He had been back in Europe five years, but he still sounded as if he gargled with rum every day. 'Where the hell are you?'

Fiona was squashing a coil of wool into a fuming saucepan. I asked her. She shoved her black hair out of her eyes. 'Kinlochbeag Lodge,' she said.

'Kinlochbeag Lodge,' I said, into the telephone.

Bon Dieu,' said Prosper. 'Have they started feeding you on seaweed yet?'

'Bacon and eggs,' I said.

'Well, watch it. They wear sandals.' I checked Fiona's feet. She was wearing hiking boots.

I told him what had happened.

'Lucky you didn't get killed,' he said. 'You want to win money, you be more careful.'

Prosper was a bad influence, but he was also my oldest friend. We had made a bet six weeks ago in Bristol when he had come down to buy wine at Avery's. Five thousand pounds for the winner of the Three Bens Race, in which the competitors race in boats between the feet of the three highest mountains in Western Scotland, and on foot to their summits.

'I mean it,' he said. 'Brown rice, the *Guardian*, Save the Whales. Ewan's mad, and Fiona's a Girl Scout. They used to live together, but they split up on political grounds, and now they just live together, if you see what I mean.'

'Oh,' I said. The windows in the gables began to make sense.

'Bean salad,' said Prosper. 'Vegeburgers. You'll lose your edge.'

'My edge is fine,' I said.

'Sure,' said Prosper, with irony. 'You want a little race?'

I said, 'Boat took a little ding. I'm going to fix it.' No sense in boosting his confidence by telling him *Green Dolphin* had her port side stove in.

'Nothing bad, I hope?' he said. 'I'm going round St Kilda on sea trials. Four days. I hoped we could have a little workout, see how the boats go.'

'Too bad,' I said.

'By the way, your office called.'

We rang off.

Prosper and I had met on his first day at boarding school. He had been four thousand miles away from his parents. I had no parents, by then. He had been a fat child, suntanned the colour of milk chocolate, with a gift for making people laugh. I had been thin and athletic. We had made friends, and my sister Vi used to take us out to tea at the Red Lion in Salisbury during the brief moment in the history of the movies when she had been a starlet in demand.

Later, we had gone to different schools. I had been a runner, and he had been a sailor, and we had written to each other from time to time. We had knocked about the Caribbean together after he had finished university and I had done my law exams. Then his father had died, and he had become very rich, and bought his house up here on the West Coast to go with the one on Cap Ferrat, and the apartment in New York, and the rest of them.

'So you'll stay for a while,' said Fiona. 'It'll be kind of dull, compared with Prosper.' She laughed, and went to her studio.

I thought about calling the office. Cyril the clerk did not believe in his breadwinner taking holidays. He would be sitting up there at his steel desk, encouraging the clients to fret, and getting ready to take it out on me. Just for the moment, I was not going to give him the pleasure. So I went down to the shore and picked my way gingerly along the stony beach towards the quay.

Green Dolphin's tall, slim mast and thick boom stuck up on the far side. The tide was out; she was sitting on dark-grey sand on the tripod of her twin rudders and retracted keel. Wet cushions and clothes and charts were pegged along the lifelines, fluttering in the small breeze from the loch. Ewan was sitting on her transom, rolling a cigarette. Hector was washing down her fat white side with a hose connected to a tap on the quay.

Hector looked up when he heard me coming. He had a face that on a good day would have been beefy. Today it was puffy and there was a bandage round his head. 'Getting the salt off,' he said. He paused, apparently locked in a struggle with acute shyness. 'The wife's very grateful to you.'

Seeing the hole in *Dolphin*'s side had brought the blood to my head. I said, 'If you showed some lights, it wouldn't have happened.'

'Bad night of the week for lights,' said Ewan, quickly. 'It was a cock-up. Bloody wind had me away before I knew Hector'd gone. Listen, though. Hector's a great boatbuilder. You'd better tell him what you want.'

He had a point. I had spent a lot of money getting *Dolphin* right, and so had Charlie Agutter. To come out even we needed to make a good impression, and it is hard to make a good impression with a caved-in boat. Hector cleared his throat, diffidently. 'We'll take it back to the clean wood,' he said. 'The timber'll be cedar?'

I nodded.

'So we dry her out, and we cut scarf, and put in new strips, with epoxy glue. Plane them fair. Then we laminate inside and out. There's no frames touched. I checked.'

His voice was tentative and quiet. So far, he seemed to know what he was talking about. Suddenly, I realised that he was grateful, and anxious to please. It was so long since I had met anyone like that that I hardly remembered how to react.

'If you'd come below,' he said.

We went below. For half an hour he took me through the repair in great detail. By the end of it I knew that he knew more about boatbuilding in composite than I did, and probably just as much as James Dixon, who ran the building unit at Spearman's.

'Will that be the way of it?' he said.

'Fine,' I said. 'Fine.'

'You fixed?' said Ewan when we went back on deck. 'I told you he was a great man. Now I have to go up the loch. Come along, I'll show you the water. Fiona will be dyeing wool. Filthy stink.'

So your boat is smashed, I told myself. It's getting repaired, free. So you're stuck on your way to your holiday. But you're stuck in a place where the mountains go all the way up to the sky, and there is no car exhaust, and no telephone, and no Cyril the clerk looking like an undertaker at a train crash and telling you that Mr Smith has just left Mrs Smith for a stripper called Zsa Zsa, and would you please secure him custody of the children.

So I said, 'Why not?'

Weed waved in the clear brown water of the loch as Ewan rowed us out. The sailing trawler had *Flora* painted on its fat transom in gold paint, with scrolls and curlicues. 'Fiona did that,' said Ewan. 'Very artistic.' We went up the side, and into the immaculately varnished wheelhouse.

The diesels started with a cloud of black smoke. Ewan told me to steer and went forward to cast off. I eased the heavy brass lever to AHEAD. Ponderously, the big wooden hull began moving down the loch.

Ewan came in, rapped the dials and frowned. 'Bloody engine,' he said. 'Saving up for a new one.' I hauled the wheel so *Flora*'s nose swung clear of a glassy patch of weed. He reached up a hand and pulled a bottle of Glenmorangie and two glasses from the netting above the fuse board.

He said, 'That collision was my fault. We'll mend your boat, good as new. Will that satisfy you?'

It was a handsome offer, because insurance companies do not like single handers. I said, 'Yes.'

'Fine,' he said. 'Dram?'

'Please.'

He poured, and handed me a glass. 'No hard feelings. *Slàinte*.' The air was transparent as crystal that day. The rocks and hills seemed to glow with a light so intense that I could see the whiskers on a seal's head three hundred yards away. Ewan showed me the marks and transits that indicated sunken rocks. On the seaward side of the narrows the swell hit us, lifting the bow as we turned north across the mouth of the bay.

'Skye,' said Ewan, pointing northwest. The Cuillins were an indigo saw blade lying across the horizon. 'Rhum, Eigg, Muck.' To the westward, the islands sat like huge green sphinxes in the hard dazzle of the sea. 'And that's Dunmurry.'

He gave me a pair of battered Zeiss binoculars. I jammed the wheel with my knee and focused them on a grey speck where a headland ran down to the water to the northeast.

I had heard of Dunmurry, and seen the articles about it in Sunday colour magazines. But the photographers had not done the place justice.

To say it was a castle is like saying that the Eiffel Tower is a radio aerial. It was the kind of castle a military architect might have dreamed up after a cheese supper: a forest of towers and turrets, garderobes and crenellations, erupting from the snout of a rocky peninsula. From an anchorage to the side, enclosed by a low promontory of rock, jutted the masts of several boats. They were tall, those masts, and carried a lot of rigging. Serious masts.

'It's a hotel nowadays,' said Ewan. 'Ever heard of David Lundgren?'

If you were interested in boats, or litigation, or both, you could not help it. Lundgren had a vision of a world in which every bay and estuary would contain a marina, and every marina would be owned by him. Recently, he had been heard to express interest in producing a new generation of super fast cruising boats. Charlie Agutter and I thought that *Green Dolphin* would suit him fine. He was immensely rich, immensely bossy, and slightly Norwegian. The Press loved him; people he did business with were generally less enthusiastic.

'Bought it the other year,' said Ewan. 'Turned the house into a hotel, and he gets his mates to come and stay there. They're the only ones who can afford it.'

I said, 'He's one of the people I'm up here to see.'

'Is that right?' For a moment, Ewan looked faintly shifty. 'Fact is, I quite like going in for a pint. Beer's expensive, but it's a stunning place.'

'Who built it?' I asked.

'Bloke called Wright. English big shot, friend of Queen Victoria. Wanted a holiday cottage.'

I said, 'It must have been built about the same time as Kinlochbeag.'

He nodded. 'The Wrights lasted a long time at Dunmurry,' he said.

'What about the Buchans at Kinlochbeag?'

He shook his head. 'Nah,' he said. 'My old man bought it in 1934. He made a load of money at the fishing. He had a steam drifter, out of Aberdeen. He caught fish, and bought fish, and sold fish, and he finished by canning fish. He made a million in the thirties, cheap herring for the guys in the slump. But million or no million, none of those kiltie bastards had a word for him, because he was only Jocko Buchan from Albert Quay.' He made a face.

'Scotland's still a feudal country, and it was a lot worse then. They used to hold their noses when they saw him coming. Hilarious.' He finicked tobacco along a cigarette paper. 'Smoke?' he said.

'I gave up,' I said. 'So he came up here to get away from all that?'

'Hard to tell,' said Ewan. 'He was a funny bloke, my old man. He loved the fishing. He had *Flora* built as a yacht, but at the last minute he told them to forget about the grand staterooms and leave in the fish hold. Then he bought the Lodge and ten thousand acres, because he reckoned that if he had ten thousand acres he'd never have to meet anyone who didn't work for him. And in case he got bored, he started a basking shark fishery. The oil from their liver's full of vitamins. That's why you've got the quay at the Lodge.' He licked the paper and lit the cigarette. The smoke hung in his beard before the wind pulled it out of the wheelhouse window. 'After he'd been here a couple of years, he got his confidence up and he went round to visit Wright, grandson of the first Wright, as neighbour to neighbour. The guy had some folk staying in the house: Fred Astaire, Oswald Mosley; you know, the whole bit in the thirties, there. Wright came down to the quay at Dunmurry with all his guests in a procession to meet the old man. The old man was pleased as anything. He brought *Flora* alongside the quay. And when he stepped ashore, Wright and all his posh guests put out their fingers and their thumbs, military precision, and held their noses.'

You could see the castle with the naked eye, now. I did not like the look of it any more.

'So the old man walked up to Wright, and he knocked him off his quay,' said Ewan mildly. 'Then he sailed away back to the Lodge, and he never set foot off of the place again.'

He paused, watching the black-and-white serpent neck of a Great Northern Diver swim across the bow. 'I had some hellish rows with the old bastard,' he said. 'He'd kill anything that walked, flew or swam. Thought I was a right Trotskyite. But since he died,

I like to go into the dining-room at Dunmurry, and have a wee spit on the parquet, *in memoriam.*'

The masts in the anchorage were growing taller above the grey wall of rock sheltering it from the south. I said, 'And what does Mr Lundgren have to say?' From what I had heard, spit on his parquet was the kind of thing Mr Lundgren would not take to at all.

The yellow teeth showed in his beard. 'Mr Lundgren has his reasons for keeping in with the natives,' he said. 'Particularly me.' He gestured to seaward. Beyond the loom of the islands a long bulk carrier was heading north, high-sided, in ballast. 'That one's away to load up at the quarry. There'll be another coming south, loaded.'

'What do you mean?'

Ewan pitched his cigarette out of the window. 'He bought a mountain,' he said. 'Ben Dubh. Cubic mile of granite. He builds his marinas with the stuff, ships it off everywhere. I run Sea Watch, which looks out for dirty water, dead seals, general muck caused by the several hundred guys round here who spend their lives trying to turn salt water into money, and never mind the neighbours. Lundgren knows his politics. He knows he can find himself in difficulties if I make a fuss about his filth at the quarry. But there's thirty jobs up there, and I know damn well that nobody'd pay any mind if I did, so I don't make that much fuss. He keeps the filth down to a dull roar, and I tease him a wee bit. It's what you could call the Caledonian standoff.'

We were passing the end of the breakwater, a horizontal finger of grey rock topped with big, closely mortared lumps of granite. The boats in the anchorage looked expensive. The biggest was a black cutter with a long counter and a spoon bow.

'*Asteroid,*' said Ewan. 'Lundgren's wee runabout. Maintenance budget like the Forth Bridge. Let's see if the man's home.'

We tied up alongside the quay and went ashore.

Chapter Four

A path of hard-packed grit led round the western shore of the anchorage, through a double gate of gilt wrought iron in a high granite wall. We followed it among species rhododendrons and flame-coloured Watsonias, upwards on to a terrace. A couple of gardeners were weeding. They greeted Ewan as if they knew him well and liked him. At the end of the terrace were tables with umbrellas whose fringes fluttered uneasily in the cold breeze. Through the French windows was a long mahogany bar and a barman in a white coat. 'Pinched the bar off the Aintree racecourse,' said Ewan.

The barman looked up as we entered. 'Good morning, Mr Buchan,' he said. The faint narrowing of the eyes in his large, bland face made me suspect that he did not share the outdoor staff's affection.

Ewan ordered a couple of pints. The room was high Edwardian, with big, dark Dutch sea paintings hung on red damask wallpaper and crossed claymores over the doors.

'It was a hotel, after Wright went bust,' said Ewan, leaning back with his elbows on the bar. 'Then it was the Commandos. Then it was some German, who shot himself. Then Lundgren.'

The French windows opened, and a small round man with ginger hair came in. He had a hard, compact look; he was wearing a guernsey and faded red O M Watts yachting trousers, 'Talk of the devil,' said Ewan. 'Harry Frazer, David Lundgren.'

We shook hands. Lundgren's hand was small and hot and dry. His face was bright sun-red, his eyes pale grey on either side of a snub nose. He looked like a miniature Viking.

'Nipped in for a pint,' said Ewan. 'Have a drink.'

'Thank you,' said Lundgren. The barman gave him something clear, with a slice of lemon in it. Tonic water, at a guess; Lundgren did not look like a morning drinker. 'So you're staying at Kinlochbeag?'

'Hector's tuning his boat,' said Ewan, tipping the last of his pint into his beard. 'Excuse me.' He winked at me so Lundgren could not see, and left the bar.

Lundgren reached over the bar, took out a box of grey, cardboard-filtered cigarettes. 'My vice,' he said. 'I had the good fortune to do a deal with Gorbachev, and he sends me some.' He smiled. It had the feel of a well-used little confidence: Lundgren puts you at your ease, while making sure you know he's a big shot. 'What's your boat?'

It was a good opening. I told him about *Green Dolphin*. He blew smoke, and nodded. 'He's a clever boy, that Charlie Agutter,' he said when I had finished. 'We'll have to see how you do. You'll be sailing the Three Bens?'

'Of course.'

'Me too,' he said. 'I've got some friends up to help me sail *Asteroid*, and a couple of Royal Marines to do the running, in case I feel tired.' He puffed smoke at me. 'Getting a little professional, the Three Bens. Nowadays it is more a test of perseverance than of sailing.' He smiled, a chilly Scandinavian smile. 'I think that is why I enjoy it.'

I nodded, to show him I was listening. He obviously liked the sound of his own voice.

'A persevering man can get a lot done in these parts. One thinks of the builders of Kinlochbeag, or this place.' He waved his cigarette at the French windows. 'The spirit that built a sun terrace facing the prevailing wind in the worst climate in Europe.' He waited for the laugh.

'Or your quarry,' I said, to provoke him.

He shrugged. 'Business with pleasure,' he said. 'I have done a lot of sailing up here, and I need a lot of stone. So I started to look for a granite mountain with a deep-water anchorage alongside it. And I found it. So now we ship Scottish rock all over the world.'

'Isn't that rather expensive?'

He sipped his drink. His eyes had the faraway look of a pocket calculator's screen. 'A big investment, sure. But demand is always good, and sea transport is the cheapest there is, per mile.' Two lean men had come into the bar. They had cropped heads, thin moustaches, and they were wearing tracksuits. He looked at his watch. 'You must come and have a look, one day.'

I said, 'I'd like to.'

'I'll look forward to making the acquaintance of your boat,' he said. They left, Lundgren strutting in front, dwarfed by the others, cigarette clamped between his teeth.

I finished my drink. The barman brought the bill. Lundgren's tonic water was marked at five pounds.

I said to the barman, 'Is that right?'

His pale face was impassive, even smug. 'Absolutely correct, sir.'

'Always working, your boss,' I said. He did not answer.

I paid and went out on to the cold terrace. The view was stunning, across the garden to the anchorage and down to the purple peaks of Ardnamurchan. It was not hard to understand how Lundgren had got where he was. Nor would it be hard to understand if the friends who had to pay hotel bills when they came to stay and the chance acquaintances who paid clip-joint prices for his Schweppes liked him less than they pretended.

I descended the terrace steps between red terracotta pots of pelargonium and agapanthus, and walked down the path through the garden. The gardeners were still weeding. I asked one of them if he had seen Ewan.

'He's away to the fish pens,' said the man. He pointed out a track that led off into a wood of Scots pine. A small wooden notice on the gate across the track said PRIVATE. I hesitated.

'Straight the way down,' said the man, encouragingly.

Pushing the notice aside, I went through.

The path was black, peaty mud, with the deep marks of tractor tyres instead of carefully raked grit. The spine of the peninsula rose on the right. Soon I was walking along the sunless southern shore of a narrow black loch. I passed an untidy huddle of asbestos-and-cement farm buildings, then a pile of tin cans and bottles and old oil drums, smouldering.

The track went round a headland where the far shore came to meet it. Beyond the headland, the loch broadened out into a wide sheet of water. It looked deep, that water. Where the tide was hurrying in through the narrows there were great boils and eddies, as if it was pouring over underwater ledges. Fifty yards ahead, a hollow square of white-painted staging projected from the shore. It was the kind of raft you see in almost every inlet on the West Coast: a walkway round the perimeter of an underwater cage, full of growing salmon. A fish farm.

Ewan was out on the staging. There was another man with him, much shorter, dark-haired, thickset. They seemed to be talking. Ewan was standing too close, as was his habit, towering over the other man. I heard his laugh booming across the flat black water. The other man shook his head. Ewan said something else.

The other man hit him.

I saw his elbow go back, his shoulder drop. Then his fist banged into Ewan's stomach. And as Ewan folded forwards, the smaller man caught the front of his jersey and slammed his forehead into Ewan's face. Ewan's knees slackened, his hip caught the rail, and he went over the side of the staging and into the water. The splash spread heavy ripples towards me. The small man's boots crashed on the staging as he ran for the shore. Another man came out of a shed, shouted something.

I stood there, frozen. Assault, I thought. That man has just assaulted Ewan.

A diesel started. A battered workboat nosed out from behind the raft. The small man was in it, and the man who had been in the shed. The man who had been in the shed had blond hair cut so short his scalp shone pink in the sun.

I shouted, 'Hey!'

Neither of them looked round. The engine noise rose from a chug to a rattle and the workboat slid rapidly towards the open sea, pushing a pile of tide in front of its blunt nose. I looked for Ewan's head in the water. There was no sign of it. It should have been showing by now. My palms were suddenly slippery with sweat. I slithered down the rocky glacis to the staging, hammered along it to the point where he had gone over the side. Hundreds of tails thrashed the water, and the torpedo shadows of a shoal of young salmon shot for the far side of the cage. I looked over the edge at the point where Ewan had fallen in. There was clear black water; no sign of him.

Something knocked against the walkway. A hand appeared, streaming water, clawed at the timber on the inside of the walkway, the side with the cage. I bent and grasped it. The hand clutched mine, convulsively. I heaved.

Nothing happened.

I thought, I have just had a drink with a Sunday supplement millionaire in his smart hotel. There cannot be a man drowning six inches under my feet. I am somewhere else, asleep, and this is a bad dream like all the other bad dreams. But the seagulls were crying, and the clatter of the workboat's engine was fading, and the hot sweat was rolling out of my hair, and the hand was cold and wet, clenched on to mine until it hurt. The pain was real, and so was everything else. I could hear the tide gurgling in the cage's mooring lines – I tore my hand free, shoved my arm over the outside edge of the walkway, and groped. I touched wet cloth. A jersey, I entangled my fist in it and pulled, hard.

For a moment, there was resistance. On the other side of the walkway, the hand still groped. I kicked at it. It scrabbled back into the water. I pulled hard on the jersey. The resistance ceased. The mass gave, coming away from the wet wall of the cage where the tide had plastered it. I found an arm. Ewan's head emerged. His fingers gripped the planking. He lay for a minute half out of the water, coughing. Blood ran from his nose and flowed across the duckboards. The water of the cage frothed as the salmon fought for the drips.

Gulls screamed on in the bright sky. I was breathing nearly as hard as he was.

When he could talk, he said, 'I am a stupid eejit.'

I said, 'Are you all right?'

'I put my arm through the netting. I could have croaked.'

'And it would have been murder, or anyway manslaughter.'

He struggled into a sitting position. 'Bastard,' he said. 'I knew he'd be at it.'

I was wet, I had been frightened, and I was very low on patience. 'What the hell are you talking about?' I said.

'Bastard looks after the cage for Jerry Fine,' he said. 'He hates seals. So he feeds them fish with strychnine in.' He pointed down the shore.

I followed the line of his finger. Something grey and bloated bumped in the ripples. A dead seal.

'Angus told me,' he said. 'The gardener. I told the wee brute I wanted a look in his shed.' His face was bluish-white, except for the crimson stripe of blood from his nose. His teeth were chattering, with shock as much as cold. 'I want to look in that shed. See where he keeps his bloody poison.'

We hobbled back along the duckboards. The shed doors were shut and locked with a big padlock.

'Give me a rock,' said Ewan. 'I'll smash the lock off.'

'I am not about to be an accessory to breaking and entering,' I said. I was getting angry, in the aftermath of the fear. He wrenched at my arm.

I said, 'If you've got a problem, tell the police. Move it.'

He moved it. We plodded up the track and through the gate with the PRIVATE sign. The walk improved his colour. At the double gates we met Lundgren, with his two men in tracksuits and a blonde woman. The woman was tall and looked like a magazine editor's version of the Nordic Ideal.

'Lisbeth,' said Ewan. 'What are you doing here?'

Her eyes were blue as twin swimming pools. They widened as they took in the stripe of blood on his upper lip.

'Hurt yourself?' said Lundgren.

I said, 'I have just been witness to an assault – '

'I cannot be responsible for what takes place in the parts of my property not open to the public,' he said.

Ewan said, 'I hope you don't know what they're at in your sheds down there.'

'That's Jerry Fine's department,' said Lundgren. 'See you at the regatta.'

We walked down the quay. There was very little else to say. Back on the boat, Ewan mopped the blood off his face, and said, 'Sorry about that.'

I shrugged.

'Lundgren's warned me off before,' Ewan went on. 'At the quarry. But he gets bored up here. So he gets all these wee neds up here, from the army and that, and they play tough guys.' His long arm went up for the whisky bottle, and he drank. 'That'll be why he's got Lisbeth down. She's assistant manager at the quarry, but he's not after her body, like any reasonable human being would be. He's got her around because she climbs.'

'What about the man who hit you?' I said. 'Will you take it any further?'

Ewan's eyes were dangerous and narrow. 'His turn will come,' he said. 'Sometime after Tuesday.'

'What happens on Tuesday?'

'It is two days after the Kinlochbeag Regatta,' he said, and showed his yellow teeth. 'In which I hope you will take part.'

He finished the bottle, tossed it out of the wheelhouse window, and hit the engine start button. *Flora*'s diesels rumbled. 'Cast off,' he said.

I cast off the shore lines feeling that I had been fobbed off. *Flora*'s fat stern moved away from the quay and her stubby mastheads pivoted against the fluffy white clouds.

Her stern began to heave and corkscrew, slewing as the seas came under her quarter. The atmosphere in the wheelhouse was fug and diesel, mixed with stale coal smoke from the saloon stove. I opened the window and concentrated on not being sick. Ewan went to change his clothes and came up looking better, carrying a new whisky bottle. 'One thing,' he said. 'Would you mind not telling Fiona?'

'If you like.'

'We used to be...shacked up. Not any more, of course.' There was a hot glaze to his pale-blue eyes. I was not surprised; in the seventeen hours that I had known him, he had drunk most of a bottle of whisky. 'But she takes things a bit seriously.'

He shuffled out on deck and wound up the sails, main and mizzen, jib and foresail, the colour of dried blood. The push of the wind steadied the boat's motion a little. The tide of seasickness receded, but not far enough to make me inclined to ask any more questions.

We picked up the mooring at nine o'clock. The sky was not yet touched with the dusk that passes for night at these latitudes in the month of July. He said, 'Come up to dinner.'

I was beginning to feel my head again, where I had hit it on the locker last night. I said, 'I think I'll go to bed, thank you all the same.'

'Tomorrow, then,' he said. 'You can't sleep on your boat, the state it's in. Kip down on *Flora*, if you want. There's food on the boat.'

I thanked him. Then I rowed him ashore, and went to look at *Green Dolphin*.

Chapter Five

I was not expecting a lot. Prosper had told me about the working habits of the West of Scotland, which he claimed were sluggish even by Martinique standards. The timber that Hector had hosed down would take days to dry out in this climate, and there was no way it could be repaired until it was dry.

I waved ineffectually at the midges and walked along the quay. Cables ran out of the shed, across the deck and into a little square shelter of grey polythene built over the hole in the side. I stepped aboard. The plastic sheeting was warm to the touch; there was a heater in there, and a dehumidifier. This might be Western Scotland, but this was the kind of service you got in Newport, R I or the Solent.

I rowed back to *Flora*, immensely cheered. I lit the stove against the evening chill and heated up some baked beans. Then I took a glass of whisky on deck, and watched a shoal of sea trout slashing at minnows in the shallows.

The midges drove me in. In the wheelhouse, the VHF said, 'Harry, this is Ewan. Your office called, over.'

I said, 'Fine.'

'And Fiona says good night.'

I said the same to her, and went below.

Flora's saloon was impeccably varnished; Hector's work, I guessed. I lit the paraffin lamp. There were a couple of shelves of books on pilotage and ornithology. Neither subject appealed. I went further a field, into a cabin that from the pair of jeans on the hook and the compass over the bunk looked as if it might be where Ewan slept when he was on board. On a shelf by the bunk there was a copy of *Small is Beautiful* by Schumacher, several learned periodicals dealing with marine biology, a Bible, and a copy of *Green Sea* by Gottfried Weber. I pulled *Green Sea* off the shelf. It seemed to be a book about marine pollution. The author seemed to be a journalist. He had signed the title page to his friend and correspondent Ewan Buchan. There was a sheaf of letters tucked into the back of the book. They were none of my business, but I had made a career of looking at things which were other people's business.

I need not have bothered. There was one about pollution caused by fish farms, another about fish ulcers caused by pollution, and a third about weed growth in water affected by quarrying silt. They were strong on references to learned articles, and weak on human interest. Ammunition for Ewan's Caledonian standoff. I took the book, got into my sleeping bag, and started to read a chapter about carbon dioxide. Three minutes later I was asleep.

Next morning, I rowed across to *Green Dolphin*. Hector was already there, grunting over his chisel. We cut, scarfed and glued new cedar strips and planed them fair. Hector worked methodically, but with the speed that distinguishes the professional from the competent amateur. I passed him tools and mixed him resins. By the end of the day we had two layers of glass cloth laminated on the new timber. 'Sand her tomorrow,' said Hector. 'Then a lick of paint, if you want it.'

'Good,' I said. It was better than good. It was going to be an excellent job. 'If you ever need work down South, just ask.'

He looked slightly anxious, then realised it was a joke. 'I'm well content,' he said. We were sitting drinking tea. The cockpit was full of mutual trust. So I said, 'What the hell were you doing out there with no lights?'

He took a deliberate sip of tea. He said, 'It was Tuesday night.'

'What do you mean?'

'Tuesday night, we went out there. Banging around out beyond Ardnamurchan. The Tuesday before, too.'

'What were you doing?'

Hector said, 'I worked for Mr Jock Buchan. And I work for Ewan Buchan. And neither of them ever explained to me one bluidy thing he did.'

'And you never asked?'

'Nobody's paying me to ask questions,' said Hector. He looked at the cheap watch on his massive wrist. 'You'll be wanting to get your dinner.' He rose, and stumped up the quay and into the rhododendrons.

I went below and pulled on clean chinos, a red shirt and a blazer out of the cedar-lined forward locker.

Fiona met me in the hall. She was wearing short, loose black trousers and a big grey sweater, with lines across it like quartz veins in a boulder. She eyed my clothes with curiosity, and said, 'Your office rang, again. They left a number.' The office seemed a very long way away. Thinking of it made me think of Prosper; I looked at her feet. She was wearing elegant green leather slippers. 'Do it in my studio,' she said.

So I sat at the white desk in the corner of a room hung with rainbow skeins of wool, and dialled the number.

It was not the office number. The high, breathless voice that answered was more my life's work than the office. It was the voice of my sister.

'Darling,' she said. 'The cards said you were in terrible danger.' Vi was a great devotee of the psychic. It was more likely that she had got a garbled account of the collision from Prosper, with whom she had flirted since she had taken us out from school at the age of ten.

She said, 'And I heard you broke your boat. I got really bad vibes from that boat the first time I saw it. I'm worried.'

I could imagine her gnawing a long red fingernail with her expensive white teeth, sighing at her reflection in the window, checking that she really did look worried. 'Nothing to worry about,' I said. 'We've fixed it already.' Her morale was subject to sudden catastrophic plunges. If you did not bolster it, she would do it herself, with bright little capsules of Tuinal, or phenobarbitone, or Seconal. 'So what's up?' I said, brightly.

As usual, everything was up except Vi. I gazed at a framed embroidery from the Yucatan and waited for the flood of words to become a trickle. She had a lot of friends, but they were expert talkers and bad listeners. At last, it came out. 'Davina,' she said. 'Davina Leyland. Well, she saw Gerald, that's her new husband, you know, at Annabel's last night with some bimbo. And Giulio followed them home, so they're definitely doing it.'

'Who's Giulio?' I said.

'Davina's boyfriend. He cuts hair at Raphael, but he's incredibly strong. Anyway, they got back to Giulio's flat, and there was this creep hanging about outside, and he turned out to be a private detective, so Giulio bashed him up. But he'd been hanging around for ages, apparently, because now Gerald says he's going to contest the divorce on the grounds of Davina's adultery. It's so *unfair*. But I told her you'd help.'

I took a deep breath. The divorce laws of England affected people like Davina Leyland the way policemen on bicycles affect Lamborghini drivers. 'Doesn't sound too good,' I said.

'But I *promised*.' Vi strongly disapproved of people who broke her promises. 'Anyway, you didn't have any trouble with Liz the Les, did you?'

I resisted the temptation to put the receiver down. When I had come back to lawyering and taken articles with Arthur Somers in Orchard Street, Vi had dropped her friend Liz's divorce in my lap, and I had freakishly managed to clear it up to the satisfaction of all. Liz the Les had been a door into the world of Vi's friends and acquaintances, which was to a divorce lawyer what the Middle East is to an oil broker. Arthur had eased his way into retirement a year later, leaving me in possession of a lot of oak panelling, a partner's desk, and Cyril the clerk. Vi never let me forget this, or any of the other things she thought I owed her.

'All right,' I said. 'When I get back.'

'For Mummy Vi,' she said.

Our parents had died when I had been a nine-year-old schoolboy, and Vi a nineteen-year-old starlet. She liked to think that in the process of dragging me out from school to fraudulent restaurants in the King's Road she had brought me up. In a way, she had. 'For Vi,' I said.

Prosper always said that putting the telephone down on her was like slamming the door of a hairdresser's salon. The feeling was intensified when I went into the dining-room. Ewan and Fiona were sitting one at either end of the table. A couple of candles made an island of warm yellow light in the dusk.

The candlelight accentuated the fine bones of Fiona's face, giving her a touch of the Cherokee. 'Have some dinner,' she said. There was the tail half of a salmon on the sideboard. On the table were a bottle of Glenmorangie and a heavy glass jug of water. Ewan pushed the bottle round. Fiona drank only water.

Fiona said, 'How long have you been a lawyer?'

'Ten years. Five practising.'

She nodded, looked across at Ewan. 'Maybe he's the man for Morag Sullivan,' she said.

Ewan shrugged. The movements of his hands were clumsy with drink as he boned his salmon. *Would you mind not telling Fiona*, he had said. I watched them; Fiona's sharp, bird-like profile, Ewan draining yet another glass. Fiona was the strong one of the pair. She had a quietness that made her unshakeable. There was something wild and restless about Ewan that reduced him.

I said, 'Who's Morag Sullivan?'

'She's one of the women who knit jerseys for me. She lives away down the coast. She's married to Jimmy Sullivan. He does some fishing. He's disappeared.'

I said, 'When did he leave?' The salmon was excellent.

She said, 'He didn't leave. He disappeared.'

I nodded. After five years in the divorce business, I was well aware that the difference was usually a technical one.

Fiona's brown hand began to pull little bits of home-baked bread off the slice on her plate and mould it into perfect cubes. 'Jimmy and Morag have got five children,' she said. 'Jimmy runs a boat. A fishing boat, the *Minnie Sullivan*. He has a few strings of pots. There are a lot of people after the lobsters. It's not the easiest way of making a living.' Her words were precise, as if she was giving a lecture. 'Jimmy told Morag he had tripped over something good. He wouldn't tell her what it was, and she didn't ask. And he went off one evening on the tide, and never came back.'

I said, 'I'm sorry to hear that,' and ate the last of the salmon. There was a pause. The huge silence of the mountains filled the room. The candle flames burned steady in Fiona's grey–green eyes. 'So are Morag and the kids,' she said.

I kept quiet. Some people become lawyers out of a burning desire to see justice done. I had become one because it was a way of supporting Vi.

Fiona said, 'Could you go and talk to her?'

I looked firmly down at the worn gilt rim of my plate. 'I don't see that there's a lot I could do,' I said.

'You could tell her how to make a claim,' said Fiona.

'Against whom?'

'Try the Navy,' said Ewan. His voice was thick. 'The place is polluted with submarines. Murdo Kennedy, there he is mackerelling, flat calm, when he gets this dirty great wave, five feet high, going like an express train, and there's Murdo in the bloody life raft, no boat, and the Navy said it was a freak wave, but Murdo reckoned if it was a freak wave it wouldn't have had the white ensign painted on the front end of it.'

I said, 'If it's the Navy, I'm not going to have any more luck than anyone else.'

Fiona said, 'Morag's in trouble. Everybody is doing what they can.' She had her chin in her hand, and her eyes were steady and unwavering.

'Please,' she said.

I found myself thinking of Ewan, turning down a perfectly good salvage claim. Of Hector, doing a day and a half's work, free. And the way Fiona and Ewan had taken me in, as if there was no question of there being any other possibility.

'When did this happen?' I said.

'Just over a week ago,' she said.

And suddenly, I heard Hector's voice again. *Tuesday night, we went out there. Banging around out beyond Ardnamurchan. The Tuesday before, too.* The skin at the nape of my neck crawled with anticipation.

'The Tuesday before last,' she said.

Chapter Six

I slept on *Green Dolphin* that night, in the after-cabin, away from the stink of solvents. Next morning I rolled out of my sleeping bag at seven. The view through the porthole was grey water and grey sky, and there was a raw bite in the air. I pulled on a couple of jerseys, and ladled Lapsang Souchong into the teapot with a heavy hand. Then I put a second coat of paint on the fibreglass patch.

At eight-thirty there was the sound of a big diesel starting. At the far side of the loch, *Flora*'s back end was spewing black smoke.

After forty minutes, there was a knocking on the hull. It was Hector, in the tender. 'We're ready,' he said.

Flora was moving into the middle of the loch, away from a little hut on the far shore. Hector pulled on with quick fisherman's oar-strokes. We came alongside *Flora*, and I went up the side with the painter. Hector came after me.

Ewan looked hung over. He grunted a good morning, which I reciprocated. We set the sails. The Narrows came and went, the ebb tide streaming in the patches of weed over the rocks. Once we were through, Ewan stuck his head out of the wheelhouse window and said, 'Take her.'

The wind was filling in as we came round the second corner in the loch and caught the razor-sharp slice of the horizon. I opened the window on its leather strap. The smell of pitch caulking rose heavily off the deck, and the sun spread the reflection of the hills across the glassy water under the shore.

The ebb ran quickly; I could feel swirls of it tugging at the rudder. The wind had gone easterly, offshore. There was very little swell coming in, which was a relief. Ewan came back into the wheelhouse and gave me a course a little south of west, shaving the Horngate, the long line of rocks off the southernmost point of the bay.

'Didn't want to come, did you? Busman's holiday, eh?'

I shrugged. He was acute, for someone who drank as much as he did. His arm went up to the netting locker where the bottle lived. 'It's being American,' he said. 'Fiona's always thinking about leverage, getting things done.' He held out a glass. It was a form of peace offering, so I took it. 'Used to drive me crazy, when we lived together. *Slàinte.*' We drank.

I do not like whisky at nine a.m., but today I had my reasons. I said, 'What happens out beyond Ardnamurchan on Tuesday nights?'

He looked at me with narrow, humorous eyes. 'Well, well,' he said. 'I bet you're good at what you do. This Tuesday, why don't you come and have a look?'

'At what?'

'So far,' said Ewan, 'at absolutely sweet damn all.' And that was all he would say.

We moved away from the coast. Against the shadowy cliffs of the cloud-shaded headland beyond Dunmurry on the northern horizon, a couple of little white triangles stood in a patch of sun. A bulk carrier was heading south, decks almost awash with the weight of her cargo.

We tramped southwards, rolling heavily. By afternoon, we were off a long knuckle of land that clawed into the sea from two thousand five hundred feet. The water at its foot was blue, and looked deep, slathered with the foam of big swells coming in from the Hebrides. But as we headed past it to the eastward, I saw that the land curled round to form a little bay, a lagoon almost, inside.

At the back end of the lagoon, facing south, was a small beach of brownish-grey sand. The sun came out, pouring down on a white single-storey building whose front consisted of a blue-painted door with a window on either side of it. Behind the house, emerald in the strong light, was a cluster of weedy green rectangles that could have been fields. In front of it, in the centre of the hundred-yard disc of the bay, there floated a big orange mooring buoy.

'Camas Bealach,' said Ewan.

A figure had come from behind the house. For a moment it stared. Then it raised an arm in greeting.

We chugged through a slantwise channel in a half-covered dam of rock that cut the lagoon off from the open sea, and Hector fished the mooring pennant out of the water with his boathook.

Close to, the Sullivan house was less than idyllic. Fragments of machinery lay in the long grass beside a wooden shed. On the hillside by a weed-grown patch of potatoes, a dying bonfire fumed in a nest of old tins and soggy, half-burned paper.

Morag Sullivan had brilliant white skin and brick-red hair that fell into her eyes. She constantly pushed it back with a none-too-clean hand, leaving dark smudges on her pale cheekbones. The smudges ran into other smudges, under her eyes, which had nothing to do with dirt. She said, 'Ewan,' in a voice that sounded tired.

Ewan strode up the beach and put his arm round her shoulders. 'How's the girl?' he said.

She tried unsuccessfully to smile. Ewan introduced me. There was a change in him; he had turned serious and solid, and he filled the place with a sense of authority and things getting done.

The woman's eyes were pink and nervous, but direct. Behind the shed, treble voices yelled. A flock of children straggled into view, calling at each other like marsh birds. She turned and screamed, *'Be quiet!'*

The children stopped, and lined up, tallest left, smallest right.

'That's better,' she said, and I could see her reminding herself to smile at them. My usual clients were richer, but less considerate.

She said, 'Come you in, and we'll have tea.'

The house had four rooms. We went into the kitchen. There was a Rayburn festooned with ragged washing. We sat down. The children crowded into the doorway and waited there. Ewan addressed the eldest, a boy of about ten with his mother's colouring. 'Arright, Jockie?' he said.

Jockie grinned and stared at his feet.

'So take out the weans and I'll talk with your Mam.'

Jockie hesitated, stopped grinning. 'What about our Dad?'

Ewan said, 'No news.' Jockie's face fell as if he had been shot. 'But this gentleman's a lawyer.'

'A lawyer,' said Jockie. 'Aye.' They looked at me with the intensity of drowning men looking at a lifeboat. Sweat broke out on my forehead. I smiled and tried to look confident.

Mrs Sullivan gave me an anxious smile of her own and sent the children away. She put a brown teapot on the table and decanted shortbread from a battered tin with a picture of Stirling Castle. Then she sat down and looked at me as if she wanted me to ask questions. So rather than sit in complete silence, I did.

'Ewan said your husband's…disappeared.'

She nodded.

'When was that?'

'Over a week ago,' she said. 'Tuesday before last, he went out in the boat to set a load of pots, lobster pots, you know. The pots were never hauled. He didn't come back.'

'When he went out before, how long did he stay away?'

She shrugged. Her breasts were long and loose in her floral overall. 'A day. Two days. You never knew with Jimmy.'

'But never this long.'

She shook her head. 'Before he went, he said he'd be back inside the twenty-four hours.'

I nodded and sipped tea, and wondered what the hell people thought a lawyer was supposed to do about someone who might have been wiped off the face of the earth by shipwreck, or submarine, or act of God, but who was probably upside down in a bar in Glasgow. I started to tell her so, as gently as I could, when she broke in. She said, 'There was something he found.'

'Found?'

She glanced at Ewan.

'Jimmy keeps his eyes open,' said Ewan. 'Gives me a wee hand with Sea Watch. Odd things floating, bits of oil, you know.'

I ate the corner of a bit of shortbread, and looked at the grease on the kitchen wall behind Morag's kinked red hair. 'So what was this?' I said.

'Some kind of scrap, maybe.' She looked down at her red hands. 'He's a great hand for the scrap. Every little bit helps.'

I looked at Ewan. 'Did he tell you?' I said.

Ewan's eyes were heavy-lidded, imponderable. 'Not a sausage,' he said.

'He didn't say much,' she said. 'Just finished his tea, got the bait out of the shed and went across to the boat, and that was the last we saw of him.' Her composure was wearing thin. Tears were sliding down the well-worn grooves beside her nose.

Ewan looked at me. I was meant to ask a question. I said, 'Had anything unusual happened?'

She frowned. 'Well,' she said. 'That Monday, Donald came over.' Visitors were rare, up here. 'They had a hell of a battle. Donald was shouting and roaring – '

Ewan said, 'What for?'

'Och, you know Donald,' she said. 'Jimmy picked something out of the sea, and Donald came to give him a price on it. And maybe the price was wrong, I don't know. But Donald went away empty.'

I said, 'What kind of thing would it have been?'

Ewan said, 'There's all manner of gear out there. Last year he had seventy tons of sawn oak off a timber ship. Another time there was thirty drums of diesel, better than a thousand quid's worth.'

'It'll be in the shed,' said Morag. We walked out of the house, across the rank grass. The shed was built of concrete blocks. It had double doors and a padlock. She opened the doors. 'The museum,' she said, with a good try at a smile.

The dark, windowless interior was jammed to the roof with flotsam: driftwood in piles, lobster pots, at least two wooden rowing boats with holes in them, and oil drums of all colours, full and empty.

'Good collection,' said Ewan.

I stared at a rainbow of oil drums, and felt useless. 'Is there anything you don't recognise?' I said.

'I don't come down here an awful lot,' she said.

I nodded as encouragingly as I could. She relocked the door. Ewan said, 'We'll be away.' His big hand dived into the pocket of his baggy jeans. He turned away from me, but I caught a glimpse of pale brown paper. It looked like a bundle of tenners; a thick bundle.

I heard him muttering to her. Morag shrugged, took it, turned away, the red kinks hiding her face. Ewan said, 'We'll do what we can. Won't we, Harry?'

'Of course,' I said.

Morag followed us to the beach, as if she was reluctant to let us go.

'Well?' said Ewan, as we rowed out to where *Flora* lay above her reflection on the blue mirror of the cove.

I said, 'Your guess is as good as mine. I'd find out what the trouble was with this Donald, whoever he is.'

'Donald Stewart,' said Ewan. 'He was the wee man knocked me off the fish cage yesterday.'

I stared at him. 'So what was he doing down here?' I said.

'Oh, we see a lot of Donald in Sea Watch,' he said. 'Usually because we get between him and some money. Would you ever give Hector a hand with the sails?'

I pulled up the foresail, and Hector pulled up the main, and we clattered out of the little harbour, waving to the small figures on the stony beach. Outside the harbour the wind stiffened the sails. *Flora* stuck her fat starboard side into the water and began to wade solidly northwest through the long blue swells.

It looked like being a beautiful evening, with fair-weather clouds proceeding like skyborne jellyfish towards the green reefs of mountain to the east. I sat on the hatch cover, away from the wheelhouse's sick-making fug, and thought about Donald Stewart, who had knocked Ewan into the water and left him to drown, and that fat roll of notes Ewan had handed over to Morag, and Tuesday night. And I got a whiff of something I usually smelled only in my office, across the desk from a shark-boned Sloane Ranger with a boyfriend half her age and an affidavit about her husband from the girl groom.

The ripe, stagnant smell of deep water.

Chapter Seven

After half an hour, Camas Bealach was a green cone sinking on the horizon astern. Ewan beckoned from the wheelhouse, waving a cup of tea.

I said, 'Were you and Jimmy Sullivan partners?'

He said, 'Why should we have been?'

'You gave Morag some money. You said it was Jimmy's share.'

He grinned. 'Bit of fiction. Proceeds of a whip-round.' He pulled a bottle of Glenmorangie from the pocket of his donkey jacket. 'Dram?'

I shook my head.

The roll had been neat, tenners only. They looked new, as if they had come from a bank. Whip-round proceeds came in flyers, Royal Bank of Scotland ones, and old French francs left over from a deal with a fishing boat.

I said, 'Were you in business with Sullivan?'

He looked surprised. 'When it suited.'

'What kind of business?'

'Anything that paid,' he replied.

'Scrap?' I asked. 'Salvage?'

'That's it,' he said.

'And Donald Stewart's in the same business?'

Ewan laughed, a hard, nasty laugh. 'He's the competition.'

He turned the fishfinder on. The screen lit up, showing a smooth, flat bottom. His hand went out, pulled back the throttles.

'Excuse me,' he said. 'Bit of business to do.' He lashed the wheel, and went on deck.

I took the teacups below, washed them in the iron galley sink, and dried them hard on the clean dishcloth. I was getting the idea that Ewan was not as keen on lawyers as Fiona.

There were bumpings and slidings from on deck. When I went up the steep companionway into the wheelhouse Hector was at the wheel, his face stolid against the glitter from the sea. Out on deck, there was a hole where the hatch cover had been. Ewan had taken the mainsail down, and rigged the boom as a derrick.

'Daft,' said Hector, enigmatically, and pulled back the throttle. 'Keep her head to wind.' He went out on deck.

The spokes were warm from his big, hard hands. I leaned against the flat wooden shelf that ran below the windows, braced against the rise and fall of the horizon.

Ewan's head came out of the hold. The sun gleamed in the sweat on his forehead. He shouted, 'Heck, get down here!'

Hector went. The sea had flattened; half a mile ahead, a smudge of white foam churned where a rock broke the force of the swell. Except for a gentle pitch, *Flora* lay steady.

Hector came back on deck and lowered the mainsheet into the hold. The boom had become the jib of a derrick, the mainsheet the tackle at its tip. Above the chug of the engine came another noise; the clack of a ratchet. Ewan was winding a winch.

Hector was gazing down the hatch with an expressionless face. Once, he looked at me, nodded absent-mindedly, and smiled. It was a perfunctory smile, full of strain. It was then that I realised something out of the ordinary was taking place.

In the hold, the clacking continued. A hook appeared, seized into netting. They're going fishing, I thought, swinging the nets up. This is a trawler: what could be more reasonable than that?

But the nets' meshes were very tight. Briefly, I wondered why. Then I knew, and suddenly my palms were slippery on the wheel, and I was swallowing hard, dry-mouthed.

The thing in the net was familiar enough. I had seen them used as litterbins on esplanades, as collecting-boxes at maritime museums. It was a dripping four-foot egg of iron, rusty, as if it had spent a long time underwater. On the esplanades, they are empty. To judge by the expression on Hector's face, this one was full: a Naval mine, vintage World War Two, packed with enough explosive to blow the QE2 to glory.

It rose above the deck. We caught a cross-swell, and it swayed horribly. Hector put the butt end of a boathook on it, and leaned into it, hard, before it could bang into the lip of the hatch. 'Keep her straight!' roared Ewan's voice from the hold.

I kept her straight.

'Go!' yelled Ewan. He came up the hatchway like a shaggy ape, attached himself to a loose line hanging from the tip of the boom, and heaved. Ponderously, the mine swung from above the gaping mouth of the hatchway until it was suspended six feet above the starboard rail, hanging half outboard, swathed in its nets.

Hector ran to the windlass. Slowly, the boom began to drop. The nearer it approached the horizontal, the further outboard it hung. *Flora* was heeled well over to starboard now, pulled down by the great weight of the mine. The sweat was pouring down inside my jersey. *This is not happening*, I kept telling myself – But it was.

Very gently, they lowered the mine into the water. Then Ewan leaped aft, his beard fluttering in the breeze, and said, as if we were sailing in Cowes week, 'Do you mind if I have a go?'

I gave him the helm without a word. Words could come later.

He banged the gears to ASTERN and spun the wheel nonchalantly to starboard. As the trawler came astern and to starboard, Hector cast the mine off the boom.

My face felt like marble as *Flora* and the mine lay side by side, rolling. Then Ewan spun the wheel back to port, until the brass-capped midships spoke came uppermost. *Flora* drifted downwind. And Hector paid out line, and the mine in its net sank, slowly and elegantly, towards the bottom. I opened my mouth to speak.

'Hold it,' said Ewan. He turned to the chart table and unhooked the mike from the VHF. He turned the dial to Channel 16, Emergency, and called the coastguard.

A thin, crackling voice said: '*Flora*, this is Oban Coastguard. How can we assist? Over.'

'Oban Coastguard, *Flora*, we are trawling by Bees Rock, and we've caught a wee mine. Have you means of disposing of this, over?'

Hector had come aft. He caught my eye and gave me a large, impassive wink. The coastguard said, '*Flora*, Oban Coastguard. Royal Navy mine hunter in the vicinity, will advise, stand by. Out.'

'Well, then,' said Ewan, pulling down the Glenmorangie. 'Help is at hand. That's a bit of luck, eh?' He drank, thirstily. 'This nasty mine has wrecked our day's fishing. So the Ministry will pay us compensation for lost fish and gear.'

I said, 'So you had it sitting at home, and you brought it out here.'

'Correct,' said Ewan. 'In a tank in the hold. Handle 'em right, they handle you right.'

He looked as smug as a big schoolboy. He had about as much common sense. I said, 'They're full of gun cotton. After fifty years, the casing looks like a colander. The holes weep nitro-glycerine. And you tied up at Camas Bealach. Give it a bump, a thump, light your fag. Good night Morag and her kids.'

'What the hell do you know about it?' said Ewan. Suddenly we were nose to nose, and I could smell the whisky on his breath.

'A hell of a lot more than you, by the sound of it.' He was staring, amazed. I realised that I had let the old Frazer slip through, the Frazer who had crawled on his belly round the bottom of the North Sea.

He shook his head. 'Bollocks,' he said. 'We trawled it up. Saved it for a rainy day, that's all.'

I said, 'Why don't I tell the Navy what you're up to?'

'It came out of the sea in the first place,' he said. 'We found it on the beach. I've just improved the lie a wee bit. And I've given the money to Jimmy's missis, and she's no getting any anywhere else.' His beard was jutting now, his eyes narrow and dangerous. 'And you'll not say a word, because you may be a prick but you're not a bastard.'

Sticks and stones, I thought. But I did not open my mouth.

An hour later a low, grey ship steamed out of the sun, lowering over the blue peaks of Skye. An inflatable dropped from her davits and buzzed towards us, nose bouncing on the black swells. The diving team came aboard.

The officer was a youngish lieutenant. If it had not been for the gold braid on his epaulettes, he might have been a recently qualified doctor. We made statements. Ewan's contained the fact that the lost trawl net had been a new one and that we had missed two tides' fishing. I thought about objecting, did not. The moment passed. The lieutenant gave the nod of a doctor signing a hypochondriac's sick note.

They lowered the mine to the bottom, very, very gently. A couple of divers went down, came up, then stood dripping and made a report in a language full of initials. It was a language I spoke. What they meant was that the mine was a magnetic-acoustic type with a jammed fuse, which was why it had rolled around the seabed without blowing up for the past fifty years, and why Ewan had managed to keep it at the bottom of his garden without it removing him and most of the garden from the face of Scotland.

'Very good,' said the officer, shoving his cap back.

One of the divers on the hatch cover had been watching me. I started to turn away. I knew what was coming.

'Wally Evans,' he said. 'You're Harry Frazer.'

He had heavy black eyebrows and red cheeks pushed out by the grip of the black rubber helmet. Last time we met had been in the North Sea, on the steel deck of Curlew Gamma, in the hot kerosene breath of a chopper taking off.

'Wally,' I said, and a lead weight settled in my stomach.

We said hello, and how the hell are you, and shook hands, and I asked him what he was doing off the rigs and back in the Navy.

'Too bloody dangerous,' he said. 'Working for the pension,' and looked awkward because he was thinking about some people on the rigs who had not made it as far as pensions. I stood there with my polite grin, looking inside my own head, six years back, to a time before I had worn that grin. To a little steel room with a floor made of black water, a thousand feet under the sea, and two sets of tubes that went out into the icy darkness. And the sweat ran down inside my T-shirt like a garden hose.

'Frazer,' said the lieutenant, cocking a single eyebrow. 'You're the diving-bell man.'

I kept the grin going on my cold, rubbery face. I said, 'It was a long time ago.'

The lieutenant looked at me hard. He could not have failed to notice the colour I must have gone. He clicked his tongue; tut, tut. 'All right, chaps,' he said. 'We're off.'

'Look after yourself, Wally,' I said.

The black folds of his neck moved as he nodded. 'You too.'

I could feel Ewan watching me as they went down the side. He said, 'I thought you said you were a solicitor.'

I said, curtly, 'I wasn't born one,' and turned away. He was not the only one who knew how not to answer questions.

The mine hunter winched the mine off the bottom and churned away, heading for shallow water. We put the sails up. *Flora* began to tramp northward.

It was warm in the wheelhouse, quiet, with the smell of coal smoke. I had too much on my mind to feel seasick. I got the whisky bottle from the locker. The sun was going down in a quiet, pink sky when we heard the *thud* of the mine to seaward.

'Up she goes,' said Ewan. 'So you're a diver, then?'

'Not any more,' I said.

'Could you change your mind?'

'Not a chance,' I said. I took the bottle below and wedged myself in beside the stove.

Hector followed. He said, 'You don't want to pay too much mind to Ewan. He's been a good friend to a lot of folk.'

I nodded, and drank some whisky. Then I gave him the bottle and went into the little slot of a cabin alongside the throb of the engine, and crawled into the sleeping bag.

The dream started in the usual way. The walls were sweating, and the telephone speakers were jabbering; Bruno's voice, and John's, tinny with the helium saturating their blood, crackling down the wires from out there on the muddy floor of the sea by the pipeline valve. Then the voices stopped, and the silence began, and I started to sweat. The silence began to roar, louder and louder, like a gong being beaten, until it hurt the ears. Behind the gong, voices were shouting. New voices from the control room up there on the surface, giving me instructions. But the instructions were too late, because the thing had happened. The walls were metal, sweating, impassive. I could not breathe. There was a thousand feet of water above me. I was alone in the cylinder, with the roaring. I had to get out. But there was no way out.

The bubble of panic burst. I began to shout, to bang at the walls, hammering, and hammering, and hammering – 'Are you all right?' said Ewan's voice.

There was light around his head. I could see it gleaming on his cheekbones above the beard, shifting as the oil lamp swung gently to *Flora*'s heel. There was no silence, but the comfortable creak of a wooden boat moving across a low swell in a moderate breeze.

'All right,' I said dully. I was off the bunk. I must have been hammering at the bulkhead. Ewan closed the door. I lay down on the bunk, and fell into a deep black sleep.

Chapter Eight

I awoke slowly, my head still muffled in the rags of the dream. The trawler was on her mooring in Loch Beag, the empty tender streaming downtide from her stern. My Rolex said six o'clock; the air smelled of pine trees, and heather, and the sea. The sky was low and grey, but the air was warm. When I leaned over the side, my reflection in the water was an old man with a grey face and black curls like greasy serpents. It wobbled with the ripples. Wobbly was the way I felt. I went into the wheelhouse and boiled a kettle and made thick, black tea. Then I undressed and dived over the side into water like liquid green ice.

On the bottom I lay on my back, dribbling bubbles up thirty feet to break against *Flora*'s dark belly in the silver shield of the surface, and felt my head clear as the cold panicked the blood round my body.

I went up the ladder, pulled on jeans and a jersey, and rowed alongside *Green Dolphin*. Hector came out of her hatch, dusting his hands together. 'I put a last coat on last night when we came in,' he said. 'Ready when you are.'

We pulled away the polythene tent and rolled up the electric cables. The curve of the side was fair, the surface flawless as an eggshell. 'Brilliant,' I said.

Hector nodded, his potato face solemn. 'One good turn deserves another,' he said. 'I'll be away to my breakfast.'

I pulled out the toolbox, and did a hard two hours' cleaning and tuning. At ten o'clock, I heard a woman's voice singing on the quay. It was Fiona, wearing baggy jeans and an old tweed jacket with a bunch of sweet peas in the buttonhole, carrying a duffle bag over her shoulder. Her skin was shining, and her eyes were clear as the water. 'My goodness, but you look hung over,' she said cheerfully. 'What happened at the Sullivans'?'

'Morag Sullivan doesn't need a lawyer,' I said. 'She needs the police.'

'If the police get to her, they'll empty the shed,' said Fiona. 'It's all she's got, that shed. Then they'll ask a lot of fool questions, and nothing will happen.'

I said, 'They should talk to Donald Stewart.'

She laughed. 'Donald spent a year in Barlinnie for half killing a guy who cut his illegal salmon nets,' she said. 'He wouldn't ask a cop for a pail of water if his house was burning.'

I shrugged. 'Too bad,' I said.

She looked at me with those steady eyes. The eyes said, All right, Frazer, you go and see Donald Stewart. But I knew all about staring, and I stared right back.

Eventually, she shrugged. 'I guess you have done...all that can be expected,' she said.

The inference was that she had not expected much. I found I did not like it. 'Wait a minute,' I said.

'What for?' she said. Her face was cold and contemptuous. 'You've done enough. That's it. Finish.'

I could not take the coldness. I said, 'I'll go and see Stewart.'

The eyes were suddenly hot and alive. 'You will?' she said.

The excitement in her voice was infectious. Fool, Frazer, I thought. But it was too late now.

'I'll tell him that if he doesn't explain his differences with Jimmy Sullivan, I'll bring an action for assault on behalf of Ewan.'

'Ewan?' she said, frowning. 'What are you talking about?'

I said, 'Where do we find Stewart?'

'Saturday,' she said. 'He'll be at the tanks.' She frowned. 'But are you sure? He can be really nasty.'

'Is that right?' I said. I could still see the short, ferocious jab of the fist that had put Ewan in the fish cage.

She smiled, a very good smile indeed, and touched my hand briefly with the ends of her fingers. I had let myself be challenged, instead of thinking it out. She was twisting me around, and I was letting it happen. Prosper had said it. *You'll lose your edge.*

But that was only one explanation. The other was the notion that, living all the way out here, she was lonely.

I liked that one better.

The breeze was blowing down the loch from inland, force two or three, hardly rippling the flat mirror of the water. I pulled out all the big, light genoa on the forwardmost of the three roller forestays. The breeze filled it with a soft *whap*. *Dolphin* glided away from the quay with her heart-quickening surge of acceleration.

Fiona said, 'That's fast.' The wind blew her dark hair around her face. She looked brown and excited.

I gave her the wheel, padded along the side deck and cranked up the mainsail. *Dolphin* heeled, and the bubble of the wake became a thin hiss. Fiona laughed, a sound of pure pleasure. 'What is this thing?' she said.

'ULDB,' I said. 'Ultra Light Displacement Boat. Sails over the water, not through it.'

'Beautiful,' said Fiona.

The beetling cliffs of the Narrows were coming up very fast, the shore sliding by, eight knots on the dial and another four of tide.

We shot out of the Narrows and into the funnel of the bay. *Flora* was moving slowly towards the point of the Horngate, canted elegantly away from the wind, a moustache of white water under her snipe's beak of a bowsprit. We went past her as if she were standing still. Fiona turned the nose northwest, bringing the wind on to the beam. I trimmed, playing the sheets on the fat winches till the sails oozed power and the wake was shooting white from the transom with the hard, whining hiss of high speed.

It was not everyone who could get her up and going like that. I said, 'You've done this before.'

She was hanging off the side of the wheel, sighting on the point at the northern end of the bay. Her hair blew across her face as she turned and gave me a flash of white teeth. 'San Francisco Bay,' she said. 'Daddy had a one-tonner.'

There was no time to be surprised, even if I had wanted to be. A puff of wind cracked across the bay. *Dolphin* lay over on her side, blasting spray out of a black wave with her port bow.

The point's snout was a crumbled ram of rock that battered the swells sugary white. She left it a couple of hundred yards to starboard, the echo sounder flicking on sixty metres.

Ahead and to starboard lay a flock of low islands, scattered across a sea that paled from deep blue to Caribbean turquoise. Along the line of the shore, I caught a glimpse of silver–white sand gleaming in the sun.

'Between the island and the rocks,' she said. 'It's your boat. You steer.'

Suddenly, the echo sounder said seven metres, and shoaling. We were hard on the wind, heeled steeply, going much too fast for the water. Fiona's cheeks were whipped red by the wind. She said, 'Isn't it beautiful?'

'Roll me in some jib,' I said. I was too busy watching the marks she gave me, and the echo sounder, and the rocks that had begun to darken the clear water to port and starboard. Beautiful was not the adjective uppermost in my mind. But we went on. And at the end, we glided between two islands and into a horseshoe of gleaming white sand.

I shoved the helm up and she came head to wind, mainsail flopping, depowered. The anchor went down.

A dory was anchored on the tide line. Footprints led up the sand to a grey concrete shed in the rocks above the high-water mark. There was an articulated lorry parked by the shed with

TRANSPORTS DRENEC – ST MALO written on the side, and a line of gulls on its roof.

'Donald's at home,' said Fiona.

'Stay there,' I said. I shoved the Zodiac inflatable over the rail and rowed ashore.

The sand of the beach was soft underfoot. The lorry was parked on a road, a narrow ribbon of potholed tarmac. There were voices coming from the shed. I put my head round the door.

There were three big cement tanks built into the shed's floor. The tanks were speckled with blue–black lobsters, rubber bands on their claws, graded by size. Donald was there, watching a man in blue overalls, presumably the lorry driver, signing a piece of paper.

'*Bon*,' said the lorry driver. '*Au revoir*.' He walked past me, nodded good morning and climbed into the cab. The engine stuttered and roared, blasting black exhaust.

Donald came out after him. 'Morning,' I said.

He had hard brown eyes with yellowish whites. His nose was long and sharp, his mouth small and lipless.

'Off to Brittany, eh?' I said, jovially.

'That's what it says on the truck,' he said.

'Caught all their own, I suppose,' I said.

'Maybe they have,' said Stewart. 'What do you want?'

I said, 'You went to see Jimmy Sullivan the day before he disappeared.' He watched me from under his brow ridge like a boxer. My mouth was dry. He stank of violence. 'You had an argument with Jimmy. What about?'

He said, slowly, 'Who are you?'

'I'm a lawyer acting for friends of Jimmy's. I want to know what you were discussing with him a week ago last Monday.'

He said nothing. His hobnails squinched on rock as he turned away, shot and padlocked the big bolts on the shed doors. The mountains soared to the sky, and little waves fell with small, violent roars on the beach. I had a bad sense that there was a lot of nature, and very few people. For the first time in years, the law seemed puny and unimportant.

I said, 'You talk to me about Jimmy, and I'll persuade Ewan Buchan not to bring a case against you for knocking him into the loch at Dunmurry.'

He frowned, screwing up his eyes at me as if he was short sighted. 'That's right,' he said. 'That's where I saw you. You're the wee Nigel that was with Buchan that day.'

His eyes travelled down my legs. I was wearing Timberland deck shoes, which are light, comfortable, and very expensive. He was wearing big black army boots. 'You can tell your friend Buchan that there's some men left who'll work for a living whether his fucking Highness says they will or no. And he can stay out of their way, or he will get caught in the machinery,' he said. 'Mind the doors.'

Then he stood on my foot.

I had no time to do anything about it. His heel came down, and his full weight pivoted on the front of my right shoe. Beach and sky blurred with tears. 'Don't you ever come near me again,' he said. Then the weight was gone, and I was sitting in the sand, and he was in the Dory, snarling for the mouth of the bay.

It was a good two minutes before I could see straight. I hobbled down the beach, rowed out to the boat and clambered on to the stern platform.

Fiona said, 'What happened?'

I took off my shoe, let the foot hang in the water, and listened to the oyster-catchers whistle while the pain went from molten to red hot. Then I told her.

I said, 'Do those sheds belong to him?'

'No chance,' she answered.

'Then who?'

'Jerry Fine,' she said. 'He runs Lundgren's fish farms, and the wholesale operation. Donald works for anyone who will pay him, but mostly Lundgren. Helping with the dream.'

'What dream?'

She said, 'I came over from the States seven years ago, because I had the misfortune to fall in love with Ewan when he came to visit with some people I know in Oregon. This place was wild as you like. I collected up a few women who knew how to knit, and gave them some designs, and they all made a living, and nobody got hurt and nothing got used up except wool. Then Lundgren came. He had this dream. Every croft was going to have a freezer and wall-to-wall nylon broadloom, and everybody was going to be real grateful. He put a fish farm in each loch, so the whole place is covered in fish shit and strong chemicals. He started up the quarry, and everyone said, whoopee, work. But most of the guys came from outside, and the ones that didn't were like Donald. I guess it's a game to him, and everybody plays by his rules. Except Ewan. Ewan teases him. Lundgren doesn't like to be teased.'

'So what does Lundgren do?'

She shrugged. 'A while ago, there was some land for sale. Ewan wanted to arrange seaweed collecting, needed to put up a building. Lundgren found out and bought it himself. No sheds, no seaweed. But I guess he's happy. Real life for Ewan, a game for Lundgren. There's ten, fifteen things like that.'

'Would he pay Donald Stewart to knock Ewan about?'

'He'd do anything to frighten Ewan he thought he could get away with. Hell,' she said. 'Let's swim.'

She bent, picked up the bag she had brought forward, and pulled out two face masks.

'I saw you dive off *Flora* this morning,' she said. 'You stayed down three minutes.'

I could feel the tension across my shoulders. 'Nah,' I said.

'Come on,' she said.

I looked at the masks as if they were poisonous snakes.

Fiona said, 'Are you all right?'

I nodded.

She caught the hem of her jersey and pulled it over her head. Under it she was wearing a one-piece bathing suit of some shiny stuff. She had a fine body: straight back, long legs, good, deep curves. The clothes she wore hid her shape. Dressed, she was good-looking. Undressed, she was beautiful.

She threw me the mask. I did not try to catch it. It clunked on the cockpit sole and slid into the corner by the bridgedeck.

She looked at me for a moment. Then she shrugged her silky brown shoulders, spat on her faceplate, pulled it on and rolled backwards into the water.

I went to look over the side. The shape of her wobbled, refracted, black and tan. The water was so clear I could read the embossed letters on the anchor. I felt fouled with dirt six years old. Rubbish, I told myself. You're doing fine. You're alive. You've forgotten about it –

But I had not forgotten about it.

I climbed over the lifelines and took my sore foot to the bottom of the sea. The water helped the foot, but it did not wash off the dirt. When I came out, she was combing her hair in the cockpit, head on one side, knees together, skin tight from the water. 'You dived,' she said.

'That wasn't diving,' I said. 'That was swimming.'

We sailed back hard, not speaking. I made a big dog-leg most of the way out to Eigg, then home in a series of short tacks, the bow sections rattling like gunfire on the small seas coming off the land.

She said, 'Regatta tomorrow. Can I sail with you?'

I smiled at her, politely. 'Of course,' I said.

By the time we were reaching into the Narrows, I had buried the shame; buried it alive, but buried it all the same.

Displacement activity, the doctors call it. Bankrupts make coffee so as not to telephone the bank. Harry Frazer works so as not to think. So I went up to the house and sat myself in Fiona's studio, and called the office.

Cyril the clerk gave me a list of the calls. Spiro Kallikratides told me I was the only friend he had, besides his coke dealer. Davina Leyland told me about a party at Annabel's, mentioning in passing that her hairdresser friend, Giulio, had lost a hundred thousand pounds of her husband's money at Aspinall's immediately afterwards. There were others: the halt, the lame, the basket cases. I told them what to do; wily, authoritative Frazer, the man in control. Then I rang the last number on the list. Cyril always left it till last, because it was Vi's.

'*Darling*,' she said, with that bellows rush of breath. She would be in the living-room of her cottage off Quay Street in Pulteney, the walls lined with photographs of her, all legs and make-up, by David Bailey, Richard Avedon. The air would be thick with heavy scent, and the heating would be turned up all the way. I listened carefully for the edge in her voice.

This morning there was no edge, and she sounded light and girlish. 'I've got a *part!*' she said.

I told her that was good.

'Listen, though.' The voice had nerves in it, but it sounded more like suspense than persecution mania. 'There's a problem with Maurice.' Maurice was her agent, an elderly namedropper with a thin moustache and wet Special Brew eyes. 'It's this TV thing, a commercial, but still. There are like these two women, a mother and a daughter, and he's not co-operating.'

The edge was back. I took a deep breath, and said, 'What's the difficulty?'

'Well naturally the daughter's just right for me. But that silly bastard Maurice says they want me for the *mother*. Can you imagine? Could you *tell* him?'

I leaned my forehead on my hand. Vi did not look like anybody's daughter. Thirty years of bombed-out nights had fixed that.

She got the silence wrong. 'Just this once?' she said, wheedling.

Just this once I had come back from the Caribbean and gone diving in the cold North Sea, so she could raise a mortgage after her first barbiturate cure. Just this once I had come out of the loony bin and clambered eagerly into the cesspool of divorce work, so I could support Vi in the manner to which she had become accustomed.

'For Mummy Vi,' she said.

That was it. Harry Frazer, the one wearing grey flannel shorts in the Lampedusa in the King's Road, paying back Mummy Vi for bringing him up.

'And by the way,' she said. 'The director's Tom Finn.'

'Who's he?'

'He directed *Charlie Running*.'

'Great.'

'It'll be nice to work together again.'

I grunted. During my third and final year in the Caribbean, Vi had had a part in a movie shot on Tortola in the Virgin Islands. She had got Prosper and me work as extras. I had no idea what had happened to the film, but as far as Vi was concerned, it was a career triumph. 'I'll ring Maurice,' I said. 'Don't get your hopes up.'

I rang Maurice. He was a desperate man who spent his days drinking up his clients' residuals in a pub in Gerrard Street. I suggested to him that the mother could have been a child bride, and he grabbed the notion like I had grabbed Hector in the fog. Then I stumped away from the grubby world at the end of the telephone and went back down to the quay, fresh air, and the boat.

Chapter Nine

Flora was back on her mooring as I moved around *Green Dolphin*'s deck, tightening rigging screws. The midges were filling in. Out in the loch, a salmon splattered water with its tail.

The wind had died. The water was like a polished shield, and the only sounds were the distant mutter of the swell in the Horngate, and the clatter of water on stone where the burn flowed into the loch.

To seaward, I heard the purr of a diesel. I looked up. A moment later, a sharp red yacht motored smoothly through the Narrows. She was fifty feet long, with unstayed carbon fibre masts, sails furled in wishbone booms like a windsurfer's, and a retractable bowsprit nestling in its socket under her bow. Her anchor plunged down with a roar of chain. On her stern was the word BONEFISH, in gold. The man in the cockpit raised both his arms in salutation. He was short and stocky, in a bright red Henri Lloyd jacket and a woollen hat in the green, orange and gold of the Rastafarian national colours. He had almond-shaped brown eyes and teeth the conventional Martiniquais white. In the homely Celtic surroundings of Loch Beag, he looked as exotic as a golden oriole in a flock of starlings.

'Harreeeee!' he roared.

Prosper Duplessis had arrived.

I put a bottle of my own into the tender and rowed it over. Prosper flung a couple of sheets into a cockpit locker and banged me on the shoulder. 'Welcome to Scotland. Meet the crew.' He put his head down the companionway hatch, and said, 'Lisbeth!'

A woman came up from below. She was wearing bib-and-brace oilskin trousers, a sky-blue T-shirt that matched her eyes, and a big white smile.

'Harry Frazer,' said Prosper. 'Lisbeth Vandekaa.'

'We've already met,' I said. 'With David Lundgren.'

'That's right,' she said. The smile did not falter.

Prosper's short, powerful thumbs were already on the cork of the Krug bottle. 'Glasses, babe?'

Lisbeth passed up three glasses from below. The explosion of the cork echoed up the walls of Loch Beag. 'I came back from sea trials last night,' he said. 'Anchored in Loch na Keal on Mull. *Asteroid* was in there. David asked me aboard for dinner. Lisbeth was there. She came back with me.'

'I have been climbing on Ben More,' said Lisbeth. 'David was very kind. But some of his friends…' She shrugged and smiled.

'Great hairy fascists,' said Prosper. 'David's feeding them raw meat before the Three Bens. Couple of them tried to take a bite out of Lisbeth.'

The glow on Lisbeth's cheeks deepened.

'She's a neighbour. So I rescued her.'

'Prosper has been very kind,' she said. 'I think David is maybe a very tough man.'

'Very small,' said Prosper. 'That's his problem.'

Lisbeth giggled, putting her fingers coyly over her mouth. Prosper patted her on the knee. Judging by past performance, he would have plans of his own for her, which would not involve climbing. 'And how are Ewan and the lovely Fiona?' he said.

'Very kind,' I said.

'Yeah,' said Prosper. 'Old Ewan's really getting up David's nose, did you know that?'

'Who told you?'

'All of them. The raw meat boys. Baying for his blood, in the nicest possible way.'

'In this case,' said Lisbeth unexpectedly, 'I drink the health of Ewan.'

'I think that goes for all of us,' said Prosper.

And for the rest of the evening, it was like being on holiday.

It was late when I rowed back to *Green Dolphin*. More boats had come in, and the anchor lights burned at the centre of whirling globes of moths. It was all very cosy. But I kept thinking of Morag Sullivan and her four children, out there by the dark sea. And I felt a fool, because I still had not talked to Donald Stewart.

Next morning I was woken from edgy dreams by the plunge of an anchor and the rattle of chain. I came on deck in time to see *Asteroid* falling back to her cable in the middle of the loch. Six hard-looking men were pulling her mainsail down on to the boom.

I made tea, and sat on the cabin top in the early chill. Over the next couple of hours, as the day warmed up and the clouds lifted off the hills, a dozen or so yachts added themselves to the fleet in the harbour. Most of them were heavy, old-fashioned cruising boats, or ocean racers with added cruising comforts. There were three weeks to go till the Three Bens race, and the real fliers were still down South, working for their sponsors.

There were a lot of eyes on *Green Dolphin*. Next to the others, her three roller forestays and high, curved mast looked lean and dangerous.

People came over. They were not your racing hard chargers. They were red-faced, affable cruising people, here for a day on the water and a bit of Highland hospitality afterwards.

By ten-thirty there were people drinking whisky on the quay. I went ashore. Fiona came through the crowd and said, 'I want you to meet Jerry Fine.' She took my arm, gave it a squeeze of complicity, and led me across to a man wearing a blue Guernsey and an old black oilskin. He had black curly hair greased back from a pale face fallen into bags of worry at the eyes and jowls. 'And Alice,' she said. Alice Fine was red in the face and sharp in the nose. Where her husband resembled a bloodhound, she was like a small, ill-tempered terrier.

'You run the fish farms,' I said, after the introductions.

'For my sins,' said Fine. He did indeed have a penitent look.

'Nice life,' I said, blandly.

'I'd rather work down the sewers,' he said, and laughed, without enough irony to be convincing.

'I'm trying to get hold of a guy called Donald Stewart,' I said. 'I understand he works for you.'

'You're out of luck, then,' said Fine, showing his first sign of real enjoyment. 'He's gone to Blackpool for a week. David Lundgren gave him a holiday, just like that. Busiest time of year, too. Henley, Wimbledon. Everyone starting to yell for salmon mayonnaise.'

'Really,' I said. 'How very annoying. And how very convenient.'

His wife's eyes were pink and snapping. 'What do you want him for?' she said. 'Because he doesn't work for Jerry. He works for David.'

'We all work for David,' said Fine, again with insufficient irony.

'And bloody hard, too,' said Alice, with vehemence. 'Not that he appreciates it.'

'Alice, please,' said Fine, with a pained expression.

'No,' said Alice. There was a glass of whisky in her hand, and it was not her first. 'The way that little *bastard* carries on, you'd think – '

At the other end of the quay, Ewan said, 'Arriiight!' and climbed on to a bollard. Alice subsided. 'Rules,' Ewan said. There was a glass in his hand, and he was grinning like an excited dog. 'It's a pursuit race. We start according to handicap. Finish together. Your starting times are in the envelopes here. I'll bring 'em round. Start from anchor, like in the great days of sail. Course is round the South Ferris buoy and back. The finish line is the Narrows. Any route you like. No ramming, no gunfire.'

He jumped off his bollard and moved through the crowd, giving out envelopes.

'Jerry,' said Ewan, and handed him an envelope. Then he was on us, breathing whisky fumes, shoving another envelope into my hand. 'I'm counting on you,' he hissed, loud enough for Fine to hear. 'Lacerate that bastard Lundgren.'

He gave out the rest of his envelopes and went out to *Flora*. The Fines paddled out to a fat Westerly with a Clyde Cruising Club burgee and started pulling up sails. My slip of paper said 13.35. Prosper's was twenty minutes earlier.

'I'm last,' said a voice at my elbow. It was David Lundgren. 'Hell of a time to wait. Still, it pleases Ewan.' His smile was a steely counterfeit of affection. 'How are you enjoying Scotland, Mr Frazer?'

'Nice place,' I said.

'Taking an interest in the local community, I hear.' He stuck one of his Russian cigarettes between his teeth.

'Sorry?'

'Asking a lot of questions.'

His eyes were grey, and hard as pebbles. I caught them full toss. 'Yes,' I said. 'I'm representing Morag Sullivan.'

'Oh, yes,' said Lundgren. 'Husband took off, I hear. And you're the fancy divorce lawyer.'

I said, 'I do other work, too.'

He grinned at me round the cigarette.

'Pity Donald Stewart's on holiday,' I said. 'There are things I'd like to ask him.'

The round sunburnt face turned up at the sky, and he laughed, a high, thin laugh. 'Needed a rest,' he said. And I knew that in this morning's round of the Lundgren game that was all I got.

Prosper was alongside. He said, 'Why are we sailing this race?'

'For the pure joy of it,' I said.

But Prosper's eyes were sleepy, and his grin went all the way from ear to ear. I knew what that meant. 'Boring,' he said. 'How about a little wager?'

'Ah,' said Lundgren. '*Now* you're talking.'

I did not say anything. I had a lot of bets with Prosper. If you gamble with the same person, and you act sensible, you usually land up more or less even at the end of the year.

But Lundgren had different things in mind. 'Good,' he said. 'Pool. Winner takes all. How much in there?'

'Five grand,' said Prosper.

'Each,' said Lundgren.

I opened my mouth to tell them to count me out. Lundgren looked at me and grinned slyly. He said, 'If I get beaten by that thing of yours, you and Charlie Agutter could be in luck with your production run.'

Hold it, I said to myself. Five thousand pounds is three months of Vi's keep that you already haven't got. Lundgren probably spent that much on three months' cigarettes.

But over Lundgren's big round head, *Green Dolphin* lay sleek and deadly alongside the quay. Never mind the common sense, said a voice in my head. Believe.

'Fine,' I said. 'Let's go.'

Lundgren's smile did not alter. Prosper laughed, and said, 'Good boy.'

'Well,' said Lundgren, 'I suppose I must go and control my crew.'

Prosper watched him go. 'He's a hard man,' he said. 'There was a guy I knew in Antigua, tried to stop him building a lot of yacht docks. The guy went bust. Stuff like that.'

'I see,' I said.

'He doesn't like losing,' said Prosper. 'Common failing.' He glanced at me sideways. 'By the way, you started diving again?'

I felt the lurch in my insides. 'No. Why?'

'I was talking to Fiona. She said had you been a diver. I said once, but not any more. What's that all about?'

'I don't know,' I said.

'They got plans for you, boy. I told you. You'll lose your edge.'

I said, 'I'm fine.'

'You better be,' said Prosper. 'Five grand's worth. May the best man win, as long as it's not Wee Davie.'

Chapter Ten

Two hours later, there were only three boats out in the middle of the loch: *Bonefish*, *Dolphin* and *Asteroid*.

Prosper started on time. His Freedom was fast, but it had a low handicap. I made Lapsang Souchong and crayfish sandwiches, put Pergolesi's *Stabat Mater* on the stereo. We sat and watched the clock, swinging to our anchor a hundred yards from the long black side of *Asteroid*.

The clock on the wheel pedestal said 13.25. *Asteroid's* windlass clacked as she came up over her anchor; she was due to start twenty minutes after us.

I pulled up the mainsail, and hit the keel hydraulics button. The pumps hummed, lowering the eight-foot blade of steel, kevlar and lead out of its housing.

Fiona said, 'Let's go.'

'Five minutes before time,' I said. 'Lundgren's watching.'

'Bugger Lundgren. Ewan would, and argue afterwards.'

'I'm not Ewan.' I had not told her about the bet.

She smiled at me. The smile seemed to imply that she was glad I was not Ewan. It was like being on the receiving end of an individual sunrise.

I leaned over and set the countdown timer above the main hatch. Then I took up the slack in the mainsheet, and pulled out some jib. It rippled hugely in the gentle breeze. *Dolphin* heeled a few degrees, shoving her lean shoulder confidingly into the wavelets. The electric windlass brought her over her anchor.

'Zero,' said Fiona.

I cranked in the last of the mainsheet. We were racing.

In a pursuit race, the boats start at intervals determined by the ratings given them under the handicap system. If the handicapper has got it right, all the boats will arrive at the finishing line at the same time. This makes it a pleasing form of race for those wishing to get to the post-finish booze-up within half an hour of each other, but diminishes the excitement of the start.

But *Green Dolphin* had long enough legs to make even that interesting.

The wind was northwesterly. The Narrows funnelled it straight at us, but the tide was ebbing hard, and we got out in two short tacks. Fiona had a delicate touch on the helm, keeping the boat hard on the wind, but not hard enough to detach the smooth flow of air over the sail. I saw the horizon widen behind the rock buttresses, and squinted at the chart clipped to the bridge-deck in the lee of the cabin top.

From the southern point of the bay the Horngate ran out in a long crescent of drying rocks. At this time of tide the rocks were awash, crunching the swell to cream. To get round its tip meant staying hard on the wind for another mile before we bore away for the South Ferris buoy, ten miles west-southwest.

A lump of wind bowled across the water to starboard. *Dolphin*'s mast dipped as it hit, and the note of her wake quickened from a chuckle to a roar as the numbers on the log flicked up to eight knots.

'Lundgren's started,' said Fiona.

I looked round. The big cutter hung framed by the cliffs of the Narrows, pinned by a shaft of sunlight. Mud gleamed on her anchor, hanging beneath the gilt scrollwork on her bow. Then a puff knocked into her cream canvas sails, and she began to move, crabbing to seaward, the ebb sucking at the long shark's belly of her hull.

Then we had other things to think about.

Over the bow the sea was dark with the racing shadows of squalls. To the west, the clouds were ripped, and big rays of sunshine spread patches of green and blue on the slate-coloured water. Ardnamurchan was lost in a curtain of rain, a heavy blue–black backdrop for the string of white triangles running down to the horizon.

The bow lifted and thumped into a trough with a *boom* and a cloud of spray. Water ran glistening down Fiona's face. Her pink tongue came out to lick the salt. I trained the glasses on the opposition.

Out at the tip of the Horngate, the slim white triangles of Prosper's sails suddenly broadened as he turned off the wind and eased sheets for the reach down to the buoy. The others were anonymous wedges of white. *Flora*'s red sails were out of sight, but then she was two hours ahead, perhaps eight miles in this wind, away under the heavy curtain of vapour masking the streaming hills of Ardnamurchan.

Now all we had to do was catch up.

I went to sit on the rail, squinting at the mountains inland, looking for the transit, the two crags you had to hold in line to clear the rocks. Fiona said, 'Ewan will have gone inside.'

'Inside what?' I said.

She pointed two hundred yards to port, where the seas rumbled and whitened in the Horngate.

'Must be out of his mind,' I said.

She laughed. For a moment, she looked almost proud of him. *Green Dolphin* worried her way through the long seas in a cloud of spray, and I concentrated on keeping the numbers on the log up around the eight knots. If I had been below, I would have been sick. Up here, I could trim the boat and concentrate. What I could see at the moment was encouraging. We were holding Prosper, the next boat ahead. But over five minutes Prosper was definitely closing the boat in front.

It took twenty minutes to thump out to the tip of the Horngate. Fiona put the helm down, and the big mass of Eigg swung smoothly across the forestay. Fiona took the wheel, and I juggled mainsheet and jibsheet, cranking and surging until the telltales blew out straight either side of the high white wings of the sails.

It was *Green Dolphin*'s favourite point of sailing. The deck kicked forward. The nose came up, and the hard fans of white wake hissed from the forward sections, like water from a hose when you put your thumb over the end. Astern, the wake lost its turbulence and became the clean white feather that meant the log needle had gone past ten. The little triangles ahead started coming back towards us as if we were reeling them in.

The wind was blowing hard and flat now, force five, out of the dark hills of Skye. It was just me and Fiona and the boat rattling across the round tops of the waves, climbing the upslope, sliding down the fronts, galloping for the buoy.

An hour after the start, the yellow-and-black South Ferris cardinal was tall on the port bow. We were crossing Prosper, who was already round, starting the leg back for the Horngate, wishbone booms cranked all the way in, the red hull of his Freedom squeezing the waves to foam.

I said, 'We're catching him.'

Fiona nodded. The wind had brightened her cheeks.

'Going down,' I said. 'Due south.'

Fiona eased the wheel gently. I gave her some more sheet, and a couple more rolls of genoa. A gust hissed across the water. Then the nose was up, and the hull was drumming, a long roaring vibration, and she leaped past the western fringes of the South Ferris between two sheets of rainbow spray, the needle sitting on fifteen, as if she wanted to run up the stegosaurus spine of the Ardnamurchan peninsula, out of the clouds now, glowing green dead ahead.

At the bottom end of the rocks Fiona put the helm up, I did the sheets, and the boom clacked neatly over. And now we were on the port tack, with the South Ferris up to port and falling astern, close-reaching after the tightening bunch ahead.

We began to take them.

Before we were halfway up the leg we passed a couple of Westerly cruising ketches, skidding on their bilge keels, forced to pinch up to windward to lay the end of the Horngate. A shower of cold rain swept through. In the sunshine that followed it, we shrugged away the trickles of water that had driven into the collars of our coats. Astern, *Asteroid* was leaning far over to starboard, her huge cream mainsail elegant as a gull's wing. Ahead, there were people running on the foredeck of a big Rival. Suddenly the Rival came upright and tacked for the open sea.

I put my glasses on her as her genoa filled.

Fiona said, 'Why did they do that?'

'Wind's headed,' I said. 'We'll get it soon.'

We got it. The winch rang as I cranked in the genoa. The speed fell back; soon, we were punching across the waves at a solid seven-and-a-half knots, and there was no way we were going to be able to lay the Horngate without putting in a tack.

'Tack now?' said Fiona.

I shook my head. With the mountains breaking and twisting the flow of the air, anything could happen. Through the glasses, I saw that three boats had tacked already. Prosper was keeping at it, hoping for a lift. That was Prosper for you; lay your money down, and push your luck until it squeaks. But for the moment it was not Prosper I was interested in.

Far ahead, right under the land, I could see *Flora*'s brownish-red sails. Ewan was about halfway between us and the landward end of the Horngate, and he was making no effort to tack.

Steadily, the distance between us and Ewan closed. We were hammering on at a steady seven knots; he would be doing three and a half or four.

We were catching him fast. But Prosper was following him too, and we were catching Prosper very, very slowly. The Freedom was a good boat to windward. *Dolphin* was mustard on a reach, but she was too wide and flat-sectioned to be any better than just good enough on the wind.

'Behind you,' said Fiona.

I glanced over my shoulder. *Asteroid* had made ground. Her bow was perhaps three hundred yards astern, close enough to see the detail of the gilt shooting star on her spoon bow, and the clawed fingers of the man perched on the end of her bowsprit, wrestling with the tack of her foresail. Seventy feet of waterline gives a boat a theoretical maximum speed of well over ten knots, and that was what she was doing.

I said, 'I'll take the helm.' If we lost, I wanted it to be my fault. The cutter would go past, tack to weather the Horngate. Prosper would tack, too. They would leave Ewan standing. And we would be nowhere.

'Maybe Ewan'll tack to cover,' I said. If he ran across the nose of the fleet on starboard, he would have right of way. But even as I said it, I knew *Flora* was too slow for it to work.

'He won't tack,' said Fiona.

His sails were four hundred yards ahead, the colour of dried blood against the white foam of the Horngate. 'He'll have to,' I said.

'It's two hours since low tide,' she said. 'He won't.'

Suddenly, I knew what she meant.

If Lundgren and Prosper went ahead, I lost five thousand pounds, and a notional production run. But it was not the money I was thinking about.

My sister Vi put an edge on her life with pills and drink. I did it by racing, and winning.

Any route you like. No ramming, no gunfire.

I took a deep breath, and did not let it out.

Flora was three hundred yards away, just off the fringes of the surf. As I watched, her sails went one behind the other. And she pointed the wrong way; not to seaward, tacking to round the point, but inland, to where the shore dived into the sea.

Behind my head I could hear the flutter of *Asteroid's* mainsail as she luffed. Quickly, not giving myself time to think, I fed out mainsheet and genoa and put the helm down. *Dolphin* turned her quarter to the waves, and accelerated hard enough to knock us off balance.

My thumb hit the button that raised the keel. The hydraulics groaned, protesting at the effort of hauling up eight feet of composite plate. The helm became light and skittery. We were sliding now, sideways as well as forwards. Gently, I coaxed the nose upwind, feathering the mainsail to cut speed. The deck surged on a quartering sea.

Ewan was fifty yards ahead. He had turned to port, heading straight for the thundering line of breakers. I glanced at Fiona. She was staring at me. 'Clip on,' I said. 'Lifejacket.'

We yawed in crookedly, my hands slipping with sweat on the wheel. We rose on a steep wave. Light showed through its crest. It broke under the bow. Ahead, in the white water, I saw a thread of black; a channel. *Flora* was in the middle of it. It was covered with spindrift and oily with tide, that channel, but it crawled into the heart of the Horngate. There were breakers all around now. Ten yards to port, the crest of the wave lifting our stern toppled and plunged down on itself with a crushing roar. Beyond, still heading out to sea, was Prosper, two trim white triangles, and *Asteroid*, immaculate, huge sails rippling as she tacked. *Stupid bastard*, I told myself. *Two minutes from now you will be a bundle of splinters.*

Flora's stern suddenly danced away to starboard, and her nose turned to port. Ewan looked back, his beard like wet red seaweed. I yanked the wheel over, came round in his wake. The wind was blowing over the port quarter now. Ahead was a wall of jumping white water from which projected evil humps of rock. *Wait for it*, I told myself. *Wait for it, and follow him in.*

But *Green Dolphin* was a racing boat, and *Flora* was a trawler, and the wind was too far aft to spill. *Dolphin* did not know how to go slow enough.

I felt a gust on my neck. The mainsail filled with a crack. A wave came under the stern, up, up. The crest curled, and I felt the heart-stopping lightness as she began to slide. *Surfing*, I thought. *This is the end.*

We flew past *Flora* as if she was standing still. Ewan and Hector stood watching, their mouths astonished black circles. Mine probably looked the same, because all I could see was the beach, a brown beach of big boulders, and we were going to hit it, seven tons of boat and God knew how many tons of water, moving at better than twenty knots.

Then Ewan's arm came up, and he waved us over, to port. I spun the wheel, and *Dolphin* rolled appallingly, and the twin rudders tore the back end off the wave, and we were shooting across the face of the next wave, parallel to that ugly beach, heading for a little gap of dark water. It looked too narrow for a dinghy, that gap. But there was nowhere else to go. The wave we had been riding exploded on the beach. I put the nose for the gap. It widened under the bow. Not enough. There were two lumps of rock, one either side, gatekeepers. They were twelve feet apart. *Dolphin* is thirteen feet wide. We were going too fast to do anything about it.

'Hold on!' I roared.

The lift of the next wave shoved hard at the soles of my feet. My hand went out, hauled the mainsheet. Dolphin heeled and accelerated, and I sank my head between my shoulders, waiting for the splintering bang as we shot, lifted on the wave, into the gap that was too narrow for the boat.

The bang did not come. Suddenly we were in black water. Smooth black water: the water inside the Horngate, at the mouth of Loch Beag. I looked astern. Our wake passed directly through the gap.

Then we were both laughing, holding on to each other, giggling like idiots.

Down to port, Prosper was tight up to windward of *Asteroid*. We slid through the Narrows with the flood tide, and into the empty loch. My knees were shaking so I could hardly stand.

As we came alongside, Fiona said, 'I enjoyed that.'

I said, 'It was a bloody stupid thing to do.'

She said, 'I don't have a problem with that kind of stupid,' and kissed me on the mouth. Then she ran forward, picked up the bow line, and jumped on to the quay.

Prosper came across. 'Nice,' he said. 'You bloody idiot.' Prosper had always had a way of saying what I was already thinking. We had a cup of tea. After he had gone, I was clearing up below when there was a knocking on the hull, and Ewan came down the companionway ladder.

His eyes were a little glassy, but no more than usual. I said, 'Thank you for showing me the way through.'

He grinned at me. 'It's one thing to show you. It's another to take it. Hector says you're a brave man.'

I shrugged, pulled a bottle of Famous Grouse out of the locker and tipped some into glasses. I had a strong feeling that Ewan was not here to chat about racing.

I was right.

'I was talking to Fiona,' he said. 'You've made a hit with Fiona. The only thing she doesn't understand is why you won't go diving.'

I started to tell him to mind his own business. He raised a hand.

'I talked to your friend Prosper,' he said. 'He told me.'

I looked into the golden depths of the whisky.

'You came through the Horngate on a wave,' he said. 'So you're not a coward.'

'Oh, I am,' I said. 'About diving.'

He stared at me. 'It's not diving you're afraid of,' he said. 'It's Harry Frazer. You'll do it, if you have to. So I'll bloody well make you.' He looked at his watch. 'Come down to the shed tomorrow morning, and I'll show you something. Then we'll go sailing Tuesday night.'

He left. I finished the whisky, and heard the bang and roar of the waves breaking in the Horngate, and tried to think of something that would make me go diving again.

There was nothing.

At half past six I pulled the Gieves blazer and the chinos out of the wardrobe, rowed ashore and walked through the fine drizzle up to the house.

The drawing-room was jammed to the panelling with leather-faced people from the boats, drinking whisky and talking. Fiona's face brightened when she saw me; I saw Ewan watching her. He raised an arm with a glass at the end of it, and said, 'The winnah!' His eyes were sardonic; he could have been talking about the race, or Fiona.

Prosper was already there, in a corner with Lisbeth and some people I did not know. They came over.

'You took a short course,' said Lisbeth. 'Not fair.' Her smile was still wide as a piano keyboard, but there was a suspicion of petulance to her lower lip.

'He sailed by the rules,' said Prosper. 'Old Harry always goes by the rules.'

There was a blast of rank tobacco smoke. Lundgren was in our midst, chewing his cardboard filter. 'Most impressive,' he said. 'Particularly the lifting keel. You can tell Mr Agutter that my people will be round at his office to take a look.'

Prosper said, 'He'll take a cheque.'

Lundgren looked at him with his pebble eyes, unsmiling. Then he said, 'Of course,' took out his wallet, and scribbled.

I smiled at him, and said, 'Thank you.'

'Not at all,' he said. 'And one of these days you must come up to Dunmurry. We'll show you how we play men's games. Maybe you'd like to join in?' He went back to the knot of hard nuts with moustaches at the other side of the room.

'Revolting,' said Prosper.

I knew how he felt.

I sat next to Fiona at dinner. I felt I had known her for twenty years. We sat in a pinkish glow, and people teased me for going through the rocks. It was all very delightful. It was almost possible to imagine I was on holiday.

Almost.

Fiona put her hand on mine. 'You don't have to go tomorrow,' she said.

I gazed into her eyes, and thought: same old two possibilities, Frazer. Either she likes you, or she wants a free lawyer.

Or both.

I said, 'I'll hang around a while.'

Losing your edge, said Prosper's voice in my mind. I ignored it.

And that was that.

Chapter Eleven

Later, I rowed back to *Green Dolphin* and made a cup of Earl Grey. The sky had come right down, and a small, warm rain was drifting across the loch. The yachts' anchor lights burned like big yellow stars in the glassy water. There was a lot of coming and going: voices murmuring across the water, quiet and unruffled, and the clonk of oars.

I went below into *Dolphin*'s meticulous cabin, hung up my blazer and trousers in the cedar-lined wardrobe, cleaned my teeth over the side and crawled into my sleeping bag.

I woke next morning to a dull grey light in the portholes, and the steady hiss of rain on water. People were moving on boats, getting ready to go. Several had already left.

My eyes ached from last night's whisky. I ate a quick breakfast, pulled on a tracksuit and running shoes, and rowed ashore. It was too early to go to Ewan's shed. It was time for what Prosper called the Hercules Hangover Cure.

I found a path and followed it up to the ridges above the loch and along the thousand-foot contour. It was a jagged scramble in the dirty fringes of the cloud base, but it set the blood running and cleared the head.

From up here, the loch was a thread of metal winding between the buttresses of the hills. I did about five miles along the ridge, towards the grey smear that masked the sea, looped up to the summit of a fair-sized mountain, and came back the same way.

At nine o'clock I found myself on a sort of pulpit of rock that plunged sheer a hundred feet to a steep slope that ran in turn down to the shore of the loch.

I paused a minute, to take in the dirty curtains of rain sweeping down the wind that had risen in the past hour. The boats had gone. A couple of gulls whisked past below, rocking to keep their grip on the air.

A man was walking along a path that ran along the shore of the loch. He was coming from the seaward end. Even at a range of three hundred yards, straight down, I could see that it was Ewan. The shed was just off the path, a small building with a pitched roof, perhaps ten feet square, the kind of place where you would keep nets and lobster pots. It looked as if it was built right out over the rocks; there was a staging in front of it where a boat could come alongside, and the water at its end was deep and black.

Ewan drew the bolt and went in. There was no padlock. I started to turn away, to look for a path down.

The loch exploded.

A blast of heat smashed me in the face and tumbled me backwards in the stink of burning hair. I felt pain in face and palms and knees as I ploughed across the ground, then I was lying looking at the dirty sky with the ring of a huge explosion in my ears.

There was an acrid reek in the air. I recognised it from diving school. Burned nitro-glycerine.

I crawled to the edge and looked over. For a moment, there was nothing but coils of poisonous yellow smoke that sank into my lungs and made me cough, big, dirty coughs. Then the wind got it, and took it away, and what I saw was as bad as I had feared.

I saw nothing.

It was as if a shark had come out of the loch, a shark with jaws thirty yards across, and taken a semi-circular bite out of the shore where the hut had been. The path was a smear of smoking rubble.

There was no hut.

Sobbing for breath, I began to slither down the side of the mountain.

It was very quiet, and it smelled like a chemical waste dump. I stumbled over the raw, peaty earth, looking for things I did not want to find. The gulls returned, and they had better eyes than me. I ran after them when they settled, shouting stupidly. But they only flapped into the stinking air and settled again, out of reach. Then I heard a voice, and I looked up. And there, standing at the end of the coast path among the splintered trees, was a thin figure in a brown raincoat that lashed in the wind. Fiona.

Away from the scar, it became possible to imagine that nothing had happened, and that the wind rattling the blue gums above Loch Beag was blowing across the same old water and rock.

But everything had changed.

I stumbled across to her. She said, 'That was Ewan's shed.' She looked surprised, that was all.

One minute someone is there. The next there is a hole in the seashore, and they are not there at all. Not at all.

She said something else. My ears were ringing with the explosion. But that was not the reason I did not hear it. I was thinking, hard. What could I say?

I said, 'Yes.'

She was not looking at the scar. She was looking at my face. Whatever she saw in it stopped her dead.

She said, 'He wasn't in there.' I gripped her arm. The muscles had gone rigid under the cloth of the raincoat.

How do you tell someone? How the hell?

You tell them. That's all.

I told her.

The colour went out of her face. It turned yellowish-white, parchment colour, the eyes suddenly sunken, so that the bones of the skull showed through. 'The gelignite,' she said, and pulled away, towards the black scar. The gulls were yelling.

I held on to her. She pulled away. Then she stopped pulling. A year later, or it might have been ten minutes, we began to walk with small, elderly steps towards the house.

When we were halfway back, Hector came running out of the trees. His face was puffy, his hair matted as if he had got straight out of bed. He said, 'What the hell was that?'

I told him, in a voice that wobbled all over the place. He stared at me with glassy, uncomprehending eyes. Then he ran heavily down the path to the scar, and the gulls' yells turned harsh and angry as they flapped into the sky.

We got back to the house. Ewan's shoes were on the hall carpet. Fiona was looking at them. She stood and stared at them. She said, 'I don't believe it. Just this morning... He slammed the door. Always that goddamn door.' She sat down on a chest.

I stood there. Harry Frazer has a remark for all eventualities, but this time I had no idea what to say.

'Seven years,' she said. Her voice was thin and tight. Her eyes did not leave the shoes. 'Fiona Campbell on a yacht. Ewan Buchan the beautiful barbarian. He went right through me like a knife. I thought he was a force of nature. Four years we lived together. Poor Ewan. He cried when I told him I was leaving.' Her eyes rose, met mine. 'But I only moved across the hall. Forces of nature don't leave you a lot of time for your own life. And then we were good friends.' Her eyes returned to the shoes. 'We were good friends.'

She picked up the shoes, and went out of sight into the kitchen. I heard the clank of the dustbin lid.

When she came back, she was crying.

Soon after that, the police arrived.

There was a sergeant and a constable, stocky, hard-looking men. The sergeant had a hard Glasgow accent that went with a thin, cynical mouth.

He said, 'So there was an explosion.'

Hector was where the hut had been. Fiona was upstairs. I was the spokesman. I said, 'That's right.'

We walked out to the scar. The policeman sniffed. 'Dirty smell,' said the sergeant. 'Kept a bit of gelignite, did he?'

Let him believe it was gelignite. Let Fiona. Telling either of them that Ewan was in the habit of collecting vintage Naval mines would do no good.

He nodded, scribbled something in his notebook. 'Terrible,' be said. 'He had a licence, of course?'

I said, 'I haven't the faintest bloody idea. He's dead. Are you going to prosecute him if he hadn't?' Calm down, I thought. Calm down.

The sergeant looked deep into my face, and asked if I would like to sit down. I was scarcely listening. My thoughts were slithering, refusing to stay still. I should have been in the shed when it blew up. I could see him now; lighting the cigarette, the match flying into the water where the little threads of nitro-glycerine hung suspended – 'Accidents will happen,' said the sergeant.

They made me run through what I had seen from the hill. They questioned Hector. Then they ate a lunch in the back of their panda car, and pottered about on the scar. I took a deep breath, and went and knocked on Fiona's door. She told me to go away. I went downstairs and made her tea, trying not to think about the gulls. Then I walked out to look for Hector.

He met me halfway. He was wearing his oilskin coat and a wool hat, and his square face was grey and tight. He asked about Fiona. He said, 'I was going up to see her. Maybe I'll leave it a wee moment.'

I nodded. We turned and walked slowly towards the quay.

I said, 'You and Ewan had been collecting mines for a rainy day. You were storing them down there. That was what went up this morning.'

Hector's face could have been moulded out of grey mud. He said, 'No.'

There was a big, terrible stillness. Even the gulls went quiet. 'Then what?' I said.

We were out of the bamboos now, on the short green turf of the foreshore. Hector stared into the grey drizzle, and spoke in the manner of one reciting a lesson to himself. 'Sure, we kept a mine. We kept it under the water, under the floor of the bothy.' The gulls were white against the black plough of the scar, fifty yards long, forty high. 'But yon mine we give to the Navy was the only one.'

More silence. Out in the loch, deep water swirled sluggishly. And in my mind.

I said, 'If there was no mine, what blew up?'

'That's asking,' said Hector, in a flat, stony voice. Drizzle blew in our faces. 'Come on out to the boat.'

He rowed mechanically across the pockmarks of the drizzle. The wind had dropped. The dip of the oars was the only sound. If it had not been for the ring of the explosion in my ears, I would have expected Ewan's shaggy head to rise above *Flora*'s high black gunwale.

But of course there was only the cry of the gulls, and the shouts of little blue figures scrambling on the scar.

There was a smell of fresh varnish in the wheelhouse, and a brush in a jar of white spirit. Hector slopped whisky into two glasses. We drank. I said, 'Did he keep gelignite in the shed?'

Hector's mouth was a dry, lipless slot. 'A few wee sticks,' he said. He jerked a thumb at the side of the loch. 'But you'd need a full crate to do that.' The big stone-coloured fist hammered down on the chart table. The varnish jar jumped and shattered on the deck. 'Some bastard put it there,' he said. 'So it would spatter the poor man up the hill like you'd butter bread.' For a moment, his mild blue eyes were full of a horrible intensity. Then he ducked away down on to the deck, and began to grope for shards of glass with his thick fingers.

I watched him across a chasm of silence. I said, 'What bastard?'

Hector swept the last of the bits of glass into a dustpan, and straightened up. 'He was after someone,' he said.

That was true enough.

'We were to be away out again tomorrow,' said Hector. 'He was in here this morning early, programming the machine.'

I looked up. The red light of the Navstar glowed above the chart table at the aft end of the wheelhouse.

I reached up my hand, and punched the buttons.

A Navstar 2000D picks up signals from Decca beacons situated on headlands and islands along a coast. It measures the difference in their phases, and produces its conclusions in little green digits on a nice little screen. It can tell you where you are, and how to get to where you want to go.

So my fingers tapped the buttons, and the waypoints came up. There were three. I pulled the chart towards me and switched on the dim bulb on the flexible gooseneck.

The first waypoint was in the bay, where the signal would reach the aerial free of interference from the rock masses of the mountains round Loch Beag. That would give a course to the second, just to the north of the Horngate. The third was beyond Ardnamurchan. It was in the middle of nowhere, that place, on the forty-metre contour, where the bottom of the sea dived away.

I found that I was staring at the square-edged figures on the display as if they were a set of headlights and I was a rabbit.

I have an excellent memory for figures, and I had seen those figures before. To within half a mile, they were the figures my own Decca had been showing on *Green Dolphin* the moment Ewan had driven *Flora* through my port side.

I said, 'What is that, out there?'

Hector said, 'I don't know.'

'What was Ewan planning to do?'

He stared at me full in the face. The whisky had glazed his eyes, but they were hot and blue and filled with conviction. 'We were out there already, day before yesterday. He gave it a scan with the fishfinder,' he said. 'We were going out tomorrow, to wait and see what happened. And after, he said he'd need a diver. He said that you were a diver.'

There was a silence. The gulls were yelling. Ewan Buchan was dead. Ewan Buchan had acted like a friend.

I climbed into the tender and rowed ashore.

Back at the house, the doctor was coming down the stairs. 'I gave her a sedative,' he said. 'She's asleep now. Is there anyone who can stay with her?'

I said there was me. Then I went into the kitchen.

The Aga needed stoking, and the fires lighting. As I spat out coal dust and fought the damp kindling, it seemed inconceivable that Ewan had done the chores this morning, a mere six hours ago.

It was quiet in the house; quiet as the tomb. I put the kettle on, for company, decided that this was no time for tea and dug a bottle of Glenmorangie out of the cupboard. I believed Hector when he said there had been no more mines in the shed. I believed him when he said that Ewan kept a few sticks of gelignite, but not enough to remove half the hill. But that meant I had to believe that someone had felt it worthwhile to blow Ewan to bits.

I shivered. The whisky burned down my gullet, but it did not stop the shivers. I tipped another two inches into the glass. What was making me shiver was what Ewan had been about to tell me, in the shed this morning.

And now he was never going to tell anyone anything, ever. The wind set up a metallic rattle in the leaves of the eucalyptus. The gust died and the house was quiet, full of the silence that flowed down the loch from the sea and the deep crevices of the mountains. At the back of the silence, there was a sound: a sound like a pulse beating; irregular, animal. Fiona, sobbing.

I picked up the telephone and dialled Prosper's number. I told him what had happened. 'I won't be coming up for a while,' I said. 'I think I'm needed down here.'

'Come when you can,' he said.

Then I went up to Fiona.

The curtains were drawn, and the room was dim. She had stopped crying. I went and sat by the hump of her under the bedclothes, and put my hand on her shoulder. The muscles were still tense, hard as iron. I said, 'That diving Ewan wanted me to do. I'm ready when you are.'

She rolled away. I went downstairs and rang the office. Cyril was there late, as usual. He told me what was going on, and we plotted a little. But the tangles of Orchard Street seemed tiny and remote next to the big, simple facts of death. So I told Cyril to open a file for Morag Sullivan, ignoring the disapproval in his voice.

'Marital?' said Cyril.

'Compensation,' I said.

'Against whom?'

I hesitated. 'Person or persons unknown,' I said. 'No fee.'

Cyril's voice became plummy and agitated. I put the telephone down on him, and spent the rest of the evening drinking whisky in the kitchen.

The next day was Tuesday.

We left Loch Beag on the tide, trudged out to the Horngate, and set a course for the third waypoint. It was raining. We moved heavily through a sea the colour of cement, the clear-view disc in the wheelhouse window whining, fug rising from the coal stove. Hector stayed below, overhauling the diving gear. I steered, watching the bowsprit rise to the big, dirty waves, point at the sky, cleave into the troughs with a heavy plunge and a cloud of spray.

The wind rose. The day turned dirtier. It was too rough for diving, even if the equipment had been ready. By mid-afternoon, we were on the waypoint. Hector switched on the fishfinder. I looked at it as little as possible, keeping my eyes out of the window, looking across the white horses to the horizon. I did not know what we were looking for. What I did know was that if I took my eyes off the horizon, I was going to be sick.

'Look here,' said Hector.

The fishfinder showed a sloping bottom, forty metres down. There were rocks down there. One of them was much bigger than the others.

'That's what you'll be looking at,' said Hector.

I nodded, and looked back at the horizon. A bulk carrier was going up for the quarry, its high sides smothered in spray.

'Now we'll see,' said Hector.

Now we would see. We would see what happened on Tuesday nights.

But first, I was going to be sick.

I went out of the wheelhouse into the raw wind and vomited over the side. Hector made tea and bacon, eggs and beans. I was sick again. The dusk came down. The wind rose; the sky cleared. The Hyskeir lighthouse blinked white, and the West Ferris buoy blinked red. Hector turned off the navigation lights. A week ago, I had been exhausted, and there had been fog. Tonight, there was no fog. Far to seaward, fishing boats showed lights. But for five miles around nothing moved except steep black waves under a high roof to the stars.

Soon after dawn, we started home.

All that day, and the next, I was tied to the house, working on the diving equipment, fending off telephone callers and taking Fiona food on a tray. At ten to six that evening I heard her radio. At ten past, she came downstairs. Her skin was the colour of ivory, and there were black circles under her eyes. She went straight to the tray in the drawing-room, poured four inches of whisky into a heavy glass, and drank it. Then she said, 'The forecast's good. We'll do it tomorrow.'

Her fingers were thin and nervous on the heavy glass. They reminded me a little of Vi's, when Vi was beginning one of her bad spells. It was Vi's bad spells that had started me on serious diving in the first place.

I smiled, a tight, dry-mouthed smile that did not help the fear in the pit of my stomach.

'Fine,' I said.

Yet again, the women in Harry Frazer's life were driving him underwater.

Chapter Twelve

By the time I left school I had had enough of Vi and her friends in and out of the hairdressers' shops and photographers' studios of the King's Road. So I went to Bristol and met Arthur Somers for the first time.

Somers was a well-intentioned family friend who ran Martin, Williams, a firm of solicitors in Orchard Street. He was a large red man who wore stiff collars, drank Madeira for elevenses, and disliked work because it cut into being a full-time gentleman. After three years of filling in for him with the obese Bristol stockbrokers and Merchant Venturers who were his clients, I had had enough. I had done some sailing in the Bristol Channel, and I had a spurious notion of the romance of blue-water voyaging. So, on completing my articles, I left Orchard Street, signed on as a deckhand for the delivery trip of a fat ferro-concrete ketch destined for charter out of the US Virgin Islands, and rolled down the Trades to the West Indies.

In the Caribbean I made contact with Prosper, just out of Princeton, who introduced me to exactly the kind of unsuitable people I wished to meet. I wore shorts for three years, perfecting the art of helmsmanship in the trade winds, and scuba diving in the warm waters off Virgin Gorda. I also ran a beach bar and managed a bareboat charter company. After the King's Road and Orchard Street, I thought it was the Garden of Eden.

Then it started hailing snakes. Vi came out to the Virgin Islands with Davina Leyland to work on *Charlie Running*. When I met her at the airport she looked like an over-exposed photograph of herself. She got me a job as an extra on the film, and I kept her out of trouble and made sure she got a good tan in the right company. By the time she left, she seemed better. Two weeks after she left, I got a telephone call from Jack Vincent, her boyfriend, who ran a Bentley showroom in Ascot, to say that she was dying in hospital and that he wanted nothing more to do with her, because the way she had been carrying on was not helping him sell Bentleys.

So I bought a pair of long trousers, and went back to see Mummy Vi.

She was in a private room at the Hampstead clinic, on credit. She had taken an overdose of barbiturates. A nice lady doctor told me she had been an addict for five years, at least. What she needed was help, of the kind available at Portway House for a thousand pounds per week. And while I was there, the administration wished to know what arrangements had been made to settle her account.

Vi had spent all the money our parents had left us, so I part paid the bill with the return half of my ticket from Tortola. I managed to check her into Portway House. Then I had to think about getting a job.

Recently qualified lawyers do not earn enough to keep themselves, let alone support their sisters in detoxification clinics. But divers were getting good money in the North Sea. So I borrowed some money and enrolled in the Loch Fyne Diving School. Next thing I knew I was at the bottom of a cold, deep loch in pitch darkness and a rubber suit, very surprised at the difference between this and frolicking in the coral off Virgin Gorda. But I went on with it, because as well as all the rest I had to pay back the loan for the diving-school fees, and there was no way out but forwards.

One of the few good things anyone has ever had to say about Harry Frazer is that, when pressed, he shows a capacity for hard work. I was pressed. So I went into the North Sea, air diving. Those were the days when you still got paid well for it. Vi graduated from Portway House clean as a whistle. But it was obvious that with the friends she had, she was going to find it hard to stay clean for more than one Saturday night. So I bought her a house in Pulteney, a fishing village much admired by yachtsfolk. And to pay for the house, I took another course, and went saturation diving.

Saturation diving is rough stuff. If you go down deep, breathing the conventional nitrogen/air mixture, on the way up you get nitrogen bubbles in your blood, and the bubbles cut off the blood supply to nerve cells in your brain and spinal cord, and after a while you have trouble walking, let alone thinking. A little deeper, and you get nitrogen narcosis, rapture of the deep; first stoned out of your mind, and then very dead. So people who wanted divers to work deeper than most sensible fish swim dreamed up heliox, a new recipe for air, in which the nitrogen was replaced by helium. Pumped up with heliox, you can go as deep as you like, provided you can keep warm, and you do not mind your hair and nails not growing, and your voice sounding like a parrot's because of what the helium does to your vocal cords; and above all as long as you do not recollect an urgent appointment on the surface. Because if you do come up in a hurry, the gases dissolved in your blood will make bubbles as the pressure reduces, and you will boil, burst, and die.

To keep you down for long enough to be useful, they provide you with a diving bell. Three of you work from the bell, which is suspended from a ship: one relief diver keeping the home fires burning, and two out there in the dark on umbilicals which supply them with heliox to breathe, and a telephone so nobody gets lonely, and hot water for the heating systems in their suits, because three hundred metres down the water is cold enough to kill you in about the time it takes to clean your teeth.

Five years and ten months ago, I was two hundred and eighty metres under the North Sea, in a diving bell with sweaty steel walls and a floor made of a disc of very cold water, all alone except for a lot of dials, and two umbilicals snaking out into the black where my mates Bruno and John were working on a pipeline shut-off valve that somebody had jammed. Up top, around the diving ship *Great Northern*, there was fog. Fog would have had no effect on our lives at all, except that churning through that fog at sixteen knots was *Rosemary Vehicle*, an eighty-thousand-ton container ship with a Filipino helmsman dreaming of Mindanao and not paying any attention to his radar.

So I was sitting down there, watching the walls, and the diving controller up top was telling me that all systems were normal, and out in the darkness Bruno was asking John for the Stillsons, because he was having trouble with a bolt. And suddenly the controller said, 'Fuck.' And at that exact moment the *Rosemary Vehicle* hit the *Great Northern* wallop on the bow, tore her off her anchors, and yanked her across the top of the sea.

My little steel room lurched and flung me bang into that little pool of icy water, no helmet, no nothing, and my fingers scrabbled for the grab handles, and hooked on. And then I tried to pull myself up. But I could not. Because the water was flowing past my legs, hard, and the bell was tilting, because we were being towed across the bottom of the sea. Very soon, I knew, the bubble of heliox I was sitting in was going to slip under the rim of the bell and wobble up to the surface, and that thousand-foot rod of water was going to ram in and be all there was to breathe.

But that was in the future, by perhaps thirty seconds. What was in the present was that Bruno and John were out there, being towed through a lot of machinery with no bell to protect them. So I yanked myself up into the gas and switched on the diver-to-diver intercom, and shouted in my stupid, squeaky heliox voice for them to come back.

And what I heard was silence.

So I went down, and checked the umbilicals.

They were still there, hanging into the round black pool, where the water had stopped moving now.

But there was nothing on the end. Somewhere in the black, Bruno and John were already dead.

The voices started in my ear, from up top. They were quiet and reasonable. 'Little local difficulty,' they said. 'Get those guys in, we'll have you up and out of there.'

The walls were sweating. I was sweating, too, but I was very, very cold. The voices went away, and there was more silence. And I knew I had to get out of this little steel room, and breathe real air. Then. That instant.

Someone started screaming in the little steel room. It was me.

The decompression took two weeks. It took longer to stop the screaming. After it had stopped, there was an enquiry. I told them what had happened, and went outside the enquiry room, and fainted. It was soon after that that I got an office back in Orchard Street, with a desk right up against the window, where I could see a big horizon, and Arthur Somers set me to work digging dirt on Merchant Venturers, and I started being a lawyer again.

That night I slept badly, in the room I had adopted in the house. When Fiona woke me with a cup of tea, the sky outside the window was grey with dawn, and *Green Dolphin*'s mast jutted from a thick blanket of mist on the loch.

Hector was moving about on *Flora*'s deck. Even at this range, I could tell he was humping the diving gear.

I took a gulp of tea, rolled out of bed and into my jeans, and trotted down to the quay. Keep moving, I thought, and you won't have time to think. But it was a queasy, dry-mouthed moving, thinking or no thinking.

Three hours later, *Flora* was slopping to and fro on a long, oily heave that banged her heavy spars with each roll. Away to the north, Rhum stood up blue in the haze the sun was pulling off the windless sea. Behind it, black in the far distance, grinned the evil saw teeth of Skye. I was in a wetsuit in *Flora*'s wheelhouse, too frightened to feel sick. Hector had the wheel and was staring grimly across the boat's stem towards the high green hills of

Ardnamurchan. Fiona was at the navigation table. On the Navstar, the waypoint alarm was emitting its thin, teeth-on-edge bleep. We were in position.

Next to the Navstar was the screen of the fishfinder. On the screen, the bottom showed as a coloured line, with bumps for rocks. Above it hung the blips of fish. On its right-hand side was the bigger thing that we had seen on Tuesday. The thing that might have been a rock, jutting from a gently sloping bottom.

Or might not have been.

'Here you are, then,' said Hector impassively. 'We've a great day for it.' He knocked out the waypoint alarm, went forward and let go the anchor. We saw it on the fishfinder, plummeting, forty metres, a hundred and thirty feet. My mouth was dry as cotton. But Fiona's eyes were on me. And I knew that I had to follow that anchor all the way down.

Carefully and methodically, I put on my tanks and strapped on the wreck belt, and set the bezel of my Rolex, and let the old ritual of the checklist take over the parts of my mind that needed taking over if I was going to do this and stay sane.

But all checks come to an end, sooner or later. My legs knew as the jerk of the chain brought her up that *Flora* had fallen back, and her anchor was holding. Hector said, 'You're maybe forty yards due west of yon thing. Tide'll be running in half an hour.'

I grinned at him with a stiff face, pulled the mask down and bit on the mouthpiece. Then I climbed up on the gunwale, holding on to the shroud, facing inboard, so as not to foul my tank. Outside the oval of the mask, spars and sea and islands swung like scenery in a goldfish bowl. I clamped it with my hand and jumped.

The water was cold enough to steal what breath I had, even in a wetsuit. A wetsuit was all there had been at Kinlochbeag. Bloody amateurs, I found myself thinking: crazy to do this without a drysuit. But thinking of drysuits and amateurs made me think of professionals and diving bells, and my mouth started to fill with cotton wool again. So I thought of Fiona, hard, and kept my eye on the depth gauge on my left wrist, the one which was not holding the safety line attached to *Flora*'s aft mooring cleat. *Ten*, I said to myself. *Eleven, clear ears*. The light was fading, now. The water was very clear. But now I was sinking from a pale limbo above to a darker limbo below. Nothing was solid; it was like dropping into fog.

My mind began to chatter. There had been fog the first time I had come here. The breath roared in my ears, and the bubbles rattled away and up. Down in my stomach, little worms of panic began to gnaw. I frowned furiously at the depth gauge, shutting them out. Thirty metres. Thirty-two. My thumb moved on the switch of the flashlight, and the heavy beam lanced downwards.

The yellow disc slid over tumbled boulders sunk in grey mud. A dogfish wriggled sluggishly away. I knotted the line to my belt, looked at my compass, kicked the flippers, and headed east. The bottom sloped away downhill.

Twenty kicks later, the darkness ahead grew darker. It had straight edges, that darkness. The left-hand end was higher than the right-hand end. And where the yellow sword of the flashlight beam stabbed it, the colour of it was blue. There was a line of little pustules in the blue. Rivet heads.

A sudden layer of cold water sucked the heat out of my body, even through the wetsuit. If I had had hot-water heating, I would have been shivering anyway. Because up there above the line of rivets was a panel of white paint, and on the white paint there were black letters.

Some of the letters were fishing boat identification. The rest said *Minnie Sullivan*.

I let out a long breath that sent a plume of bubbles wobbling up into the fog. Then I checked the line, and began a circuit, treading gently with the fins.

I moved all the way from bow to stern, my breath regular in my ears. All the way down the starboard side, there was nothing amiss.

Then I came under the stern, and the sound of my breathing stopped.

The port side went on in a nice straight line to a point four feet forward of the wheelhouse. Then it curved violently in, and became a jagged mass of metal that showed naked red edges where rust had already formed on the plating. It looked as if someone had smashed in the port side dead centre with a great big axe.

I looked at my watch. Ten minutes before I should start up. I took another deep breath, hitched up the diving rope, and swam up on to the deck.

It was tangled with gear, that deck. The masts had come down; the hatch cover had been blasted off by the impact; there were nets tangled half in, half out. This is where we trip over a mine, I thought. And my foot hit something big and roundish and soft on the deck.

I shone the flashlight down. The bubbles roared at my shout of horror. It was a body. There were teeth, long and grinning. My heart slammed inside my wetsuit. But no humans had canines like that. It's an animal, I told myself. A seal.

Things had been eating the seal. I wondered how it had died, hot with relief that it had not been anything worse. The beam of my flashlight played over the rest of the deck. There were two more seals, tangled in the nets.

I swam forward, searching inch by inch. There was a tumbled confusion of gear under the nets. There were boxes and drums on deck. I rolled one of the drums. It was yellow, with stencilled numbers. Whatever had caved in the fishing boat had just about torn it in half. Probably spare fuel.

I looked at my watch. I did not want to go aft, because aft was where the wheelhouse was. But I only had five minutes left, and I had to get it over with. So I raised the beam of my torch, shone it square at what had been the wheelhouse windows, and stared in.

Something stared back.

It had eyes, and a mouth, and shoulders. It was a terrible whitish thing, ragged and torn, and it grinned in places it had no right to grin.

But there was enough of it left for me to know without a shadow of doubt that its name had once been Jimmy Sullivan.

I kicked convulsively backwards. The lifeline caught against a tooth of jagged metal. I could not move. And suddenly they were all down here, Bruno and John and the rest of the dead men, waiting.

I was shuddering. I could not control it. My hands went forward to the lifeline, pulled. Calm down. Mustn't break the link. It had ravelled itself into a tight knot. Easy, I thought. Breathe slow. Panic uses air. Then, slowly, trace the turns of the rope – The thing in the wheelhouse moved. I yelled in the mask. Panic hit me like a truck.

My hand went to the big knife on my leg, yanked it from its sheath and sawed violently. The rope parted. I jumped away from that filthy deck in a cloud of bubbles that spewed from round the mouthpiece as I screamed. I kicked upwards, until I could not see that black shape underneath –

Then I stopped. Because the movement had only been a stirring in the currents, and I was being a fool. The gauge on my wrist said I had come up ten metres. In my blood, the nitrogen dissolved under pressure would be coming out of solution, forming bubbles. I had to wait, alone, suspended in the fog, while my lungs adjusted the gas balance of my blood. There were knots on the guide rope, at five-metre intervals. But the guide rope was gone, lost.

No guide rope meant no position. The panic swelled in my chest. Then I heard the instructor, back in the cold steel classroom on Loch Fyne. *If you want to die, panic.* It was only air diving. Only thirty metres. I had done ten times that.

I began to swim, maintaining depth, in a series of square turns, quartering the fog. And on the fourth turn the flashlight caught the rope.

The rope was old, pale Terylene, but as far as I was concerned, it could have been braided from platinum. I went up beside it and hugged it. And when my minutes were up, I climbed to the next stage.

The last stage is the longest wait of all. I hung there a hundred feet above the horror of the *Minnie Sullivan*, under the big dark shadow of *Flora*'s hull. The thing that had made that hole in the fishing boat's side must have been a ship. But how, in the whole of the sea, had Ewan known where to look for it?

The light was bright on the deck, and the air tasted like dry Martini after the stale, rubbery stuff in the tank. They pulled the tanks off me and gave me a towel. When I was dry I went into the wheelhouse, where the heat and stink from the coke stove was billowing up the companionway, and poured boiling tea down my icy throat.

'Well?' said Fiona.

I told her what I had seen.

She closed her eyes. The lids were dark and papery. 'Poor Morag,' she said. 'We'd better go and see her.'

Hector was already stumping aft from the anchor windlass. He pushed the throttles forward, and set the nose southwards.

The wind was getting up. *Flora* bucked as she went down in a trough, and spray clattered against the wheelhouse windows. To seaward there were fishing boats. I was beginning to feel sick.

Fiona said, 'For Christ's sake, what is happening?'

Her eyes were glassy with tears. Two violent accidents, I thought. It was possible for a ship to ram a fishing boat and not know about it; or for a fishing boat to get hit by a submarine. But it was not possible for a man to get blown up by a mine that was not there. I said, 'I don't know.'

She gripped the edge of the chart table, teeth bared, as if she was in physical pain. 'Then find *out*,' she said, and went quickly down the companionway to the saloon.

Hector said, 'The time we hit you. Ewan was looking for another boat.'

'What other boat?'

He shrugged. 'He never told me anything. So I wouldn't have to answer if anyone asked, he said.'

'And you never asked.'

Hector turned a heavy, solemn face on me. 'I worked for him,' he said. 'Why would I ask him?'

I stared at him. In his bleak gaze was the fiery cross, Bonnie Prince Charlie, the whole mad Highland baggage of duty and allegiance. There was nothing you could say.

I rowed Fiona across the little bay in front of the Sullivans' house. Morag was standing by the green-painted front door. She waved, a half-hearted lift of the arm. We carried the tender up the beach. Fiona took her aside. I went into the house.

There was a confused sound of fighting coming from the room on the left of the back door, opposite the kitchen. It seemed full of beds, and the beds seemed covered in children. I went in as far as I could. The fighting stopped, and the dark-haired girls scuttled away from the dark-haired boy they seemed to have been trying to stifle with a pillow. You poor little devils, I thought.

'Evenin',' said a voice from the corner. It belonged to a fourth child, larger than the rest. This one had his mother's freckled, dead-white skin, pale red hair and pale blue eyes. Jockie. One side of his face was marred by a huge red weal.

I said, 'What have you been doing to yourself?'

'Jellyfish,' he said. 'Poisonous ones.' He pulled down his sheet and pulled up his pyjama shirt. 'Look.' The blue–white skin of his chest carried more weals, a foot long, standing in angry scarlet ridges.

'That looks nasty,' I said. 'What kind of jellyfish?'

'Didn't see him,' said Jockie, with a negligence that seemed forced. 'Mam put on some stuff. Did you come about Daddy?'

A chill of dread settled in my guts. Yes, I thought: I have seen your father, and he has been underwater two weeks, and things have been eating him. I grinned, the best grin I could manage. 'Your mam will tell you what I came about,' I said.

'He's dead,' said the boy. 'He must be.'

And they all got into bed, and lay down, quiet. I turned away and went out, so they could not see my face. Lawyers should not cry, but Harry Frazer was crying.

In the parlour there were antimacassars, portraits of stiff men and women in blue suits and black dresses, and a plastic Virgin Mary with a flask of Lourdes water at her feet. Morag was not crying. She was biting her lips inwards. Fiona was sitting beside her on the ceremonial sofa. The room felt as cold as if it had been embalmed for burial.

Fiona said, 'I was telling Morag what an excellent lawyer you are.'

Morag looked up at me and said, 'But I suppose you'd not have the time, with your work and all.' She had stopped chewing her lips. She looked white and shrunken, made suddenly old by the destruction of hope.

I shoved my hands in my pockets, and looked out of the window. The room faced to seaward, at the view that nobody ever saw, except on days of family celebrations and family funerals, beyond the rotting tractors and the piles of driftwood, where the sun was smacking white sparks out of a sapphire sea. But it was only a view.

Suddenly I felt very tired, tired with the diver's ache of nitrogen in the blood. Tired with the memory of being nine years old, reading about the plane crash compulsively in all the papers. With the certain knowledge of what it was like to be Jockie Sullivan, hoping against hope that what you knew had already happened would not happen, and that you would wake up and everything would be all right again.

I said, 'I'll do what I can.'

She stepped forward, and shook me by the hand. Her palm had the texture and hardness of stone. 'Thank you,' she said.

When we had rowed out to *Flora*, I got on the radio and called out the coastguard. We went back to the wreck site, and stood by while the choppers circled and the fast launches came out and dropped their divers over the side. Then they came and took my statement.

'Poor bastard,' they said. 'Someone went straight through him. Can't have known what hit him. Neither will anyone else.' They stabbed their thumbs downwards, at the deep water, where the submarines cruised.

The choppers clattered off, and the launches slid away. As the sun sank like a bag of blood into the fire-and-ebony sea, *Flora* began to shoulder her way back to Loch Beag.

Chapter Thirteen

It was raining next day as I drove Fiona in the Land Rover through the lunar outcrops of the glen to the grey kirk. She was pale and grim-faced, wearing a blue–green sweater that matched her eyes. There were cars parked for three-quarters of a mile down the side of the main road. I dropped her off at the door and watched through the streaming windows as she made her way through the black-clad crowds at the kirk door like a kingfisher through crows.

The congregation piled in behind her. When I came back from parking the car, she was alone in the front right-hand pew, straight as a sword-hilt beside the pale oak of Ewan's coffin. She turned as I came in, caught my eye, and made a tiny movement of her head. Prosper beckoned, but I went past him and Lundgren and Jerry Fine and the rest of them in their dark suits and dresses, acutely conscious of my blazer and pale grey flannels, and stood next to her. I could feel the eyes on the back of my head. The new fancy man, some of them would be thinking.

She turned her face up to me and smiled. 'Thank you,' she said, quietly. I began to feel better.

The minister was brief. Hector and five men I did not know carried the coffin out and into the churchyard. The rain turned the black earth to mud. Hector came alongside in a stiff dark suit. He said, grimly, 'There's a few here not as sorry as they make out.' I looked at the faces, and wondered which were which. The service ended. Fiona was in the middle of a knot of condolers. After ten minutes she said, 'Drive me home.'

In the Land Rover, she rummaged under the seat, found one of Ewan's half-empty bottles of Glenmorangie, and drank. The diesel roared as we ground off the main road and on to the battered track leading down to the house.

She said, 'Thank you for that.' There was silence, full of the clatter of the pistons and the bang of the suspension. Then she said, 'That wasn't Ewan. Ewan's on the hill.'

She was not being romantic; it was literally true. The coffin we had buried had been empty.

We drove in silence across fifteen miles of lunar rock and heather, up to the pass that cuts off Loch Sallach from the sea. We passed the rush-fringed lochan, and started to grind slowly down the hairpins towards sea level. As we came round the last hairpin, Loch Beag was spread below us, its grey surface frosted with patches of black ripple. On the grey were a host of black motes.

'Look at the boats!' she said.

There must have been a hundred of them. Most of them were fishing boats, small trawlers and gill netters and pot boats. But there were yachts, too, and even something black-and-white and rusty that might have been a ferry taking the day off work.

Fiona covered her face with her hands. I drove on. As we came to the first of the trees beside the river she straightened up, blew her nose, and looked across at me. 'Don't go too far away,' she said, in a strange, choked voice.

Then we were at the house.

Kinlochbeag Lodge was full of people. They spilled on to the drive, and through the bamboos and the rhododendrons, and on to the quay. They all wanted to shake Fiona's hand and drink whisky. God knows how much whisky they drank, under the baleful black eye of the scar on the mountainside.

They stayed there all afternoon, while the tide ebbed and turned. As the flood licked over the sand, I found myself standing with Fiona on the quay. The rain had stopped, and there was no wind. On the foredeck of a rusty trawler, a bagpiper played a lament. The thin skin of the pipes pulled at the throat. Fiona's fingers were clenched on my arm.

The last notes of the pipes died away, and the tendrils of the echoes sank into the high slopes of the hills on either side. Silence pressed like a blanket over the water, and the mountains, and the trees. It seemed to go on and on, that silence.

I was gazing out over the loch, at *Flora*. A figure was walking slowly aft, along her deck; Hector. He went into the wheelhouse.

Into the silence blared the sound of the foghorn.

It blew a long blast. There was a split second of silence. Then, raggedly, every foghorn in the harbour came in after it, and a great grief-stricken wail rang in the hills.

I stood on the quay, the skin of my back and forearms crawling with goose pimples. Suddenly I was not on Kinlochbeag quay. I was back on *Green Dolphin*, watching the black wall of *Flora*'s side bearing down out of the fog. And hearing the bellow of the foghorn.

I had thought the foghorn was *Flora*'s. But it bore not the slightest resemblance to the horn *Flora* had just sounded.

The night when *Flora* had hit me, at the same position where someone had hit Jimmy Sullivan a week earlier, there had not been two boats milling around at close quarters in the fog.

There had been three.

The fleet pulled out on the tide and the cars ground unsteadily up the road in low gear. I caught Hector as he came up the quay steps. 'You weren't looking for another boat, the night you brought me in. You'd found it.'

He stared at me impassively. There was at least a bottle of whisky on his breath. 'Aye,' he said.

'Who was it?'

'That was what we were trying to find out.'

'Why didn't you tell me?'

He sat down heavily on a bollard. 'It wasn't up to me,' he said. 'It was up to Ewan.' He looked across at the scar, and stuck out his chin. 'And after...well, I didn't know you.'

I resisted the urge to shake him. 'I'll tell you what happened,' I said. 'Someone was trying to ram you. You were taking evasive action.' There had been that wave; the sudden lump of sea, coming across the run of the other seas, as *Flora*'s high black side bore away in the murk. 'His wake. It was his wake knocked you overboard.'

'That's right,' said Hector.

'Who?' I repeated.

'I don't know,' said Hector.

'A fishing boat?' I said. 'What did you see, for God's sake?'

'Bigger...I don't know. It was foggy as hell. There was no lights. I seen the side of him. It was a bluidy great slab of iron, was all. Black iron.'

'And Jimmy Sullivan wasn't so lucky. Is that it?'

He shrugged. 'That's what Ewan said.'

'And Jimmy was out looking. For Sea Watch.'

'Aye.'

'So why was whoever it was trying to ram you?'

'Ewan knew. But he reckoned I didn't need to know, so he didn't tell me, the way nobody could give me any trouble because I knew what I shouldn't know. He was like that.'

I said, 'So what about Jimmy Sullivan?'

'Jimmy was different,' he said. 'Jimmy had his own boat, and he did his own dealing. It was just that from time to time, he told Ewan things.' He got up, with difficulty. 'I'll be away,' he said. 'Will you be staying long?'

'As long as it takes,' I said.

'Aye,' said Hector. 'Well, then.' He turned, and stumped off down the track.

The house was quiet except for the kitchen, where there was a light on and a murmur of voices. As I walked past the window I saw Fiona, Morag Sullivan and three people I did not know. Morag's children were in bed somewhere. There was a bottle of whisky in the middle of the table. The faces looked warm in the yellow light, but strained, as if they were all having to think hard to remind themselves that Ewan would not be coming up from the quay. They looked like people who had known each other well for a long time. I did not disturb them.

Instead I padded through the hall into Ewan's side of the house, and into the dark-panelled room he had called his office. The floor was covered in envelopes, most of them untouched: his deep-litter filing system. On the roll-top desk, papers lay in mounds.

Paper is my element. I turned on a lot of lights and started skimming, piling the papers on a bare patch of floor as I read them. It was the desk of a man whose affairs were in acute disorder. There were bills, letters from creditors, threats from the bank manager, angry letters about pollution incidents to and from environmental organisations, forms for seabird censuses. There were also a couple of life insurance policies, big ones, made out in Fiona's favour, tucked away between Fisher and Lockley's Sea Birds and the 1964 catalogue for Berry Bros and Rudd, wine merchants.

I spent an hour at it, getting nowhere. From the drive there came the sound of car engines, receding. The door opened. Fiona was standing there, leaning against the doorpost as if she was exhausted. There were dark circles under her eyes. I suddenly realised that I was in Ewan's desk, rummaging, and that I had not asked anyone's permission.

She said, 'What are you after?'

I said, 'I don't know.'

'Don't play games with me.' Her voice was thin and exhausted.

'Whoever rammed Jimmy Sullivan tried to ram Ewan.'

'And then blew him up. And we lived in the same house, and I helped him with Sea Watch. And not once, ever, did he even hint that he was doing anything that could get him anywhere like this.' She sounded drunk, but I knew she was only tired. She leaned her head against the doorpost. 'You're a good guy, Frazer,' she said. 'A very good guy. I'm going to bed.'

I sat and listened to her footsteps go up the stairs at a slow, weary shuffle. Then I went and tried Ewan's bedroom. It was cold and bare, as if he had hardly used it. There was a narrow iron bed, a shelf with more books on ornithology. I was tired myself now; going through the motions. I was not surprised when I found nothing. Bed, I thought.

I went up to the room in the attic, and lay down. My thoughts began to drift towards dreams; dreams of fog. Suddenly, the foghorn was roaring through my head again, and I was all the way awake, staring at the moonlight on the ceiling.

I lay there, rigid as a plank, eyes cranked wide open. The house was deadly quiet. Too quiet; I missed the shift of the boat, the lap of waves. My watch said two a.m. Soon it would be light. There was no chance of any more sleep. It was easier, on the boat –

On the boat.

I swung my feet on to the floor, pulled on a jersey, and went down the stairs at a run. Don't be stupid, I said to myself as I trotted across the drive and into the rhododendrons. Lawyers do not go chasing intuitions at two o'clock in the morning.

But I kept running, down to the quay and into the rowing boat. The moon glared down out of a silver sky as I pulled over the shallow water by the quay. A Great Northern Diver wailed, and a sea trout shot out of the water and fell back with a splash. I went up *Flora*'s side fast, found a torch in the wheelhouse, and flashed it across the cluttered shelves and lockers. *Ludicrous*, said the lawyer. *Intuition is a fancy word for bullshit.*

There was nothing in the wheelhouse. I clattered down the companionway steps. Ewan had used the starboard cabin. There was a crumpled sleeping bag on the bunk, a pair of jeans hanging from a hook on the bulkhead. And in the fiddled shelf by the head of the bunk, the books.

There was a cigarette lighter by the paraffin lamp. I lit the lamp, took out the books one by one, and flipped through the pages.

The letters were still inside the cover of *Green Sea* by Gottfried Weber. I rifled through. There was nothing new. Nothing until the end.

At the back of the pile, attached with a paper clip, was a Polaroid photograph. It had been taken at Kinlochbeag, and recently; you could see the blue gums in the background, and *Green Dolphin*'s mast alongside the quay. But it was not a landscape. It was a photograph of a yellow forty-five-gallon drum standing on a staging outside the door of a shed. The shed which had blown to smithereens the day after the regatta, and taken Ewan with it.

I had seen drums like it before. There had been one in the shed at Camas Bealach, and another stove in on the deck of the *Minnie Sullivan*.

I shoved the photograph into my pocket, climbed into the tender and rowed back to the quay, pulling the boat across the last twenty yards of mud, where the tide had gone out. It was time to go to the police. But I did not trust policemen unless there was a case tied up with ribbons. Very interesting, they would say. So you followed your intuition and you found a photograph of an oil drum, and you've got it with you. The hard-faced Glasgow sergeant would be smiling, his thin, seen-it-all-before smile. Thanks for your co-operation. he would be saying. But he would be thinking, We've got a right one here. The moon was sinking as I walked back to the house.

What I had to do was get my hands on one of those yellow drums, and find out what Ewan and Jimmy had found so interesting about them. And what it had to do with both of them being dead.

Chapter Fourteen

Next thing I knew the room was full of drizzly sunlight, and my watch said ten-thirty. My clothes felt sticky as I rolled off the bed and stumbled down the stairs.

Something was happening outside the front door.

There was an ambulance in the drive, incongruously clean and square-sided against the dripping dark green of the rhododendrons. Children's voices squalled. The drive seemed to be full of Sullivans; three of them fighting each other and weeping, Morag even whiter than usual. And, on a stretcher, Jockie.

I found myself standing very still, staring at Jockie. Last time I had seen him there had been a red weal on his face. Now, from the collar of his shirt to his forehead there spread a crescent-shaped raw patch, the skin yellowed and dead-looking at its edges.

The ambulance men lifted the stretcher. One of them said, 'Ready when you are, missis.'

Morag Sullivan followed them out and climbed into the back of the ambulance after the stretcher. The doors slammed. Its light flung blue stripes across the grey leaves of the gum trees, raced down the drive and lost itself among the tangled boulders of the glen.

Fiona stood there, looking after it.

I said, 'I thought he was stung by a jellyfish.'

Fiona said, absently, 'So did he.' She shivered. 'All the skin's coming off the weals he had. Poor child.'

One of the other children said, 'It wisnae a jellyfish.' It was the dark-haired boy. We both looked at him. His face reddened.

'What do you mean?' said Fiona.

'It wisnae a jellyfish.'

'What was it?' said Fiona, gently.

'I canna tell ye,' said the child.

I opened my mouth to put the question more forcefully. Fiona glanced at me, shook her head. 'You can,' she said.

'I'll get a whacking.'

Fiona said, gently, 'There's nobody here's going to whack you, Angus.'

Angus eyed her narrowly. Her face had a confidence-inspiring openness. She did not look capable of whacking anyone. 'Promise?' he said.

'Sure,' said Fiona.

'There was no jellyfish,' said Angus. 'There was a kind of a tin lid in Daddy's shed. We was playing discus with it. And Jockie got a skelp of it across his face, and put it down his shirt, and took it away.'

'What kind of lid?' said Fiona.

Angus was not up to describing subtle variations in tin lids. 'A wee yin,' he said.

I had an idea. It was not an idea that I liked. I pulled the Polaroid of the oil drum out of my pocket. 'Was it that colour?' I said.

He said, 'Just like the top part of that.' He started to cry. It was hard to blame him. I took his hand, and we went back into the house.

I told Fiona I was going to Camas Bealach, and fetched Hector from the workshop, where he was stripping down an old Land Rover.

We took *Green Dolphin*, because she was fast. We were off Camas Bealach at noon.

The sea was brilliant green on the bar. Hector piloted us gingerly through the narrow channel into the circular cove. We tied up to the buoy in the middle and went ashore.

There is something that happens to a house when the family moves away. I have seen it often in divorce cases: the lawn seems to grow six inches in a couple of days, the paint to peel off the shutters and weeds to spread in the paving at unnatural speed. Not that Camas Bealach had a lawn, or any paving except a rudimentary concrete slipway; but it stared across the bay with peeling green window frames, its white pebble-dash stained with damp as if it had lain uninhabited for years.

'An awful lot can happen in a wee while,' said Hector, grimly.

It was not something I wanted to be reminded of just now. I walked away from the shuttered house and down to the shed.

It was padlocked, the shed. There was a strong galvanised hasp and a big brass padlock. We had no key. I said to Hector, 'Have you got a crowbar?'

Hector said, 'Jimmy kept the tools in the shed.'

All that way for nothing, I thought. The hasp was bolted all the way through the door; no chance of unscrewing it. I put out my hand, grasped the cold metal of the padlock, and gave it a futile tug.

The padlock came away in my hand.

Hector said, 'Dear God.'

I flicked off the hasp. The door sagged open. I looked down at the padlock in my hand.

Someone had got here first.

Whoever it was had sawn through the hoop of the padlock. They had done it recently, because the steel was still bright.

The shed was unchanged: the battered deep freeze, the piles of driftwood, the outboard on the trestle. I walked over to the collection of forty-five-gallon drums.

Hector said, 'If it was me breaking into Jimmy's shed, I'd pay myself for my trouble by pinching his bloody outboard.'

In the dirt and spilled oil by the drums, something had left a ring. Something the right size for a forty-five-gallon drum.

There were the marks of wheels leading through the diesel puddles to the door. A sack trolley, perhaps. On the concrete slipway outside, at the high-water mark, there was a scratch of blue paint. Hector bent, and picked at it. A little lump of it came away under his nail. 'It's not been here long,' he said. It was the colour of the battered workboat that Donald Stewart drove.

We went back to the boat, slowly, picking our way across the big schist pebbles. On the tide line, my eye caught a flash of colour in the wrack of weed and old plastic.

It was a disc of metal, perhaps three inches across, painted yellow; the lid of a forty-five-gallon drum. There were clips round the edge, and a black serial number across the top. On the paint was scratched in wavering lines the linked rings of the Olympic symbol.

I caught it in a fold of black polythene and picked it up.

'What have you got there?' said Hector.

'Jockie Sullivan's discus,' I said.

We climbed into the tender and rowed out to the boat. I stowed Jockie's discus carefully in the cockpit locker. The breeze was up, a fresh westerly. It cracked into *Dolphin*'s sails and sent her shooting across the blue roller coaster of waves that heaved between the green cone of Camas Bealach and the grey ramparts of Loch Beag.

Angus and his sisters were in the studio, helping Fiona wind skeins of lichen-red wool. Fiona looked up and smiled. I got a feeling of homecoming. She said, 'Get out and play,' to the children. There was the smell of wet wool in the house, and skeins drying on the rack above the Aga. She was working again.

I said, 'How's Jockie?'

'Morag says they say it's an allergic reaction. Or it was; that's what caused the blistering, then the skin came off. They're talking about skin grafts.'

'Allergic to what?'

'They don't know,' she said. 'But it wasn't jellyfish.'

I said, 'I've got the thing that hurt him in a plastic bag out there. Maybe Hector could take it up to the hospital.'

'Of course.'

Not that there would be much of anything left on a piece of metal scoured by sand and tide.

I rang the hospital, and asked to speak to Morag. She told me that Jockie was a lot better. I said, 'Did you go into the shed, this past week?'

'No,' she said.

'Did Jockie?'

'Oh, aye,' she said. 'I sent him out for some fish from the freezer.'

'Oh,' I said. Jockie could have collected the fish, spotted the drum lid on the way, carried it out and stashed it where it would have come in useful to an athlete.

'Jimmy had a row with Donald, you said.'

'That's right.'

'About a drum.'

'A kind of oil drum,' she said.

'What was the row?'

'I told you,' said Morag. She sounded tired. She would be tired, poor woman; too tired to remember the details of arguments that had happened in another world.

'Try to think,' I said. 'I need to know exactly. It's important.'

'Oh, dear,' she said. 'Donald was offering twenty quid for the drum. Jimmy said someone else would give him more. I think that was it.'

'Who else?' I could not stop the sharpness.

'Ach, I don't remember.' She sounded distracted. 'Would it have been somebody up the quarry?' I could imagine her in the hospital, the clean, white, hot rooms. Her and Jockie, shut up, a long way from Camas Bealach. 'I don't remember anything much about it at all.'

'How did Donald know Jimmy had the drum?'

'Jimmy maybe told him. Maybe it was overboard from a ship. Listen, Mr Frazer, Jockie's calling me.'

I said, 'Send him my best.' But she was already gone.

Fiona had stopped fiddling with her wool. She was watching me. She said, 'What was all that about?'

I said, 'I want to find out if Donald's back from his holidays.'

I rang Jerry Fine's number. When he answered, his voice was as gloomy as his bloodhound's face. 'Oh, hello,' he said, as if he was surprised I was still alive.

I told him I was looking for Donald Stewart.

'Blackpool,' he said. 'Bloody awkward time, too. He's due back today or tomorrow.'

I said, 'Where would I find him, if he was back?'

'There's a shed we use at Dunmurry,' he said. 'By the fish cage. He keeps some stuff in it. You might find him there.'

I thanked him, and put the telephone down, and sat there, looking at it. Two people had known that Jimmy had the yellow drum: Donald, and someone else Jimmy had offered it to. So two people had a motive for breaking into Jimmy's shed and helping themselves.

I remembered Ewan at Dunmurry, rattling the padlock on the shed door. *'I want to look in that shed. See where he keeps his bloody poison.'*

And now, so did I.

Fiona was in the kitchen, in a cloud of steam. I said, 'Do you want to come out to dinner?'

'No,' she said. 'Thank you all the same. I'll stay with the children.'

I picked up the telephone, rang Prosper, and arranged to dine at the Dunmurry Hotel. And I left Fiona presiding over a table full of Sullivan children wolfing cereal, and headed out into the high-gloss world of the Holiday Highlands.

Chapter Fifteen

At seven o'clock that evening, I slid *Green Dolphin*'s nose past the grey breakwater of Dunmurry Castle, brought her head-to-wind, and scuttled forward to pick up the mooring buoy marked V for Visitors. Prosper's *Bonefish* was on another mooring. There was no sign of life aboard. When the sails were down and tied, I went below, carefully shaved my face in hot water from the calorifier and eased myself into a dark blue silk dinner jacket out of the wardrobe. Then I rowed ashore.

The gardens smelled of geranium leaves and lemon verbena in the early evening air. There were a few midges, but not enough to be intolerable. Prosper was at a table on the balcony with Lisbeth Vandekaa and an ice bucket. He poured me a glass of Krug. Lisbeth smiled with her china-white teeth and her china-blue eyes. Prosper said, 'Christ, you've been having a time,' and looked pointedly at my feet.

I stuck out my black Sebago loafers and said, 'No sandals.'

'Yet,' said Prosper. We both laughed. The toes still ached vaguely where Donald Stewart had trodden on them. I cut the laugh off short, because it seemed disloyal. Lisbeth smiled uncomprehendingly. 'What a bloody week, though,' said Prosper. 'First Ewan. Then that bloke they pulled out of the trawler. I hear you're making yourself useful down there.'

I shrugged.

'Lisbeth!' said a voice behind me. It was David Lundgren, red and round in a tracksuit and running shoes. There was a towel round his neck. The man with him looked like one of the usual tough guys, except that he did not have a moustache. He had a big, sun-reddened face and blond hair cut short. He looked hard and fit, and his head ran straight down into his shoulders without benefit of neck.

Lundgren's grey eyes were gleaming, his red shiny jaw jutting. 'Mr Duplessis, Mr Frazer! Breaking training for the Three Bens, I see!'

'Pure fruit juice,' said Prosper, his eyebrows innocent arches on his coffee-coloured forehead. 'Have a glass.'

Lundgren said, 'Thank you, but Kurt and I have been running.' The blond man nodded, unsmiling, watching the horizon. 'Taking the training seriously. Kurt keeps himself in shape, don't you, Kurt?'

The blond man nodded again. I had the impression that I had seen him before.

'Oh, by the way,' said Lundgren. 'Very sad about Ewan.' He said it smooth as cream, as if by way of polite conversation.

I said it was. Then I said, 'I'd like to take up your invitation and see round the quarry one of these days.'

'Really?' said Lundgren. 'I didn't think you Kinlochbeag people were very keen.' He allowed his stone-cold eyes to rest on me. 'Lisbeth, could you fix it?' He smiled, then led Kurt towards a table down the terrace where a table full of hard looking, crop-headed young men were sitting in front of glasses of lager.

The sun came out from behind a cloud. There was a sudden burst of laughter from Lundgren's group, like the sharp bark of a pack of dogs. I glanced round.

And stared.

Kurt was sitting with his back to the sun, which was shining full on his head. The hair was so fine that the scalp showed pink through the blond stubble. And I remembered where I had seen him before.

He had been the man in the boat with Donald Stewart the day he had knocked Ewan into the fish cage.

At dinner, we drank another bottle of champagne and ate lobsters, and talked about sailing and life in the Caribbean. For an hour or two, it was almost like being on holiday. I said so.

Lisbeth frowned. 'But what I do not understand is why Prosper comes here to spend the summer. He could be in Martinique, or the Côte d'Azur.'

'Solitude,' said Prosper. 'And no hurricanes. About now, a chance to bust my ass on some hills, and sail against my old pal Harry.'

'And stalking deer?' said Lisbeth.

'I let it,' said Prosper, with his grin. 'To David and his muscular companions. Mind you, it's good stuff. You ever see a stag in rut? Death or glory. Shoot him, he doesn't even notice. Like you, climbing.' He shook his head. 'Human fly,' he said. 'You beautiful iridescent creature.' She punched him on the arm and left her hand there. 'Or Harry in the Horngate. The way you went through the inside channel, you're dead. You just didn't notice yet.'

Soon after that, we threaded the garden paths back to the harbour. There was a breeze now, rattling the halyards against the masts of the shadowy boats. 'Drink?' said Prosper.

'Early bed,' I said.

'See you tomorrow at the quarry,' said Lisbeth. 'Any time.' Her teeth gleamed in the moonlight.

'And come up to the house after,' said Prosper. 'It's only five miles.'

I rowed out to *Dolphin*, arranged the dinner jacket carefully on the hanger and hung it in the wardrobe. Then I pulled on a navy blue guernsey and black jeans, and wriggled into the rubber seals of my sailing drysuit. I shoved a pair of sneakers and a knife into a watertight bag, and turned out the light. Quietly, I climbed back into the cockpit.

Anchor lights burned at the masts of the other boats, their reflections dancing on the ripples kicked up by the breeze. One or two cabin lights were on, dim behind curtains. Wisps of Beethoven floated across from the direction of Prosper's boat. Courting music, Prosper called it. I moved aft, down *Dolphin's* bathing ladder and into the black water.

The drysuit floated me. I paddled gently for the land.

Asteroid's black hull went past. Weed brushed my shins. Then I was ashore, on the rocks where the garden wall cut off the neck of the peninsula.

The midges were bad. I pulled the bottle of Jungle Formula from my waist-bag and slathered it in my hair, so the sweat would bring it down over my face. Then I struggled out of the drysuit, put on my sneakers and started along the wall.

The ground went up steeply, became a rocky spine. When I looked back, I was a hundred feet above the anchorage. To seaward, the Hyskeir light flicked at the cloud base. My mouth was drier than it need be; nobody was going to see me. Groping for a handhold, I pulled myself over the crest of the ridge.

I was looking down over the loch. The fish farm was a square of bluish floodlights, neatly marking the shed. I went down gingerly, prodding the ground before I chose a foothold. A broken leg here would be hard to explain to David Lundgren.

The rocks became grass and heather. The ground fell away. A black mass came between me and the floodlights. The shed.

My hand went into my bag, and came out with the flashlight. I am not a burglar, I told myself. I am pursuing enquiries on behalf of my client. It did not make my mouth any less dry, or slow down my heartbeat.

In the dead ground behind the shed, I turned on the flashlight. The wall was made of concrete blocks. The cement between them was of uneven thickness; Gulf Stream craftsmanship. There was no window in the wall. I moved round to the side furthest from the hotel.

This time, there were three windows. They were high and small, steel-framed, the kind you see in a public lavatory. Too small to climb through. The wall was deep in shadow. The double doors and the fourth wall, the one closest to the hotel, were brightly lit by the fish-farm floods.

I put the torch between my teeth, jumped up, and hooked my fingers over the sill of the closest window.

Whoever had built it had known little enough about building not to have sloped it outwards. The water would flow in when it rained, but it gave the fingers a good grip. Grinding *Green Dolphin*'s fat primary winches had made my arms strong enough to haul me up until my chin was level with the sill, and the flashlight in my mouth drilled a circle of yellow through the window's dirty glass.

The shed was yellow inside. The drums in Sullivan's shed had been yellow.

I squinted through the glass. My stomach became heavy with disappointment. The yellow things were plastic fish boxes. I could read the black lettering: DUNMURRY FISH FARMS – WESTER ROSS. They were stacked in piles of a dozen, filling the shed. I let myself down and stood flexing my cramped fingers. Fish boxes were what you would expect to find in a fish farm. Wild goose chase.

But as Arthur Somers used to say after a couple of glasses of the office Madeira, all good solicitors are methodical. Even if it means prowling round other people's private property in the black of the night.

I put away the flashlight and pulled out the knife. Then I walked round to the front of the shed.

The floodlights cast a blue–grey glow over the black-painted double doors. I was black myself, hair and clothes, but I still felt naked. The padlock hasp was screwed, not bolted.

The knife had a screwdriver blade on its end. The screws came out easily. The hasp folded back with a grate of unoiled hinges and the door swung open. One step inside; torch on.

There were the teetering piles of boxes, the stink of fish, and the big fridge humming in the corner. Your standard fisherman's shed, same contents from the Faeroes to the Falklands.

I moved forward quietly, in an aisle between the rows of boxes, wide enough for a wheelbarrow. At the back end of the shed the boxes were older, wooden, stained with years of fish blood. The disc of light slid over something yellow; moved on. I brought it back, not breathing.

The yellow thing was a forty-five-gallon drum. There were wooden fish boxes piled up against it, in a perfunctory attempt at camouflage. I pulled the boxes away. There was a line of letters and numbers stencilled down the side in black paint. I had seen the line before, in the Polaroid photograph aboard *Flora*, and on Jockie's discus, and on the deck of the sunk *Minnie Sullivan*.

But Ewan's drum was blown to shreds and Jimmy's had been ripped apart. This one was merely battered. Its cap was on. I jammed the screwdriver under the cap, and levered.

There was a little clatter as it flew off. Hard on its heels, I thought I heard another sound. My heart banged. I turned. As I turned, something that felt like a flying anvil slammed into my right ear. My knees went and I fell sideways across the drum. I felt metal on my cheek. Suddenly someone was pointing a flamethrower down my throat and pulling the trigger. There was no breathing. My face was wet, but whether it was blood or tears I did not know, because the whole of me was concentrated in the flaming agony of my throat, trying to grab air.

There was a heavy concussion somewhere around my ribs. I felt myself sliding on to the floor. My head hit concrete with a crack and started to roar. Still the breath would not come. Another concussion. Boot, I thought with the tiny part of my mind that was still working. I was being dragged, but I could not see where, except that it was light.

There was a grunt, and a heave. Then I smashed face down, mouth open, into icy water.

The world was black as ink, but the water eased the burning. I rolled, thrashing. My head came to the surface and I got a choking apology for a breath. The floodlights were still on. Against the line of them a man was standing. There was something in his hands, something long and thin, which thrashed over and at me. There was a burst of pain in my shoulder. Pole, I thought. He's got a pole.

I swam away, gasping. There were lights all around. You're in the fish farm, I told myself. Perfectly all right – He had run round the edge. The pole came down again. I rolled away, put my feet down, looking for the bottom.

There was no bottom; only the slither of close-packed fish.

I went for the far side. But he got there before me, a black silhouette against the light. The pole came again. This time he was using it as a harpoon. The end of it snarled in the wool of my jersey. He leaned on the pole and I went down, a long way down. My hand wrenched at the pole. Fabric tore, and I was free. *He wants to hurt me*, I thought. *He wants to hurt me very badly*. I was on the surface, breathing.

The pole whacked across. I writhed away, my breath coming in agonising sobs across the raw flesh of my throat. Wherever I went, I was within reach of the pole. I was getting heavier. Soon I was going to sink. The bag round my waist was dragging me down. I tore at the buckle. The pole came again, shoved me to the bottom, pinned me against the netting. I wriggled frantically, my ears roaring. The pole was a boathook. I wrenched the end out and shoved it hard into the net, felt the jerking as he tugged. Stuck in the net, I thought, kicking for the top –

The net.

The pole came free. I dived again, before he could swipe at me. The buckle of the bag was undone. But I did not throw it away. My oxygen-starved fingers wriggled in the interior. They found what they were looking for. The knife.

I kicked hard for the side of the cage. The world was choking water, filled with racing blocks of maddened fish. The net came at me, a taut wall that tried to bounce me back. I hung on to it with the clawed fingers of my left hand. With my right, I swept the knife down and across.

It was a proper knife, ground like a razor blade. The taut wall slackened. I kicked hard, tumbled outward. Slimy bodies whispered past my skin, gushing for the open water. The grey light of the floods had gone. My lungs were bursting.

I swam for the surface. My head broke water. The air tasted like sugar, and there was no pole.

Chapter Sixteen

The floodlights were a patch of grey behind me. I kicked legs that were suddenly like rubber and the lights slid further away. I remembered the swirl of the tide through the narrow neck and into the body of the loch. It would be ebbing now, pouring to seaward. I started to swim where I thought south must be. My throat was burning. I breathed through my nose, and kept kicking.

Dark cliffs rose on the shore. They put power back into my legs. Boulders came under my hands. Then I was not swimming but crawling up a rocky beach.

Behind me in the dark an engine started, the metallic clatter of an old diesel. I pressed my face into the boulders of the beach. A boat passed perhaps twenty yards behind me, moving rapidly down the tide through the choke of the Narrows. The stones were comfortable. I would have liked to stay there and sleep for a long time. But I climbed to my feet and stumbled up the beach, over the track and on to the ridge.

By the time I reached the top, my lungs felt as if they were full of broken glass. I coughed and spat. On the other side, there was a blur of white lights. Anchor lights, burning serenely in the bay. I slithered down the far side, retrieved the drysuit and crawled over the beach. The tide was a long way out, and the mud of the bottom stank of bad eggs as I waded through. There were only ten yards to swim at the end of it. They were ten bad yards.

In the cockpit, I took my clothes off. Naked, I struggled below and drank half a pint of milk from the fridge. The throat abated, became sore, but not worse than sore. There was a foul chemical taste in my mouth; the taste of what had been in the drum. Then I sat down on the bunk.

Next thing I knew the sun was shining in my eyes and seagulls were screaming. I was lying sideways on my bunk, where I had fallen. My throat was sore, and I was aching.

The throat improved slightly when I dripped coffee over it, and the aches responded to a hard swim across the harbour. Prosper had left; getting the lady friend to work. I cleaned the mud out of the cockpit. Then I went ashore, and propped myself in the telephone box by the landward end of the quay.

I rang the office, reverse charges. Outside, gulls were jockeying for a grip on the wind, and cloud-shadows hung on the green faces of the mountains. In the box, there was Cyril's soupy murmur, with the drowsy hum of Orchard Street in the background. At that moment, Orchard Street felt like an oasis of tranquillity.

Cyril laid the day's mail before me like a verbal banquet. I got rid of it, item by item. Then I said, 'Ring James Charrington, and find out about the ArdnaBruais granite quarry.'

'Granite quarry,' said Cyril, with the mild surprise that was his version of incredulity. 'And file under Morag Sullivan, I suppose.'

'Ring me back,' I said. 'In ten minutes.' I put the telephone down, and rang Fiona.

She answered quickly. She said, 'What's happened to your voice?'

'I found a drum of chemicals,' I rasped. 'Same as the one Jimmy had, and the one Ewan had. I took the top off and I got a little sniff of it. It gave me a sore throat.' I did not tell her that afterwards someone had tried to drown me, because I did not want to worry her.

'Are you coming home?' she said.

'I'm going to the quarry,' I said.

'Look after yourself,' she said.

'And you.'

I rested my head against the cool glass, and watched a man rereeving a deadeye lanyard on Lundgren's cutter. There was no queue outside the box. Exactly ten minutes after I had rung off, Cyril called back.

'The granite quarry,' he said. 'Supplies Mr Lundgren's marinas. Mr Charrington pointed out that most of the world's conurbations are situated in swamps. Mr Lundgren ships aggregate to such places, notably the Netherlands. It is a flourishing business, Mr Lundgren is very rich. He would be hard to proceed against with any expectation of success.'

Particularly if we were not being paid for such proceedings, was the unspoken message. Cyril was the voice of my conscience, or anyway my bank manager.

I said, 'Thank you,' and put down the telephone. Fair means looked expensive and time-consuming. Foul would have to do.

I wanted a look at Donald Stewart's shed. I stood outside the telephone box, irresolute. A powerboat roared into the harbour and stopped hard alongside the quay. Jerry Fine jumped out, and walked quickly towards the garden gate.

'Morning,' I said, as he passed.

His bloodhound face was grey and drawn. 'Morning,' he said. 'Can't stop.'

I fell into step beside him. 'Problems?' I said.

He nodded, without slackening his pace.

'Nice morning for it, though,' I said. 'Going down the fish farm? Mind if I tag along?'

He said, 'Do what you bloody well like.' We went through the gate marked PRIVATE and down the track. There were a couple of men standing by the cage, shaking their heads.

It was not hard to see why.

The hole I had ripped in the net had not let all the fish out. A few had stayed in. They were floating belly up on the surface, the sun glinting on their scales. All the way down the shore towards the Narrows the weed was brown and seared. The air smelled putrid. Between the rocks, dead crabs and shrimps were already beginning to rot.

The shed door was open. I glanced down at the far end. The drum was not there.

On the floor of the shed were parallel lines, heading for the door. Lines that could have been made by the ribs that run round a drum. Whoever had found me in the shed last night had recapped the drum, pushed it over on its side, and rolled it out of the shed. A full forty-five-gallon drum weighs nearly a quarter of a ton, so if he had been alone he could not have loaded it on to his boat. He knew I would be back to look in the morning. So he had lightened the drum in the only possible way, by pouring its contents into the loch.

Jerry Fine sat down on a rock, and put his hands over his head. I went back to *Green Dolphin*.

ArdnaBruais quarry was a hard mark to miss. The pale scar of the workings extended halfway up a short, jagged peninsula to the northward. The sun had gone, but the cloud was high, a mottled grey roof under which blew a crisp force four westerly. *Dolphin* cracked along at a fine old pace, doing her best to cheer me up. I sucked antiseptic lozenges from the medicine chest and the throat calmed down. The quarry grew out of the sea.

From top to bottom, it must have been two thousand feet high. Close to, the jumble of shapes at its base resolved itself into a huddle of big grey sheds on the terraced remains of a hillside. There were a couple of ships tied up at a loading berth. The scale of the place was so huge that they looked like models. As I drew closer, I saw one of them was about fifty thousand tons. The other looked like a coaster, rusty and battered, barely two thousand. A man in a dirty singlet was fishing off her stern with a rod, in the outfall of what might once have been a burn. It did not look as if he was going to catch anything, because now it was more like a drain. There was a dirty scum where it hit the sea, and a slick drifted away to join the tide.

I tied up *Green Dolphin* to a tyre-edged pontoon, and walked across a grey plain of rock and dried mud to a collection of Portakabins, the only buildings with any windows.

Lisbeth was sitting in a room with a computer, a coffee mug, and a lot of paper. She gave me her smile, squeezed my hand, and said, 'Goodness! You do not look so well.'

I muttered something about sleeping badly. 'So,' she said, waving her hand at the window, 'here you are in the largest granite quarry in Europe.'

'Here I am,' I said. She smiled brightly, her brown skin blooming with health as if she had not been up half the night with Prosper, and followed it with a brisk early morning sail to get to work on time. 'Listen, you're busy. I'll show myself round. I'm quite happy.'

'Oh, no,' she said. 'Mr Lundgren insisted I take you round personally. It will be much more interesting.'

I said, with as good a grace as I could muster, 'Are there things Mr Lundgren wants me not to see?'

She laughed brightly at the absurdity of the idea. 'Of course not. It is only insurance.' She lowered her eyes. 'I enjoyed last night very much. Prosper is a wonderful person.'

I said, 'Yes.' I had known him long enough to have a good idea what happened aboard his boats when there was him, a beautiful woman, and Beethoven on the stereo.

'Now we go,' she said, recollecting herself.

The grey plain smelled of dust and chemicals. Its surface was scored and rutted with the wheels of big machinery. A couple of hundred yards inland, it turned into a steeply sloping hill of sand and scree, which rose perhaps a hundred feet to another plain and another cliff. At the top of that cliff was another plain, and so on. They rose from the sea like a flight of gigantic steps. Over to the left were grey-painted sheds, and two or three big dragline cranes, dwarfed by the steps, so they looked like children's toys. Beyond the sheds were huge molehills of what might have been crushed stone, and long, spidery catwalks and conveyors. Distant machinery rattled noisily.

Lisbeth's face was full of a sort of missionary enthusiasm. 'Hundred-foot benches,' she said, pointing at the cliff faces. 'And over here, in these sheds, the graders. We can sort you out anything from fine sand to big rocks, mix them, blend them, process them.' We were walking towards the sheds. She moved with the grace of a mannequin on a catwalk. One of the men on the smaller ship whistled at her. She ignored him. 'The shiploader,' she said, pointing up at a long, scaffolded nozzle that projected from a grey steel shed. 'It can deliver one ton per second into a ship. Three thousand six hundred tons per hour.' The nozzle was prodding at the hatches of the bigger of the two ships like a giant mosquito. 'So this ship will take roughly ten hours to fill.'

We were under the sheds now. The roar of the machinery was almost too loud for normal speech. 'Now I will show you the Glory Hole.'

We climbed into a Land Rover. There were big coils of rope in the back, and a climber's helmet. She started the engine and we roared up a zigzag of ramps that travelled along the face of the benches, climbing so fast that my ears popped. After half-a-dozen benches, we came out on to a track, which crossed a scarred waste that still looked like a Scottish mountain if you crossed your eyes. At the top, the jeep stopped and she climbed out. The breeze was blowing up here. It stung my throat. At the foot of the slope, tiny diggers butted at the steps of the quarry.

Inland was a funnel-shaped depression, a hundred yards across and fifty feet deep. There were a couple of diggers on the slope, feeding buckets of rock into the hopper of a vast machine that shook and roared. A conveyor belt came out of the machine and led to the centre of the pit, the deepest point of the funnel. In the exact centre was a circular hole, perhaps fourteen feet across. A continuous stream of crushed rock rattled off the conveyor and plunged into the hole.

'The Glory Hole,' said Lisbeth. 'Just begun. Phase Two of the ArdnaBruais Project. The machine is the crusher. Crushed rock falls three hundred metres down the hole, on to a conveyor belt in the horizontal shaft at the bottom. This carries it to the grading sheds, from which it goes into storage bins, and so on.'

I said, 'Why not just dig away the mountain?'

'That is just what we do,' she said, smiling as if at a favourite pupil. 'The reserve is one billion tons of granite. But we seek to minimise environmental impact. So instead of digging from outside, we dig from inside.'

I turned my back on the hole and looked down at the raped hillside and the slick of God knew what snaking away with the tide from the burn's foot. 'Beautiful,' I said.

The jeep howled down the benches. We walked through endless sheds, following a river of crushed stone that fell over ledges and sieved itself through grids and was washed in streams of water, until it landed up, graded by size, on the huge conical piles from which the shiploader could suck it up and squirt it into the ships.

At last we came out into the grey daylight. My ears were singing with the noise. Over to the right were a couple of long, low sheds. I said, 'What's in there?'

She glanced across. 'Storage only,' she said. 'Of no interest.' A jeep pulled up. The driver was wearing a silver hardhat. He said, 'Lisbeth.'

'The boss. Excuse me.' She gave me her dazzling white smile, and trotted over like a gazelle.

Contrary to her view, the storage sheds were of enormous interest. I edged away, hands in pockets, towards the nearest one.

It was big, and the door was open. There was an aisle down the middle, wide enough for a fork-lift truck. There was a fork-lift operating at the far end, closing up to a pallet with bags of something on it. I wandered down the aisle, whistling, trying to look like a tourist. On either side the floor was piled with pallets of sheet steel, bits of machinery, bags of cement and chemicals. No forty-five-gallon oil drums. I waved at the man driving the fork-lift. He waved back. The far doors were open. I went out, turned sharp left past a couple of big diesel tanks, and into the second shed.

It was exactly like the first. There was another fork-lift operating down at the far end. I wandered down towards it.

The fork-lift driver had his back to me, and so did the man he was talking to. They were both wearing yellow hard hats. The fork-lift driver nodded, and reversed out into the aisle. On the forks of the truck was a pallet, and on the pallet were four forty-five-gallon drums. The drums were yellow. The same yellow as the one in Donald Stewart's shed. There were numbers and letters stencilled on them in black paint, but at this range I could not make them out.

I started forward again, taking it easy; nothing suspicious, not really interested. Just Harry Frazer on holiday, taking a little private excursion from the main tour. The fork-lift truck spun. And I stopped, dead.

Because the driver of the fork-lift truck was Donald Stewart. The other man turned. He had a big, sun-red face and a thick neck. He was Lundgren's friend Kurt.

For a moment, nobody moved. Donald's eyes were narrow and black under the rim of his yellow hard hat. I said, 'Morning.' The word was hollow in the big shed.

Kurt said, quietly, 'Hurt him.'

Donald did not answer. Instead, his right foot stamped on the truck's pedal. The truck came straight at me.

I jumped backwards. But what was behind me was a wall of packing cases. So I scuttled sideways, looking for clear space so I could start running. I saw his hands move on the controls, and the forks with the drums on them swung sideways after me, faster than I could run, and something caught me a smashing blow on the big muscle of my left thigh. I went down, rolling, shouting with the pain, as the forks swung. I tried to scramble away, but my left leg was dead, dragging. The yellow drums toppled and hit the floor with a crash. The forks were coming straight at me now. Stewart's face was twisted sideways, looking at something. There was wet on the floor. Metal screeched, and the motor whined like a cat. I got ready to roll, once again. Above the engine and the screeching was another noise: swearing. Stewart swearing. The forks had stopped advancing. I heaved myself up on the packing cases. My left leg was still not working, but I knew it was not broken.

The shed door slammed. Kurt had gone. I saw that one of the yellow drums that had rolled off the pallet had jammed itself under the forks. One of the blades had run through the metal, and liquid was gushing out on to the concrete. I started to think what a fork that had run through a steel drum could have done to my torso. Then I began to think about what something in a drum this colour had done to my throat and Jockie Sullivan's skin and the fish at Dunmurry, and I began to wipe my hands on my oilskins, hard, waiting for Stewart to get off the truck and come at me.

Stewart was very pale. He had stopped the truck.

I stared at him, too shocked to speak. Then I understood.

The shed door was open again. There were black figures against the light, making noises like alarmed geese, Lisbeth's voice among them. Stewart came towards me. He said, 'Goodness, sir, are you hurt?' in a loud voice. His eyes jinked from side to side. He was evidently paralysed with fear.

I found my wits too late. By then he had bent right forward to offer me his hand. Suddenly, he brought his head back a little, then hooked it hard down. I twisted aside, but not soon enough. There was a violent pain in the bridge of my nose as the visor of his hard hat pecked into it. His voice grated, 'Last warning. Keep your nose out, poof.' My eyes filled with tears, and I fell into the stuff on the floor with my hands over my face.

It was maybe twenty seconds before I could think straight enough to get up out of the puddle. I could hear Stewart's voice, raised in explanation or self-justification. I got up. There was the iron taste of blood in my mouth. People gathered round: Lisbeth was there, and the man in the silver hard hat. They put out their hands. I said, 'Don't touch me. I'm covered in it.' I started for the exit, running clumsily on my bad leg, towards water, where I could wash it off.

'Covered in what?' said the man in the silver hard hat.

'Stuff out of the drum,' I said. 'Irritant.'

The man in the silver hard hat put out his hand. It was a plump white office hand. The stuff would burn it to a crisp. He put it on my shoulder. 'Relax,' he said. When he took his hand away, I could see that it was slimy with the liquid. 'You're fine.'

I stared at him stupidly, the blood dripping off my chin.

'Detergent,' he said. 'Washing-up liquid.'

The drums were the same colour as the one I had seen last night, and they bore the same serial numbers. What had been in the drum last night had not been detergent. But there were iridescent bubbles on the shed floor. The man in the silver hard hat was right.

And something was very badly wrong.

Chapter Seventeen

There was a lot of flapping of hands. They took me to the office washroom, and I dripped blood into the basin. The face in the mirror was bony and haggard, with a red weal across the bridge of the nose. It was the face of a fool. I told it so. Then I went back to the main office.

The quarry manager had hung his silver hard hat on a peg and was standing looking out of the window, his jowl resting on his collar. 'I really can't apologise enough,' he said. His voice was Home Counties, ex-military. Through the door I could see Lisbeth reading a sheaf of notes in the next office. She was not smiling; the manager would have been giving her hell for letting me wander off on my own.

I grinned at him. It was meant to be reassuring, but it hurt my nose. I said, 'I'd like to speak to Donald Stewart, and the man who was with him.'

The manager said, 'What man?'

'Yellow hard hat,' I said.

'All the men wear yellow hard hats.'

The pain was affecting my temper. I said, 'I have just been assaulted by two of your employees.'

He said, 'Oh, come now.'

'The man on the fork-lift,' I said. 'His name's Donald Stewart.'

The manager frowned. 'Honestly,' he said. 'I mean if it happened I'm most terribly sorry, but are you sure?' He pulled a portable VHF off his belt. 'Jones to site office, please. It's a dangerous place,' he said. 'Lisbeth shouldn't have let you go wandering off by yourself. I really can't be held responsible.'

Jones arrived, fat and out of breath. He took off his hard hat. 'Who's up in Storage West?' said the manager.

'One of them's Donald Stewart,' I said.

Jones looked at me. 'That's right,' he said. 'He took a guy up there off *Marius B*. They were stacking some cargo.'

I said, 'Do you employ Donald Stewart?'

'No,' said Jones. 'He does some cargo handling for *Marius B*. He comes over from Dunmurry.' On the manager's face there was the faintest trace of smugness. Assault or no assault, it was not his problem.

The squat funnel of the smaller of the two ships spouted black diesel smoke. I picked up the pair of binoculars hanging on the door, and focused them on her. She was loaded deep. The derrick between her hatches was pulling the hatch covers over the pile of granite chippings in her hold.

'Got to get out on the tide,' said the manager. 'Had engine trouble. Been cluttering up the dock for days.'

The disc of the glasses had moved away from the hatches, and on to the rust-streaked white paint of the superstructure aft. There was a man on the starboard wing of the bridge. He had taken off his hard hat. There was no mistaking the big red face, or the pink shine of scalp through the close-cropped yellow hair.

I said to the quarry manager, 'What day does that ship come in?'

'Eight day round trip,' he said. 'Different day each week.'

Hurt him, the blond man had said. I put the binoculars on the *Marius B*'s bow. It was tall, and rusty. The rust looked old and well-established. Nobody had used that bow to hurt Jimmy Sullivan.

A stripe of dirty water appeared between the *Marius B* and the quay. Her propwash writhed briefly as her engines went astern. Then her rusty nose was pointing at the horizon, and she was away.

A stocky figure was walking across the rutted grey plain towards the quay. I ran through to Lisbeth's office, swiped the Land Rover keys off her desk, jumped into the driver's seat and roared after him.

He turned at the sound of the engine, and walked round the side of a shed, out of sight of the Portakabin. I turned after him. He started to run, looking over his shoulder, his face short and red, the eyes and mouth hiding in deep creases of raw-looking flesh.

'Stop!' I shouted over the howl of the engine.

He kept going. This time, I was going to talk to him, and he was not going to use the rules of the jungle, because I was going to use them first.

I brought the bonnet level with him as he ran. He could not peel off to the right, because the wall of the shed was in the way. I yanked the wheel over. There was a thump. He fell between the bonnet and the wall. I braked. Too hard, I thought. Killed him. When I looked back he was lying on the ground, knees drawn up, whooping for air. I backed up to him, gently, so the tyres were pressing a little on his ankles. I said, 'You can tell me what I want to know, or I will drive over your legs.' I blipped the throttle, slipped the clutch enough to show him. He roared like a bullock, down there on the ground. It was a disgusting noise. I was doing a disgusting thing.

His eyes swivelled up at me. Sweat was rolling down his forehead in big, fat drops. I said, 'Where were you last night?'

He said, 'Canna harbour.'

I said, 'Prove it.'

'I was on the buoy with Michael McCrimmon and Ecky Harris. You can ask them.'

'I will. Now you can tell me what you were fighting about with Jimmy Sullivan three weeks ago.'

'Go to hell,' he said. I blipped the throttle. He roared again. 'Jimmy picked up some drums,' he said. 'They'd gone overboard off a ship. I gave him a price on them. But he wouldn't have it.'

'Who else would he sell them to?'

'Nobody.'

'That's not what his wife said.'

He said, 'I met a bloke. He had a container go adrift. He wanted a bloke who knew the tides to collect them up. The boss told him to come to me. He was paying out.'

'So Jimmy could have sold them direct. For thirty quid. You were paying twenty. What was this guy's name?'

His head thrashed side to side in the mud. 'Kurt Mancini. He works for a chemical company in Rotterdam. Bach AG.'

'That was him you were with just now.'

'That's right.'

'And you went down to Camas Bealach last week and you stole the drum out of the shed.'

'I never did.'

'There was paint from your boat on the slipway.'

'Bollocks. I was in Blackpool. Anybody could have used it.' He had a point.

I said, 'Why did you knock Ewan Buchan off the fish cage?'

'Because I hated his guts,' said Donald. 'He was a nosy rich wee bastard. And so's that American woman of his, and so are you.' His eyes were pits of bile. 'But you're out of your league, kiddo. You're being watched, you and that woman.'

My foot hit the throttle. He yelled with pain. I was sweating, and my heart was pounding. 'Who's watching?' I said.

There was a lot of Land Rover on his leg now. He said, 'You can break every bone in my body. There's people will do worse.'

'Like Mr Mancini.'

'It was you said it.'

I should have driven over him. I could not. I rolled the Land Rover forward. He sat up, rubbing his legs. 'You're on the way back to Barlinnie,' I said, and drove my sore throat carefully down to the landing stage.

He was the kind of man who would use violence and threats of violence, and be governed by them himself. A hard man.

But a frightened hard man. Not a killer.

Out on the broad sea, the *Marius B* was climbing towards the horizon. The day was warm and humid, but I was cold. If it had not been Donald who had put me in the fish cage last night, who had it been?

Deep water, I thought. Full of sharks. At least one of the sharks was watching me, and its eyes were the cold eyes of Kurt Mancini. I sailed down the coast to Prosper's house. I wanted someone to confide in.

The house was a miniature of Dunmurry, complete with battlements, pepperpot towers, and stuffed salmon in glass cases in the hall. My throat was getting worse.

Prosper noticed. He looked worried, and made me drink a large glass of malt whisky. Then he said, 'What have you been doing?' I told him.

He said, 'Harry. Why don't you tell the police?'

'It looks like Ewan died broke. If anybody gets the idea he was storing mines, the insurance won't pay out.'

He watched me with his large, slightly protuberant eyes, then leaned over the table. 'Words of one syllable,' he said. 'Call the cops.'

I said, 'There's Fiona.'

'Fiona?' he said, and looked at me hard. 'What about Fiona?'

'If I call the cops, she'll have to sell up Kinlochbeag.'

'So?' said Prosper.

'I aim to spare her the necessity.'

'Oh, dear,' said Prosper. His face split into his huge, melon-slice grin, and he reached for the whisky bottle. 'She has got all the way through to you. Boy, you is doomed. And here was me thinking it was going to be death or glory this summer.'

'Death,' I said. 'Not much glory.'

He said, 'You came up here so you and me can go racing. There's two weeks to go before the Three Bens. The smart move is to call the cops, and do some sailing, and not get hurt. Right?'

I sat there and nodded, and contemplated the wreckage of a summer's racing. 'Right,' I said.

He sighed. 'But you're staying with it,' he said.

I nodded. 'I'll sail the race,' I said. 'And I'll win.'

He smiled, the cynical Prosper smile. I got up to go. He put a hand on my shoulder. His face was serious again. He said, 'I want to sail that race. You be careful. And if you need any help, you say the word.'

I thanked him, and left.

The whisky made the throat feel as if it had been attacked by killer bees. I put *Green Dolphin*'s nose on the end of the Horngate, clutched in the autopilot and slumped up in the corner of the cockpit, breathing through my nose to keep the raw wind off my throat. All I could think about was what Donald had said. *You're being watched, you and that woman.*

By the time I had anchored, stowed the sails, and rowed ashore, it was all I could do to walk. I stumbled up to the house. Fiona was in her studio, working at a miniature loom.

She turned. Her mouth opened, but she did not say anything at first. Then she jumped up. 'Harry!' I found her voice infinitely comforting. She said, 'What have you been doing?' in a voice that crawled with worry. I sat down, hard, in an armchair. *You're being watched, you and that woman.*

But I was too ill to understand anything but the fact that Harry Frazer was among friends.

I said, 'Breathing jellyfish.'

'Jellyfish?'

'Jockie.'

I had very little voice left. What remained had to be rationed. 'He's all right.'

'Same stuff,' I said, and opened my mouth. Must look like a dying fish, I thought. A tired dying fish.

Then I fell asleep.

Life became vague and hazy. Hector seemed to be helping me up the stairs. I tried to tell him that I was all right, but I was hampered by the fact that my voice had now gone completely, and my knees were only working one step in four. Then there was a doctor, frowning from behind the pen light he was shining in my mouth. And a lot of sleep: night, day and another night, disturbed by the burning of my throat, and the feeling that out there, in the daylight, things were happening beyond my control.

It was all jumbled together out there: yellow drums, and fork-lift trucks, and Donald Stewart. And most of all, the big, pink face of Kurt Mancini, shrinking in the round eye of the binoculars.

After a certain length of time it was daylight again, and Fiona was sitting by the bed, and I was able to turn towards her with my eyes open. When she saw me, she smiled. It was a smile that was like someone drawing the curtains and letting the sunlight roar into the room. She said, 'Don't talk,' grabbed my hand, and squeezed it, hard. I squeezed back. I seemed to have become alarmingly weak. There was a disgusting taste in my mouth, chemical and toxic.

I whispered, 'What the hell's wrong with me?'

'Shut up,' she said. She did not stop smiling. It looked anchored on her face, that smile.

'What?'

She sighed. 'The doctor doesn't know. He reckons you have managed to inhale a vapour which has burned your larynx and polluted your system. He said it was unusual to get two cases of poisoning, source unknown, in the same week. He's got one at Inverness hospital.'

'Jockie,' I whispered.

'Jockie's doing well,' she said. 'He was worse than you. They reckon he had contact with the stuff itself, not just the vapour.'

I nodded. It hurt my neck. If Jockie could get better, so could I.

'Get some rest,' she said. 'I brought you tea.'

I lay there and looked at her. Her eyes were as calm as flat water, as if it was the most natural thing in the world that she should be nursing someone who had dropped into her life fourteen days ago. It felt natural from my end, too. Kinlochbeag was no longer somewhere I had dropped off on my way to stay with Prosper. It was the right place to be. I had come back not only because Donald had been uttering his threats, but because I wanted to, very badly.

I said, as best I could, 'I love you.'

Chapter Eighteen

Her eyes became green searchlights. A tide of red rose from the collar of her jersey and covered her face. She put out her hand halfway towards me. Then she jumped up and ran out of the room.

I lay and watched the door, and thought about the blush, and the movement of her hand. I felt weak and ill, but for the moment extremely happy. I dozed off, and woke up a couple of hours later. This time I was strong enough for the happiness to get my feet on to the floor, my clothes on, and my spinning head down the stairs. Fiona was in her studio. She looked up as I came in, and began to say something. She stopped. The pupils of her eyes looked big and deep, and her face was suddenly young and vulnerable. She came across the room to me, and I put my arms around her, and she put hers around me. It was very good. But I was well enough to take things seriously.

You're being watched, you and that woman.

The telephone began to ring.

She said, 'Ah, shucks,' pulled away to answer. 'It's for you,' she said. I pointed at my throat.

'He can't talk,' she said. 'Can I take a message?' The telephone yammered in her ear for some time. When she rang off, her face was solemn. 'That was your office,' she said. 'They had a call from a hospital in Pulteney.'

'Pulteney,' I whispered. The happiness congealed. My skin was cold with the knowledge of what came next.

'Your sister,' she said. 'She's in intensive care. Overdose of barbiturates.'

I stared at her, frozen-faced.

'They think you should be there,' she said.

I nodded. My head felt heavy as lead.

That was why Vi did it; to convince other people that I should be there. It was her method of reaching out and gathering me in, so I would light her cigarette and pore over her photograph albums. Mummy Vi.

What they had told Vi when she checked out of Portway House for the third time was that she had to think about her life in a new way. She had to stop being Vi with the glass in her hand and the pills to soften the hangover. She had to be a new Vi, stand-alone Vi, swimming through life without her raft of little brown bottles. So Vi had said, Of course, darling, and gone to Narcotics Anonymous meetings, and moved back to the house in Pulteney I was paying for with the money from the broken marriages of south-west England. She had started taking walks on the beach before breakfast every day, and telling people who asked if she was lonely that she was getting into solitude.

That had been the year before last. Then she had picked up a nice pink young 505 champion called Georgie in the Yacht Club bar one evening, and brought him home to her big soft bed in her nice little whitewashed house, and shown him things he had never dreamed of out there on his trapeze. He had come back for more the next night. For five nights after that, Vi had clucked and cooed, and spun her rusty enchantments. But the only one who had fallen for the enchantments was her. On the sixth night she had seen Georgie in a dim corner of the Yacht Club bar, very close to a very pretty girl who was not only helmswoman of a nationally rated Hornet, but also half her age. And Georgie had said some unkind things about sixties throwbacks and the age beyond which short skirts should not be worn. So she had gone to see her friend Cynthia. Cynthia was married to a property developer who had two Mercedes, a Sunseeker Tomahawk, and a villa in Tenerife, but felt there was something missing from her life. Cynthia had given her a handful from her stock of little helpers to cushion the hammer blows of lost love. Three weeks later, Vi had left the intensive care unit of Plymouth General, very pale and pumped empty, and I had shipped her back to Portway House. At Portway the doctors let it be known that this time was her last time, and that if Vi showed up with barbiturate in her urine again, she could go and get well somewhere else.

There was nowhere else.

Fiona said, 'Can I come with you?'

I hugged her. We packed.

On the way to the airport, we stopped in at the Inverness Hospital. A bemused doctor said, Yes, of course, he had the drum cap that had come in with Jockie Sullivan, and I was welcome to it. So we wrapped Jockie's discus in a polythene bag, dropped a couple of Mars Bars on to the pile of *Beano*s on his bed, and caught the afternoon plane from Inverness. And at six o'clock we were rolling in a hired car between the fuchsia hedges of the Pulteney Cottage Hospital.

It was a low, white building. Fiona said, 'You see her. I'll wait in the car.'

The doctor was young, with brown curly hair and a harassed expression. 'She's been a bit…excitable,' he said.

I had spent the journey dozing and drinking mineral water. My voice was coming back. 'What happened?' I said.

He said, 'She came in with acute barbiturate poisoning yesterday night. We pumped her out.' He paused. 'I believe she has had…problems before in this direction?'

He had read the notes. There was nothing to discuss. He led me up the stairs and into a ward with French windows beyond which green Devon hills fell away to a glittering blue line of sea. Curtains were drawn round the beds. 'I've given her something,' said the doctor. 'To keep her quiet. But…well, it's a problem.' He pulled back her curtain.

She was lying dead straight in the bed. Her skin was the colour and texture of blotting paper. Her hair lay on the pillow like dyed black snakes.

The signs were all there. The bones of her small model's face looked as if they were about to pierce the skin. They had not got all the make-up off; the brown shadows round her eyes were smudged with mascara, and the lurid bars of rouge on her cheeks were random diagonals. Prosper had once pointed out that you could always tell when Vi was off the rails because her make-up would be half an inch off-centre.

Her eyelids lifted, slowly, like heavy trapdoors. She said, 'Hal.' Her voice had a saloon-bar slur.

I said, 'What have you been up to, Vi?'

She did not seem to hear. Instead she said, 'Good little Hal popped down to see Mummy Vi.' She smiled, a doper's smile. When I had been younger, I used to treasure those smiles. It was only later that I had found out it was the pills smiling.

The doctor said, 'I don't know how much she'll, um, register. Er...have you considered where we go, as it were, from here?'

What he was trying to say in the nicest possible way was that the Cottage Hospital was not equipped to deal with a barbiturate addict in withdrawal, and she was upsetting the broken hips and varicose veins. 'We're getting there,' I croaked.

'Getting where?' said the slurred voice from the bed. Vi had years of experience of fighting the effects of strong drugs.

'You were back on the pills,' I said. 'We'll have to get you some help.'

'I *know*,' said Vi. She started to cry, a weak, cat-like mewing. 'It's not *my* fault.'

It never had been. Life was a series of conspiracies to deprive her of parts, grow wrinkles under her eyes, make her oversleep, get her fired.

The doctor said, 'If you could pop by on your way out?'

'I won't be long,' I said.

'Going away,' said Vi. 'Always going away.'

'Not yet,' I said. 'Not going anywhere.'

'I stayed with you,' she said. 'Always, always.' She reached her hand from the sheets. It was as cold and thin as a lizard's claw. I thought of small Harry Frazer staring at the Street lights on the ceiling of the mansion flat, and expecting every taxi to be Mummy Vi. Once, when I was ten, she had stayed out for three days.

'You're fine,' I said. 'What happened?'

'Spiked me,' she said. 'Bloody Eric spiked me.'

I said, 'Who's Eric?'

'Bloke. Big and nice.'

'Oh.' Lately, her life had been riddled with Erics.

'By the way,' she said. Her grey tongue came out and moistened her lips, and her long nails tickled my palm coquettishly. 'I've left my handbag at home. My make-up, you know.'

I knew. I said, 'I'll nip down to the hospital shop and buy you some more.'

'No,' she said. Her hand was suddenly clammy. 'It's special.' What was special about her handbag was not the make-up, but what was in the pill bottle. 'Not yet,' I said.

Something horrible happened to her face. 'You fucking bastard,' she said.

I tried to quiet her. But my voice was fading again. As it faded, hers rose till she was screaming, a torrent of filth that merged word into word, and became a long, dreadful yell of agony. The doctor brushed the curtains aside, scrubbed her arm, and shoved in a needle. Her eyelids fell, smooth and slow as hydraulic gates. The doctor and I walked slowly down the ward together. 'We haven't got the facilities,' said the doctor.

Nor had Portway House. Nor had anywhere but Mabbacombe, which they used to call the County Asylum. Mabbacombe had tiled wards with beds jammed in six inches apart. Vi had been in there once before. She had tried to kill herself on the third day. 'I'll think about it,' I said.

'The sooner the better.' The doctor looked embarrassed. 'Actually, by tomorrow morning.'

'Tomorrow?' I said.

'I'm afraid I must insist,' he said. I could see his point.

Pulteney is a pretty village, with a horseshoe harbour, a lifeboat station and tiers of granite cottages once inhabited by fishermen, but nowadays serving as holiday homes for the kind of people who could afford the subscriptions for the new cedar Yacht Club they had built on the old Fish Dock at the quay. I was not in the mood for new cedar Yacht Clubs, but Fiona and I needed a drink. So we went down to the other end of the quay to the Mermaid, which had successfully resisted the rising tide of horse brasses.

It was still early evening, and the pub was empty except for a couple of fishermen at the bar. Kids in bright wetsuits were windsurfing in the harbour outside the window by our table. I rested my heavy head on my hands and said, 'Why did she have to start again?'

'What do you think?' she said.

It was good being with Fiona. She had a way of slowing things down to a manageable pace. 'She doesn't like herself,' I said. 'She wants to get away.'

'She wants you,' said Fiona.

I laughed. I had spent a good part of my life as Vi's main chore, and the rest of it as her bankroll. 'Needs, possibly,' I said. 'Wants, no.'

The bar door opened and a man came in. He had a low-cheekboned face, brown with a seagoing tan, dented with hollows and crowned with spiky brown hair. He looked as if he had just got out of bed. Charlie Agutter always looked as if he had just got out of bed. 'Harry,' he said, as if we were in the middle of a conversation. 'Vi's had a turn, I hear.'

'Charlie Agutter,' I said. 'Fiona Campbell. Charlie designed *Green Dolphin*.'

Charlie looked at Fiona as if he was measuring her.

She said, 'You did a nice job.'

Charlie raised his eyebrows and looked faintly sheepish. I went to the bar and got him a Famous Grouse; when I came back, he was talking, and Fiona was smiling at him. I envied him the smile, but not for long, because I got it next, and a hand on my hand under the table. 'What happened to Vi?' I said.

Charlie was not one to beat about the bush.

He shrugged. 'It was very quick,' he said. The Agutters were an old Pulteney family, and not much happened in the town he did not know about. 'Otherwise I would have rung. One minute she was coiled round some bloke. The next thing, she was upside down in the Yacht Club bar. Then they carted her off to the hospital. She all right?'

I said, 'She's going to need looking after.'

Charlie said, 'Particularly if she stays here.'

'What do you mean?'

He pointed out the window. A man with a deep tan and blond hair was unstrapping a windsurfer from the roof rack of a BMW.

'Nicky Charleston,' he said. 'One of our cocaine heroes. The young set, my deah. Dope in every orifice. Vi hangs about with them.' He looked grim, drank his whisky. 'They have a laugh at her. Call her the Barbie Doll. They like her house, though. I told her not to be damn stupid a couple of times. Did me more good than it did her.'

I said, 'Do you know someone called Eric?'

'No,' said Charlie. 'But you can lose count of the little darlings. They're all down from London at the weekends, poncing round the harbour. Then they nip back up to fiddle around with the stock market. Go and ask Nicky.'

'We haven't been introduced,' I said.

'Come here.' He pulled me out of the door. The wind was cool off the harbour. 'Nicky!' he said. 'Pop over!'

Charleston smiled, a charming smile full of white teeth and empty of meaning.

'Ever heard of someone called Eric?' said Charlie.

'No,' said Charleston.

We went closer. 'Nicky,' said Charlie. 'When's the court case coming up?'

'Tuesday week,' said Nicky.

'Possession of marijuana,' said Charlie. 'Assaulting P C Weatherall while under the influence of lager. Pulteney magistrates are not a friendly bunch. To you, that is. I've known 'em all my life. What you need is a character witness.'

'I've got some,' said Charleston. The smile was gone now, and he looked mean and sullen.

'Not from Pulteney, you haven't. I'd like to be able to get up myself and say you were a nice, helpful boy.'

'Hang on,' said Charleston. 'Do you mean Eric Waters?'

'Friend of Vi Frazer,' I said.

'Barbie,' said Charleston. 'That's Eric.'

'His number,' said Charlie.

Charleston rummaged in his Filofax. 'There,' he said, and handed over a slip of paper. 'Thanks a lot.'

'See you in court,' said Charlie.

Charleston seemed to have changed his mind about windsurfing. He strapped the board back on the BMW and drove away.

'Chairman of the Bench hates my guts,' said Charlie. 'Here.' He handed me the paper. 'Boat going all right?'

'Like a train,' I said. I had told him about the Kinlochbeag Regatta. 'If we do a good Three Bens, we're in business.'

'See you up there,' he said.

He said goodbye to Fiona and went back to the converted warehouse he used as his office. Fiona and I walked up the steep cobbles of Quay Street. 'I like your friend Charlie,' she said. 'I'm not sure about the town.'

The whitewash of Pulteney was very white, the baskets of geraniums excessively vivid. 'They think it's pretty,' I said. After Scotland, it all looked too small and too cute.

'Maybe I need to get my eye in,' she said.

Vi's house was in a terrace off Quay Street. I opened the door with my keys. It smelled of dirty dishes, un-put-out-garbage, and stale scent. Dozens of photographs of Vi wearing miniskirts and riding in Mini-Mokes gazed down from the walls, glacially cool behind pale lipstick and false eyelashes. Her handbag was among old coffee cups and used Kleenexes on a low table. It contained crumpled money, spilt make-up, and a brown bottle with four orange capsules. The label said Seconal. I flushed them down the lavatory. When I came back, Fiona was gazing with a sort of fascinated horror at the photographs and the shocking-pink upholstery. 'It's like a womb full of mirrors,' she said. 'She can't come back here.'

I shrugged. 'Where else can she go?' I went into the kitchen and started to stack plates. When I came out, Fiona was picking lipstick-smeared butts off the carpet. She smiled at me, and I smiled back. There was nothing to smile about, except being in each other's company.

Two hours later, the house was straighter and the guilt was riding me like the Old Man of the Sea. I found a crumpled packet of Earl Grey in the kitchen, and made tea. We sat at the Formica table in the kitchen. It was small and claustrophobic, but it was a long way from Donald Stewart and Kurt Mancini. The adjective was safe.

I had to talk to people at Bach AG about what was in their yellow drums. When I knew about the yellow drums, I would be in a position to help Morag Sullivan, and make Kinlochbeag safe for Fiona.

I said, 'I've got to go to Holland.'

Fiona said, 'And you're worried about what to do with Vi.'

'That's right.'

'I'll stay with her.'

'You'll *what*?'

The light fell downwards, casting shadows under her cheekbones, hiding her eyes. 'Listen,' I said. 'She'll come out of there stark raving bonkers. She'll be swearing, and screaming, and running round the walls.' Fiona stared at me, silent. My throat hurt again. I had been talking too much. 'And the first time you turn your back she'll be down Fore Street putting a brick through a chemist's window.'

She said, 'There aren't any chemist's shops in Kinlochbeag.'

I said, 'You can't go back to Kinlochbeag.'

Her eyes widened. 'And why the hell not?'

In Scotland, I had not told her about my conversation with Donald, because I had not wanted to frighten her. I told her now.

She said, 'That's ridiculous.'

I did not want to spell out two dead men, and twenty-odd miles of single track road, and big mountains all around. I said, 'I've got to go abroad. Just till I get back.'

She was quiet for a moment, looking down at her brown, competent hands. She was spelling it out to herself. Finally, she said, 'I want you to know that I am not staying in this doll's house one minute longer than I have to. So you hurry back, Frazer.' Her face became solemn. 'And make sure you come back safe.'

I went round the table, and suddenly we were kissing each other on the mouth, hard.

After a little while, she pulled away. 'Stop,' she said. 'I want to know about you.'

'What you see is what you get,' I said.

'What about all this?' she said. Like the living-room, the kitchen was full of photographs. Of Vi.

'I'll show you later,' I said. 'Come upstairs.'

Her eyes were suddenly hazy, and her face looked twice as alive as usual. 'Now?' she said.

It was difficult to talk. 'Now,' I said.

'All right.'

She looked at me sideways under her lashes, and smiled, a deeply ironic smile. 'I'm a very obedient person,' she said. 'Just as well, eh?'

I took her hand. It was if hundreds of new nerve endings had suddenly developed in the skin. We walked up the stairs slowly.

Vi's bedroom was pink, with frills everywhere. Neither of us were looking at the decorations.

Fiona's body was warm and brown and her skin was smooth as satin under the new nerve endings in my hands, and her mouth was a wet, hungry sucker moving on my face and chest. Somehow, we were on the bed, and she made a small noise of satisfaction and moved herself under me. She opened up and pulled me in. She said, 'I love you.'

I loved her, too.

Later, we lay and watched the seagulls squabbling in the slice of sunset above the roof of the house across the street. It should have been peaceful. It was not, because for some reason I was thinking of Ewan. I was thinking of whoever had blown him out of a world that contained Fiona, and friendship, and the yell of gulls in the evening, for their private convenience. And I was angry.

Fiona burrowed her head into my neck. 'Hunger,' she said. We went to a restaurant on the quay, and gazed into each other's eyes a lot. For a while there was no Vi, drugged in her bed at the hospital, needing to be looked after; only the candle flames standing in the green–grey lakes of Fiona's eyes, and the faint, good weariness that had taken the place of my poisoned exhaustion.

We drank Sancerre and ate turbot. Vi and Ewan and the yellow oil drums hung around the horizon like cloud round the calm eye of a hurricane. Afterwards, we went back to Vi's house and drank some brandy we found in the drinks cabinet. 'Your early life,' she said, and pulled a photograph album from the sixteen in the purpose-built shelf above the television. 'Tell me who's who.'

I gave her the rundown. There were the black-and-white pictures of the parents, waving goodbye at Heathrow Airport three hours before the Comet 4 carrying them had fallen apart in the sky. Then there were pictures of Uncle George, the guardian, grinning a loose grin under his strawberry nose, dying of drink by inches. After that, Vi, disguising herself as a grown-up before she realised it was fashionable for grown-ups to disguise themselves as

153

children; and me, a gloomy child with black hair hanging in my eyes and an expression of dogged determination.

'Poor little guy,' said Fiona, kissing me.

'I was fine,' I said. Which was true; I was fine, because I had no idea that life could be any other way. I had friends instead of family. I did well at school. And in the holidays, Vi was kind, when unstoned, and her friends were at least polite.

I tipped some more brandy into the glasses and pulled down the album of Vi's stay in the Caribbean. There were a lot of shots of her on the beach, naked, waving her bottom in the air; one of the last jobs she had done for *Penthouse*. Then there was the movie.

'*Wow*,' said Fiona.

There were me and Prosper, posing with tanks and fins on the beach at Virgin Gorda. And there was Vi on Tortola, her brown Spanish skin shining with sun, her eyes glazed with happiness and Tuinal, clinking glasses with Rock Hudson at the wrap party. There were dozens of brown, shining faces at a long table under the palms. On the blue sea in the background, schooners lay at anchor.

'Looks practically unendurable,' said Fiona dryly.

I was not listening. I said, 'Let me see that,' and twitched the photograph out of its mounts.

One of Vi's methods of killing time between her agent's three-monthly calls was *petit point*. Since she was too vain to wear spectacles, she used an illuminated magnifier. I pulled the magnifier down, switched it on, and looked at the photograph.

Vi's teeth were huge, and so was the dimple in Hudson's chin. Further down the table, my own face came out at me, laughing drunkenly as I fed a girl a banana. Down at the end of the table, far away from the camera, faces were very small, but not so small as to be unrecognisable. I blinked, hard.

There was Tom Finn, the director, pepper-and-salt hair and dark glasses. But it was not Tom Finn who was interesting. It was the man he was talking to. A man with shoulder-length yellow hair and a big, sunburned face. I had seen him last week. True, his hair had been crew cut, and he had shaved the beard. But the face was unquestionably the face of Kurt Mancini.

I took the photograph out of its mounts, folded it carefully, and stowed it in my pocket. Any ammunition was going to be useful ammunition, where I was going.

Chapter Nineteen

Next morning, I picked up my old Merc station wagon from Neville Spearman's marina and drove up to the Cottage Hospital, where the staff handed Vi over with the National Health equivalent of a sigh of relief. They gave us some pills that would keep her calm for the next seventy-two hours. We took her home and put her to bed. ' 'Svery clean,' she mumbled, and went to sleep. I rang the Legal Affairs Director of Bach AG in Rotterdam, and made an appointment for the following morning.

'What are you going to do?' said Fiona.

'Find out what is in those drums,' I said. 'And why, and who it belongs to. And do my bit for Morag.'

'Take care.'

'Same to you,' I said. She fitted neatly into my arms.

At the time, I thought it was her who was going to have the trouble.

Later that morning, I stopped off at my house in Clifton to pick up some clothes. Dolores the Chilean lodger was drying her underwear on the rack in the kitchen. This week she was wearing scarlet. The Oriental carpets in the living room were clean, the floor-to-ceiling books dusted, the geraniums watered. All was ready to receive the hermit Frazer and throw him towards the office.

I ran up to the bedroom and pulled some clothes out of the walk-in cupboard. Then I went out of the front door without a second look.

The Merc was going well. It was half past three when I reached the M25 junction. At this rate, I would be ridiculously early for the ferry. So I headed on into London, stopped at a telephone box in Hammersmith, and dialled the number Charlie Agutter had got out of Nicky Charleston.

A languid girl's voice said, 'Raphael.' There was music in the background.

I said, 'Is Eric there?'

'He's cutting right now,' she said. 'Who's that calling?'

'Never mind,' I said. 'I'll pop round.'

She gave me the address, in a little street to the south of Knightsbridge. I ditched the Merc and found a taxi.

Raphael was a hairdressing salon. It had a big glass window, and the inside had been built out of sandblasted boiler plates and ice cream parlour chairs. There were Vogue tearsheets on the wall, models with swan necks and sculptured topknots. Two girls with hair like moulded polythene interrupted their conversation long enough to point out Eric.

He was a large man in his early twenties, with slate-grey trousers and shirt and a pudding-basin haircut. He was smearing evil-smelling paste into the hair of a pretty girl and telling her what he had said to somebody the night before.

I walked through the hair clippings on the floor and said, 'Got a minute?'

He stopped in mid-sentence, mouth ajar. He had a pale face, spaniel eyes and a thin, conceited mouth. Next to him in the big mirror I looked lean and brown and threatening. That suited me fine. 'Now,' I said.

He began to object.

'Now,' I said again, pitching my voice so everybody in the shop would hear. 'You know Vi. You probably call her Barbie.'

'Yeah,' he said. A cocky grin started on his face. 'Weird old thing.'

'I came in to tell you something,' I said. 'I came in to tell you that if I ever again hear that you have been giving her pills, or smack, or cocaine, or any other form of dope, I will make sure you go to jail, and pull you apart when you get out.'

They were all looking at him now. His face was red and sullen. 'Ooh, butch,' he said. A man with a large black moustache had laid down his scissors and was coming across the room, a professional peacemaker's smile on his swarthy face.

'She says you spiked her.'

'Why would I do that?' he said. 'She didn't need any encouraging.'

He had a point.

'Is there a problem?' said the man with the moustache.

I said, 'Your little snipper's been feeding people heavy drugs. You want to watch him.'

The man said, 'Is this right, Eric?'

'Ah, shit, Giulio,' said Eric. 'I don't believe this.'

'I believe it,' said the man with the moustache. 'Is not the first time. Asleep in the mornings. Locked in the lavatory. Now this. You make a disgrace of my good salon. You fired. Get out, before I call the police.'

The scissors had fallen silent. It was good theatre; everyone in the place was watching. I had achieved what I had set out to do, not that it would help Vi. Bach AG would not be so easy.

Out in the purer air of Knightsbridge I took a taxi back to the Merc, and headed for Sheerness.

I slept like a brick, alone in a double cabin. Next morning, I disguised myself as Henry Frazer, solicitor: close shave, charcoal-grey worsted double-breasted suit from Hammond's of Stamford Street, blue-and-white cotton poplin shirt from Hilditch and Key, black Church's brogues, Royal Ocean Racing Club tie. In my black briefcase there were several file folders, and the plastic bag containing Jockie's discus.

In Flushing I passed between polite Dutch customs men, and turned out of the town and on to the flat green polder and the motorway that jumps, bridge after bridge, across the Rhine delta towards Rotterdam.

Bach AG inhabited a tall white building beside a straight road flanked by neat beds of red-and-yellow antirrhinums and other tall white buildings. The receptionist was blonde with a smile that showed not only white teeth, but a quantity of pink gum as well. The coffee table was covered in company brochures and copies of *Eco*, to show that the company's heart was in the right place.

It took only three minutes for a stern-looking secretary to appear and conduct me to the lift, and the eleventh floor.

The office of the Legal Affairs Director overlooked most of Holland and a fair amount of the North Sea. The Director himself sat so he was silhouetted against the window. He rose when I entered. 'Hendrik Pienaar,' he said. 'Won't you sit down?'

He was plump and pale, with a manner as portentous as his title. He had a big red moustache, as if to compensate for the hair that was fighting a losing battle against a flashing dome of scalp.

He shook hands and waved me to a chair. There was a long pause. I knew I was meant to fill it with words. He said in barely accented English, 'You have some sort of problem, I understand.'

'Not really a problem,' I said. 'Merely a matter arising peripheral to some enquiries I am making, on behalf of a client.'

He nodded, his fat fingers like a bunch of white bananas round the pen with which he was making notes. 'Who is the client?' he said.

'Morag Sullivan,' I said, and left a beat. 'Wife of James, deceased.'

The fingers wrote smoothly on. 'And what is the nature of the enquiry?'

I wrote the serial number from the yellow drum on a sheet of paper from my notebook and passed it across the desk. 'Could you tell me the contents of yellow drums bearing this code?'

He unfolded a pair of half-moon spectacles, put them on his nose and raised his head to peer at the paper. Then he tapped the keyboard of the computer next to him, and waited a second. The mouth under the moustache smiled. 'Detergent,' he said. 'Like washing-up liquid. Used for cleaning, and also to clear oil spills. Here at Bach we are manufacturing chemicals with a conscience.'

I nodded and smiled, in tribute to the PR copywriter who had written the line. 'So there's no way that chemicals with this serial number could be harmful.'

He laughed, a hearty, beer-drinker's ho-ho. 'Well,' he said. 'If you drink it, you maybe get a little problem with your belly. But nothing to kill you.' He had got his confidence right back now, which was precisely the way I wanted him.

I said, 'You might be interested to know that the contents of some drums marked in this way have proved to be violent irritants, highly toxic to marine life.'

His smile did not shrink. He said, 'This is not possible.'

I reached into my briefcase and brought out Jockie's discus. 'This is the lid of a drum in the possession of my clients, the dependants of James Sullivan. I have medical evidence that whatever was in the drum from which this came caused severe irritation, followed by local blistering and skin loss. We are talking about a child.' He stopped smiling. Behind the red moustache his mouth had become a thin, unforgiving line. 'Before removal, the lid was sealed. As you will see, it bears the serial number we have been discussing.'

He looked at me. Then he peered at the drum lid in its plastic wrapping. 'Well,' he said. 'Excuse me a moment.' He picked up the telephone, and spoke in Dutch. Then he put down the receiver, and said, 'Bach AG of course deny absolutely any harmful consequences from the product under discussion.' He shrugged; gave me a winning smile. 'I have called our Product Manager, Mr Smit, to speak with us.'

The Product Manager arrived. He was a lean, stringy man with a worried expression on a grey face. He tried to look relaxed as Pienaar said his piece. When he had finished, Mr Smit said,

'Irritant, you say?' His accent was thicker than Pienaar's. 'So somebody's reusing the drum, I cannot say for what.'

'It was with a consignment *en route* for the ArdnaBruais quarry. Some of the drums contained detergent.'

'Then I don't understand,' he said.

I picked up the plastic-wrapped package and handed it to him. He unwrapped it, and examined first the bottom, then the top. His face cleared. He said something to Mr Pienaar in Dutch. Mr Pienaar stroked his moustache, deliberating. Then he said, 'Would you excuse us a second?'

They put me in a dove-grey room with the day's *Financial Times*. I would have liked a cup of tea, but I could not face a tea bag. I did not read the paper. Instead, I worried. I was sure that Bach AG was capable of mistakes, but I was equally sure that they were not into deliberate mislabelling of corrosive substances. What I wanted to do was frighten them so much with the flannel that they would not even notice the real questions.

When I was called back into the office, both men were standing alongside the desk, the drum lid between them on a blotter, with the indefinably smug air of a couple of expert witnesses about to turn the prosecution's evidence upside down.

'We have a problem,' said Pienaar.

I waited.

'Somebody has been tampering.'

'With what?'

Mr Smit beckoned me over. Close to, he smelled of aromatic pipe tobacco. He had a ballpoint in his hand, which he held like a conductor's baton. With it, he tapped the drum lid. 'Look,' he said. 'Listen. This is not off a detergent drum.'

I said, 'The serial number is right.'

'Observe,' he said. 'Here where the paint is abraded. There is paint under.'

I bent and looked. The stones of Camas Bealach had knocked off some of the yellow. Under it, there was bare metal. Between the bare metal and the yellow was a narrow stripe of red.

'We do not use this colour,' he said, using his ballpoint to indicate the red stripe. 'At least, not for detergent.' He smiled, as if he had proved something important.

I said, 'What do you use red for?'

'Rubbish,' said Smit. 'Dirt chemical. What you call toxic waste.'

Chapter Twenty

There was a silence in which I could hear Smit breathing, and my heart beating. Ewan's Polaroid photograph; Jimmy Sullivan's argument with Donald Stewart; the weals on Jockie and the fiery breath of the drum in the shed at Dunmurry. They had been unrelated, those things, meaningless. But suddenly they were like words in a language I was beginning to understand.

I said, 'How can a drum of waste carry the serial number of an industrial detergent?'

Pienaar said, 'It is not possible to speculate at this moment.'

Right, Frazer, I thought. Time to make these people sweat like public fountains. I said, mildly, 'I seem to recall there are laws against painting drums of waste a new colour, giving them a false label, and shipping them across borders.'

Suddenly, Pienaar was very pale, and his spare chin was wobbling. He said, 'That is an accusation I will not dignify with an answer. There is a law of slander in Holland, as in England.'

Smit said, 'We are a responsible company.'

'Enough,' said Pienaar. 'This interview is at an end.'

I shrugged. 'By all means,' I said. 'Throw me out of the office. I will stop at the first public telephone and call five environmental journalists, and the police.'

'There will be nothing to print,' said Smit.

I looked at Pienaar. His eyes were remote. They were looking at the fact that however innocuous the answers might be, it was the questions that would do his company the damage.

I looked at my Rolex. 'The time is twelve-thirty,' I said. 'I shall return at two.' Smit started to say something, but the office door was closing before he could get it out.

I drove in a relaxed manner to a restaurant, ordered myself fried mussels with fried apples and onions, and a beer. I ate slowly. In the Bach AG offices they would not be eating at all.

When I got back to the building, Mr Pienaar looked older. His white hands left sweaty prints on the walnut veneer of his desk as he got up. He was smiling. Someone would have told him to smile. 'Mr Smit is on his way,' he said. 'I think we are in a position to point you in the direction of sources of information which will be of more benefit to you than ourselves.'

I smiled at him. What he meant was that he was going to pass me on down the line. Which was precisely where I wanted to go.

Mr Smit came in. His pipe was going nicely, and he had the drum lid in his right hand.

'Well,' said Pienaar, in the manner of a showman.

Smit said, 'We have made an X-ray. We have found a new serial number under the yellow paint.' He paused. 'It is certainly a serial number for Bach AG waste.'

I smiled at him and Mr Pienaar. Mr Pienaar smiled back. We are being frank and open with you, the smile said. We could have covered up, and sold you any old bill of goods. But Bach AG cannot tell a lie.

'However,' said Smit. 'This serial number gives a problem. Because it is of a consignment taken from us by a disposer under contract. And as such of course it is not our responsibility.'

'Quite,' I said. There was a pause. 'Though there must be doubts about the wisdom of using a disposal company which can allow this to happen.'

Smit said, 'We are deeply concerned.'

I said, 'Perhaps you could tell me who this disposer is?'

'There is a duty of confidentiality in the contract – '

'On a purely informal basis. To assist me with the further conduct of my claim. Since it seems that Bach AG are in no way culpable in this matter, and are indeed anxious to co-operate.'

Pienaar's eyes added it up, and were satisfied with the total. 'Very well,' he said. 'You will sign a release.' He spoke into his intercom, then sat back in his chair. Smit filled his pipe.

I said, 'By the way. Do you have a Kurt Mancini working for the company?'

Pienaar tapped his computer. 'No,' he said. 'Nobody of that name.'

'Too bad,' I said. Now that I had seen Bach AG in action, I was not surprised.

The secretary came in. I signed a release enjoining me to confidentiality, and exonerating Bach from all blame. It was not worth the paper it was printed on, but it was a face-saver for Pienaar. Then they gave me a blank envelope.

Inside the envelope was a slip of paper that said CLEAN-UP WASTE. There was a telephone number in Geneva.

'Anything we can do to help,' said Pienaar.

I smiled at him, and shook his soggy hand. He smiled back. For a moment, the room was practically full of teeth.

Then I left for the airport.

Ten thousand feet below the aeroplane window, Geneva was shrouded in a dirty evening haze on the edge of its lake. It was no place for grey worsted suits. By the time I got from the air conditioned airport building to the taxi, I was pouring sweat.

The lake looked nice and cool and blue. They were sailing out there in dinghies with bright stripes on their sails, kids having a good time after school. I slumped in the back seat and felt corrupt, and sticky, and old.

The Hotel du Rhône is not a bad hotel, if you are working. I took a workmanlike shower, ate a workmanlike dinner in a restaurant by the lake, and stared out of the window at the big fountain. Then I went running, to prove to myself that I was still in training for the Three Bens.

Next morning I donned the suit, gripped the briefcase, and took a taxi to 14 Rue Chailly. It was an unlikely spot for waste disposal: no chimneys, no incinerators, just the words CLEAN-UP WASTE on a brass plate among other brass plates by the glossy black front door of a discreet eighteenth-century building. I made my way through the door into a gilded wrought-iron lift.

On the fifth floor, a very pretty secretary in a short, expensive-looking black dress smiled at me sweetly and told me I was Mr Frazer. I was pleased to admit that I was. She led me down a passage and into a panelled office with a big vase of lilies on the side table. The man behind the desk had a pleasant, oval, schoolboyish face, sandy hair, and a long nose. He got up, beaming, and stuck out his hand. 'God Almighty,' he said. 'It's *that* Harry Frazer.'

I stood there grinning a grin that felt as if it had been cut out and stuck on. 'George,' I said. 'Nice to see you.'

He said, 'Siddown,' and turned to the secretary. 'Harry is a genius,' he said. 'You remember I was having that trouble with goddamn Trisha? Well, it was Harry got her off my back.' His hand planted itself like a meat spider on the secretary's *haute couture* buttock. 'Harry, this is Hélène.'

There were no rings on Hélène's brown fingers. She leaned gently against him, and gave me a smile that was eighty per cent business and twenty per cent pleasure, which was twenty per cent less business than most smiles I had seen so far in Geneva. I had handled George's divorce from his wife Trisha. George had lived in Wiltshire, near Swindon, and worked as an oil broker in London while Trisha, as it had turned out, distributed her favours among the horse-owning classes of the Cotswolds.

'So what the hell are you doing in Geneva?' he said. 'You must be out of your mind.'

I sat down. I had not expected Cleanup to be run by a client who had become a friend. I wondered how much to tell him. While

I wondered, I said, 'Why out of my mind? I'm just visiting. You live here.'

He said, 'Boredom capital of Europe, not counting Zurich. I had enough of England for a while.' He frowned. The Trisha business had upset him badly. 'And it was a nice job.'

'Waste disposal,' I said.

He smiled. It was a pleasant, schoolboyish smile. 'Not very fashionable, is it?'

'Not very.'

'These Greenies,' he said. 'They make me puke. They keep their yoghurt in refrigerators. They listen to music on plastic machines. Then they say we're not allowed to send refinery waste to purpose-built incinerators.'

I nodded. I said, 'And the money's all right?'

He laughed. 'Had to be, to pay your fees.'

George Hayter was a shrewd man, except when it came to choosing a wife. The way to get sense out of him was to approach him on the level. I said, 'George, you've got a problem.'

'I have?'

'Some weeks ago, you took a consignment of chemical waste off Bach AG, Rotterdam.'

He stared at me. 'Bach?' he said. 'It's not possible.'

'What isn't?'

'I've had them on the horn half the night,' he said. 'Some bloke turned up with a drum lid.'

'Me,' I said.

'Well I'll be blowed,' he said, shaking his head heavily. 'Talk about a small world. What are you doing, running around with tin lids?'

'Just interested,' I said. 'There could be a compensation claim.'

'Oh, no,' said George, hands up, palms out. 'Spare me that. Bach are bad enough. Yelling writs, and Greenpeace, and God knows what all. Something turned up on the West Coast of Scotland in drums repainted to look like a Bach detergent, someone said.'

'It was me that said it,' I said. 'I'm trying to find out how it got there.'

I pushed over the memo I had knocked up on the hotel typewriter, with the black numbers Mr Smit had discovered when he had X-rayed the drum lid. 'You've seen the numbers already, I suppose. Those are the waste codes. Any idea how it happened?'

Creases of skin deepened under his jaw as he studied the paper. Then he pulled a keyboard towards him, and banged out a sequence of digits. From where I was sitting, I could not see the screen. 'Password,' he said in a high, chanting voice, going through what looked a familiar ritual. 'Morning, children. Bach. Yep.' He looked back at me. The schoolboyishness was gone from his face; there were grooves on either side of his mouth, and bags under his eyes. 'How much do you know about the waste business?'

I shrugged. 'You get rid of nasty stuff for nice people.'

'Okay,' he said. 'Let me explain. I call myself a waste disposal company. But what I am is a trader. Someone with waste for disposal calls me. I tell him a price for taking it off his hands. Then I find someone who will dispose of the stuff, and I sell him the contract. Now, then. If you've got waste, there are a lot of ways of getting rid of it. In the old days, you could tip it down the drain. But there was a lot of fuss about that, quite right too. So now you dispose of it by landfill or incineration, depending on what you've got. For something nasty like PCBs – polychlorinated biphenyls – you will get quotes between fifty dollars and three thousand dollars a ton. For three thousand dollars, you get squeaky clean licensed incineration. For fifty dollars, you get some guy to ship it out to a place maybe in Africa. He will show you evidence under the Great Seal of Bongo Bongo Land that there is now a shiny new disposal plant down there. What he is actually going to do is tip the stuff on the beach, or down a nice deep hole, and clear off before people start to dissolve. But this kind of thing is beginning to excite comment. Not all that Green, you know.

'Bach AG are a nice tidy bunch of Dutchmen who want to keep their consciences clear, or anyway their reputations good. So I fixed up a contract with an outfit called Piranesi – Italian, not too cheap, but scrupulous. Totally scrupulous. And I arranged the shipping, and the stuff went into the incinerator…let me see…four weeks ago. I've got the paperwork here.' He tapped a bundle of papers in his in-tray. 'I'd guess that someone's been fly-tipping up there in Scotland.' He laughed.

'But not me, and not Bach. You have to understand about drums.

'If you are a works like Piranesi, you get maybe ten thousand drums a week, which is ten thousand dollars a week. You are not meant to reuse drums that have contained waste. But if you reckon an empty drum is worth a buck, Piranesi's empties are worth ten thousand dollars. My guess is that Piranesi sells its waste drums to a scrap merchant who reclaims 'em, caps and all, and sells 'em off. Even if you only get a dollar a drum, that's serious money.'

I said, 'So someone is going around painting illegally reclaimed drums in Bach AG colours and filling them with toxics.'

He spread his hands.

'There are a lot of funny guys around Italy,' he said. 'Guys with friends with shiny new plants in Africa.'

'Or Scotland,' I said.

'Or Scotland.'

I said, 'Are you trying to tell me that toxic waste drums go from Bach AG to be reclaimed in Italy, and are sold to someone who by coincidence fills them with more toxic waste, paints on bogus Bach codes, and sends them off to be fly-tipped?'

'It needn't be a coincidence. Bach produce a lot of drums. They have an excellent reputation. If I was doing it, I'd use their name. How big's your sample?'

'One drum cap,' I said.

'There you go. It's like picking an oil can out of a litter bin. Would you be amazed if it said Shell on it? And of course, if someone really naughty was getting hold of the red drums, someone who wanted to pull a cover-up, they would paint second-hand Bach red drums with the Bach detergent livery, and sit back and watch people get confused. People like you.' He smiled. 'It's a bloody minefield,' he said. 'Anyway, I'll institute urgent checks at Piranesi. I know the guys there. We'll find out. I'll let you know.'

'Thanks,' I said. I meant it.

'So where now?' he said.

I said, 'Have you got *Lloyd's Shipping Index*?'

He sifted papers on the table by his desk. 'Day before yesterday's,' he said.

'Fine.'

Lloyd's Shipping Index looks like a slim telephone directory. It is published daily, and it contains a record of every significant shipping movement in the world, with owner's name, latest reported movements, and cargo carried. The *Marius B* had sailed for ArdnaBruais yesterday. Her owners were listed as Monoco, Rotterdam.

'Hell,' I said. 'By the way. Have you ever heard of someone called Kurt Mancini in the world of waste disposal?'

'Never. Why?'

'Wondering,' I said. Mr Mancini was beginning to fit, but not well enough to be discussed in public. 'He's showing up on the West Coast at the same time as this muck.'

'Don't know him,' said George. 'Don't want to. How did you get mixed up in this? Bit out of your line, isn't it?'

'I was on holiday,' I said. 'Sailing. I ran into the stuff.'

'Horrible,' he said. 'Worst of it is it gives a perfectly good industry a bloody awful name.' Then his face lost its lugubriousness, and he became boyish once again. 'What are you doing this evening?'

'Going back to Holland,' I said.

He said, 'You'll never get a flight. Stick around. I've got a 470 on the lake. There's a race. Not up to your standards, of course. Only a club do. But...well, come and have a helm. Get pissed afterwards.'

I said, 'Let me use your telephone.'

He was right about the flight. I booked for the following morning, went back to the hotel, and had some lunch. It was a good lunch, *ris de veau* and half a bottle of Côte de Léchet. I hardly tasted it.

The *Marius B* was bringing consignments of perfectly legitimate Bach chemicals to David Lundgren's quarry. Camouflaged with the consignments were other drums, containing chemicals not as per label. Those other drums were being disposed of by methods as yet unknown. Some of them had been washed overboard. Most of those had been retrieved by Donald Stewart, who had handed them in to Kurt Mancini. Others had been picked up by Jimmy Sullivan and Ewan Buchan, who had not handed them in to Kurt Mancini. Jimmy and Ewan were dead.

It was a beautiful theory, but there was a problem with it. Running down a fishing boat means damage to the ship that runs it down, and the *Marius B*'s bow was undamaged. Also, the dates did not fit.

After lunch I went to my room, dialled International Directory Inquiries, and found Monoco's number. A girl's voice answered. I said, 'I'd like to speak to a clerk.'

She put me through to a man who sounded very young, with a thick Dutch accent. I said, 'Seymour here, Yarco Pumps. I've got a couple of pallets of machinery for Mallaig. Can you help me?'

'Of course, I hope,' said the clerk.

'Do you have a sailing tomorrow for a cargo FOB Rotterdam?'

'Alas I am sorry not,' said the clerk. 'We have only one ship this month. She is sail yesterday.'

This month. I drew in my breath. I said, 'You've got more than one ship?'

'Sure,' said the man. I held my breath. 'We have *Marius B* and *George B*. *George B* will be back in service in a couple of weeks, maybe. *Marius B* make the trip in four days, round trip eight. *George B* is faster. Three days, round trip seven.'

'What happened?'

'Hull damage,' said the youth. 'We have her back soon.'

'A week, with turnaround,' I said. 'What day does she get to Mallaig?'

'Wednesday morning,' said the youth.

'Thank you,' I said. 'I may call.' And I put the telephone down, gently, as if on eggs, and got some oxygen back into my lungs.

For of course, Wednesday morning is the day after Tuesday night.

Chapter Twenty-One

I rang Cyril in Bristol, and told him to look up the company details of Monoco, Rotterdam. He wished to draw my attention to office matters, but I cut him off and went to the Bibliothèque du Léman. There I stole the ship repairers' section out of the Rotterdam classified directory, and took it back to my room. It took me sixteen calls before I found a company called Ford, and a voice with angle grinders in the background said sure, *George B* was nearly ready. I asked what the damage was, but the voice did not seem to understand.

It was not important. I already had my flight booked to Holland in the morning.

When I rang Cyril, he told me that Monoco was registered in Gibraltar, with a solicitor and his clerk as directors. There was no hope of further information, unless I wished to use excavating equipment. Then he told me about two cases that could not wait and the next thing I knew I had been dictating letters down the line for half an hour.

At six o'clock I pushed my way through the hot, wet air to the yacht club.

The car park was full of new BMWs and Mercedes. There was a wooden building with a terrace and tables with yellow umbrellas under which clean-looking young men and women were drinking teabag tea. The lake looked dark and cool beyond a pack of dinghies.

George stood up and waved. He was wearing a Lacoste shirt and white shorts from which his red legs bulged meatily. Among the brown, sleek Genevans, he looked like a Wiltshire village tennis champion. He said, 'Drink?'

I shook my head.

'Good,' he said. 'Nice breeze out there.'

Hélène was sitting at the table behind him. The gold chain around her neck made her smooth brown skin look positively edible.

I said, 'I hope I'm not doing you out of a sail.'

She smiled, and crossed her long, delicious legs. Outside the office she seemed to have gained in authority, and George somehow to have diminished. 'Hélène comes for the social side,' said George.

We went down to the shower block by the dinghy park. I climbed into a pair of shorts in a smart tiled-and-panelled changing room with showers off and lockers down the wall.

George said, 'Date of birth,' and punched the combination lock. We put the sails on, wheeled the boat down the hard and floated her off the trailer and into the water. Hélène waved from the terrace. There were a couple of other people at the table, out of the same sleek, dark-haired mould. 'Waiting for me to be gone,' he said, and laughed, a laugh with too much self-dislike in it to be entirely convincing. 'You helm, me on the wire.'

I took the tiller, squinted up at the mainsail. After *Green Dolphin*, it was like taking the helm of a toothpick. I cranked in the mainsheet. The rudder hardened as the flow picked up, and the 470 took off across the water like a bazooka shell.

'Wonderful girl,' said George.

I glanced at him. He had that wounded look I had seen become fixed on his face as Trisha stripped him down like an onion. 'Yes,' I said. 'Where are we going?'

He pointed out the line, two big orange buoys on the water.

'Go on,' he said, glancing back at the clubhouse. 'I'd like to do well, for once. Hélène would like it, too. Bit of a frost, usually. Chap who crews is no good.'

'We'll do our best,' I said.

There was more of a breeze out in the middle, pouring down the lake from the mountains to the northeast. The 470 got up on its hind legs and planed. George was built like a rugby forward and his weight on the wire flattened the boat so it banged across the ripples like a bobsleigh. The messages began to flow from the sail through the tiller to the mind.

There was another boat over to port. Two men were crewing, wearing matching floral shorts. 'Anton and Fritz,' said George. 'They usually win.' One of the men turned and waved, his teeth white in his face. George waved back. 'Oily bastard,' he said. 'Anton, I mean. He's chasing Hélène. Poor girl.' He looked as if what he really thought was poor George. I began to understand that Frazer was the ringer who was going to fix Anton.

A gun banged on a cabin cruiser anchored out in the lake. 'Ten minutes,' said George. He was sweating. 'Let's do it.'

The triangle behind the starting line was filling up with dinghies. It looked like a mess. I said, 'We'd better stay out of that,' sailed round to the wrong side of the line, and sat there, on the starboard tack, spilling wind, going nowhere.

Time passed. The Blue Peter went up on the start boat. On the other side of the line, people were shouting at each other in French; neat, businesslike shouts. At the right-hand end, the boats were packed together like sardines. George was impatient, looking at me anxiously, fiddling with the jib sheet. 'Three minutes,' he said.

The sound of rattling hulls came from among the sardines. The shouts became more passionate, less businesslike. None of them had a clear wind. I said, 'We're off down the middle.' I shoved the tiller away from me. The sails snapped across. We left the committee boat to starboard. Water began to fly out astern as we reached away to the southeast.

'Gybe,' I said.

The 470 is a light boat. We turned 180°, and accelerated fast, up on to the plane. The committee boat came up on the starboard bow, rocking in the wavelets the wind kicked up. This time, we were the right side of the line, astern of the sardines under the lee of the committee boat.

'Going down,' I said, and turned the nose for the orange inflatable buoy at the left-hand end of the line. The boat was charging along, spray fizzing from halfway down the hull, nose all the way out of the water.

'Five,' said George. 'Four. Three.'

There was another boat up to starboard. A face peered under a silver boom. Then it had flashed astern. I hardened up, keeping the nose on the buoy.

'Two,' he said. 'One. Zero.'

There was a horrible pause. The buoy was charging down on us. Then the gun banged.

I ladled in the mainsheet, easing the tiller away with my knee. We shot past the buoy.

'Tacking,' I said. The wake roared as I shoved the tiller.

'Brilliant,' said George. He planted his feet on the gunwale. I heard him grunt as he shoved himself out, suspended parallel to the water by the trapeze wire on the harness.

We were on port tack, crabbing away from the line towards the first mark, an orange dot in the blue water under the green mountains beyond the lake. The sardines had got themselves straightened out, and were straggling towards the middle of the course on starboard.

I squinted down the sightline the mast made with the forestay. We were going to pass well ahead.

'Wonderful,' said George. 'Bloody marvellous.'

We shot under the bows of the fleet. In Britain, someone would have tried a hail, or ostentatiously changed course to make it look as if he had been obstructed. But this was not Britain.

We tacked quickly. And there we were on the starboard tack, twenty yards in front of Anton and Fritz, who were lying second.

'Wow!' said George, his pink face gleaming.

We had the fleet covered. At the next buoy, we increased our lead. The 470 went like a train on the reach, squirting water up from under the sides, George all the way out on the wire, keeping her flat. But it was not the moment to get overconfident. Something was happening to the wind. Out there in the lake, there were glassy patches; the evening calm setting in. Pretty soon, the calm was going to reach us, too.

Halfway to the second mark, what had been a crisp force three to four collapsed to a limp zephyr. George came off the trapeze and crouched over the centreboard casing. 'No bloody good,' he said. 'We're too heavy.' He was looking astern.

I did not look back, but I knew what he was seeing. Together, we weighed in at twenty-seven stone. Anton and Fritz were a good five stone lighter, and that will make a lot of difference when you are being wafted along by a breeze like a gnat's breath.

'Bugger,' said George. His face was sullen.

Ahead, a lake steamer had pulled away from the tall white buildings of the city. Its rails were crowded with sightseers, and it was nosing gently across the line of the course.

'Better duck under,' said George.

I looked down at Fritz and Anton, twenty yards to port and ten yards behind. A puff turned the blue water from sky to navy blue. The dinghy shot forward. 'We'll see,' I said.

George opened his mouth to speak. Then he shut it again, and licked his lips as if they had suddenly gone dry.

We converged with the steamer on a collision course. Half of me was saying: *Duck under; it's a silly little dinghy race on a silly little lake.* But the prudent voice was drowned by the roar of pure adrenalin in the ears.

My hand on the tiller did not move. The steamer's bow towered overhead; its siren was roaring, rattling in the buildings by the lakeside. Then there was a rail, with heads leaning over, mouths black holes in the faces. The bow-wave rolled us. We shot under. Then we were the far side, rocking in the wash.

George said, 'Wow!' again. This time there was a look on his face as if he did not quite know whether what had happened had been a slap on the back or a rabbit-punch.

'Look at your friends,' I said.

Fritz and Anton had had to bear away to avoid the steamer. They were a good way down the track, now, and to lay the mark they were having to sail too far up to windward to use their spinnaker.

George cheered up. 'Mad bastard,' he said, and glanced at the distant terrace.

We came in first. Given the general standard, that was no big deal. But George stuck his chest out, and Hélène wrapped herself round him, so all in all it seemed a satisfactory result.

Sixteen of us jolly mariners had dinner in a restaurant with a lawn running down to the edge of the lake. George was overexcited. He bought a lot of drinks. With dinner he drank a lot of good Burgundy, which converted the elation into gloom, and made him confidential. 'Trouble is,' he said. He waved a hand at the floodlit geyser of the fountain and the lights of the city swimming in the lake. 'Trouble is, it's not the same.'

'What's not the same?'

'My second life.' He laughed, a drunk's ironic yelp. 'About the only bloody thing I can remember about the kids is their bloody names.' He put on a high, self-mocking voice. 'Hello, boys. Tacka-tacka-tacka. Certainly can't think what they look like.'

I shook my head. His children were at boarding school in England. He and his ex-wife had them alternate holidays.

'Poor little fellers,' he said. 'Still, you did your best.'

I nodded, wishing he would shut up.

'Bloody hopeless, innit?' he said. 'We're in the same racket, you and me. Cleaning up the mess.'

'Sure,' I said. I had not drunk nearly enough to start getting poetic.

Soon after that I walked back to the hotel across the quiet, clean city, and went to bed.

It was raining in Rotterdam. The motorway was wet, and the dark roads were fringed with long, filthy puddles that squirted from under the Merc's tyres like *Green Dolphin*'s wake when she was up and going on a reach.

Forel was a dirty little yard out towards Maasluis. There were some tin sheds dripping rain, a couple of slipways and a smallish dry dock. I stopped the Merc between two puddles, and rolled down the window.

There was a ship in the dry dock. She was a two-thousand-ton coaster, reasonably modern. The name on her slab stern was *George B*. Where the name should have been on the bow, there was only red primer. Further down her bow there was scaffolding, and a welding torch flared blue in the grey rain.

There was a dirty little bar by the entrance to the yard. I went in, and ordered a glass of gin from the fat man behind the bar. The fat man told me I was English, and reminisced about riding through Nazi road blocks with dynamite in his saddlebags. I asked him about the ship in dry dock. He said she had hit a pier. That was what would have been said. We parted friends, and I drove to Flushing and caught the ferry.

Next morning I stopped for breakfast at a hotel, and called Vi's number in Pulteney. There was no answer. Out on the beach, I thought. Try later. I got some more change from the reception desk and started to look for Tom Finn.

People who work in television get a lot of divorces, so I had good contacts in BBC West. Jamie Neville of the Wildlife Unit had heard that Finn was working with *Get Afloat!*, a yachting programme. I rang the producer and he told me that he was spending a week filming at Waterfront, in Southampton. So I climbed back into the Merc and fought my way round the M25 and on to the M3.

Waterfront was one of Southampton's favourite projects. The developers had organised the bulldozing of some derelict sheds by a black and evil stretch of Southampton Water. On shore, they had built what looked like a giant greenhouse, incorporating a nineteenth-century shot tower at one end, dozens of apartments for executive leisure, and too many shops and offices. The place was no more than three years old, but it felt as if people were not buying enough in the shops, or finding much work to do in the offices. A cold northwest wind was hissing through the old crisp packets in the crevices of a World War Two anti-aircraft gun concreted into the car park, and rattling the halyards of the boats moored in the dredged-out harbour.

At the end of the pontoon, bright lights were shining through the smoked-perspex windows of a sailing cruiser with a deck saloon and a mast the thickness of a drinking straw. It was the kind of boat that builders construct to lie alongside marina pontoons while the owner drinks gin and tonic and polishes the chrome. 'The Padmore and Bayliss Merganser,' a voice was saying down there by the lights. 'A tidy little craft for the weekend seagoer who wants exhilarating sailing without getting the wife and kids wet.' There were a couple of men on the pontoon. One of them wore corduroy jeans and earphones. The other one had a clipboard and whisky breath. 'Exhilarating,' he said. 'Bleeding boat's water soluble.'

I said, 'I'm looking for Tom Finn.'

The whisky man said, ' 'Ang about.'

The wind blew. A voice said, '...and cut.' Two men came into the cockpit. One of them was tanned, with the artificial look of someone who spends a lot of time in front of cameras: Tony Crutch, a yachting journalist and diarist's nark well known for his lust for money and his dislike of getting wet, who had hung around the sheds at Pulteney when we were fitting out *Green Dolphin*. The other, with close-cropped iron-grey hair and a primrose-yellow polo neck, was Tom Finn.

Crutch looked at me and smiled automatically, showing an expensive line of caps. 'It's the sea lawyer!' he said. 'Heard you had a prang. Going all right now, eh?'

I nodded, and said to Finn, 'I'd like a word.'

Finn smiled, one of those television smiles. 'I'm tied up right now,' he said. He had little black eyes like chips of anthracite.

'I'd like to talk about Kurt Mancini.'

For a moment his face did not move. Then he frowned. And I felt a surge of joy. Because the motionlessness was controlled, and so was the frown. They were expressions put on the way you put on an overcoat because it is raining.

He said, 'I don't think I know him.'

I said, 'Yes, you do. You met him when you were filming *Charlie Running* on Tortola.'

Muscles knotted at the hinge of his jaw, and his Adam's apple bobbed as he swallowed. 'No,' he said. 'I don't think so.'

I pulled the photograph from Vi's album out of my pocket. 'Him,' I said, pointing.

'Good party,' said Crutch, looking over his shoulder.

There was sweat on Finn's upper lip and his skin had turned a nasty yellow. 'I told you,' he said. 'I don't remember seeing him. Ever.'

I took him by the arm, and led him down the pontoon, away from Crutch's big ears. 'What are you frightened of?' I said.

He yanked himself free. 'Nothing. Look, I'm busy.' He marched away down the pontoon after his crew.

I followed him, slowly. Crutch fell into step.

'Our Gladys has really got a hair across,' he said. 'Did I hear you mention *Charlie Running*?'

I nodded.

'Interesting stories about that,' he said. 'I did hear that the reason our Tony's not making features any more is that there was a muddle, and when they opened the film cans in the States they found that some of them had cocaine instead of film inside. And while there was nothing that could be proved, the idea was that he had to have known something about it. You've been up at Dunmurry, I hear. Three Bens? Because old David Lundgren put a bit of money into the movie. Funny you should be talking about it.'

'David Lundgren?' I said.

'You know. The rich one.'

I managed to say, 'I know.' Lundgren and Mancini, sitting in the bar at the Castle. Mancini, moving about the quarry sheds as if he owned them.

'You all right?' he said.

I said, 'Fine.'

'Well,' he said. 'Remember who gave you the word, eh?'

I walked ahead, and caught up with Finn. He did not look at me. I said, 'I'm seeing Mancini any day now. I'll tell him I saw you.'

He turned round and looked at me. There was no television left in his grey, haggard face. He said slowly, as if he was talking to a child, 'I think that would be a bit silly. Because it might give him the idea that you are curious about his business. And if that is the idea he gets it is quite possible that you will land up dead. Which is fine by me. But leave me out of it.'

He walked away and climbed into a silver Volvo estate with the crew. He had done a good job. I was convinced.

Seven years ago, David Lundgren had put money into a film on whose set Kurt Mancini had frightened the wits out of Tom Finn. Now, David Lundgren and Kurt Mancini were in business again. And once again people were frightened. Frightened, in some cases, to death. And I was in it, and worse, so was Fiona.

There were two things I had to do. I had to find out more about Kurt Mancini. And I had to wait for George's urgent enquiries at Piranesi to bear fruit. Then I had to follow them up. Because if you were going after somebody as powerful as Lundgren, it was as well to have your facts straight.

Chapter Twenty-Two

Orchard Street is a charming eighteenth-century backwater, close enough to the hub of Bristol to be full of piranha-toothed solicitors and architects. I had rung Davina Leyland from Southampton, and she was on her way. I trotted past the brass plate with my name on it, past Enid the receptionist, and up the eighteenth-century oak staircase to my office.

It was like a room belonging to a stranger. The desk was horribly tidy. It smelled of polish, and old files. I stood in the doorway and felt that it was too small and too dark, and did not contain enough air.

Things became familiar soon enough.

Cyril found me hovering on the edge of the carpet and shoved a sheaf of papers in front of me. He was short and plump, wearing a black jacket and striped trousers, with the smooth skin of a man who never got any fresh air except on his annual trip to Weston-Super-Mare. Orchard Street was Cyril's life. He was a thorough-going cynic, with a lofty moral code that he never had any scruples about compromising.

I said, 'Anything dangerous?'

He said, 'Dross, Mr Henry.' Dross meant stuff that needed to be signed, but did not need to be read. I scribbled signatures, while Cyril told me what was going on. This was very little, because it was July, and most of my clients were off on the holidays which would lead to the rows which would bring in the work later in the year.

'Lady Davina is in the waiting-room,' said Cyril, with a pursing of his small red mouth that managed to express disapproval of Davina with appreciation of the vast fees she paid.

There was the click of heels on the linoleum in the passage outside, and a high, upper-class woman's voice calling 'Cyril! Cyril, blast you!'

'I believe her ladyship is with us already,' said Cyril, impassive as a pink jade idol.

Davina made her entrance.

She was very tall, and very blonde, with a mouthful of carnivorous teeth under cheekbones high and remorseless as Genghis Khan's. She had bright green eyes, and dancer's legs, and the general outlook of a wolverine on heat. *'Darling,'* she said. She called everyone darling. 'I've been *longing* to see you.'

I took refuge behind the desk. 'Really?' I said. The office had shrunk further.

'Yes,' she said, speaking as always in italics. 'What have you done with Vi?'

I told her she was in Pulteney.

'I know,' she said. 'She rang up yesterday. She said you'd left some keeper with her. She sounded *desperate.'*

I had known Davina a long time. There was no point explaining about Fiona. 'It was a toss-up,' I said. 'Either she spends a while being desperate, or she spends for ever being dead.'

The word fell like lead. Davina shuddered theatrically. *'Ugh.'* She flung her big Gucci handbag down on the desk, crossed her legs with a flash of thigh that went all the way to the top. 'I've got to rather dash,' she said. 'I'm meeting Serena at the Arnolfini.'

I said, 'You remember when we were on Tortola, filming.'

'With that poor old faggot Hudson,' she said.

I said, 'There was a man there. A big guy, with a blond beard. Kurt Mancini.'

She frowned, picked at the red cushion of her lower lip with the red claw of her fingernail. Then she said, 'Oh, God. *Him.*'

I said, 'Do you know what he was doing out there?'

'He was some sort of money man, I think. But he liked to mix with the roughnecks. You know the type. Gold American Express, and still wants to Indian wrestle. I thought he was queer, at first.'

'At first?'

'One has one's methods,' she said. 'He wasn't. Not very, anyway. But he certainly liked hurting people.'

'What was he *doing*, though?'

She shrugged. 'God knows. He just sort of slid around. He was always talking to that Tom Finn chap in corners, then oiling round the girls on the beach. Bit reptilian, really.' She gathered her handbag, and uncrossed her legs.

'Nothing else,' I said. 'No idea who he was working for?'

'None,' she said. 'By the way, what have you been doing to Giulio?'

'Giulio?' I said.

'Don't be silly. You know. My Giulio.'

'Nothing, as far as I know.'

'He said you burst into his salon the other day and started shouting your head off.'

I remembered the man with the black moustache at the hairdresser's. 'That was him?' I said. I told her about Vi and Eric.

'Quite right too,' said Davina. 'Jolly masterful. Quite a coincidence, though.'

Cyril came into the room. 'Facsimile transmission, Mr Henry,' he said. 'Excuse me, your ladyship.'

I said, 'Bloody hell.' I wanted to get to Scotland. Cyril was doing his damnedest to ravel me in the office routine. I glanced at the fax.

Cyril said, 'Is there something wrong, Mr Henry?' The fax was short, typewritten. It bore yesterday's date.

Fiona Campbell and Violet Frazer ate breakfast at eight forty-three.
After breakfast Violet Frazer cried for half an hour. They then went to
Quay Street, where Fiona Campbell purchased a green handbag. Then they
returned to the house, and drank a cup of coffee. Violet Frazer took two
spoonfuls of sugar. Fiona Campbell took none.
Any more questions?

It was not signed. The number on the paper belonged to a Geneva fax bureau.

I read it again. This time my hands were shaking. I knew the format. It was a surveillance report.

I had thought that persuading Fiona to stay in Pulteney would keep her out of the trouble zone. I had been wrong.

'God,' said Davina. 'You look ghastly.' She rose to her feet, walked round the desk, and looked over my shoulder. She had had enough private detectives and Sun journalists after her to know what she was looking at. 'Narks,' she said. 'Well, they're out of date.'

'What do you mean?' I said.

'When I talked to Vi yesterday, she said they were off.'

'Off?'

She raised a well-plucked eyebrow. 'Yes.' she said. 'To your girlfriend's house in Scotland. They should have left first thing this morning.' She handed me back the fax, kissed me on the nose, and swayed out of the room.

The Kinlochbeag number rang for a long time. The telephone receiver was sweaty in my hand. The fax sat on my desk and looked at me with its bland buff face.

Eventually, Hector answered. I told him who I was, and said, 'Have you got Fiona there?'

He hesitated. 'Aye.'

'Can I speak to her?'

'Aye.'

'And Hector – keep your eyes open.'

'That's why she's making me answer the telephone.'

He went away. Fiona came on. She said, 'Hello.' She sounded apprehensive.

'You went to Scotland.'

'I couldn't stand that place. Vi's happier here. Hector's around, and so are Morag and the kids. What's been happening?'

I said, 'I've found the ship that killed Jimmy Sullivan. Now I'm after the people who run it. But there are...complications.' She knew that there was trouble. But I did not want to tell her that someone had been following her round Pulteney closely enough to know what colour handbag she had bought.

She said, 'Why did they ram Jimmy?'

I told her. She said, 'Dumping? Here? My God.'

'You'll have to keep quiet about it,' I said. 'Not for long. But don't say a word.'

'But – '

'Not a word.'

She said, 'So we have to sit here while they keep right on doing it?'

'If you start a fuss, direct action, they'll stop, and they'll carry right on somewhere else. If we can keep quiet, I can roll the whole thing up.'

There was a silence.

I told her about George and Piranesi. 'So when we find the drum salvors, we'll murder them. Did Ewan have an address book?'

'I've been sorting out his stuff,' she said. 'I've got it here.' Suddenly I could smell the leather armchairs in Ewan's study; see the panelling.

'There were some letters he wrote to a man called Weber,' I said. 'Gottfried Weber. Have you got his number?'

She gave it to me, then said, 'Who is this George Hayter?'

'An old friend,' I said.

'And a toxic waste trader?' Her voice was sceptical.

'Somebody's got to do it.'

'Depends what they're doing,' she said sharply.

And suddenly, we were on the edge of a row. I did not want a row. To sidestep it, I said, 'I'll ring Weber.'

'I prefer new friends,' she said. Her voice was soft again.

'Me too.' I paused. I said, 'Keep Hector close. And don't do anything that could put you in the way of an accident. I'll be back.'

She said, 'We'll be all right. Look after yourself.'

I put the receiver down. For a moment I sat in my office in the middle of the big city and felt lonely. Then I dialled Gottfried Weber's number.

When he answered I said, 'You corresponded with Ewan Buchan.'

'From Scotland,' he said. His voice was quiet and cultured, with a faint German accent. 'I remember.'

I said, 'I'd like to talk with you.'

'About what?'

'About a consignment of toxic waste.'

'What's the problem?'

'It went via a trader to Piranesi, in Italy. I want help checking what happened to it after Piranesi received it.'

He said, 'It will be difficult. Have you been reading the newspapers?'

'No. Why?'

'Because the Piranesi plant has been burning since four days ago. An explosion. The administration offices, everything. All gone. There is a picture in the *Financial Times*. Listen, I have a deadline. I am in Geneva tomorrow. Dinner?'

'Of course,' I said, through lips that felt stiff and cold. 'Restaurant Palmyre,' he said. 'By the lake. Eight o'clock.' I told Enid to bring the *Financial Times* from reception. On page nine, there was a picture of smoke billowing across an industrial estate. The caption said the fire had been burning for four days.

George Hayter must have known Piranesi was burning when he suggested I follow the consignment through.

An old friend, George. But a toxic waste trader. As Fiona had pointed out.

Chapter Twenty-Three

By the time I got to Geneva at midnight, and checked back into the Hôtel du Rhône, I was tired. The receptionist gave me the welcome-home smile. It did not cheer me up.

I was a lawyer, and lawyers operate inside the law, or they stop being lawyers and become like anyone else. But tomorrow morning I had to insinuate myself into George's office, which was trespass, and violate the privacy of his records, which was burglary. Without Fiona's voice on the other end of the line, it was less easy to believe that George, with whom I had been sailing only a couple of days ago, had sold me a bill of goods.

I lay in the Hôtel du Rhône's nice soft bed and stared at the ceiling with red-hot eyeballs. At five o'clock I swung my legs out of bed and pulled the *Financial Times* out of my briefcase. The waste disposal plant was still there, still spreading its dirty black smoke across Genoa.

Outside the window, the streets of Geneva became light and began to hum in their businesslike manner. I felt separate from them, an alien.

There was a café opposite the offices of Cleanup. I went in there at noon and sat with a pile of newspapers. The Piranesi story was there. Still burning. Administration and records destroyed. Pennies from heaven for George.

Sweat leaked out of my hands and into the paper. People bustled up and down the steps of the narrow building like bees on

190

the flight-ledge of a hive. He's not having lunch today, I thought. There was a jumpy hollow in my stomach. Sandwiches in the office, and I am wasting my time. The air was wet and heavy, and thunder crawled in the hills. I began almost to hope that he would not come out.

But at ten to one, with the café filling up around me, he trotted down the steps, his big brownish-pink face sticking out of the top of a blue seersucker suit, swinging a briefcase. He came straight across the street towards me. I cowered behind La Suisse. He looked as if he was coming to lunch in this café. But he shook hands with a man at one of the tables outside, and the two of them walked away towards the lake.

I took a deep breath, and felt the sweat running down my back inside my shirt. Then I paid my bill and strolled across the street and into the door of the office.

Hélène was at her desk, dark and businesslike and so beautiful that when I kissed her cheek I felt like Judas. 'You have missed him,' she said, with the expression of exaggerated worry that Swiss people use when a matter of routine goes awry. 'Alas, he is having lunch with a client.'

'Bother,' I said. 'Oh, well. Can't be helped. Can I leave a note on his desk? It'll have to be a longish one.'

She smiled. It was like someone setting off a magnesium flare in the small, panelled anteroom. 'Of course,' she said. She blushed, looking down at her long brown fingers. 'By the way,' she said. 'We are getting married.' A diamond the size of an olive glittered on the third finger of the left hand. She laughed. 'He asked me the day after you won the race. I think it was because he was so happy.'

So happy.

I smiled at her. 'Good,' I said. 'I'm glad.' The words were like lumps of coal in my throat. Go on, I told myself. Get in there and ransack the files. All the guy's done is trust you, and take you sailing, and feed you. And she's so happy she can't think straight. Take advantage.

So I took another deep breath, as if the oxygen would dull my conscience, and went through to his office. I sat down at his desk and turned on the computer. It whirred as the hard disk loaded the program. It told me it was dBase IV, and said PASSWORD?

I had been thinking about the password. I had watched him key it in the first time I had come to the office. Accountants learn to read upside down, so they can see what is on the tax inspector's desk. In the electronic age, solicitors get good at keystrokes.

There had been three words. The middle word had three letters, the first four or five. I had lost count with the last one. But I remembered something he had said when he had been typing: *Morning, children.* And later, when he had been drunk: *about the only thing I can remember about the kids is their bloody names. Hello, boys. Tacka-tacka-tacka.*

His children were large and fair-haired. James and Daniel, they were called.

I keyed in the names.

The prompt said: SORRY I DON'T RECOGNISE PASSWORD.

My hands started to sweat again. God knew what alarms he would have built into this thing. Then I remembered. It was not James and Daniel. It had struck me at the time; he had called his younger son Daniel, unabbreviated. But his other son had not been James. He had been Jamie.

I typed in Jamie and Daniel, and hit return.

The screen said HI DAD, faded, and changed.

I was in.

dBase IV is a big, expensive database. Solicitors use it too. I told it to go looking for Bach AG. It hummed to itself for a moment. Then it popped up a list of transactions.

Cleanup had done a lot of business for Bach AG, stretching back over three years. I used the cursor to run through, looking for a good date.

Found one.

On June 16th, ten days before Jimmy Sullivan had had his argument with Donald Stewart, Cleanup had agreed with Bach to dispose of five hundred tons of mixed filth, in red drums bearing the serial number the X-rays had exposed on Jockie Sullivan's discus, at a price averaging seven hundred and fifty pounds a ton.

Heels tapped in the passage. I turned the screen away from the door, pulled out a sheet of paper and a pen, and started to write. Hélène put her head round the door. 'You're being a long time,' she said.

'It's a long note,' I said.

'You want some coffee?'

'No,' I said. 'I'm on my way to lunch. Thank you all the same.'

'Okay,' she said, and beamed at me.

I grinned and mumbled something and hoped she could not hear the hum of the fan in the hard disk casing. She closed the door. I wiped my palms on my trousers and went back to the screen.

Fiona had been right. George had not taken the contract to Piranesi of Genoa, whose plant was still spreading dirty smoke across the blue Mediterranean. Instead, he had sold it to another dealer, Enzo Smith, at an address in the Rue St Pierre, in Geneva. Smith had bought it from him for five hundred pounds a ton, leaving George a margin of two hundred and fifty pounds a ton, total one hundred and twenty-five thousand pounds.

Enough for a really cute engagement ring.

I wrote down the Enzo Smith number and the names of the chemicals disposed of, and switched off the computer. Then I wrote a polite note to George, thanking him for the race and dinner and congratulating him on his engagement. After that I said goodbye to Hélène, and left.

I went back to the hotel. The first thing was to find out if there was a direct link between Enzo Smith and Monoco. The direct approach would be best. Failing that, there would be Gottfried Weber. It was hot and humid; a two-shirt day. I put on a clean one, and made a copy of the information I had taken off the screen of George Hayter's computer. Then I walked through the sweltering streets to Rue St Pierre, where Enzo Smith Brokerages had its being.

The office was in a 1960s block, faced with grey granite. The boards on the ground floor must have held a hundred company names, and the lobby was crowded with tight, inward-looking faces. I went up in a grey steel lift with seven other people, got out on the seventh floor, and pushed open the thick mahogany door that said ENZO SMITH – RECEPTION.

If George Hayter's office had been Old Geneva, Enzo Smith's was New Milan. The air conditioning froze the sweat on my skin. The reception desk was made of white marble and black wrought-iron tree branches. A small, greasy-looking man with a black moustache was reading a newspaper in an angular chair. In contrast to the furniture and the man with the moustache, the woman behind the desk looked scrubbed and wholesome.

I said, 'Mr Smith, please.'

She said, 'Have you an appointment?' A slight shadow marred the smooth planes of her shining forehead; the Geneva equivalent of a frown.

I said, 'He will want to see me.'

She opened her mouth, probably to tell me to go away. But at that moment one of the stove-black doors opened, and a man came out; a small man, with very short black hair, a box-jacket suit of buff linen, and four gold rings on the fingers of his right hand, the only one I could see. His eyes skidded over me. And mine skidded over him, into the office he was leaving.

For in the office, gazing out of a floor-to-ceiling window with a view over the rooftops of Geneva and across the ruffled blue surface of the lake, was another man. A big man, with a head that ran down from ears to shoulders without benefit of neck.

'*Monsieur Smith,*' said the receptionist. '*Voici un monsieur qui –*'

I did not hear the rest. Because the big man had turned round. The sun made a yellow halo of his hair, which was cut as short as Smith's. The pink scalp showed through. His eyes locked with mine for a split second, then he was coming through the door at me. It was horribly quick, the instantaneous reflex of a wild animal. I went out of the office door backwards, as fast as I could.

The man who had been looking out of the window was Kurt Mancini.

As I came out, the lift doors were closing. I let them close. To the right, a door said ESCALIER. I ran for it, fast. The stairs were white concrete, plunging down in a big square helix. I was sweating again. Somewhere in my mind, I was yelling *Got it!* But much louder was the voice that said *Get away!*

I went down the stairs at a controlled fall. A door slammed above. I saw a head leaning over. A small, dark head. Enzo Smith. Feet were coming down the stairs, in big bounds. Not Enzo Smith's. I did not have to look round to know whose feet they were.

The number on the next door said three. The steps behind were gaining. My heart was crashing in my ribs as I cannoned off the wall, jumped the next flight in one. Two, said the next door.

He was one flight behind now, a yellow-headed animal I could glimpse out of the corner of an eye as I went down the last flight. The footsteps stopped. In front of me was the door that said one. My shoulder hit the middle of the painted figure at the same time as my fingers found the handle. Something slammed into the door by my ear. Then it was open, and I was falling forwards, stumbling into a lobby filled with people, treading on toes.

I turned. The door swung slowly to. As it closed, I saw the thing that had hit it by my ear. A good way off, now, but I saw it with great clarity, every detail crisp and neat.

It was a knife. It had a handle bound with dark green insulating tape, and a thick, silvery blade ground on both edges. It was stuck two inches into the door. If it had been six inches to the right, it would have hit my neck at the point where the skull stops and the vertebrae begin. It would have cut my head off.

I turned round, walked quickly into the street on legs that were suddenly made of jelly, and hailed a taxi. I told the driver to go out along the lake shore. Then I sat back and kept my head down, and shook for a while.

You stupid bastard, I told myself. You stand in front of the mirror and you tie your tie, and you tell yourself you will stroll into the lion's den and check a few facts, everything nice and legal. And it just does not occur to Harry Frazer, the ace lawyer in the smart shirt, that men like Mr Smith, men who are responsible for the deaths of Jimmy Sullivan and Ewan Buchan, may have their own techniques of making out-of-court settlements, using knives.

The lake unreeled outside the taxi window. It was hazy today. The mountains had a brown, thundery look.

Harry Frazer was not on the case any more. He was in the case. There was not a shadow of doubt in my mind that ten minutes ago, Kurt Mancini had tried to kill me. Which confirmed two hypotheses. One, that Cleanup was selling its disposal contracts to Enzo Smith, who was shipping the waste in Monoco ships, under the supervision of Kurt Mancini, for illegal disposal in Western Scotland. And two, that there was enough money in it for Mancini not to mind permanently silencing anyone who got in the way.

I took off my jacket. It did not stop the sweat. I had received a warning in the storage shed in Scotland. He had tried to finish the job today. And there was no reason to suppose he would not try again.

Chapter Twenty-Four

I went to a café and drank two glasses of brandy, fast. Then I went to a cinema, and sat in a seat in the middle of a full row. I do not know what film I saw. It was late in the afternoon that I went back to the hotel. I mixed myself up with the rush hour and walked the broad pavements, out of crowds but near groups of people, staying within sight of a policeman wherever possible. At the hotel I got a bell-boy to come with me up to the room, and made him wait while I packed. The idea of being alone was so horrible that I could not look it square in the eye. I changed into a dark-blue linen suit, yellow shirt, no tie. Then I checked out, booked myself on to the ten o'clock flight to London, left my bag with the porter, and took a cab down to the lake shore and the Restaurant Palmyre.

The thunder was closer now. The air under the plane trees was sticky with heat and sap loosed by aphids. I sat at the back of the terrace, shoulders against the wall, and sipped nervously at a cup of tea. After ten minutes, the waiter brought over Gottfried Weber.

I had been expecting somebody along the lines of Ewan. But Weber was wearing an off-white cotton suit with a red silk handkerchief in his breast pocket and carrying a discreet black leather briefcase. He had a neat black beard, cynical grey eyes, and a smile he did not use much. He ordered German beer. 'Excellent,' he said, sipping. 'And how is Fiona?'

I told him she was well.

'Good,' he said. 'An amazing woman, from what Ewan used to say.'

I agreed.

'Ah,' he said. 'But I am sure she has not told you about the Welshman's Creek project.'

I said she had not.

'A big project to make a lake, flood the valley of a river in Northern California,' he said. 'Obliterate the river, some birds, you know. To the developers a swamp, to the birds a home. The developers were making maybe fifty million dollars. She got the President to stop them.'

'The President?' I said.

'Of the United States. Her father was a senator, I think. She got the President to go fishing in the river, and talked to him. After that, no problem.' He sipped his beer. 'But of course she did not tell you.'

'No,' I said. I tried to be surprised. I was not.

Weber permitted himself a smile. 'There are many things she does not tell people. There were even more things Ewan did not tell her.' He sighed. 'So Ewan is dead,' he said. 'It is a horrible thing.' He looked up at me. His eyes were extremely shrewd. 'How did it happen?'

I said, 'He got blown up.' I told him the story.

Weber nodded. 'If I was a paranoid person, I would say I was not surprised.'

'Oh?'

'He was writing me letters until, well, three weeks ago. He was asking me whether I thought it would be possible to tip waste in Scotland, and get away with it.'

I said, 'Three weeks.' Three weeks ago I had been in the fog, and Ewan had been closing in on the *Marius B*. He had suspected, even then. 'What did you tell him?'

'I said that any substance financially worthwhile to tip would persist in the environment. Money or not, you would have to be crazy to tip. In ten years' time you could have a place that was completely dead.'

'In ten years, the people who are tipping will be long gone.'

'Sure,' he said. 'It's possible.'

'It's happening,' I said.

The crowds shifted constantly on the boulevard; out on the lake, the tourist steamers glided, the Jet d'eau gleamed, and bright-sailed dinghies jostled. The patterns they made were the aimless loops of people enjoying themselves, doing business, drifting. Somewhere in the tangled skein was a hard, clear line of intention: *Kill Harry Frazer*.

I pulled from my breast pocket the paper on to which I had copied the consignment details on George Hayter's computer. Weber looked at the paper, then at me, eyebrows raised on his high forehead.

I said, 'This is the kind of thing. What is it?'

He laid the paper on the table, tapped the entries with his ballpoint. 'First,' he said. 'Acid tars. Waste product of oil refining. Black, sludgy stuff. Very corrosive. You can drum it but if you get any water near it, it will explode. It's so hard to get rid of that actually it's now kind of old-fashioned. Hmm.' He was looking at the next entry on the list. 'Goodness me.' He sipped his beer delicately.

'What?'

'PCBs. Used to be supplied to the electrical industry, coating for transformer windings, still a lot of them around. Toxic, irritant, carcinogenic. Brings you out in terrible rashes, minimum. And persistent. You need a high-temperature incinerator, with scrubbers for the smoke. Would cost you maybe two thousand pounds a ton to get rid of, with a reputable disposal company.' He ran the pen down the five remaining entries. 'Cyanide. Mercury. Cadmium, heavy metals. Mixed shit, corrosive, irritant.' He smiled, a twisted, unamused smile. 'Run-of-the-mill poison.'

I said, 'How would you get rid of this stuff, cheaply?'

'There is no cheap way. Incinerating is expensive. Reduce it to ash, simpler compounds. Landfill the ash, maybe reclaim the simple stuff.' He tapped the paper. 'This is a consignment?'

'I think so.'

'Who is doing this dumping?'

I said, 'Have you ever come across Enzo Smith?'

He was raising his glass to his lips. At the name he stopped for a second, still as a waxwork. Then he set the glass down on the table. He said, 'Ewan was making research into Enzo Smith's business?'

I said, 'He didn't know it was Enzo Smith's business.'

Weber sighed. 'Jesus,' he said. 'I'm not surprised he is dead.'

My heart was beating unpleasantly fast. I said, 'What do you mean, you're not surprised?'

'Last year, Enzo Smith was going round all the companies telling them he had an incinerator in Guinea-Bissau, offering stupid rates to get rid of very bad stuff. I made enquiries. Of course, the incinerator did not exist. But by that time, a company had given a load to Smith and he had sent it out of Trieste. And two weeks later, the Gulf of Taranto was full of dead dolphins.'

I said, 'So he's killing dolphins. Not people.'

Weber sipped again at his beer, as if to wash the taste out of his mouth. 'Smith said the cargo had diverted to an incinerator in Palermo. Had all the documents, the paperwork, no problem. Which of course is a big clue to his activity.'

'Corruption,' I said. 'Still not murder.'

'All toxic waste movement is the subject of internationally agreed regulations. But in Italy, you want something from a bureaucrat, you hand over the *tangente*, the bribe, and you get it. I guess this is how your Cleanup man got his papers from Piranesi. And if you are a member of some organisation, maybe you do not even pay the *tangente*.'

A cold cannonball of fear had lodged in my stomach. 'What evidence do you have?' I said.

'I have evidence,' he said. 'But you do not speak of your evidence in a café when you are dealing with the Mafia.'

There was a horrible pause.

I said, 'Why should the Mafia be interested in something as cumbersome as chemical waste?'

'Money,' he said.

'What about drugs, prostitution, protection?'

'That is the old Mafia,' he said. 'Besides, there is not so much money in drugs as there used to be, or if there is it is going to a lot of Pakistanis and Iranians and Colombians. So the guys who used to make the heroin factories in Southern Europe are looking for new ways to make some fast money. What a drug seller understands is desperation. So these drug people realise that all over Europe there are companies who are desperate to get rid of this dirt that they possess after they have made their oil, or their transformers, or whatever it is that they make. And of course, most of these companies are greedy; there are new methods that don't make dirt, but the new methods cost big capital money, so they stay with the old ones. But there are big rules about disposing of the dirt, so it is very expensive. So anyone who will do it cheap is going to get a lot of business. To do it cheap, you have not to care too much about what happens to it, or anyone who lives where you dump it. Like drugs again. Enzo Smith has a big connection with people in Italy and New York. They are a powerful group of people.'

He looked at me steadily. I looked back. But I was not seeing him. I was seeing Ewan, and Jimmy. I was seeing the expression on Tom Finn's face, hearing Mancini walloping down the stairs, and the knife hammering into the wood of the door by my ear.

I said, 'Why Scotland?' What I meant was, how would an Italian drug baron find the patch of grey water north of Ardnamurchan, and decide it was the right dump for his filth.

Unless someone showed him the way. Someone who knew the area well.

'You look at a map,' said Weber. 'You find a remote place. You tip it in the sea, drop it in a quarry – '

I said, 'What kind of quarry would you need?'

He raised an eyebrow. It must have been my voice. 'Doesn't matter,' he said. 'Ideally, a deep hole, impervious rock. Granite, maybe. And bury the stuff.'

The Glory Hole. I thought of the hole, like an ant-lion's burrow, the slick of filth winding down the tide from the burn's foot. I said, 'I must make a telephone call.'

He shrugged, said, 'More tea?'

'Beer,' I said.

As I went away between the tables, he was summoning the waiter. The telephone was in a glass booth by the bar. I got through to Kinlochbeag without difficulty. Fiona answered. I said, 'They're dumping it in the quarry.'

'What do you mean?' She sounded tired.

'They're dropping their waste in the Glory Hole.'

'So what do I do?' She was not tired any more.

'Police,' I said. 'Journalists. Environmental Protection Officers. The bloody lot. Tell them anything. Get them there.'

We rang off. This was no time for telling people you loved them.

As I paid for the telephone call, something was happening outside. There was the sound of glass breaking, and a woman screamed.

Night was falling. The restaurant's terrace was a pool of brightness, its tables big white water lilies. The evening was brownish and murky, with a hot wind that flapped the tablecloths and brought in the flat, watery smell of the lake.

I stopped in the door. A knot of people had gathered round the table where Weber was sitting. The crowd eddied, parted. My mouth became suddenly dry as blotting paper.

Weber was not sitting any more. He was lying across the table. His hands were clutching for the edge, and his cheek was pressed into the white tablecloth. His eyes were open, and he was looking straight at me. But he was not seeing me. His face and lips were a terrible blue, and the eyes were glassy.

The waiter was at the table, waving his hands, talking hard. He looked round. His face was white. But his eyes were black, moving fast. They settled on me. He raised a hand, pointed.

I turned, and went back into the restaurant.

My knees were like jelly, and my heart was hammering. Weber was dead.

A woman's voice shouted '*Gift!*' Poison.

There were going to be questions. A lot of questions. Slow, Swiss questions. *So you were the last man with Mr Weber. You left the table to…er, telephone, you say… Relax, Mr Frazer. We have nothing but time…*

But I had no time. Because Fiona knew what I knew, and there was no point in trying to silence me unless they silenced her as well. She was in a lonely house full of the sick and young, in lonely Scotland. They had silenced Weber in a busy café.

I walked to the back of the room and stepped through the kitchen door. There were people in white uniforms, dark eyes under chef's hats. The outside door was by the dustbins. I slid through it, and out into the hot dusk.

Sirens were wailing. I moved between the big, clean garbage cans. Back to the hotel, I thought. There was no way they could identify me –

A man came round the brick corner of the restaurant. He was small, with a moustache, wearing a waiter's white coat; his black hair was slicked back. This afternoon he had been in Enzo Smith's waiting room, reading a newspaper.

There was something in his hand; something that caught the light of the mercury bulb lamp above the kitchen door, and glittered nastily. A knife. A kitchen knife. He was holding it like a butcher, not a waiter.

My skin crawled. Kurt Mancini did not want me to talk to the police, either. I found I was breathing in quick gasps that did not satisfy the lungs. I turned and started to walk quickly away from him.

I went past the dustbins behind the restaurant, fast. There was an alley leading to the road. My feet took me down the alley, past the terrace of the restaurant next door to the Palmyre. There were crowds out there; good, solid crowds of people, taking the air. Nothing could happen under those hundreds of pairs of stolid, law-abiding Swiss eyes.

The man with the moustache had hidden the knife. He had taken off his white coat and thrown it away. He was strolling now, hands in pockets, fifteen yards behind, a man in shirtsleeves minding his own business on a warm evening. He caught my eye as I turned. His small, foxy face was without expression. I stopped. He stopped. I sped up. He sped up. I knew with a sinking in the guts that he could stay there all night, and that sooner or later he would catch up.

Blue lights were flashing in front of the Palmyre. There were more lights ahead; swags of jewels, multi-coloured, and a sign that said PROMENADES EN LAC. A loudspeaker was saying in polite tones, '*Attention messieurs dames, c'est le dernier appel.*' The lights were looped down a gangway. There was a tourist boat at the end, a big, old-fashioned pleasure steamer like the one that had won the race for me and George. Deckhands were on the fore- and afterdecks, letting go mooring lines.

I started to run. Faces turned to me, pale as moons in the dusk. The hot wind buffeted my face and my shoes clattered on the duckboards of the gangplank. A man in uniform loomed up in front, arms spread, shouting that it was too late. I dropped my shoulder and caught him in the stomach, full weight, and he spun against the gangway railings with a crash. Then there was the end of the gangplank, and a gap of water with fairy light reflections, and the boat's side, moving away.

I launched myself across the gap and tumbled over the rails, landing among people's legs, apologising. They drew away. The gap of water grew. Already there was that feeling of safety, the sense of isolation you get from a boat's rail as the land recedes. Under the light of the boat-trip notice I could see the waiter, gazing at the boat, his eyes shadowed till they looked like empty sockets in an Inca mask.

I did not want to look. I made my way through the crowd to the other side, away from the shore. There were fewer people there. It was possible to breathe. It was even possible to think.

Weber was dead. He was dead because he was a well-known journalist and he had been seen talking to me. They were taking no chances, these people. When the boat came back to the landing stage they would be waiting, with faces like stone and shadows in the sockets of their eyes.

The lights of the shore wheeled as the boat turned. The wind blew across the deck like the breath of a boiler room. And I knew I had to go up to the wheelhouse, and ask the captain to radio the police and tell them to be waiting on the landing stage when I got back. Then I would have to give them the whole story. And they would check it out, and that would be the end of that.

If they believed me.

But that was the chance I had to take.

I drew in a deep breath. Most of the passengers had gone inside, to be out of the wind's flat, stagnant smell. I turned to walk towards the bridge.

I half saw an arm, and a hand, and something that was whipping at my head.

I jerked my head away. The thing in the hand sliced into my cheek instead of my neck. There was a big, burning pain that blotted out the night in a red haze. I went down, rolling. Something slammed into my ribs. I twisted, hurling myself away. The pain yelled at me, but I could see. And what I saw was a man, silhouetted against the lights of the city. His neck ran straight down into his shoulders from his ears.

Mancini.

I had my back to the rail. He was coming towards me. Behind and below was another, smaller deck, railed off from the passengers, with the mooring bollards, and a winch. I rolled backwards over the rail and landed with a crash on the steel plating next to the winch. I crawled behind it. My face was aching and burning. Something wet was running down inside my collar. Mancini's silhouette came to the rail. I waited for the whip of the flung knife.

It did not come. Instead, he grasped the rail and vaulted over. He landed in horrible silence, like a huge cat. I kept the winch between us. Heads appeared at the rail above. I shouted, '*Au secours!*' but the heads did not move. They stood there, stolid, watching.

Mancini came over the top of the winch with a sort of crawling spring. I jumped away. My heel caught on a coil of mooring rope, and I fell backwards, slam on the deck, arms out flat.

Something rolled under my hand. Something round and wooden. I grabbed it. Broom handle. Boathook.

Boathook.

I twitched it up the moment he jumped. He came through the air at me, hands out. It caught him just below the left collar bone and went in. The blunt end was wedged against the deck. The sharp end must have been grinding into his top ribs. It stopped him dead. He screamed with pain.

The lights came on.

Suddenly the little deck was flooded in a bluish glare. It shone in the whites of Mancini's eyes and the red splodge where the boathook stuck out of his chest like a cocktail stick out of a sausage.

He was screaming. He tore the butt loose from the deck. He came on, crabwise, good hand first. I circled away.

What I knew was that I had to get to him before he got to me, because he was going to kill me, the way he had killed Weber; there was no doubt about that. So I ran at him, hard, and my shoulder hit him in the middle of the chest. He lurched back. He fell over backwards, still screaming, into the black water where the stern wave swelled along the side, just before the propeller churned it white.

He hit the water with a great splash, and suddenly the note of the propeller changed, labouring *chunk chunk chunk chunk* as if something big and solid was caught down there. In the white lights, the wake of the boat was pink, and things rolled, terrible things, before they sank.

The propeller stopped. On the passenger deck, women started to scream. I stood there, sobbing for breath, pinned like a rabbit by the hard blue lights. My right cheekbone felt as if someone had gone digging with a pickaxe. But that was not the problem.

The problem was that I had killed a man in front of a crowd of perhaps twenty people, and that the man I had killed was the second person it looked as if I had killed in the past hour.

Chapter Twenty-Five

For a moment, everything was very still. Then a voice from the upper deck shouted something in a language I did not understand. But the sound was enough. Suddenly it was not only my mind that made me realise terrible things were happening. My legs shook, and my stomach turned to water. Think, I told myself. Think, Frazer.

The lights of Geneva were a thick crust of brilliance astern, tapering off on the north and south shores of the lake. We had not travelled more than half a mile.

I ran to the rail and jumped overboard.

The splash of my entry was blinding in the floodlights. The water was warm. I kicked down hard into the black, until I was under the thermocline and the water felt cold as ice. Then I swam underwater until I had counted a hundred strokes, and headed upwards.

When my head broke surface the boat was fifty yards away, a wedding cake iced with light. People were shouting. There was a searchlight on the upper works, and somebody was sweeping the water with it, on the wrong side. I got out of my jacket. The wallet was still in my breast pocket. I pulled it out, took a look round, saw what I wanted to see, and went down again.

This time, I did a hundred and fifty strokes before I had to come up, and when I surfaced, I was on target. Three-quarters of a mile across the dusky water to the north was George Hayter's sailing club, its long window a cheerful yellow dash against the crawl and whip of head and tail-lights on the road inland.

I laid myself flat across the black waves, and began to swim. It would not have been a hard swim, under normal circumstances. But there were a lot of boats out now, and several of them had searchlights. The lights whizzed over the water, their beams illuminating big swathes of the haze the wind was sucking out of the lake. Once a boat came straight at me, its light glaring like a cyclops' eye. I breathed all but a teacupful of air out of my lungs and sank into the deep black. The boat's propeller set up an angry ticking in my ears, and its wash buffeted me like a shirt in a washing machine. I kicked my way back up to the surface and gulped air.

After that, the boats stayed out of the way, snarling like angry chainsaws in a confusion of light towards the middle of the lake. Presumably they had found some bits of Mancini. I kept swimming, doggedly, hampered by my shirt and trousers.

I was getting tired. I am a strong swimmer, and fit; the problem was my face. The water had set up a big, dull ache that attached itself to me like a leech.

I gripped the wallet between my teeth, struggled out of my shirt and trousers. The water did not feel so warm any more. It seemed to be dissolving the heat out of my body, and with it the strength. The lighted rectangle of the clubhouse window was closer, but it wavered like a quarantine flag in the wind.

I kept my arms and legs moving in an easy breaststroke, and tried to keep my mind off what was happening back out there in the lake. Instead I thought of what would be happening ashore: aperitifs being drunk in the clubhouse; then some dining, dark, sleek girls, men in clean shirts. The thought became depressing. No place for a sodden fugitive with his face hacked open.

But the clubhouse was a landmark. I needed landmarks. I kept it in my eye, and swam for the window in the gathering night.

Some time later, the dim shapes of moored boats reared against the sky. A jetty loomed out of the darkness. I put my feet down on to mud and stones and walked on rubbery legs out of the water.

A dull roar of conversation and the clatter of cutlery was coming from the clubhouse. It was a beautiful sound; the sound of humans, warm and alive, eating. It did not stay beautiful for long, because I was shivering in the dark, propped up on the side of a Wayfarer dinghy, wearing only a Gucci wallet and a pair of blue-and-white striped boxer shorts, one hour after I had been seen to kill two men in public places in downtown Geneva. I was cold, and weary, and hungry, and very, very lonely.

And I was very, very angry with George Hayter. Good old George, client, friend, and lying bastard, who slapped people on the back and reposed philosophical confidences about clearing up mess, in order to get rid of them while he went on making money out of poisoning children. The anger unstiffened my legs enough to propel me across the dark, slimy beach towards the dark mass of the changing-block.

The door was open. I went in, and across to the lockers. It would not be sensible to turn the light on. Enough light came in at the windows for me to see the combination locks, little calculators welded to the doors.

Date of birth, he had said. Good old George, with his running commentary on his life in case you lost interest. A life made up of computer passwords, and combination numbers, and cheques for engagement rings.

I had filled in a lot of forms about the bastard George Hayter, and I knew his date of birth like I knew my own. Even so, my fingers were so cold that it took me three stabs before I made contact with the right numbers.

The door swung open. I pulled the contents on to the floor. There were battens, a suit of sails, two sets of Musto oilskins, two lifejackets. There was also a pair of Bermuda shorts, a nylon pile jacket with a sailor's knife in the pocket, and a pair of ankle-length rubber boots. I struggled into the jacket, and felt instantly warmer.

Then I pulled on the larger of the two pairs of oilskin trousers, bundled the rest of the stuff back into the locker, shut the door, and locked myself into the lavatory cubicle.

Now that the blood was moving round my body, it was easier to think. The small problems were that I was hungry, and I had nowhere to go. The big problem was that the Swiss police probably had a very good description of me, which meant they had two courses of action. Either they could assume that I had drowned out there in the lake; or they could assume that I had swum ashore. Knowing the Swiss, they would assume both, and not take any chances.

So I had to find a way of getting away from the lake. Short of stealing a car, that would be impossible. And stealing a car was not sensible, because there would be road blocks.

There are borders all the way around Geneva. Even if I got mobile, I was going to have to cross a border. I had some money. My passport was at the hotel. That was not a disaster; being in possession of Harry Frazer's passport might do more harm than good.

I sat down on the floor, and tried to shut out the fear that was beginning to gnaw at the pit of my stomach. Think, I told myself.

But lawyers think on rails. I was off the rails. I felt alone, and panicky. And suddenly I knew what it would be like to be Vi. Before, I had stood on the sidelines and watched people live, and made decisions as to whether or not I would join in. But now life had yanked me aboard, and there were no brakes I could apply. It was a feeling close to vertigo. Vi's solution was drugs. Tossing a pill down her throat gave her the illusion of control.

I leaned my forehead against the cool tiles, and thought of Fiona. There was another way through the vertigo. That was to keep going, and stay alive, and enjoy the ride. I wondered what Fiona was doing. Learning *petit point* from Vi. Two little old ladies, in their lonely house –

There was a rattling at the outside door. Someone was shouting. The vision faded. What now? I thought. What the hell do I do now?

Then I realised that whoever was shouting was asking if there was anyone there. It was the clubhouse porter, locking up for the night.

His key clattered in the lock. I took a deep breath of disinfectant, old soap, chlorine, all the dank bathroom smells of this little block down by the lake. To me, at that moment, they were the smell of freedom.

I washed my cut in the basin by the light coming in from the little windows up near the ceiling. My face was ghostly white in the mirror, the cut about two inches long, well back on the cheekbone in front of the right ear. If I pulled my hair forward it more or less hid it. When I had finished the first-aid, the bleeding was no more than a trickle. I took the wet money out of my wallet and stuck the bank notes flat on the wall tiles to dry. Then I took the sailbag out of George's locker, pulled out the sails, and made myself a bed in the changing area. It was not the Ritz, but it was better than sleeping on the mud. I looked at my watch. Ten o'clock. I put my head on the hard Terylene cloth, and fell immediately into a deep, exhausted sleep.

It did not last. I woke suddenly, bug-eyed, staring into the dark. My watch said two-thirty, and my stomach was complaining that I had not eaten anything but a cup of tea for eight hours.

There were noises outside: the yelp of dogs, the jabber of radios, and blue lights sweeping through the frosted-glass windows and across the textured ceiling.

Suddenly my hunger was gone, my mouth dry. The voices were outside the door. Shirt, I thought. They've found my shirt. They've got dogs. But I was in the water. Can a dog smell you when you've been swimming for three-quarters of an hour?

Something was whining at the door, scrabbling. I heard the latch rattle. That's it, I thought. Inside you go, and God knows when you'll be out.

A voice said, *'Fermé a clé.'* Locked. It sounded bad-tempered and weary, the voice. *'T'es con, Eiger.'* He did not believe his dog. My heart bounded with hope. *'Bien, on va le piger sur la route.'* We'll get him on the road.

There was a sound of a choke-chain being yanked, footsteps receding. I thought: Frazer, you are a lucky, lucky bastard. Luck is a relative thing, when you are locked in a lavatory with a hole in your face.

I lay and stared at the ceiling. It was not only the police who wanted to see me. From what Weber had told me, Enzo Smith did not seem to be the kind of man who would forgive and forget.

The blue lights kept flashing on the ceiling. I got up, climbed on to a urinal, carefully opened one of the slit windows, and peered out. There was a distant view of the big road that runs along the lake shore. The flashing lights were a road block. Geneva itself would be swarming with policemen, alert for men with carved-up faces. Similarly, the inhabitants of the hinterland were not going to take in their stride a man wearing yellow oilskin trousers, a blue fleecy jacket, and a two-inch gash on his right cheekbone.

I turned to get down. The sails were spread out on the floor in a big, crumpled triangle, pale in the darkness of the changing room. I stopped for a moment. Then I climbed very carefully down.

There was a way out. It was a route for which no passport would be needed. All it required was a bit of a breeze.

I lay down on the sails, and fell into a fitful sleep. Some time later I woke, worrying about Davina Leyland's divorce. Must ring Cyril, I thought. Then I remembered that there were more serious things to occupy my attention. It was five o'clock by my Rolex. I got up, breakfasted on water from the tap, and bundled the sails, a lifejacket, and the battens back into a bag. I pulled the Bermudas on under the oilskin trousers. The fleecy jacket had a hood. I tugged it forward so it would hide my cheek. Then I undid the latch of one of the frosted-glass windows on the lake side of the changing-room, and gently, very gently, pushed it open.

Ten feet away, aluminium dinghy masts rose from a mat of fog. Beyond them, the lake was hidden under a pearly floor of vapour; beyond the lake, the buildings of the city rose white and clean in the early sun. There was no sound but the lap of oily wavelets on the mud beach, and the thin squawk of radios from the police road blocks on the blind side of the building. There was not a breath of wind.

I needed wind.

I peeled the money off the tiles and stowed it in my wallet. Then I pushed the sailbag through the window, squeezed after it, legs first, and pushed the window to. Picking up the sailbag, I scuttled down into the dinghy park. The fog lapped up and covered me over. I held my breath, waiting for the shouts of the pursuers.

There were no shouts. Slowly, keeping my head below the surface of the fog, I made my way down to George Hayter's boat.

On a hot night, there are worse places to sleep than a tiled floor. But the fog was cold, and clammy, and though it was daylight I could not see what was happening. Also, while Geneva tap water is doubtless clean and alpine, it makes a very light breakfast.

So I sat in the mud by the boat and shivered, and waited, and tried not to think about coffee. There was a rattle of keys as the janitor unlocked the shower block. Cubicle doors slammed as he did his cleaning. He did not seem to notice anything amiss. Half an hour later, at seven o'clock, a car pulled into the car park. Several more followed. Voices sounded: young, well-off voices, full of breakfast.

I swallowed hard, pulled up the hood of my nylon jacket, and started to unlatch the cover from the dinghy.

As I took the last loop of shock-cord off the last hook, there was a hissing of shrouds and a rattle of halyards. The wind had arrived.

It pulled the fog from between the boats and swept it off the beach and across the water, leaving it in a big grey pile between the two shores to the northeast. The sky was clear and blue, reflecting in the mirror-like calm. The halyards rattled again. Heavy matt stains began to spread on the surface of the lake.

'*Va faire ∂u vent,*' said a man in a one-piece suit to the woman helping him put together a 505.

Wind. Wind was what was required.

I got the sails on quickly. I was assuming that George started work early enough on weekday mornings not to come down for a spin in the boat, but I did not want any jolly clubmates asking me who, and what, and why. I shoved the launching trolley down the hard, hoisted jib and mainsail. Then I took the trolley back to the park, walking nice and slow. There was a policeman watching idly from the road block, a queue of early cars held up at the document check. It was going to be a bad day for taking a spin to France.

A bad day by road, anyway.

I climbed into the 470 and pushed off. The wind cracked into the sails. The wake gurgled. The shore shrank. Nobody shouted.

Now came the hard part.

There were already three or four boats out there. I reached to and fro, getting the feel. The wind was freshening from the northeast, cool, with the smell of big mountains in the night. Gingerly, I clipped on to the trapeze, planted my feet on the non-slip on the gunwale, eased myself out over the water. The boat came flat, got up, started to plane. If I had had some breakfast, it would have been exhilarating. As it was, it was just practice.

There were a good dozen boats out now, all shapes and sizes. Racing, I thought. Very keen. The line was up. Someone in the clubhouse fired a gun. All the boats started to move. I followed them, so as not to stand out. We went down on the line quickly, full of the spirit of seven o'clock on a working morning; twelve hard chargers from the Club Nautique du Léman, and one double murderer with a stolen boat and a knife-slash down the cheekbone.

There was a lot of ill-tempered barging on the line. I held off; there were other things on my mind than club racing. I crept up to the right-hand end of the line behind the main bunch, and eased over a full twenty seconds after the gun. But the 470 is a quick boat, and the breeze was still only force three, and there was only one of me, so weight was not a problem. Without spilling wind and drawing attention to myself, there was very little I could do to stop myself moving up the fleet.

So halfway up the first leg, I found myself on port to windward of another 470. The helmsman turned, saw me. He shouted, 'Where's George?'

My heart turned over. I said, 'Working!' My voice felt rusty from long disuse. 'Trying to pay off the engagement ring!'

The helmsman laughed. I recognised him as Anton, the man we had scraped off on the tourist boat's bow in the race last week. Fritz was crewing, grinning. He had enjoyed the crack about the ring. Three weeks ago, they would have been nice guys from my world, good for a laugh and a drink. Now they seemed alien and shallow, brittle shells full of false bonhomie and bad jokes.

I smiled, as best I could with the hole in my face. Inside, I was weak with hunger, and raging. The last thing I needed was a serious race with these people. 'See you,' I said. The mark was up to port. So I shoved the tiller away and ducked under the boom, moving on to the starboard tack, heading out for the left-hand side. There was clear water ahead, now, with grey piles of fog.

But astern there was the clank of the boom going over. My heart sank, and I turned my head. Fritz and Anton wanted to play.

Anton cranked the sheet in. Fritz went out on the trapeze. A puff came over the water at the right moment for them. They accelerated up under my stern. I had no time to get myself on to the trapeze, so all I could do was heel, spilling wind as they came through and under and went into the lead. Anton grinned, a triumphant sportsman's grin. He yelled, 'Mast abeam!'

I knew what came next.

It came.

His shoulder dropped as he pushed the tiller away. His sail came across my bows as he luffed. I luffed too, turned it into a tack, so I was heading away from him. He tacked too.

Blast you, I thought. Has nobody ever told you that playing silly buggers with one boat in the fleet means that the rest of the fleet sails past you?

Obviously nobody had. They came through on the next puff, with big grins all over their faces.

I tacked again. We were well out on the lake now, and the fogbanks were smooth-sided grey hills on the water.

They tacked too.

Out here in the middle, the wind was less strong than close inshore. This time, it took them longer to catch up. But they caught up. Giving the foreigner a hard time; getting their revenge, and having a bit of fun.

But the foreigner was not up for a bit of fun. The foreigner was getting desperate.

I heard the chuckle of their wake as they came through to leeward, established their overlap. Anton pushed the tiller away.

According to the rules of racing, I had to follow suit and luff too, to avoid a collision. But Frazer was out in the jungle now, where sticking to the rules got you eaten. As their side turned across my bows, I kept right on going.

Fritz's face turned. He was on his way out on the trapeze, knees bent. My forestay caught him and flicked him sideways. Suddenly he was dangling like a spider on a thread, in mid-air. There was a crunch of fibreglass as my bow hit their side. Fritz yelled something that did not have any words, and tumbled into the sail. Then they were over, flat on their side in the water. And I was clear.

I eased the tiller towards me, unclipped the extension, sat out. The bow lifted to a gust. I aimed it for the grey wall of fog, two hundred yards away. Tendrils of the stuff reached out at me. Suddenly there was no wind. But the boat's momentum carried me forward.

The shore and the sky vanished, and the fog bank swallowed me in.

Chapter Twenty-Six

The fog was clammy and still. There were tiny breaths of wind, boxing the compass. The 470 crept along, sail slatting, making scarcely visible seams in the water at rudder and transom. The sounds of the road and the shouts of the racers had vanished. It was like being in a boxful of wet cotton wool.

The collision did not seem to have done any damage. There was a little steering compass sunk in the thwart. I kept it on 50°, a little east of northeast. Down to starboard, the lake shore was trending away northeastward, towards Hermance, maybe ten kilometres down in the fog. And at Hermance, the lake changed. On the map in the hotel room there had been a yellow line, edged with dots and crosses. At Hermance the lake became French, and I was over the border, and into the European Community, where passports were fading into history.

But in this wind, ten kilometres could take all day.

It was cold in the fog. I was shivering. The hunger was like a crab taking handfuls of my belly, and the wound in my face was throbbing angrily.

Lack of food makes you gloomy. I could see myself out here, drifting, till the Swiss sent out whatever they use for a lifeboat on the Lake of Geneva. And they would have their double murderer, dropped into their hands like a ripe plum.

A rather shrivelled plum.

It was not a great joke, but I grinned at it. Grinning makes you feel better; releases endorphins into the blood. Aloud, I said to the wind, 'Come on, you bastard.'

That could have been a mistake.

The fog stayed where it was. There was a small breeze, now, from the north. I managed to make some ground to the northeast. After half an hour, the fog began to thin. Something had happened to the air. It felt hot, now, hot as the breath of a kettle.

All of a sudden, the horizon ran away. One moment I was sitting on the centreboard case, heading northeast in a breeze force two or three, at the centre of a circle of grey. The next, the wind was up to force four to five, and the lake was a ruffled blue sheet, spreading away to shores whose trees and houses were as crisp as if they had been painted by Canaletto.

But it was not the same view as before.

For a moment, I could not work out why not. Then I realised that the mountains at the far side of the lake had disappeared. In their place was an indistinct, yellowish haze. In the haze, thunder muttered.

Astern, the race boats were white nail-clippings of sail, on the final leg. Soon they would be in the shower block, talking. Talking about me, more than likely. What was he doing, all the way out there? Better send the rescue boat, see if he's all right.

I turned back to look the way I was going.

The shore had changed again. The Canaletto trees and houses had vanished. In their place was a wall of vapour, yellowish-brown. The thunder sounded very close.

The wind dropped. The blood roared in my ears. I scrambled forward, took the jib off, rammed it under the half-deck. Then I pulled the boom off the mast and rolled the mainsail down until it was as fat as a wrestler's thigh and the sail was the size of a cheese sandwich. As I was making fast the halyard, a drop of rain fell on the foredeck with a sound like a tomato falling on an oil drum.

A pall of darkness drew across the sky. The rain came.

It came straight down, that rain, with a bang of thunder like the crack of doom. It knocked the wind flat as a pancake. The boat rolled, aimless.

Then there was wind.

It came so fast that there was hardly time to let go of the mainsheet. The sail roared like a kettledrum, and the hull stood on the lee rail. I clung to the weather rail, pushing the tiller away to bring the nose head to wind, into the short, nasty sea that had come up from nowhere.

My breathing was coming fast and hard. The water was black and very deep, and the shore was a long way away. The thunder was continuous, like a herd of giant horses galloping round and round the head. Somewhere there must have been lightning, because the rain and water were lit with a brilliant blue flicker. I could see a tin can bobbing on a wave. I thought: Tin can, you are going to get struck. And then hooked up at the mast, reeling against the overcast, and I thought, Harry Frazer, you are going to get struck, too. But the hammers of the thunder were so big, and the cold was so bad, and the gnaw of hunger was so sharp, that the brain did not register anything but numbness.

So I put the compass needle back on 50° and plugged on up the lake, hanging over the weather side against the heel. The waves were very short and very square. If I took them straight on the bow, the bow dug in, and shovelled water into the bottom of the boat. If I ran off, to take them on the corkscrew and get up enough speed to work the self-bailers, it would not make the course. So I compromised. I went bang into the waves for as long as it took to get the boat so full that it began to wallow. Then I kicked open the bailers and bore away until enough water had drained out. We made progress. Not necessarily progress in the right direction, but progress nonetheless.

My mind went walking. I was not Harry Frazer the fugitive, crouched in the deluge. I could see myself as if from a great height: an insect on a leaf, floating imperceptibly across the black lake; the lake connected to Geneva, and Geneva connected to Enzo Smith;

and Enzo Smith connected to the repainted drums from the hold of the *Marius B*; and the *Marius B* coming into Rotterdam to load, and slather more filth up the coast of Scotland. And Harry Frazer, the insect, who had to stop his insect crawl, and start moving; travel the thousand miles to Rotterdam to catch the *Marius B* red-handed, loading filth for Mr Lundgren's quarry, and roll up the whole picture like a carpet.

The boat's nose rose on a wave, lurched into a trough, stopped dead. Water poured over the bow. I eased the tiller towards me, ran off again, clipped down the self-bailers, cleared the water from the boat. I did it ten, a hundred times. I tried to think, but staying afloat was a full-time job. Thinking was out.

The thunder stopped. The clouds were getting higher. There was fog that was not fog any more, but a kind of steam the hot wind was sucking out of the lake's surface. The wind itself was moderating; force five, perhaps, sinking to four in lulls.

I needed to get a start. Get a long way up the lake. A long, long way up the lake. The map had shown the odd village dotted up the southern shore. There was no sizeable town till Thonon-les-Bains. In a sizeable town, they might not ask too many questions of a man with a hole in his face who came out of the lake in Paisley Bermudas. In a village, it would give rise to comment and discussion.

But Thonon was twenty miles up the lake, and twenty miles is a long sail in a 470. Too far.

Come on, I told myself. Brace up. Get organised. You've done five miles of the twenty already. The voice was partly my own voice, but it held echoes of Fiona's. The thought of Fiona had a tonic effect, though not as tonic as a steak and chips would have been. I turned the boat head to wind, clipped the jib to the forestay and took most of the rolls out of the mainsail. My fingers were working badly, but I swore at them until they did as they were told. Then I settled back to the tiller.

Now she began to sail. She began to sail so well that the nagging voices in my head stopped nagging, and I was not tired any more, and nobody had got chopped up in a pleasure steamer propeller. There was just the wham and rattle and hiss of a shark-bodied dinghy slicing waves, and the glitter of light in flying water.

The sun came through. The wind settled steady, force four, shoving the fat piles of cloud down towards Geneva. I had passed into French waters in the wind and the rain. Now the French shore spread away to the northeast, a low headland of woods and fields, and beyond, across a blue bay, a jumble of white buildings that had to be Thonon.

I took a tack inshore; no need to excite curiosity by appearing out of the middle of the lake. There was more wind there. The houses of Thonon grew out of the shore like mushrooms. Twelve o'clock, my watch said. Nearly lunchtime. The thought of lunch was agonising: big complacent French people, tucking themselves under white tablecloths. The feel of the bread under the hand –

Shut up. You'll be there any minute.

I should have kept quiet. The 470 leaped off a wave, landed wrong on the next, tripped on her lee rail. Suddenly I was in mid-air, flying into the middle of the mainsail. There was a bang as I hit it. Then I was inhaling fresh water, and the boat was over, capsized.

I came up, swam round to the centreboard. Without the exhilaration of forward movement, I was nearly too tired to swim. I was certainly too tired to lower the mainsail, stand on the centreboard, get the boat upright, and bail it out all over again.

Five hundred yards away, the first houses of Thonon sat neat, white and bourgeois as their owners in their immaculate gardens.

I made my decision.

I kicked off the oilskin trousers. Then I started on the boat. First, I pulled the bungs out of the buoyancy compartments. Then I stabbed their fore ends with the spike of George's sailing knife. The composite was thin foam sandwich, and they went through easily. After that, I enlarged the spike holes with the blade. There was a satisfactory rush of bubbles. Now there was a hole at either end of the buoyancy chambers; I did not want the boat coming ashore tonight, serial numbers and all, buoyed up by trapped air.

The hull rolled, and sank away into the dark water. I was violating the rules of a well-ordered life. *Never abandon your boat. Never kill anyone in Geneva.* I was alone, a dark speck under the shuttered windows of the houses. Forcing my reluctant legs into motion, I kicked for the shore.

I swam round a point, towards the town. There were umbrellas on a brown beach. A fat old lady in a rubber hat averted eyes that reminded me of Cyril's. My feet touched bottom.

It took me a full three minutes to get the mastery of my knees. I scraped the hair over my scar, and wobbled up the beach. At the stall selling windmills and ice creams, I bought a tote bag. Slinging the bag over my shoulder, I strolled drunkenly through the quiet suburbs and into the town. I saw my reflection in the window of a chemist: heavy black stubble, matted hair, skin the colour of old oak. I did not look like Davina Leyland's solicitor. I looked like a minor saint in Paisley Bermuda shorts. The slash along my cheekbone was more pink than red, washed by gallons of water. I shrugged into the hooded coat, went into the first chemist's shop I saw and bought some sticking plaster. This might be France, but Geneva was just down the road, and people would have heard about the bodies, and the man with blood on his face.

I patched up my face in an alley, walked on, bought a pair of jeans from a shop. Then I slid into a telephone booth and pulled open the directory.

My eyelids were collapsing over my eyes and my stomach felt like a burst paper bag. I talked to the Hotel Adelphi, the Choisy and the Desmarais. Full, full, full. As I dialled the Fouché, I heard the scream of sirens, and a Citroën police van come round the corner of the road on two wheels.

It passed. It took my confidence with it. I was in a perspex box in a strange country, where the police would soon if they did not already want me dead or alive, and the friends of Kurt Mancini wanted me dead. Harry Frazer, Bristol's Mr Fixit, had become about as real as a soap bubble.

The vertigo got me. I began to shake. I shook like an alcoholic in a drunk tank.

The Fouché had a room. I quavered along there, in my sticking plaster and my jeans. They showed me a room with a bed and a telephone. They brought me a steak, and some chips, and some salad, and a bottle of red wine. Things began to look better. I could think about Fiona, for one thing. The sun was shining outside; I was alive. Then I sat and stared at the raised pattern on the wallpaper. Brown peonies, there were, and eau-de-nil grass. I was a long way from my friends.

And then I suppose I must have gone to sleep.

Next thing I knew it was dark, and I was lying sideways on the bed with the taste of old socks in my mouth and a non-specific sense of impending doom.

It became specific quickly enough. My watch said ten o'clock. I had slept for eight hours. I walked out into the hot, dark streets, and found a bar, where I drank coffee, and tried to work out what to do next.

I was in France with two hundred pounds in Swiss francs, no passport, a coat, a pair of jeans and a pair of rubber ankle boots. The odds were that the police would have my photograph by now. They might possibly be under the impression that I had drowned in the lake, but there was no sense in relying on it.

I got another cup of coffee and thought about the *Marius B*, and tried not to think about Fiona.

The *Marius B* had left Rotterdam last Friday. An eight-day round trip meant she would sail on Saturday. Today was Wednesday. I had two clear days to get to Rotterdam, without a passport.

I went out into the thick, humid night, turned back towards the hotel, and began walking.

Then I stopped.

Four or five shadowy figures were standing on the pavement by the hotel door. Behind them was a van, with its engine running. It was a square, boxy van, with something on the roof. A police light. One of the figures moved against the lighted plate-glass door of the hotel. He was wearing a square topped blue peaked cap.

There was still enough left of Harry Frazer, solicitor, to make it hard to believe that this was happening to me.

But it was.

My heart was beating so loudly I could not understand why they did not hear it. I turned left down a dark street, Staggering a little; a man who had spent some time in the café.

It went on, that street. There were no streetlights and no turnings. I walked quickly and quietly in the rubber boots. At the end, the houses stopped. There was an alley off to the right, running along the backs of a row of houses. I went down it, quickly now, my heart hammering, because I knew that when they found nothing in my hotel room but a beach bag and a still-warm bed they were going to start looking in the town.

I was travelling past a row of garage doors. As I went, I tried the handles. Must hide, I thought. They can't search the whole town. Sweat was pouring off me; I was close to panic.

One of the garage latches gave. It sounded loud as a pistol shot.

I stood still for a moment, listening. No sound but the distant wail of a tomcat. Then I went inside, pulling the door after me.

There were no windows. It smelled of old oil. I felt around, carefully. My hands found smooth metal; a car. Opening the driver's door, I turned on the sidelights.

In the dim yellow glow there appeared a workbench covered in a quantity of metal junk, and a pile of lit magazines, and an old, greasy beret. I pulled the beret on. It fitted. In one corner was a motorbike, covered in dust, missing its engine.

In the other was a bicycle.

It was a middle-aged bicycle, but the chain was oiled, the tyres pumped up. It looked as if somebody used it for going to work.

There was no lock, and no lights; it would not be wanted before morning.

Not by the owner, anyway.

I switched off the car's sidelights. Cars made too much noise. I needed to travel quietly, and be able to hear. I pulled the door open, pushed the bicycle into the alley, and very quietly eased the latch shut behind me.

Out in the alley, everything was quiet. I climbed on to the bike and pedalled back the way I had come.

The night was dark, but not too dark to see. I took the first turning on the right. Houses passed on either side, big lumps of town-centre building. A couple of people shuffled along in the lights of shop windows.

At a fork in the road, the sign on the right fork said GENEVE. It was a big road, with white stripes down each side. I did not want to go to Geneva, particularly not on a big road that stank of road blocks. So I forked left, down a road that said ANNEMASSE. The road was smaller, and I had never heard of Annemasse. But it was away from the police, and that was the main thing.

Almost immediately, the road dived under a railway line that ran away southwest towards Geneva. I began to pedal, hard. Gaps appeared between the houses. There were a few lights on, mostly bedrooms. The intimate yellow gleam was encouraging. It made me feel that it was late enough for the world to have its eyes closed. A couple of cars whizzed past, their headlamps fading into the hills that rose ahead. I began to feel an odd elation, as if the night was my private possession. I had not shaved for two days. My beard grows fast and dark, and the beret made me just another local pedalling back into the hills from an evening in the café.

Another car was coming up behind. The road ahead lit up in the beams of powerful headlights. I began to swerve a little, for local colour, like a man who had drunk maybe a couple of glasses too many in the café. Then there was a huge blue flash, and the scream of a siren. Oh, my God, I thought. Police.

I sank my head into my shoulders and pedalled on, waiting for the slowing engine note that would mean the end.

Tyres squealed. The headlights cut the sky, and the front wheel of the bicycle swerved and jolted across the verge and into a ditch. I went over the handlebars. My shoulder smacked a bank. I scrambled up, tugged at the bike, knees shaking, nailed in the lights.

A window opened. A voice yelled, '*T'es saoul, con!*'

Hope dawned, brighter than the lights. I put out my hand, a hand dirty from the oily muck in the garage, and rocked it from side to side; the universal gesture, maybe, maybe not.

'*Attention tes phares!*'

The window slammed. Tyres screeched again. No time to prosecute peasants without lights; better things to do. The van rocketed off between the hedges, slapping blue blades of light across the sides of the hill. I stood and breathed deeply, waiting for my heart to get back into my ribcage. Then I slung my leg back over the saddle, and pedalled on.

The road began to run uphill. The saddle was low, but my legs were good, so that was not a disaster. What was a disaster was the knowledge that sooner or later I was going to hit a road block, and someone was going to ask me for my papers.

I turned off the main road, on to the lanes that threaded the steep hillsides to my left. I navigated by the big red glow of Geneva in the sky ahead and to the right. Most of the night, I struggled across cart tracks in the black. Flies bit me, and there was a lot of mud left over from the rain. I slept a couple of hours in a barn, which made me feel worse. At dawn, I was freewheeling down a winding road signposted to Ampéguy. I found a café, drank coffee and ate bread and butter. I went and leaned on the marble counter, to pay. Because Harry Frazer was a known non-smoker, I bought a packet of Gauloises *papier maïs*, for camouflage.

The face in the mirror behind the bar was an ill-tempered mask of stubble with a dirty-yellow cigarette sticking out of it. I was on my way to work in some bad garage, or in the back quarters of a shop. Maybe I had killed somebody; but it would have been in a bar in Marseilles or Dakar, not an expense-account paradise in Geneva.

There was a pretty girl in the bar, blonde, with blue eyes and a carefully made-up mouth. She glanced at me. I caught her eye, and she looked away quickly. I thought of Fiona's steady grey–green gaze. She would have seen straight through the stubble and the Gauloise. Luckily, there were not many around like her.

The girl turned her back on me, crossing her slim legs. I grinned at the bandit in the bar mirror, a grin of complicity. Then I picked up a copy of *La Suisse* from the pile by the Gaggia, shoved some francs over the counter, and climbed back on the bicycle.

It was on the front page. They had used my passport photograph. It looked nothing like the face behind the bar. DEUX MORTS A GENEVE, it said. It was suspected that I was in Switzerland or France, or maybe (said a creative police source) Italy. Gottfried Weber had died of cyanide poisoning. The other dead man, Kurt Mancini, had a criminal record that featured extortion and grievous bodily harm. There was very little new in it except the cyanide. Or maybe the police were letting very little new be known about it.

I pedalled slowly down the road to Annemasse. When I got there it was nine o'clock, and the station was jammed with people going to work in Geneva. I bought a ticket for Bellegarde. Then I elbowed my way through to the other window, and bought another for Bonneville, with one for the bicycle. I lit a cigarette at the *guichet* and blew smoke through the glass at the girl inside. She scowled. She would remember me.

I took the bicycle to the *consigne* and checked it through. I told the man in the office it was raining. He looked at me as if I were crazy, his eyes screwed up against the brilliant sunshine streaming in at the window. He would remember me, too. Then I strolled out on to the platform and hid behind the newspaper. Ten minutes later, the Bellegarde train came in. I climbed aboard and locked myself in the lavatory.

In Bellegarde I stepped out and bought myself a blue canvas workman's suit and a pair of running shoes, changed, and ate lunch. Then I rang Fiona.

The telephone rang for a long time. Finally, she answered. She said, 'Where are you?'

'Somewhere,' I said.

'The quarry,' she said.

'What about it?'

'We went up there. We looked. There's nothing there.'

I felt as if I was standing in a lift, and the lift had suddenly gone into free fall. 'What do you mean, nothing?'

'Rocks. Stones. Dust. Water. No chemicals.'

I said, stupidly, 'Then they must be putting it somewhere else.'

'Yes.' Her voice was small and desperate. I had never heard it so small. The sound of it made me realise exactly how bad things were. 'What do we do?'

It was a good question. An excellent question. I said, 'Relax. I'm on my way.' Then I lit a yellow Gauloise and blew smoke at the glass of the box and stared inside my head at a world which had fallen apart.

I was not a lawyer any more. I was not even someone under suspicion of murder, who had a way of explaining everything. I was a man in a blue canvas suit in the middle of nowhere, with less than two hundred pounds, no passport, two dead bodies, and no excuses at all.

Chapter Twenty-Seven

The TGV hissed into the station like a metal snake. I got a window seat and stared at France unrolling green and empty beyond the glass, and knew what a fox feels like when the hounds chase it back to its earth, and it finds that a big, brave human has rolled a stone over the hole.

But the workman's suit was working, and my face was not the kind of face that most people like looking at. The nicely dressed passengers did their best not to sit anywhere near me. In Paris I changed some of my remaining money into French francs and the rest into guilders, filled a bag with food from an *alimentation*, and took the Metro to the Gare du Nord.

I tried to eat lunch in the station buffet, without success; there were two frontiers to cross, and EC or no EC, the police and customs would be checking. Then I caught a train for Aulnoye-Aymeries, just south of the Belgian border.

The train rattled across the low, rolling hills of Picardy. I dozed fitfully, my stomach jumpy with nerves, dreaming I was feeding money into a payphone and dialling the office, but running out of coins as soon as Cyril came on the line. I awoke. There was no rush, I told myself. The ship was not sailing till tomorrow. Plenty of time to find her, check her cargo, and arrange a reception in Scotland.

As the train roared into Aulnoye, the man opposite me pulled out his passport. Further down the carriage, the other passengers started reaching for theirs. I got up, walked quickly between the seats and off the train. I bought a large-scale map in the *tabac* by the station. There was a bicycle shop in a side street. The owner sold me an ancient black trade-in for four hundred francs. I climbed aboard and rode out of town, up the road towards Bavay. The houses fell away. Rain was filtering out of a low sky; the country was flat, with fields of cabbages. The other side of Bavay there was a lane, straight and flat and empty. I looked for the striped barriers of a frontier post. There was none. Only the map and a change in the lane's surface told me I had entered Belgium.

It was about twelve miles to Mons. By the time I got to the station, the drizzle had become a cold, northern rain, and I was soaked. I bought a ticket for my bicycle and ate a sandwich until the next train came in.

The tannoy blared in Flemish. I did not hear the French, because I was too busy heaving my bicycle into the guard's van. I climbed in, found a seat. Other passengers followed. As usual, I noticed that nobody seemed to want to sit next to me. So I lit a cigarette to discourage them still further, and studied the leaflet with the rail map I had picked up in the station.

The train went all the way to Rotterdam, about a hundred and twenty miles. I was planning to get off at Antwerp, cycle to Roosendaal on the other side of the Dutch border, and catch the next train through. Meanwhile, I had a good hour and a half before I needed to do anything.

The country was grey and monotonous beyond the rain-splattered window. It was hot in the carriage. My clothes began to steam. My head nodded. Stop it, I told myself. Stay awake. I started to recite precedents in matrimonial law. But the precedents got mixed up with the waypoints west of Ardnamurchan, which were at the same time the locations of road blocks between Geneva and Bergen-op-Zoom. I fell into a jolting sleep. I woke slowly, the way you wake when you have been ten miles down. Straight away, I knew that there was something badly wrong.

A grey platform was sliding past the window. We were drawing out of a station. My watch said five thirty-five. A notice on the end of the platform said ANTWERPEN.

Suddenly I was fully awake. At the far end of the carriage, a man in dark blue uniform was walking between the seats. I saw him ask someone a question, open a passport, check their face against the photograph, hand it back, walk on. *What now?* I asked my sleep-clogged brain.

No ideas came.

I watched the man in uniform. He was only asking for about one passport in five. I lit a cigarette, put my lunch bag on my lap, and slumped back in the corner, beret pulled over my eyes. I was not in France any more. I was in the scrubbed pink North. I stood out like a lighthouse.

There was a short woman on the other side of the train. She was wearing a flowered dress, and her skin was pink, as if she scrubbed it with pan-scourers. Her button nose sniffed once, twice. Then she leaned over and stabbed a fat finger at me, and said something I did not understand. *'Quoi?'* I said.

She said it again. I blew more smoke in her face. She screwed up her nose. The immigration man was three seats down, now. She pointed at the ROKEN VERBODEN sign above the window.

'Ah!' I said. *'Pardon. Je m'excuse!'*

She sat back, folded her arms on her huge bosom, and stuck her chin in the air. I got up, slung my bag over my back, stuck my Gauloise into my mouth, and walked back down the train.

The immigration man was inspecting the passport of an Arab-looking man. I pushed by, said *'Pardon.'* He did not even look round. I went out of the carriage and stood in the gap between, leaning against the wall, dizzy with a mixture of nicotine and relief.

The immigration man did not come back. An hour later, we pulled into Rotterdam. I picked up my bicycle, wheeled it over to the tobacco stall, and bought a pouch of Drum tobacco and some rolling papers. I was becoming a firm believer in the power of the cigarette. Then I went to the telephones, called the Docks office, and asked for the *Marius B*.

The man gave me a booth number. 'If you've got anything for her, you'd better hurry. She sails in two hours.'

'Two hours?' I said. But he had rung off.

Two hours meant eight-thirty. I had expected to have until the next morning. I wheeled my bicycle out of the station, and managed to persuade a stout taxi driver to put it in the back of his Mercedes. He took me under the Maas tunnel. I told him to drop me off half a mile short of the dock, and got him to give me precise directions.

The rain had given way to a steady drizzle. Lorries swished past, trailing plumes of diesel-flavoured spray. It was time for the shift change; there were drifts of cyclists, lunchboxes on carriers, heading to and from the apartment buildings that stood like a ring of gravestones round the flat, dirt-coloured horizon.

I pedalled slowly between puddles rainbowed with spilt oil towards the city of sheds and upperworks to the westward.

Down here, the quays ran in parallel lines to a murky vanishing-point in the drizzle. The ships alongside were small, some of them no bigger than barges.

On the stern of the ship in berth nine was painted MARIUS B PANAMA. Her hatches were open. A crane was lowering a container into her forehatch. Another lorry with a container on its back end was waiting its turn.

I pedalled on through the rusty chain link gate, past the long shed that ran along the quay, and parked the bike under the overhang of the roof. Then I pulled out the Drum, rolled myself a cigarette and lit it, watching the crane through the smoke.

I was here, and the *Marius B* was here, and the cargo was going aboard.

Methodically, I locked up the bicycle, took off the lamps and stowed them in my bag. The ship would be sailing in an hour and a half. In this desert of rain and stone and rust, it could take at least half an hour to find a telephone. And God knew how long it would take to organise the reception committee.

Besides, I was a double murderer, and there was no way back to England that did not involve long explanations.

Except one.

I watched the next container go down into the hold. The crane came up; the second lorry moved forward. The crane locked on. The driver jumped down to uncouple the container from the chassis, and the crane bore it up and across, and down into the hold.

But I was not watching the container any more. I was looking at the driver of the lorry. The driver of the lorry was the man I had seen in Geneva, in Enzo Smith's waiting-room, and again, knife in hand, by the dustbins of the Palmyre.

The driver walked round and stuck his hand in the air, two fingers up. A figure in a trilby hat standing on the starboard wing of the bridge raised a curt hand in acknowledgement. The driver nodded and walked across to the shed, and pulled open a blue door that said MANNEN.

I swallowed, hard, in an unsuccessful attempt to fill the hollow that had opened below my breastbone. Then I threw away my cigarette, and walked across to the lorry, and climbed in at the driver's door. Someone was shouting on the ship. I glanced up, quickly. The container was in mid-air. The shouting was because it had clipped the hatch as it swung, not because of me.

It was a long-distance lorry. There was a curtained-off bunk in the roof of the cab. Two days ago, I would have died before I would have done anything like this. But that had been before I had stopped being a lawyer and become a murderer. I climbed up into the bunk and pulled the curtains behind me.

It smelt of sweat and cigarettes. On the wall someone had pasted a picture of a girl with a pink tongue and pink nipples. The lorry door opened. I held my breath and watched a nipple. The engine started. I heard the driver grunt as he spun the wheel. Centrifugal force piled me up on the end of the bunk as we turned in a tight circle. The engine roared, the wheels spinning on the unloaded back axle. He went through the gears, down the road away from the dock, paused at the end, out on to the main road. There was a window, a little square of grey sky. We snaked through a maze of turnings. The brakes went on; we stopped. Through the minute crack in the curtains, I saw that we were in front of a chain link compound. On the gates was a notice that said MOUNT PLEASURE FORWARDING SA. A man in dungarees opened them. The lorry drew up next to a rank of containers. There was a crane; in the far corner of the yard was a ready-mix concrete lorry.

A container settled its weight on the trailer. I pressed my forehead against the greasy glass of the little window. Down at the far end by the concrete truck, a man with a fork-lift was driving pallets of forty-five-gallon drums into a container.

Yellow drums.

The driver climbed in again. He wound down the window. '*Una mezz'ora!*' he yelled. 'Ship, she goddam sail!' The clutch went in with a bang. The truck ground out of the gates and flung itself through the maze back to the docks. I stared at the nipples and breathed the sweat.

Una mezz'ora. Half an hour. I hung on grimly as the truck laboured round a bend.

The bunk stank. The stubble on my chin itched, and I was sticky from long travelling. Harry Frazer, the old Harry Frazer, wore Turnbull and Asser shirts that he changed twice a day, and flew first class at his clients' expense. Harry Frazer took beautiful, well-dressed women to marble restaurants where they put the sauce under the food, and got up between courses to telephone the office.

The new Harry Frazer had not changed a shirt or called the office in days. He was in love with a woman who would think that a smart restaurant was a joke unless the food tasted as good as it looked. And he travelled second class, if that.

I had thought of Rotterdam as the end of the journey. It was not an end. It was a beginning. The only person who could follow the

Marius B and the yellow drums in the containers she carried was Harry Frazer.

The lorry stopped and the driver got down. I watched him out of the little window. A man came down the gangplank with a piece of paper. They both looked at it, arguing. Little bullets of rain rattled on the roof of the cab; the drizzle was becoming heavier. The driver looked at his watch, squinted at the sky, jerked his head at the ship. They went up the gangplank. Up in the cab of the crane the driver had swivelled his seat away from the window, arranged sandwiches on a table, and was pouring something out of a thermos. *Everything stops for tea*. Very gently, I climbed down, opened the driver's door, and slipped out into the rain.

Silly bastard, Frazer, I thought.

But even as I said it, I was strolling across the concrete to the gangway, strolling through the lashing rain; a man in a beret and dungarees, with a faceful of thick black stubble, slinging a bag over his shoulder, rolling a cigarette as he stepped on to the gangway, even though the rain made the cigarette a tube of pulp. Sticking the cigarette between lips that had a tendency to tremble. Finding a steel ladder that led down into the hold. Going down the ladder. The hold empty, except for cargo. Putting himself behind a pile of chemical drums, stacked neatly in the corner.

Silly bastard, Frazer.

But it was too late now, because there were men in the hold again. The grey, rainy light was blotted out by something coming down through the hatch. Container. Ten minutes later, another container. I huddled in a cold steel corner, wedged between a pallet of cement bags and the battered steel side of the ship. Four days of this, I thought.

Four days back to Fiona.

Things were happening. Crouched in my cold, cheerless slot, I felt a new vibration coming through the hull plating. The ship's main engines had started. A shadow crossed the cement bags in front of me, and they vanished. Shutting main hatches. They closed with a hollow boom.

Four days in the dark.

Silly bastard.

I lay in my cold slot and listened to the vibrations in the hull. Ahead, then astern, then ahead; moving off the dock, out into the Nieuwe Maas. A confused rolling and pitching as we hit the waterway, and the wakes of dozens of ships, crossing and recrossing. The tick of many propellers as we moved down the Nieuwe Waterweg, past the sardine-jammed quays and the docks where the ships and barges nosed in together like pens in a civil servant's breast pocket. Maasluis, on the right bank. Then to port flat, deadly dykes, and the tank farms and white superstructures of the Europoort. Night would be falling now, the channel buoys flicking red and green, the lights of ships steady ruby and emerald to seaward, enigmatic white flashes from the Noorderhoofd radar tower. And finally, three hours after the first movements away from the dock, the lift and sink of a low North Sea swell, pocked with drizzle to the indistinct grey horizon.

I climbed painfully to my feet and groped in my bag for the bicycle's front lamp.

The hold was a room the size of a church, walled with metal scarred and abraded with sharp edges of aggregate, splashed with patches of red lead. The hatch covers were big, windowless skylights above. Forward, there was a blank wall of steel. Aft, the wall was pierced by two metal doors, which would lead to the accommodation. It was a huge, cold room, echoing with the bang of the cross-sea, and as cosy as the business end of a gravel lorry.

I shrugged my shoulders inside the nylon pile jacket, trying for more warmth. The flashlight's little white disc slid over pallets and crates and drums. I picked my way over the close-wedged cargo to the containers that lay below the hatch covers.

There were six of them. They were the kind of containers you see used as sheds on a dirty quay, or rotting in the back lot of a scrapyard, full of old sewing machines and bicycle frames. As the flashlight beam slid over their bulging sides it lit flaking paint slapped over cancerous patches of rust. Somebody had closed the doors by hitting the metal with a sledgehammer until it fitted, and then banging home the latch. Everything else in the hold looked new, and shiny, and consumable. The containers looked fit only for throwing away.

For throwing away.

I went closer. From the cracks in the doors, something was oozing, gleaming dirty grey in the flashlight's beam. My foot squashed in a pile of something on the floor, something grey and gritty. The smell of it was earthy, with a faint chemical edge.

I leaned against a pallet and thought about lying in the truck's bunk, peering out of the little greasy window in the Mount Pleasure Forwarding compound. And in particular, about the ready-mix truck parked in the corner, its drum revolving slowly.

The grey stuff was concrete. Nobody was filling forty-foot containers with concrete to stop them keeping the helmsman awake with their rattling.

If there had been anyone with me, I would have slapped them on the back. But it was three days now since I had been anything but an animal, skulking in a dark corner with my antennae bristling. So I limited myself to a hard, nasty grin. Then I did a tour of the hold, rounded up some odds and ends of polythene bubble-wrap and tarpaulin and a bucket, and found a tap that dispensed fresh water.

With the bedding I made myself a rat's nest between a frame and the hull plating. There I divided what remained of the food I had bought in Paris into eight portions. The portions looked very small, but I did not allow myself the indulgence of looking at them for too long, because there were no spare batteries for the flashlight. I thought about eating one of the portions on the spot. But I had had a nominal lunch, and that would have to do for the moment. So I rolled a cigarette and smoked that instead, cheered by the little red glow of the ash. I was smoking a lot. Harmful to the health, Frazer. Along with a lot of other things at the moment.

I knew why I had been wrong about the quarry. It was the concrete that had put me right.

Mount Pleasure Forwarding was repainting red drums yellow, and stencilling on the false codes, and loading them into containers. And then, on the way up to the quarry, they were simply dropping them over the side.

I was guessing after that. But they were good guesses.

They had not always padded the containers with concrete. They had started when one of them had burst, and the drums had gone adrift, and started to perturb the smooth running of the operation.

Mancini had used Stewart to collect them up, because Stewart knew the tides. But Jimmy Sullivan had known the tides, too. He had worked out where the drums were coming from, and when, and gone looking, that Tuesday night. He must have seen the loom of the ship, and the containers going overboard into the dark water. But someone had seen him, too. And they had run him down, and he had gone to the bottom on the slope down to the six-hundred-foot pothole where the rusting containers lay piled in the gloom.

It was not the kind of place where anyone with any sense went trawling. It was a nice little glory hole, where Mr Smith and his friends could dump their filth, a hundred and fifty tons a week, as a bonus to the general cargo they were taking to the quarry, and the aggregate they were bringing back. And by the time the fish and seals were coming ashore dead and the bathers were being skinned alive, Mr Enzo Smith would be elsewhere, in a big, shiny car with the windows rolled up. And so would the man who had brought him there in the first place.

I was angry. I was going to collect my evidence, and get to the quarry, and I was going to get out of the ship. And then I was going to turn the whole dirty rabble of them in.

Chapter Twenty-Eight

The warmth of the anger did not last. I sat in the dark, and tried not to look at my watch, and not to eat the next fraction of food. It was cold. Polythene bubble wrap is warm to the touch, but it makes you sweat. Outside, the North Sea slid past.

After fourteen hours by my watch, the sea began to kick up. There was a lift to the bow now, and a corkscrew roll, as if the ship was butting into a shortish, steepish head sea. From time to time, the bow came down flat with a *boom* like the roar of a giant gong. Bad smells crept in on me: the stink of spilt diesel and some kind of sour chemical, and the clammy stone smell of cement. With a sinking of the heart, I recognised the symptoms. I was getting seasick.

The only way I have ever managed to dodge seasickness is by going on deck and taking exercise. Going on deck was out of the question. Exercise was easier. But as the rolling increased, doing press-ups began to seem less desirable. In fact, everything seemed less desirable. My horizons shrank. I was being bloody stupid, and I felt very sick, and there was nothing I could do about it.

I was sick. I was immensely, horribly sick, somewhere as far away from my bedding as I could get, down between two drums of diesel on a pallet. Afterwards I crawled back to my bedding and pulled some polythene over me, and wished pathetically that I was anywhere but here. The bucket was within range. I was not sick any more, because there was nothing left to be sick with. After a while, I fell into an exhausted sleep.

When I awoke, it was dark. It was always dark in the hold. I felt as if I had been filleted. The ship was moving, always moving, shouldering through a sea that felt as if it might be lengthening out; a deep-water sea. Thirty-six hours, now. Three hundred odd miles. Aberdeen down to port, or Exmouth up to starboard. Choose one; matter a damn.

My throat was dry and raw, and I was very thirsty. I clambered laboriously out of my corner and made my way wobbly-legged across the cement bags and the drums to the tap. It was awkward going; the bicycle lamp seemed eye-achingly bright, and I was weak enough to have to use my hands a lot, so I kept dropping it.

But at long last I got to the tap, and turned it on. The water went down my neck and into my ears. Some of it trickled down my throat. It tasted sweet as honey. I turned off the tap, and straightened up.

The sun exploded in my eyes. I stood there with the water running down inside my shirt. My mouth was open. I could not shut it. Something hummed in the air and slammed into my head, along the right side, above the ear. No, I thought. Too hard. The pain was dreadful. It sucked the strength out of my knees; they unlocked. I pitched forward. My chin hit a sack and my teeth snapped shut, biting my tongue. There should have been more pain, but I could not feel any because it was all zooming away from me down a long, dark tunnel, and I felt too sick to catch it.

Lights out.

Things went bump in the night. They did it a lot, and when they did it they made me feel as if there were jagged stones rolling in my head.

Gradually, matters began to take shape. There were white walls and a ceiling, and blue curtains on a porthole. I could not see out, because I could not move my head without a spear of pain jabbing through both eyeballs, a pain that had something to do with the big, pulpy lump on the right-hand side of my head above the ear.

The cabin was full of things and people. There were Fiona and Vi, sitting on a chintz sofa. There was also *Green Dolphin*, anchored in the middle of the green fitted carpet, and a man in a trilby hat. I shouted at them all to do something. Someone brought me a cup of coffee. After I had drunk it I began to perceive that some of the things I was seeing were there, and some were not. As soon as I became aware of this, the things that were not there faded away. *Green Dolphin* was the first to go. Then Vi. And finally, Fiona. I cried when Fiona went, because I wanted Fiona very, very badly. But she faded out all the same.

That left the man in the trilby. He was wearing a dirty white oiled-wool sweater and smoking a cheap Dutch cigar. I knew he was real because I could smell him. I studied his face closely. It had grey, coarse-pored skin, a mouth as lipless as a tortoise's, drawn down at the corners until the creases spread on to the grey, leathery neck. His eyes were dull, sceptical slots above his flat cheeks. It was a face with the texture and emotions of a slab of cement.

And suddenly I knew exactly where I was, and why. And I felt very weak and very, very ill.

The man said, 'I am the captain of this ship. You want some food?'

There was nothing I wanted less than food.

He said, 'Yeah. They knowed you was down in the hold because they could smell the puke. You will have more coffee.'

I drank the coffee.

He said, 'How did you come on board?'

There was no harm in telling him. 'Up the gangway,' I said. 'It was raining.'

His muddy eyes rested on me like two slugs on a cabbage leaf. He nodded. 'Okay,' he said. 'What's your name?'

Relief warmed me like a hot bath. There was no reason anyone on this ship should know who I was. I said, 'Joseph Crecy.'

'What you doing on my ship?'

I said, 'I was going travelling.'

'Not on my ship, you're not,' he said. 'I give you to the police when we land.'

Thank you, I thought. Yes, please. The captain reports a stowaway. The captain is on the side of law and order. The captain is unaware of my special interest in what he has got in six containers in the hold.

The cabin door opened. A head came round. '*Capitano*,' it said. '*Momento –*' The eyes strayed to the bunk. I met them with mine. '*Dio*,' said the head round the door, and smiled.

It was a cold smile, with a lot of teeth in it. It did not alter the tight skin over the cheekbones, or the stony black eyes. Mine was probably even less convincing.

Because the head in the doorway belonged to Enzo Smith.

'Mr Frazer,' he said. 'This is a big pleasure. A really big pleasure. Captain Pauwels, we must talk about this.'

Pauwels got up. They left the cabin. I heard the solid click of the door lock. I lay there and waited. There was nothing I could do. For the first time since Geneva, I felt real fear.

When he came back, Captain Pauwels' face was more like granite than cement. He said, 'You been telling lies.'

I said, 'You have been dumping waste into the sea.'

The eyes were slits of mud. 'The sea is big,' he said. 'Nobody see. Nobody know.'

Fuzzily, I realised that Harry Frazer was not the only frightened man in the cabin. I said, 'James Sullivan saw you. Ewan Buchan saw you. They're dead. You killed them.'

He stared at me.

'There's a big weld on the *George B*'s bow where she hit Jimmy Sullivan,' I said. 'The police will be looking.'

The slits blinked. He gazed at me for a moment. Then he went out, and the door slammed behind him. Over the hum of the engine I could hear his voice outside the door, low, like the doctor outside the sickroom. Discussing my health. My stomach hollowed out, and my bowels became liquid with terror.

Enzo Smith came in. He was smoking an Italian cigarette that smelled of cardboard. He said, 'I hear we have been dumping waste in the sea.' He might have been discussing a movie at a cocktail party.

'That's right,' I said.

'And the police will be looking. Maybe your friend Fiona Campbell will tell them where to look.'

Terror made me sweat. 'No,' I said. 'She doesn't know. I haven't told her anything.'

He smiled at me, the tender smile of a father jollying along an awkward child. 'Of course,' he said. 'Never tell the woman.' He blew smoke at the ceiling. 'But I think we must make sure.'

I said, 'What do you mean?'

'You will find out,' said Smith. 'Goodbye, Mr Frazer.'

I knew I had been right. But I also knew that I was dead. And so was Fiona.

Nobody brought me any more coffee. I lay there and listened to the pulse in my head banging. Every time it banged, it said, *die. Die. Die.* It said it for hours. But with every bang the pain improved. And as the pain improved, that ugly syllable in the blood shed a little of its terror, because I was beginning to look for ways to prove it wrong.

The ship's motion had changed. The roll had stopped, and given way to a strong pitching. From time to time the nose came off a wave and walloped flat into the next, and the whole of the *Marius B* shook and shuddered, and the propeller-shaft sent spastic vibrations up through the frames, quivering, until she got going again. Pentland Firth, I thought. Wind on tide, and everything standing on end.

The pounding turned my shredded mind to outside. And the thought of outside got my feet off the bunk and on to the floor, and my hands to my head so I could carry the head off the pillow and upright.

There was a pause after that, while I got used to the tides of blood slopping in the cranium. When I could use my eyes again, I took a better look at the cabin.

It had white walls, and a green carpet. The door had the solid feel of heavy steel. When I tried the handle, it was locked. Behind the curtain was a square window. Outside the glass was white-painted metal. Someone had put up the storm covers. The other orifices were a couple of six-inch gratings, for ventilation.

I sat down on the bunk, mouth dry. It might as well have been a safe.

At the far end of the bunk was a plywood hanging locker and a couple of drawers. I pulled open the cupboard. It was empty, except for a couple of coat hangers suspended from a bar. I gripped the bar, and tugged. It came away easily in the hand. It was not the usual chromed tube, but an eighteen-inch length of steel piping that might have come out of the engine room. It had a confidence-inspiring heft in the hand, that pipe. Though confidence was about all it was good for, in the circumstances; I was not going to get far against perhaps five fit men, at least one of them a murderer, with a length of scaffolding pipe. But I shoved it inside the waistband of my trousers all the same.

The bottom drawer was empty. The top drawer contained a box of Kleenex and two copies of *Hot Car* magazine. I pulled out the magazines. Underneath the bottom one, wedged in a corner of the drawer, was a disposable cigarette lighter.

I picked it up and looked at it, and wondered if it would do anybody any good if I set fire to the cabin. But there was nothing flammable except magazines and the mattress, and if I lit the mattress the fumes would save Captain Pauwels some trouble.

There was a rattling at the door. I slipped the lighter into my pocket. Pauwels came in. Smith was with him. They ran their eyes over me as if I was a thing, not a person. Smith brought the flat of his hand round and smacked me on the bad place above the right ear. I was too groggy to duck. The pain was spectacular. It knocked me over on to my left side on the bunk. Through the blood-coloured haze I knew that something was happening to my wrists. A rope looped round them, twice. I heard Pauwels grunt as he yanked it taut. The door banged.

The head subsided enough for me to turn over. I rolled, and heaved myself into a sitting position. My heart was beating too hard, and I kept swallowing. I was not about to go through a steel door with my bare hands. So they had tied me up because something was about to happen. *Dead*, said the pulse in my ears. *Dead, dead*.

I twisted my shoulders, fighting to get my hands round to the trouser pocket. The lashings were tight. Very soon, my fingers would be numb, and that would be that. My right hand went into the pocket, closed on the lighter. The fingers were as manoeuvrable as a pound of pork sausages. I flicked the wheel and played the flame on the back of my left hand. There was the smell of burning hair. It hurt. It hurt like hell. Then the pain lessened, and the smell changed. Now it was burning plastic. Burning Terylene rope. The smoke wavered in the air, was caught in the suction of the vent, dragged away. Stay out, Pauwels, I thought. Stay out. Otherwise you'll do it again, and there will be no lighter –

The heat increased. There was no time for thinking any more. The Terylene was burning. Burning plastic was stuck to the back of my hand. It felt as if it was going all the way through.

It was too much. I rammed the hands into the mattress, and clamped my teeth together so as not to shout. For a moment, I thought the mattress was going to catch fire. But the heat lessened, and the smoke rushed away through the vent. I lay on the bunk with the sweat streaming off me and a left hand that was blazing with pain.

And I tried to pull the ropes apart.

They held.

That, for the moment, was that. I lay on the bunk and stared rock bottom in the face with streaming eyes.

It must have been twenty minutes later that the door opened again. This time it was Pauwels and another man. They each took one of my arms, and walked me out of the cabin. Outside the cabin was a corridor. It led through a door, on to a deck. Wind was pouring over the deck. It was dark out there, cold after the cabin, and it smelled wet and salty, a smell I had always associated with holidays. A light was flashing where the horizon must be; a white blink, the glitter of the beam's sweep on the black facets of a low swell. I knew the pulse and sweep of that light. It was the Hyskeir.

There was a rattle and a roar forward, at the end of the pale stripe of the deck. The anchor had gone down. Against the overcast sky, a pale, gibbet-like structure moved: the derricks.

'Come,' said Pauwels. 'Nearly ready for you. Mustn't hold us up.'

We went down an iron companionway and into another door. Down here the decks were diamond-pattern steel, and the air was hot and full of diesel. My eyes were grabbing at things, gulping them down: a pair of rubber boots at the entrance to the hold, a picture of Diego Maradona taped to the bulkhead by a rack of oilskins.

Then we were in the hold, and they were dragging me down an alley that ran through the middle of the cargo. Overhead there was a grinding boom. The hold filled with wind, and a slot of lesser black appeared in the black of the roof. Taking the hatches off.

The hard fingers on my arms jerked me to a halt. A flashlight beam lanced ahead. It glanced over the hard face of Enzo Smith and hit the bulging, rusty side of one of the containers. The door of the nearest was open. We walked round the side. There was a grey wall of concrete in it, raw, moulded where they had poured it in to keep the drums in place. They must have filled the container through a hole in the roof, and welded it up later. There were bubbles and crevices in the concrete. By the open door, there was a crevice big enough to have taken another drum.

Or a man.

And suddenly, I knew what was going to happen.

Chapter Twenty-Nine

Someone was shouting. It was a nasty, raw noise, and it echoed and bounced off the metal walls of the hold. Something hard landed on my head, the old place, above the right ear. More pain. The shouting stopped. The shouter had been me. I was picked up and shoved into that little hole. And the doors, double doors, heavy steel, slammed shut with a noise like the crack of doom. The latch went in. They banged it home with a hammer, like a nail in a big steel coffin.

The doors did not fit. There was a good-sized crack. I put my face against it and started to tell them what I would do if they let me out. What I would do if they let me out was exactly anything they wanted. I yelled it loud, in case they could not hear, because the derrick motor was whining now, up on the deck.

They laughed. Enzo Smith laughed, anyway. Then he turned away, him and Pauwels, and stood back. Pauwels lit a cigar, a new one. I stopped talking. Talking was not going to get me anywhere. Instead I concentrated on the rope on my wrist, particularly on the back of my left hand.

I could feel a hardness there: melted Terylene. The edge of the concrete was sharp and rough. I shoved my hand against it, and ground.

Something gave.

Sweat covered me in an icy sheet. I tugged, hard.

Nothing gave.

Something clanked on the container's roof. Crane hooks. Under my knees, the floor stirred, then settled. I squirmed until I could feel the cigarette lighter and pulled it out. Again the heat on the back of the hand; the stink of burning flesh, burning plastic. I shouted. This time I did not stop. They were used to me shouting, out there. The shouting helped.

Pull.

The rope gave. I could see the back of my hand, now. It was lit by the molten Terylene stuck to it. I banged the speck of light with my right hand. It went out. There was not a lot of feeling in either hand, now, so the pain was not too bad. Outside, somebody else shouted, and the whine of the derrick rose to a scream. And the concrete under my knees was rising, and I was rising with it.

I grabbed the edge of the door. I could get my fingers through the slot, but not my knuckles. The latch was a straight bar of metal across the slot. My fingers clawed at it. Something straight crossed the gap, descending. The hatch coaming. A hammer, I thought. A hammer. Because down there is the hole. The long, wet hole. I have been in little steel boxes before, steel boxes with a wire joining you to the surface. I know what it is like to have a big column of cold water waiting to come ramming in and spread a little man-shaped blob of hot flesh and bone over steel walls. I know exactly what it is like.

I wanted a hammer.

I had a hammer.

The realisation came on me so quickly that I nearly laughed, a big, mad guffaw. And my horrible fingers scrabbled like bananas after the piping I had pulled out of the wardrobe, wrapped themselves round.

The sound of the derrick stopped. The container swung to the roll of the ship. Ah, I thought. Ah-ha. Craftiness. I could hear breath hissing in and out between my teeth. Fear, I thought. Fear makes animals cunning. Fear saves animals from death.

The derrick began to whine again, a staggering, lumpy whine, engine braking. Under my knees, the concrete sank towards the water. Shoving the piping through the crack, I began to pound upwards at the latch.

It was an old latch, bent and mangled with years of rough treatment. Every scratch on it, each fleck of rust stood out in perfect detail in the mind's eye. *Give, you bastard*, I screamed at it in my head. *Give*.

I hit it again, full weight of shoulder in the bar. The bar was bending.

Give.

It gave an inch.

The sea hit the container's base with a thump. Icy water sluiced in, covering my legs. One more bang.

The latch kicked up. I flung myself against the door. It swung outwards a fraction, enough so the latch could not re-engage through force of gravity. But there was water outside now. Heavy, cold, black water. Inside the container there was air. And until the airspace was full of water, the doors were not going to move.

By that time I could be full of water, too.

The light went. Now it was all black, and the jet of water shooting in the doors, hard as a sheet of steel. My hands were over my ears. My breath was coming in big, stupid gasps. Because it was the diving bell all over again. The smell of seawater and wet metal. The urge to climb into the skull and run away, down into the middle of the brain, to a place where it was all cosy and red and safe. And the place not being there; the only thing there the icy cold and the hard steel and that black bitter world of water –

Shut up, I said. Someone said. My voice. Fiona's voice. I was not asking. What I was doing, all of a sudden, was breathing, hard, in, out, in, out, the air that was left, up by the rusty metal ceiling.

Then, lungs full, my shoulders were against the doors, legs braced against the concrete, pushing. Pushing the solid doors.

The not-so-solid doors.

The metal against my back gave. The doors sagged open. I was out, kicking, in open water.

The blackness was complete. I gave myself a second for the buoyancy of my lungs to assert itself, point me upwards. Then I began to kick.

Muffled drums boomed in my ears. How far down? Fifty feet. Sixty. Not that much. There was no point wondering. Air trickled from the mouth. Blackness before the eyes, with red shapes, floating. What if I came up under the *Marius B*?

Keep swimming. Think later.

I swam. The ears were roaring, now. It was all focused inward, on that pinpoint in the mind. Ignore the panicky signals from the chest. Pay no attention to the spastic heavings developing in the ribs –

And suddenly, my head was clear.

I breathed. I breathed a lot. I used enough air to fill an airship.

Over to my left, a derrick motor whined. In the darkness was a darker patch; darkness made solid. The *Marius B*. Anchored. Dropping big time bombs of poison into a neat pothole on the sea floor.

I was angry. I began to swim. The water must have been very cold, but I did not notice. I swam out in a loop, to clear the place where the derrick cable ran down into the sea, and in towards the bow. My eyes were working well now. I could see the bow clearly, a squared-off cliff of inky black against the greyer black of the sky. There was a four-foot sea running. But I am a good swimmer, and I had just got myself out of an iron box fifty feet under the water, and nothing was ever going to be difficult again. I homed in on the bow as if the sea were flat.

Under the flare I trod water and twisted my neck, squinting at the rail high above. Not that high; twenty feet, maybe. Ten feet away, a knobbed black line descended from the sky. Anchor chain. Laid out so they could drop back, watch the echo sounder, find the hole, drop the filth dead centre, nice and gentle. Then pull up the anchor and go and get your money. Like falling off a log.

My hand closed on the chain. The links were big enough for a determined man to get his hands into, and his toes. Big enough to snip off fingers and feet if the boat fell back and snubbed at the chain.

I went up it.

I squeezed and wriggled through the hawsehole, and lay flat on the foredeck, breathing like the bellows end of a blast furnace. Cold water ran out of my clothes and on to the deck. I was grinning, not because anything was funny, but to stop my teeth chattering.

In front of me, the hatch covers were off. Beyond the forward hatch, the derrick motor was whining. A container was coming out of the hold. Time had no meaning; it could have been the second, or the sixth. There were no working lights, no running lights. *Marius B* was dark, the way she had been dark in the fog the night Ewan had been out looking for her, and had bounced *Flora* off *Green Dolphin*.

But my eyes were used to the dark. The deck was a pale shadow, terminating in the cliff of the accommodation. I knew what I was going to do back there. I was angry enough. There were maybe five crew, and one of me. But they would not be expecting to see me.

Another gust of wind. *Marius B* fell back. Behind me, the anchor chain jerked, clanking in the hawsehole. I did not even think about what would have happened if it had done that when I was halfway through. Instead I got up and ran crouching down the port side, the side away from the derrick's cable. Nobody would be looking over there.

As I arrived at the accommodation block, the wind blew another gust, a hard one, that rattled the Dutch flag on the ship's mast and set up a grief-stricken wail in the aerials. It smelled raw, that wind, and there was a spatter of rain in it. I stood for a second outside the heavy steel door on the port side of the block, and counted crew in my mind. Two in the hold. Probably one more steadying the containers. One on the derrick. Enzo Smith. Five in all.

I twisted the handle, pulled the door open, and slid inside.

Dim lights were burning in the corridor. The air was hot, scented with diesel. I locked the door behind me, ran across the width of the ship, locked the starboard side door. Then I went down the steel steps to the lower deck.

The sliding door to the engine room was half-open. I went down on to the gridded catwalk above the bilges. Down in the bilge, the motionless propeller-shaft shone with oil. The roar and rattle of the engine was deafening. To drive the derrick, you needed a generator, and to drive the generator, you needed an engine.

Halfway down one side of the engine was a control console. I went for it, my rubber soles slipping on the oily grid, clothes beginning to steam in the heat. There were dials for RPM, oil pressure, charge. There were a lot of buttons, and a couple of fixed-position switches. One of them was labelled CONTROL. There were two positions: BRIDGE and DIRECT.

Out of the corner of my eye, I saw movement. I spun round. A man in a filthy white boiler suit and green ear-protectors was coming round the forward end of the engine. His lips were moving, but I could not understand what he was saying, because of the racket. The gin on his breath cut through even the smell of oil. There was a big spanner in his hand.

I switched the switch to DIRECT and pulled back what looked like a throttle lever. The man frowned. He came for the board, tried to barge me out of the way. The engine note faded. I pushed him off. He looked at me with eyes like goldfish swimming in booze. For the first time, he registered that I was not somebody he knew.

He went straight from bafflement to aggression. The spanner swung in the general direction of my head. It probably felt smooth and agile to him. To me, it looked hopelessly clumsy. I stepped aside. The spanner went on round. I ran to the after end of the engine. There was a clang, and a hissing. The note of the engine became ragged. The man yelled, a hoarse, agonised yell. When I looked back, one of the brass pipes was off the cylinder block, and something was jetting into the overheated air with a sound like an angry snake. From *Green Dolphin*'s engine manual there bubbled up a caution: *Do not allow high pressure diesel to come into contact with skin.*

The engineer was on the floor. His hands were over his eyes. He was screaming, a horrible, deep, grating bellow. The air was pearly with diesel mist. I yelled, 'Fuel cut-off!'

He bellowed some more. I put a foot on his neck and said it again. He pointed at the console with a finger that shone with oil. It was a red button, above it a red stopcock. I hit the button. The engine faded, and died. I turned the stopcock clockwise until it stuck.

The hissing had stopped. I said to the engineer, 'Get up.'

He got up, clutching his face. I led him up the steps and down to the door in the hold. The door opened outwards. I kicked him out, slammed the door and locked it. He was bellowing again. I found a hammer and went down the side of the engine, smashing the neat brass tubes off all the injectors. Kill the ship, I thought. Leave it dead in the water. Then get help. There was another engine, an auxiliary generator. I smashed that, too. Then, slipping in the diesel on my boots, I ran up the iron stairs.

There was nobody in the rest of the accommodation. I locked all the bridge doors. Outside, the whining of the derrick had stopped. Through the doors there came a confused sound of shouting. Inside the bridge it was warm, and little lights glowed, powered by the ship's batteries. The wind was well up, wailing in the aerials. Rain was clattering against the bridge windows. The radio was on, a plastic tranny on the shelf; Radio 2, Herb Alpert mangling *Stranger on the Shore.* It was all very cosy and homelike.

There was a Decca over the navigator's table. It was older and more complicated than my trusty Navstar, but it had a button marked PUS. I hit the button. Beyond the window the Hyskeir light was nearly in line with the West Ferris buoy. I wrote the transit down neatly in the notebook, and added the Decca position and the sounder reading. After that I trailed salt and diesel into the radio operator's shack, pulled down the handset of the VHF, and twiddled the dial to channel 16, emergency. 'All stations,' I said. 'All stations, this is—'

The lights went out. One minute the radio shack had been glowing with the red and green cat's eyes of LEDs. The next, it was pitch black.

I groped my way back on to the bridge. The lights were out there, too. It was a black cave, lined on its forward wall with the grey squares of windows. Only the transistor was still working. Main batteries out, I thought. They've blown the fuses, to stop me using the radio. No chance of getting help. I had knocked out the engines and the generators; there was no way of getting more power, since they were locked out of the engine room.

We were stuck at anchor. The winches needed electricity. So did the derricks. The *Marius B* was paralysed. I was inside, they were shut out. There would be flares, a handheld VHF. I could still get help.

'Well,' said the disc jockey. 'Beautiful world, right? Thanks, Herb.' There was a jingle like tinned treacle. Then a plummy voice said, 'The Meteorological Office issued the following gale warning to shipping at 2000 hours…There are warnings of gales in Rockall, Maim, Hebrides, Bailey.'

The voice was soothing, with as much urgency as it could summon up, given its closeness to bedtime. It worked its way through the consequences of a depression like a junior hurricane whirring up at Iceland: force eight and nine in Rockall and Malin, moderating six. 'Hebrides, westerly severe gale force nine increasing storm force ten, imminent.' The Rolex said 0205 hours. Imminent meant any minute now.

Something hard and metallic hit the starboard door of the bridge. A sledgehammer. I could see a man-shaped hole in the sky out there. My mouth dried out again. The bridge door was steel, and the windows were presumably toughened glass. But even toughened glass was not going to hold up long against a sledgehammer. Another bang.

255

The wind buffeted at the bridge windows. The rain was like machine gun bullets. The Hyskeir light was nothing but a pale glimmer now. In front of it, the West Ferris buoy had vanished. I went for the door. *Bang* again, on the steel this time, down by the lock. I clenched my teeth. Then I twisted the handle and tugged it open.

The man outside was a dark shape, hammer up. I kicked at the middle of him, hard as I could. My foot hit something yielding. He staggered backwards. The hammer clattered over the rail and on to the steel deck. His nails raked my face, grabbing not to hurt but to save himself. It did not work. He went backwards after the hammer, twenty feet, headfirst. Then I could not see him any more.

I could see something else. I could see the West Ferris buoy, which five minutes ago had been in line with the lighthouse. The wind was up in earnest, screaming. The West Ferris was not in line with the lighthouse any more. It was off the dark loom of the starboard bow.

The wind lulled. I yelled, as loud as I could, 'She's dragging!' Then I went back into the bridge, locked the door, and watched.

The sea was getting up. The nose of the ship bucked as the waves came under. From time to time a big one came and blasted itself to shreds whose last remnants battered the bridge windows. The West Ferris drew ahead with each of those waves. The anchor was dragging fast, ploughing through the soft mud bottom. And the wind was barely gale force yet.

I stared out of the window. The adrenalin had gone. The clothes hung on me cold and wet in the growing chill of the dark bridge. If I went out, they would kill me. There were three of them left, perhaps four.

A metallic roar came from forward. Partly it came on the wind, and partly it came up through the deck. It seemed to go on for ten minutes. It ended suddenly, with a great bang that sent a shudder through the whole ship. Ahead, the pale deck rose like a white rocket on a huge wave. I clutched the chart table as the ship slid sideways, landing with a plunge and a roll, blasting a hundred-foot sheet of spray out of the trough. I did not know anything about large ships. But I knew what that roar and plunge meant, and the one after it, and the fact that the West Ferris buoy was on the port beam now, and the *Marius B* was wallowing beam-on to the waves.

It meant that the anchor was not dragging any more. It meant that to stop her dragging, Captain Pauwels had tried to veer more anchor chain. But there was no power, and no hydraulics, so he and the men remaining had done it manually. They had knocked off the ratchet pawl, and the chain had gone out all the way. It had gone so far that the bitter end had gone down the hawse pipe and flicked into the sea.

I stood very still, dry-mouthed, hanging on against the buck and twist of the deck. Another roar came up through the deck, followed by a thump. Second anchor. The thump was the pawl catching. I said it aloud, for company. Dragging. Catching. Dragging again. There was another series of thumps. Too little chain. Veer some more.

Again the roar through the deck. *Out of control*, I thought. Up on the foredeck, tons of six-inch chain thrashing and writhing like a mad snake in the saturated dark –

Bang.

Marius B reared free and easy, slicing a long white curve from the upslope of a wave. There were no anchors left. She had God knew how many tons of toxic waste in her belly, no engines, no nothing.

She was adrift.

Chapter Thirty

After that, things on deck began to move very fast. Someone lit a flare; a white one, not red. They would not send up a red flare, because they did not want to attract attention; not that anyone would see a flare here anyway. By the white flare, I saw them piling into a lifeboat on the lee side, little figures moving very quickly. I saw them wait for a lull. The flare fizzled. The lifeboat launched.

And I was alone on the *Marius B*.

The motion of an unpowered ship in a seaway is a horrible thing. The seas had lumped up, big hills of water cruising in from the far west. The *Marius B* took most of them beam-on, with a big, fast roll that filled her open hatches with wind and slewed her diagonally up the next wave, or skidded her down the black slope and slammed her into the trough.

My mind had frozen solid. Now it began to unfreeze. With the slowness of crevasses forming in a glacier, ideas began to take shape.

They were not very big ideas. The first one was *light*, and the next one was *compass*, and the one after that was *chart*. It was not possible to think more precisely, because the noise was dreadful, and the wind was going on up, flinging solid blocks of water back down the deck to smash against the windows with a bang worse than the sledgehammer. I tried not to think about the fact that if that much water was finding its way aft to the upperworks, a lot of it would be going into the hold, and I began a solemn rummage.

I started on the bridge, running my fingers along the rail and the ledges behind the navigator's table. There was a box of matches behind the Decca. I lit one and went through to the radio shack before it burnt my fingers.

The deck was twitching and leaping like the skin of a horse attacked by flies. A shambles of loose gear was slithering from side to side as she rolled. No flashlight in the radio shack. I moved on into the captain's cabin. It was funereally tidy, and smelled vilely of cigars and sweat. There were bonuses: a flashlight, in clips by the bunk.

The flashlight was a big encouragement. I went quickly back to the bridge. The light meant I could not see out of the windows. Perhaps it was better that way, because there was a big roaring out there now, and I did not need eyes to know that those long, smooth swells out of the west had turned steep, and their tops were exploding under the lash of the wind.

Hanging on to anything that looked as if it would take my weight, I led the white pool of the flashlight over to the chart table.

The only mark on the chart was a circle with a dot in the middle over the ring of contours that marked the dumping ground. Decca fix; useful starting point.

Wedging myself against the back of the desk, I slapped a straight edge on the Decca fix and lined it up due east, straight downwind. The edge crossed some big soundings. But further inshore the soundings were in the low teens. In this weather, the low teens meant breaking waves. And inside the breakers there was worse: a chain of islands, the gaps between them jagged with the little hatched circles of rocks, with the soundings underlined, to show heights above the lowest astronomical tide.

I looked at the wall behind the chart table. Uncontrolled, the *Marius B* had about as much chance of coming out in one piece as of drifting beam-on through the eye of a needle.

A gust hit. The bridge caught it on the starboard side, and the ship heeled steeply to port, yawing.

I staggered to the wheel. It was locked. The indicator said the rudder was fore-and-aft. I whipped off the lock. The pale blade of the deck rose as a wave came under, and the stern drove through the trough. The wheel spun. Without power to drive the hydraulics, steering had to be manual: perhaps fifty turns to drive the hydraulic pumps where one would have sufficed under power. The deck yawed as the stern went up; the pressure of the water came off. I wound the helm back amidships. In the green glow of the betalight, the compass card had swung until it was 275°. Another wave came under. I watched for the nose to yaw sideways.

It did not go.

The muscles in my cheeks were aching with the clenching of my teeth. Got you, I thought. Got you, you bastard. The wind roared a full-throated force nine roar. It was music to my ears. Because we were sailing. The wind had the *Marius B* by the upperworks, and was blowing her stern-first. She was deep enough loaded not to skid across the surface of the water; her hull was a keel, tracking.

The third wave came. It was high, a wall of pitch darkness blocking the lower third of the sky. The top of the wall turned grey, and there was a bellowing roar. *Marius B* caught it on the starboard bow. A plume of grey water rose, bent, thundered on to the foredeck. She slewed to port, rolling steeply. The exhilaration vanished. Down there on the deck the hatches were open, and the water would be pouring in.

The trough ran under, and the stern lifted. I began to spin the wheel, not pausing for breath until the indicator read forty-five degrees port rudder. The next wave did not break. As she rose, diagonal in the trough, I felt the wind's shove on the upperworks, the heel of her. The compass card was moving again, 255°, 260°, 275°, as she came round. I wound furiously, brought the helm amidships. She took the next wave straight, and the one after that. On the third, she began to yaw again. I corrected. She straightened. Easy as that.

Then I went back to the chart.

It had been twenty minutes by my Rolex. We had come straight downwind of the Decca fix. A mile at three knots. That left two miles to go to the fifteen-metre contour. I pulled an almanac out of the shelf above the table, and focused my eyes on the tide times. Tide flowing. Carrying us north, at maybe three-quarters of a knot.

The pitch became a roll. That meant the ship was wallowing, trying to broach. I ran for the wheel, waited for the roar of the wind on the bridge, gave her forty-five degrees of starboard rudder. She straightened. I went back to the table.

Sailing-school stuff. Tide running northish at three-quarters of a knot. Boat's speed, assume three knots. Draw track. Lay off tide with the plotter provided, three little arrowheads. Other end of plotter on the gap between the islands. Draw the vectors. Measure the angle. Course to steer –

Glass exploded on the starboard side. Wind and rain shrieked in. My stomach jumped with terror.

Then I saw that it was only the bridge door that had blown in, the one the man had crazed with his hammer. I laughed, making it loud, so I could hear myself above the screaming din of wind and sea. At her three knots, bow jumping at the black sky, wind battering at the rusty white tower of her upperworks, *Marius B* drifted and wallowed her way on towards the rocks.

I tried to keep the compass between 280° and 300°, the reciprocal of the course I needed to lay off the tide. Ten degrees either side was better than I could do, because the ship's course had become a series of yaws, thirty degrees either way. When she rolled, there was a nasty sluggishness to her recovery. I had never steered a ship before, let alone a ship full of poison sailing astern into a lee shore in a force nine gale. But it seemed to me that she was behaving like a ship with a lot of water in her hold.

I knew what happened when you got water in your hold.

It was the same thing that had happened in dinghies on the reservoirs of my youth. A couple of inches of water is no problem when the boat is on an even keel. But when it runs over to one side, into the turn of the bilge, you get a lump of the stuff, each gallon weighing ten pounds, concentrated on one point. And over you go.

Perhaps the bottom was the best place for the *Marius B*: deep water, out of reach of the smash and surge of the waves, waiting for the divers.

Water blasted aft. It was too late now. Too shallow. If she sank here the waves would grind her to iron filings on the bottom, and spread her tons of filth up the beaches to Skye and beyond. I clenched my teeth, and put my shoulder to the wheel.

The rain seemed to be easing. To seaward, the black roof of cloud lifted and split, showing long leads of paler sky. But the waves were steep now, hollow, their tops curling, ready to break.

I got her straight, ran and stuck my head out of the broken door. The wind tried to pull my head off. I braced my shoulders against the frame.

Four hundred yards astern and to starboard, the sea became a cauldron of boiling white. There was a dark hump that might have been an island. Tongues of white water were kicking up it, falling back, being chased up again and smashed to smithereens. Dead astern, in our line of drift, the sea was darker. It is always difficult to tell from seaward how a wave is breaking. In the darker alley, they seemed to be breaking less. Certainly there was no island in the way. Hope spread through my veins like whisky. The ship started to yaw. I shuffled back to the slavery of the wheel.

We were passing over the first of the shallows now; twenty feet of water and us, plus the tide, maybe six feet. *Marius B*'s bottom would be shaving it. All I had to do was keep her straight, and she was through.

All I had to do.

Ahead, a big wave began to lump up. An unusually big wave. It was twice as high as the rest. Its crest reared and trembled. The bow started to rise to it. The wind was stilled, hidden by the wave. Up and up it went, the bow. Somewhere below, things were breaking loose, sliding and crashing. The wave grew a grey crest that projected from its top like a cornice. The bow strained to meet it. For a period outside time, the world stopped ticking, and hung suspended.

The wave broke.

Something hit me like a hammer on the upper arm. I was flung away, down the deck of the bridge, which had suddenly become a precipice. My head thumped into the port door. Sprawled in the angle of the chart table, I watched the bow of the *Marius B* stand vertical, kick hard to port as the wave curled and nonchalantly dropped a million-ton curtain of water on its grey upslope. The deck vanished under a boiling white torrent. The body of the wave picked her up, swung her sideways, and pushed her beam-on towards the shore.

Water was coming in at the starboard window. Torrents of water. I was actually underwater on the bridge.

The smooth forward rush faltered. There was a grating, then a trip and a hard, nasty bang from forward. Water poured over the starboard side. *Rock*, I thought. *Hit a rock*.

The crest roared away towards the land, and was gone. The ship lay heeled thirty degrees. She felt motionless, dead. On the bottom. I crawled up the slope. The next wave was gathering, shoulders growing. It covered her bow. Here we go, I thought: the water sweeping over open hatch covers. She fills. The rocks hold her up, like a bully's friends, so the waves can smash her into little bits –

She moved. I distinctly felt her stir. The bow rose to the wave. It rose sluggishly, but it rose. She had taken on a list to port. My mind had been battered to a point where it hardly worked any more. Crawl up to the wheel. Spin –

No movement. Jammed.

Through the bridge windows, I saw the islands like stone whales in the half-light. Water leaped and spouted around them. Something was wrong. The seas seemed smaller. The white water was on the wrong side of the islands.

The far side.

Under my cheek, the deck grated and bumped. Bottom again. With a final, huge effort I pulled myself upright.

The *Marius B* was lying inside a bay guarded by islands. To seaward, waves were tearing themselves apart in the gap she had come through, wallowing in the troughs. As I watched, she pivoted on the rock that had speared into her bow, until she was head-to-sea. Sounds of hissing air and buckling metal came from her bowels. She settled on to the bottom, decks awash. The four-foot waves banged almost cheerfully against her upperworks.

The light grew. The wind dropped. The tide turned, and began to ebb. Very slowly, like an old man, I walked through the cabins of the island that had been the upperworks of the *Marius B*. In a locked drawer in the radio shack, I found a handheld VHF transceiver.

Half an hour later, a yellow Sea King helicopter clattered round the headland at the end of the bay.

Chapter Thirty-One

I was a felon, of course. They put me in a police car, and the police car haled me over to Inverness. In Inverness they put me in an interview room, and a pipe-smoking detective called Swan invited me to tell him all about it. He had friendly grey eyes that must have been worth a fortune to him in his profession. I told him precisely what had happened since I had left Switzerland, and had the satisfaction of watching the scepticism give way to amazement.

They brought me tea while he did some checking.

He came back shaking his head. He said, 'The crew of your ship came ashore this morning. They've one man in the hospital with diesel burns to the eyes, and another without his fingers.' That would have been the anchor chain. 'Maybe you'd identify them for me?'

We went to the hospital. Pauwels had lost his fingers; his face was as grey as the hospital's stone. The rest of the crew were there, too, except Smith. When I told Swan he said, 'We'll look into him. Where can we find you, if we want you?'

We were back in the station lobby. Outside in the granite streets of Inverness, the sun was shining on fresh rain. I gave him the Kinlochbeag number. 'But I'll be away on a race,' I said. 'A yacht race. The Three Bens.'

He looked at me and shook his head. 'You're certainly a glutton for punishment,' he said. 'Good luck.'

I thanked him. Good luck was one of the things I needed, besides a shower, and a shave, and a twenty-four hours' sleep. His eyes travelled over my shoulder. I turned, following them. Someone was standing against the rainy light from the street.

Fiona.

I went and put my arms round her. She put her arms around my neck. I felt as if I could have held on to her for ever, right there in the pale green lobby of the police station, in the faint smell of her perfume.

She said, quietly, 'I've missed you.'

I wanted to say it back, but there was no way round I could put it that carried enough force. So I said nothing, and we walked into the bright afternoon light. Outside I looked at her: the straight shoulders, the small, arched nose, grey–green eyes very pleased about something. About seeing me.

Serpents of traffic were winding along the Great Glen, with caravans instead of heads. Her fingers moved on the back of my neck. 'So that's it,' she said. 'This Mancini put a bomb in Ewan's shed. But it's finished. We can start again.' She looked at me. There were new lines of strain at the corners of her eyes. 'Can't we?'

I nodded. She had been living between the hammer and the anvil for too long. Now, I wanted her to be happy.

But it was not finished.

We turned off the main road and on to the single-tracker that wound down the glen towards Kinlochbeag. The ground on either side began to lose its skin of peat and heather so the bare rock thrust through. It was a harsh, hostile place, set with pools of black water. Today it felt familiar, even welcoming. And when we came over the pass and the angular gables appeared in their grey–green cushion of eucalyptus, the sensation was definitely one of homecoming.

Hector raised a hand from the shed, and Vi was waiting in the drive. I looked at her with anxiety that turned quickly to surprise. She was wearing very little make-up, and the skin of her face had a brown, weather-beaten look. She said, 'Darling,' and embraced me, her usual long-distance kiss, first one cheek, then the other. But it struck me that the first syllable of the 'darling' was shorter than usual, and the kiss less powdery and butterfly-like.

I said, 'You look terrific,' cautiously. Vi had been known to go into a spiral decline because she disagreed with a compliment somebody paid her.

She said, 'I'm into *health*, man.' She pivoted on a high heel. Her legs were terribly thin inside her blue jeans, and I could have put my thumb and forefinger round her upper arm. 'It's her.' She pointed at Fiona. Look out, I thought. Here we go. Jealous screams, and eventually pills.

But Fiona winked at her, marched between us, put an arm round each of our shoulders, and took us into the house.

'She makes me go for walks,' said Vi. 'Really *hearty*, you know.'

She gave Fiona a look I had never seen her give anyone. It was a child's look; it said that she wanted approval, she was trying hard, and would Fiona please take note. Fiona smiled at her, the beautiful smile. And Vi looked happy, for the first time I could remember.

Or perhaps it was just that nowadays, I was actually noticing these things.

The silence of the house was so loud that it droned. We did not talk much. Vi seemed to have forgotten how to be Mummy Vi. She read a book, something I did not remember seeing her do before. I showered, and shaved the dense black beard off my face. The scar on my right cheekbone was a long, deep groove, with a scab. It should have been stitched a long time ago. It was definitely a knife scar; not the kind of scar to inspire confidence in a client. Lawyers do not have scars.

Lawyer or not, I called the office. When Cyril answered, he sounded short of breath. He said, 'The Sullivan Compensation Claim. We have an *ex gratia* payment of one hundred thousand pounds. From Bach AG, of Rotterdam.'

I said, 'Subject to what?'

'Nil publicity.'

'Cash it,' I said. 'Send the money to this address.' I gave him the address.

'I shall include certain important items requiring your immediate attention,' he said.

'Do that,' I said. 'And you can send in your notice.'

'Notice?' he said. For the first time since I had known him, he sounded surprised.

'I'm closing the office,' I said. 'Moving to Scotland.'

Silence.

'Goodbye, Cyril,' I said. 'Come and stay some time.'

And I put the telephone down on Orchard Street, and the wreckage of other people's lives.

Fiona came down to see *Green Dolphin*, rocking gently at a mooring in the middle of the loch. Exhaustion had stretched my mind like chewing gum. I felt drugged; not dazed, but sharpened, as if everything I looked at was bathed in a new kind of light. We walked with fingers hooked together, like lovers in the park. The black peat of the explosion's scar was already greening with weeds.

We all cooked the dinner. We laughed in the kitchen, and threw French beans at each other. Charlie Agutter rang, and said he was bringing the Three Bens' crew up tomorrow. We might have been on holiday. I suppose we were on holiday. Vi pottered around with a cheerfulness I had not realised she was capable of. Fiona and I laughed at each other's jokes, and leaned on each other, and fitted together like Fortnum and Mason. It was as if we were swimming in a charmed lake, where everything was warm and made you want to laugh. I had forgotten about laughing, except as a means of telling myself things were not as bad as I knew they were.

At dinner we drank water, for Vi's benefit. Fiona and I both talked to her, because what was happening between the two of us was too powerful to need words. Vi giggled a lot, and ate what for her was a vast meal of venison stew and crayfish Hector had caught in his pots.

After dinner, she said, 'I'm going to bed.'

It was half past nine. Vi never went to bed before three a.m. I said, 'Never.'

She said, 'I bloody well am.' She smiled. It was a new sort of smile, as if she was looking outwards, not at what was happening inside her head. 'I am keeping you from getting your hands on each other.' Once, she would have said it to hurt. Now, it was almost wistful.

We looked at each other, and laughed, because she was right, and there was no point in denying it. We said good night. Her high heels clicked up the stairs. We sat apart, in a sort of glow. But not for long. Ten minutes later, we went upstairs ourselves.

The bed was big, made of brass that glowed in the red light of the low sun. There were windows on three sides; the room had the lingering warmth of a place that has had the sun all day. We undressed quickly, almost shyly, one on either side of the bed. She said, 'I wanted you when we went diving. The first time.'

Her breasts were heavy, her stomach flat. I said, 'Me too.' It was not eloquent, but it had the merit of being true.

She smiled her infinitely understanding smile. I put my arm around her narrow waist, and pulled her to me. Her fingers held my head precisely. We kissed long and delicately, for what seemed like a year. Her breath was hot on my face. 'Now,' she said. It was partly a word, partly a noise that an animal might have made.

We took each other. It was good, and slow, and it went on and on, while the night wind got up and rustled the leaves of the eucalyptus outside the window; a rustle that joined the rustle of our breathing, and the hot pounding of blood.

It became dark. We lay side by side. She ran her fingers over my face like a blind woman. They paused on my right cheekbone, the scar. She took a deep breath and let it out. It was the first unhappy sound I had heard all evening.

I stroked her smooth flank with my hand. She burrowed in closer. Her mouth was a hot snail on my neck. I did not want her to be unhappy, not this evening. That was why I had not told her who had really killed Ewan, or what I had to do in the morning.

She said, 'Stay with me.'

'Of course.'

'For ever.'

'You too.'

Quite a lot later, we went to sleep.

I slept like a rock, obliterated by blackness, ten miles down. Waking was like coming up through warm, dark water. When I finally got my eyes open, it was light. Not only was it light, but the sun was pouring in at the window, lying in pools on the American rag rug on the floor. The pillow beside me was empty.

I rolled out of bed, pulled on a pair of trousers and stumbled down to the kitchen. It was tidy; breakfast long gone. The Rolex said ten o'clock. There was a sound outside the window. It was Vi, weeding the border.

Vi, weeding the border. Fiona, I thought, you are a genius. I felt excessively happy. Whistling, I heaved up the sash. 'Coffee?' I said.

She looked up. Her face was flushed with work and fresh air. 'Not yet,' she said. 'Thanks.' And she smiled again, a smile without malice or artifice. 'Surprised?' she said.

I wanted to say that it was amazing to see her out of bed before lunchtime, and even more astounding to see her two-inch fingernails cut, grovelling in the soil after the roots of ground elder. Once, I would have gone ahead and said it. Now, I said, 'Of course.' There was a pause. I could sense her waiting for it, like a blow. Bastard, Frazer. 'You look very well,' I said.

She said, 'I feel very well. Fiona's, like, an amazing person.'

'Where is she?'

'She went out.'

'With Hector?'

'No,' she said. 'By herself. She took Hector's little boat. Somebody rang.'

'Oh?' Put Vi on a desert island, and she would gossip about the turtles.

'From the quarry,' she said. 'I think it was someone called Lisbeth.'

The birds stopped singing. The rattle of the eucalyptus was suddenly cold and deadly. 'What did she want?'

Vi's face was losing its openness. Things were twisting up, in there behind her eyes. 'You,' she said. 'She wanted to meet you. Fiona said she'd tell you. Then she said to me that you were tired, she'd let you sleep, she'd go instead.' She stopped. The tight lines were coming back around her eyes. Her big black pupils gnawed at my face. 'Is there something wrong?'

I kept my voice smooth and calm. 'Nah,' I said. 'It's fine.'

Sounds of beaten metal were emanating from Hector's garage. 'You stay here,' I said. 'Various people are arriving, to come sailing. Hector will look after you. I've got to go out in the boat, a minute.'

She smiled. It was a weak smile, but at least it was a smile. 'Okay,' she said. As I walked away, I heard the clink of her fork in the tiles of the flower bed.

As soon as I was out of sight of her, I began to run.

Chapter Thirty-Two

Green Dolphin's engine started first kick. I put on full throttle, then I aimed the nose at the Narrows, shoved in the autopilot, and ran along the coachroof to get the cover off the mainsail.

Through the Narrows there was wind, the rags of a depression spinning northeast five hundred miles off the Hebrides. It cracked the mainsail full and bore *Dolphin* over on her starboard side. Advocates of safe single handed sailing would have said that she was carrying too much sail. Today, safe single handed sailing came a poor second to getting there.

There was a long, slow heave to the sea, the remnants of the groundswell from the *Marius B* storm. It was not big enough to stop *Dolphin*, or knock her out of her stride. She moved across it at a steady canter, blasting a white road across the deep blue–green. Out beyond Ardnamurchan was a dark speck; a floating crane, at work on Enzo Smith's Glory Hole. There were a lot of other sails; some of them had the drab ochre look of Kevlar. Serious racing sails. The Three Bens was ready to take place. *Green Dolphin* was supposed to be part of it.

But over at the quarry, things were happening that made any racing difficult to take seriously.

There were two ships on the quarry wharf: big ships, maybe forty thousand tons each. With a chill, I saw Hector's whaler tied up at the small boat pontoon. I tied up astern and ran ashore. Though it was mid-week, the conveyors were silent.

In the office, a sleepy-looking man was eating a sandwich and reading the Daily Record. A VHF set glowed green in the corner, tuned to Channel 16. Beyond him, Lisbeth's desk was empty. He said, 'It's the annual holiday,' surprised to see me.

I said, 'Where's Miss Vandekaa?'

The man waved his sandwich at the quarry benches rising outside the window. 'I didn't see her,' he said. 'She called down on the radio. The other lassie went on up after her.'

'The other one?'

'Miss Campbell from Kinlochbeag.'

'How?'

'What d'ye mean, how?' He took a bite at his sandwich. 'On her two feet, how else?'

I nodded. There was a Land Rover outside the window. I could see from the office that the keys were in the ignition. 'I'll find her.'

'Ye want to be careful,' said the man, champing his sandwich. 'There's some terrible loose shooting up there.'

'Shooting?'

'Some loon got the stalking,' he said. 'Wild as a hare. Bullets all over. It's early for stags, yet. I doubt he'll be practising.'

He looked as if he was ready to say more. But I was out of the door and into the Land Rover. It was Lisbeth's; I could smell her perfume, and her climbing gear was in the back. Through the Portakabin window I could see the man's face, staring at me, mouth open, half-full of sandwich.

The Land Rover started second try. I banged it into four wheel drive, high range, and shot across the muddy plain for the first of the ramps that went up the benches. It was possible that Lisbeth had wanted me for a chat about the weather. Possible, but not at all probable. She would be concentrating on saving her skin, and to save her skin she would tell me things.

I stamped on the throttle, but it was already flat on the floor. There was a thought in my mind that was so bad I did not even want to give it room. There was another reason she would want to see me at the top of the quarry. It had to do with silence.

The Land Rover roared up the final ramp. Ahead, the flayed surface of the mountain became rock and heather. A figure was standing four hundred yards away, by the machinery on the edge of the funnel-shaped depression leading down to the Glory Hole. I went across. It was Fiona. Strands of dark hair were plastered across her forehead with sweat. When she saw me, she smiled. It was a quick smile, but it brought back last night.

I said, 'Where's Lisbeth?'

'God knows,' she said. 'I've looked all over the place. Top to bottom.'

'Get in,' I said. The emptiness of the plateau was oppressive.

She turned, her face surprised at the urgency in my voice. The sun had brought her freckles out, and the green in her eyes. She took a step forward.

There was a sharp crack from inland. Her face slackened, and her eyes and mouth opened wide. She slammed forward, face down into the mud.

The cries of gulls were thin as sheep's wool in brambles. Bees buzzed in a little island of heather. She lay there.

Some loon got the stalking.

I threw myself to the ground, put my head close to Fiona's. Her skin was white. I said her name. She answered with a small sound. A terrifyingly weak sound. I put my hand on her back. There was a hole in her jersey under the right shoulder blade. The blue wool had turned reddish-black and wet, glistening in the sun.

Something cracked overhead. The Land Rover's radiator let out a long, angry hiss. There was steam everywhere.

Some loon.

My mind was slipping gears. Fiona was sliding. Sliding away. We had found each other, and now she was off, slithering out of life. Target practice. I tried to remember what was on the right-hand side of the body, under the shoulder blade. Ribs. Lungs. Big arteries, heading for the heart. Bad, dangerous stuff. Oh, Jesus. Don't let her die.

The fog cleared. I lay still beside her, exposed in the grey bowl of rock and mud. Back at the lodge, Vi was weeding. Charlie Agutter and the crew would be driving down the road, fresh from the airport, ready for the start.

And Fiona was halfway up a mountain, dying.

Do something, I thought. *Somebody should do something*.

But there was only me, and Fiona, and the ordinariness of being alongside someone you loved. And the horror of the someone you loved, large as life, lying with the blood leaking out of them.

'Fiona,' I said.

Her eye was close to mine. The lash fluttered. The pupil was a black pit in the grey–green iris. 'Whoops,' she said, in a voice so small it was hardly there at all. I found I was smiling. She was dying, but she was making me laugh. I was not going to let her die.

I said, 'I'm going to get you out of here.'

She smiled, the merest flicker of a smile. I smiled back. Her eyes closed. A thread of blood ran from the corner of her mouth. Lung, I thought.

I was shaking. There was a lump in my throat. It was anger that had put it there. Childish anger. I lay with my face in the mud, and thought, Grow up, Frazer. Think.

So I thought, and raised my head, and looked.

We were on the western rim of the saucer-shaped depression that led down to the Glory Hole. The bullets were coming in from the east. Beyond the rim of the depression the hills rose in ridges, pale and misty, like a Chinese painting. The closest ridge was four hundred yards away. Then there was dead ground, and another ridge, two hundred yards further back as the raven flies. The rim of the saucer was clear. So the shots were coming from the ridge. Probably the first ridge; possibly the second, if whoever was shooting was using a telescopic sight.

All we had to do was move across the saucer until the ridges disappeared behind its rim; where the sniper could not see, his bullets could not travel.

I said to Fiona, 'Can you move?'

Her closed eyelids did not flicker.

I took a deep breath to stop the butterflies that were flapping and crawling in my stomach. Then I sat up, took Fiona by the arms, and dragged her to the back of the Land Rover.

At the back, we were out of sight of the ridge. Circling her chest under the arms, I heaved her up and slid her along the bed of the truck. Her breathing had a nasty bubble to it. Quickly, so as not to have time to think, I skirted the side, opened the driver's door, and climbed on my hands and knees into the cab, keeping below the level of the windows.

Which was just as well. The wing-mirror made a sharp cracking noise and evaporated. He was still there. Hands slippery with sweat, I twisted the key in the ignition. The engine started first time. I shoved down the clutch pedal with my hand, put the gear lever into four-wheel drive, high range, first. Carefully, I gave her some gas with my right hand, and let out the clutch with my left. The Land Rover lurched forward.

The windscreen went. Something stung my cheek, and when I put my hand to my face it came away bloody. I was sick of blood. The sight of it made me furious. I accelerated, keeping the steering wheel steady with my shoulder. Grinding and lurching on its flat tyre, the truck crept downhill.

I put my head up. The first ridge had gone behind the lip of the saucer. Good, I thought. That's him – Another bullet whacked into the engine. The temperature gauge was all the way up in the red, and there was the stink of burning. But it was fine, because the ridge was slipping behind the lip of the saucer.

Smoke poured out of the bonnet in a sudden, surprising cloud. The engine stopped dead. A bullet cracked overhead. A safe distance overhead; the ridge had gone. I sat for a moment and let the smoke blow away, and worked out the next move.

To go back down the benches on foot, I would have to traverse the grey mud of the plateau, two hundred yards of it, under the powerful glass eye of the telescopic sight on the ridge. If I got shot, Fiona would die. Out of the question.

There was another answer. It was at the bottom of the saucer, thirty feet away. There was a crane next to it, and the big metal frame of a mobile crusher. The Glory Hole.

I went round to the back. Fiona was a bad colour. Her breathing was shallow, pulse thready. First-aid said you left her up here and went for help. But first-aid did not take account of people with rifles who could come over the brow of the hill and finish off what they had started.

I worked fast, breathing hard, the sweat running. First, I took off my shirt, tore it in strips, tied the thick pad of cloth tight over the hole in her back. Then I unscrewed a grating, six feet long, three feet wide, from under the railings of the crusher. I moved Fiona on to the grating, gentle as if I was carrying eggs. She groaned as I tied her on with the Land Rover's winch rope; face up, one rope under the arms, another round the waist, another round the legs. I said, 'Hold on. Getting you home,' and smiled, hoping I was not showing the fear that was making my mouth dry and my knees shaky as aspic. I pulled up the sides of the grating, so they met in front of her face, and she was encased in a mesh tube. Then I went round the back of the Land Rover again.

Lisbeth's climbing gear was in an untidy heap in a corner. There were three fat coils of rope and a crash helmet. I pulled them out, undid the coils and measured them, thumb to nose.

It was good, strong rope. There was three hundred and twenty metres of it.

I said to Fiona, 'We'll get you out of here.'

She did not answer. Her face was grey. There were dark circles under her eyes, which had sunk back into her sockets. The bones of her skull showed under the skin. I felt a desperate impatience. If she did not get to a doctor soon, she was going to die.

I strapped Lisbeth's helmet on to her head, slid the grating to the lip of the hole. It was scoured and polished by the rocks the crusher poured down it, a hundred tons a minute, eight hours a day, five days a week. I found a smooth place, lined the grid up carefully. The mouth of the shaft whispered at me. *A thousand feet down*, it said. *Anything can happen.* I ignored it, took a round turn with the climbing rope round the front axle of the Land Rover, and tied the short end to the grid above Fiona's head. Then I took the long end in my right hand, and with my left I pushed the grid like a sledge over the edge and into the black gulf.

The rope tautened. She swung, feet down, head hanging forward. Unconscious. At best unconscious. I stopped myself thinking about the worst, and began slowly and smoothly to feed the rope to the turn over the Land Rover's axle.

The pile of rope grew smaller. I began to worry that it would run out before the bottom. But that was only one of a dozen worries. The worst of them was that any minute now the rim of the bowl was going to sprout a little head with a glass eye and a mouth that spat heavy little slugs of lead. And when that happened, and I went down, the rope got out of my fingers, and flew away. And Fiona, down in the shaft, would plummet –

The weight was off the rope.

I pulled in three feet, let it go. The hole was three hundred metres deep, Lisbeth had said. There were about sixty feet left in my pile. Fiona was on the bottom, not stuck on a ledge. Quickly, I added two half-hitches to the round turn on the Land Rover's axle. Then I looped the rope between my legs and over my left shoulder, the way Andy Cooper had taught me on a weekend halfway up the Avon Gorge the day after he had come to see me about his wife.

In the Gorge, it had been easy. But in the Gorge the drop had been fifty feet, not a thousand. My stomach was watery, my knees showed a strong tendency to shudder, and my flesh to crawl. I told myself to shut up, took the strain, and walked backwards over the lip of the hole.

I swung sideways, lost my footing, and smashed into the rock. My legs went up and my head went down. I was hanging over a thousand feet of nothing at all. My right shoulder yelled as the weight came on it. For a moment, I was hanging by one hand. Then I got the other one up there, and I was hanging by two. I stopped myself being sick. *If you can't make it, climb down a wee way. Get yer bottle back*. Andy had been no good with his wife, but he was a useful man on a cliff. So I climbed down the rope like a monkey, hand over hand, ten feet, which left a mere nine hundred and ninety feet to go. Then I got the rope between the legs and over the shoulder. And down I went.

Andy had gone down in big, bounding leaps like a gibbon. I went down like a little old lady. The hole was new-cut, but already it had had enough stone down it to polish the sides smooth. It had also had a lot of water down it, and the water had bred slime. Legs straight. Take the weight on the bottom hand. *Walk*.

The disc of daylight above shrank to the size of a dustbin lid, then a snare drum, then a dinner plate. The rope cut into my shoulder and my thigh.

There were ledges. There were little piles of rubble on the ledges. I found out about them just after I had passed the knot where I had joined the first two ropes, four hundred feet down. I kicked a pile of it off, and it plunged into the gulf with a roar and a rattle. My heart turned in my chest. Fiona was lying down there, and even a small stone was going to be bad at this height.

Thinking of the bottom made me think of where I was. Thinking about where I was jellied my legs. My shoes slid on the algae. I pitched sideways, and my face banged into the wall with a wallop that made my ears ring. I hung there like a spider on a thread. No more abseiling, I thought. Go down, hand over hand. But I knew that if I went hand over hand, everything would start to go too fast. So I hung there and breathed the tombstone smell of the shaft wall until my heart was out of my mouth again, and I could hear myself think above the roar of my breathing.

And I went on.

It got darker, but as it got darker, it got easier, because I was getting in practice. When I looked up next, the entrance was the size of a saucer. On, on; down, down.

I ran out of wall.

One moment I was trudging down. The next I was swinging wildly, because my feet had found air instead of rock, and my hands were burning, because this time I was going for sure. My thrashing legs found the rope. My hands burned like fire. But they were the only ones I had. So I clenched them on the rope. There was a consolation. I knew that at the base of the Glory Hole, there was a great big chamber, fifty feet high. And the reason I had missed my footing on the wall was that it had widened into the chamber.

Between five seconds and a month later, my feet hit bottom. I did not waste any time breathing. I followed the slack of the rope along with my hands. There was the kind of light you get from a small window in a big, cold cellar. Fiona's face was a pale patch on the darker grey of the rock. Her skin was warmer than the rock she lay on, but only just.

I said her name. My voice boomed in the cathedral spaces of the chamber.

No answer.

I put my face close to hers. In four weeks, we had spent a lifetime together, and we were only at the beginning. It wasn't going to end now.

It had not ended. She was breathing. Getting that fear out of the way made room for the next one, one that had ridden my shoulders all the way down the shaft. I grabbed the grating and dragged it away, towards the deeper gloom at the sides of the chamber, away from the feeble glimmer of the entrance.

It happened.

In the centre of the chamber there was a crash that boomed in the vault. The air filled with the stench of dust. More crashing.

But we were out of the line of fire, now. I did not go back, to look up at that little hole, and see the little dark tick in its rim, silhouetted against the light. The tick that was the head that had done the shooting, and was rolling stones into the abyss.

There were two reasons. For one thing, I did not want to take the chance of getting a rock in the eye. For another, even if I had been able at this range to make out the features, I would not have gone to see who it was.

There was no point.

I already knew.

Chapter Thirty-Three

The control-room door was fifty yards down the passage, on the right. It was not locked; there was no crime at ArdnaBruais, except attempted murder. I barged in, found the lights and the telephone. When he heard my voice the watchman gasped as if someone had stabbed him.

Ten minutes later, he came down the track alongside the conveyor belts in a Toyota pick-up. 'Chopper's coming,' he said. The lights shone on the climbing rope snaking down out of the darkness like a bell rope at the back end of an evil cathedral. He stared at it. He said, 'You never came down there.'

I said, 'Hurry!' I could hardly speak. There were terrible chasms of shadow on Fiona's face.

Carefully, we lifted the grating, and slid it into the back of the pick-up. I climbed up after her and held her hand. It was frighteningly cold. Then we drove slowly back down the track, a full mile, the rough-hewn rock of the walls flinging hard black shadows in the yellow glare of the headlamps. The watchman was asking me questions over his shoulder from the cab. I did not answer them, because I did not hear them. My stomach was a tight, agonising knot. Faster, I thought.

But faster would have meant jolting. Jolting meant more bleeding. And the helicopter would take time. There was no hurry. Either Fiona died, or she did not die. There was nothing I could do about it.

Except go after the person who had tried to kill her. And succeeded in killing Ewan. And bring that person back, before it happened again.

Outside, the glare of daylight blanked out vision. Down by the sheds, I covered her with blankets. I took the helmet off her head, smoothed her hair. She said, 'Cold.'

I said, 'You're off to hospital.'

She smiled. It was a terrifying smile. In the space of an hour, she had become old. But you could still see the amazing sweetness in her face. Stop it, I told myself. You will bloody well not start to weep.

She said, 'Love.'

'Don't talk,' I said, in as steady a voice as I could manage. Tough guy, Frazer. She is dying, but it is her trying to cheer you up. 'Race,' she said. 'Do the race.' Her eyelids sank over her eyes. Far away up the glen, I heard the *whock* of rotors. The chopper came over the hill like a big yellow beetle, filling the benches with deafening clatter. A doctor jumped out of the door in its side, examined her, nodded over the pad I had strapped over the hole, replaced it with one of his own. Two men in green immersion suits moved her on to a stretcher with quick, certain movements, folded a down quilt over her, strapped her on. I said to the doctor, 'What do you think?'

He gave me a smile that failed to soften the bleakness in his eyes. 'Wait and see,' he said. 'Wait and see.'

'How long?'

'Lost a lot of blood,' he said. 'In shock. Accident, was it?'

'Stray bullet. Stalkers,' I said.

His eyebrows went up. 'Bit early in the year,' he said.

One of the green suits said, 'Okay, Doc.'

'Excuse me,' said the doctor.

'Where are you going?' The pilot was throttling up. I had to shout.

'Inverness,' he said. He ran under the rotors, pulling on his helmet as he went. The Sea King lifted, pivoted, and raced nose-down for the dark hills to the eastward.

It was quiet again, except for the cry of the gulls.

The watchman said, 'Will you go after yon fool with the gun?'

I shook my head. 'Too late,' I said.

'What do you mean, too late?'

I turned towards the sea. A speedboat was drawing parallel lines across the wrinkled slate of the water, heading south for the steep hills that rose from the tiny grey drum of Dunmurry Castle. 'That's him,' I said.

The watchman squinted in the glare of the grey, diffuse light on the water. 'But yon's Donald Stewart. He's a careful man with a gun, Donald.'

'Maybe he's got passengers,' I said.

I walked slowly down to the pontoon, where Hector's boat was moored, the boat she had climbed out of hale and hearty this morning while I had been trailing behind with a headful of sleep, and the sniper on the ridge had been filling his pockets with cartridges.

I climbed aboard *Green Dolphin*. The watchman cast off. I pointed her south. After that, I drank half a tumbler of whisky, and looked at the sails massing towards Ardnamurchan. Winds westerly, force five, the forecast said. Depression well out in the Atlantic. Associated fronts.

Sails were up off Dunmurry: a couple of Kevlar flyers, the twin triangles of Prosper's *Bonefish*. And Lundgren. Everybody dipping to the fresh breeze driving big blue patches of sunshine across the water.

Lovely weather for a race. Even if you were not going to finish it.

There was a pile of seabags on the quay at Kinlochbeag. I tied up, and ran to the house. Charlie Agutter's rusty old BMW was in the drive. Charlie himself came out of the house.

'Blimey,' he said, looking at me. 'What have you been doing?'

I did not want to talk about what I had been doing. I said, 'We're running late. Boat's at the quay. I'll follow you down.'

The other men were in the drive, now: Scotto Scott, a vast New Zealander, and James Dixon, a taciturn Pulteney timber merchant and boat builder who had won a Round the Isles Race in his own catamaran, and liked running up mountains.

Vi came out after them. She looked less sure of herself than she had this morning, a lifetime ago. She said, 'Where's Fiona?'

I did not want to tell her. I did not even want to tell myself. 'She had an accident,' I said. 'She's in hospital.'

The tan vanished from her face. She looked thin, and white, and terrified. The old Vi.

'It'll be all right,' I said. The old way, tell Vi anything to shut her up. 'We'll give them a ring.'

'You should have gone with her,' said Vi.

I nodded, went into the hall, picked up the telephone and dialled the hospital. The doctor said that Fiona was in the operating theatre. They were taking a bullet out of her right lung. He would not tell me what he thought her chances were.

'What am I going to do?' said Vi.

It was a general question, but I took it as particular. 'Hector will look after you,' I said. 'We'll be back.'

'Not for *days*,' she moaned.

'Sooner than that,' I said.

'How can you go *sailing*?' she said. 'I need you.' Cunning leaked into her eyes. 'Fiona needs you.'

I said, '*Fiona* needs doctors. And when she gets better, she'll need you.'

'Need me?' said Vi. It was a new idea for her.

'I've got to go,' I said.

'Enjoy yourself,' she said. She looked remote, puzzled.

I ran down to the quay. *Green Dolphin*'s engine was already running, her sails on. Charlie was looking nervously at his watch. I tossed the shorelines over, pushed the bow off the quay and jumped aboard. Water boiled over the rudder as Charlie put the helm down. *Green Dolphin* swung for the Narrows.

The tide had turned. The ebb swept us strongly into the bay. The sails went up with a speed and smoothness dazzling after all my short-handed sailing. The wind was westerly. *Green Dolphin* leaned hard over, spat clods of water from under her bow and hammered past the snout of the Horngate towards the little splinters of sail gleaming off Ardnamurchan.

Scotto made corned-beef-and-chilli sandwiches. We sat up on the weather rail and gnawed at them. I said, 'We're late at the line.'

Nobody answered. Everybody knew.

Charlie said, 'Forecast's westerly six, seven.'

'We'll catch up,' I said.

We were catching up already. Start time was six o'clock, two hours into the ebb. The line was off the white tower of the Ardnamurchan light. The sails were growing as the boats jilled about behind the line. Prosper was there, two identical-sized triangles, hard on the wind, heading to seaward. So was Lundgren, in irons, head-to-wind, waiting.

Charlie punched the buttons on the readout by the wheel. The timer said 1753. 'Avoid the rush,' he said.

Ardnamurchan rose on the port bow. The log said nine knots. 'She'll do better than this when we free off,' said Charlie.

The Point of Ardnamurchan was opening down to port, the black swells turning to cream in the rocks. A puff of white smoke drifted from the forward guns of the grey frigate off the Point, followed by the dull, wind-flattened *whap* of the report.

'Gone,' said Charlie.

We bore off, to shave the point close. Scotto went up to the foredeck at his gorilla crouch, and pulled up the big asymmetric reaching kite. Dixon steered; he was a good helmsman in catamarans, and *Dolphin* had a lot in common with a cat. The numbers on the speedometer flicked up to ten and twelve, and the wake roared aft.

'Moves all right,' said Charlie laconically.

I nodded. I could not think about the way the boat was moving. There was a hard ball of tension in my stomach. All I could think about were the sails ahead, and Fiona in hospital.

Particularly Fiona.

I went below, unhooked the VHF mike, and got hold of Skye Radio. They put me through to the hospital. She was out of theatre, the doctor said, as well as could be expected. No, he could still give me no idea of her chances.

I disconnected, went up the companionway, stood with my head out, watching the sails ahead.

Charlie was watching me with his sunken eyes. He said, 'Who's that?'

'You met her,' I said. 'Fiona.'

'What happened?'

'Accident.' I did not want to talk about it. I wanted to catch up with those boats ahead, and beat them. And then I wanted to have a long conversation with the Managing Director of Mount Pleasure Forwarding and Monoco Shipping about accidents.

Charlie nodded, tweaked the spinnaker. I said, 'I'll do the Ben Nevis run. Everybody happy?'

Dixon grinned. He said, 'Delighted.'

I went over the chart with Charlie, propped at the table against the long lope of *Dolphin*'s progress. At this speed, we would have the ebb all the way down the Sound of Mull, and pick up the flood off Lismore Island. The flood would carry us all the way up Loch Linnhe to Fort William at the foot of Ben Nevis.

'Wind looks like it'll stay put,' said Charlie. 'Seven hours.'

'Eight,' I said.

He shrugged. 'It's your boat,' he said. 'Got anything to drink?'

I pulled down a bottle of Famous Grouse, dealt out the glasses. We all drank. Then I went below and lay on the bunk, resting, trying to ease the aches the ropes had left in my body this morning. After a while, I went to sleep.

Chapter Thirty-Four

I woke. Someone was shaking my shoulder. It was dark; through the porthole, I could see sodium glare streetlights. There was rain on the perspex.

'Coffee,' said Scotto's voice. 'We'll be anchoring in ten minutes.'

The coffee was full of sugar: it gave a hard, slow hammer to the pulse. I pulled on Lycra tights, shorts and a singlet, and a light, warm sweatshirt over the singlet. I stuffed more clothes into the pack, and food, high-carbohydrate sandwiches, orange juice and water, glucose tablets. I laced up the shoes carefully. They had a long way to go.

The anchor went down with a roar. I climbed on deck. There were other masts; four multihulls, and the faster of the monohulls. *Asteroid* was there, and *Bonefish*. We were two-thirds of the way up the fleet.

'Tender,' said Charlie.

I said, 'Ring the hospital in Inverness, would you?' I paused. 'And if there's good news, you can fly the ensign at the masthead.'

He nodded.

I went over the side into the inflatable. The race rules said no engines, so I rowed us to the stony beach, the exercise warming the blood. On the beach, a race steward waved a flashlight. 'Follow the marshals through the town,' he said, in a thick Aberdeen accent. 'Then pick your route. There's seven ahead of you, a marshal at the top. Good luck.'

I said, 'Thank you.' Then I went.

I took it easy at first, at a gentle trot, letting the muscles warm up, getting used to the balance of the pack. The ground rose gently as I passed among the rain-wet houses of Fort William and crossed the River Nevis. There was a faint greyness in the sky: two a.m., the first glimmer of dawn.

I passed three stewards. The fourth said, 'There's one maybe a minute ahead, and another ten minutes ahead of him.' I could feel my legs under me now, shoving me up the slope against gravity. I accelerated from a trot into a run. The path branched off left, slanting across the face of a steep slope. Ahead, indistinct in the darkness, was a small, dark figure.

I pounded after him, my feet kicking loose stones out of the path. I could hear his breathing before I got to him, a hard, heavy panting.

He grunted. His hair was cropped close against his head and he had a small moustache. I had never seen him before; he was moving forward at a dogged, military run. I went past him quickly, the effort speeding my heartbeat. Bloody idiot, he would be thinking: going to knacker himself before he gets to the top.

He was right, of course. But there was no way for him to know that getting to the top first was not the reason I was going so hard.

I ran on. The light grew steadily, and it started to rain. The track grew steeper. Above and to the left, crags of rock jutted through the covering of heather. To the right the glen fell away a thousand feet to the river. The big muscles at the front of my thighs were aching with the constant upward push. I ignored them, pounded on. There were drifts of fog, now; two thousand feet was cloud base. The track zigged, flattened. A sheet of water opened out on the left. Then it zagged, and began to climb again. I splashed across a burn. A couple of hundred feet above me, the hillside vanished into thick cotton wool.

It was a bleak, green, lonely place. The only sounds were the sigh of the wind, and the croak of a raven in the mist, and the pant of my breath.

I was running under the face of a cliff. Above, something made a slight sound. I looked up, caught a glimpse of a dark object, toppling. Then I was flat against the side of the cliff, and a mass of stone and boulders fell with a crunching roar into the path where I had been a moment before.

I watched it for perhaps a second. Then I ran on along the base of the cliff until it stopped being a cliff, and turned back and up, on to a steep slope of grass and heather and stones. There I paused, and peered up the slope, my heart hammering in a way that was only partly because I had run four miles uphill.

A ragged veil of mist hung across the green slope. Caught by the wind, it writhed, then shredded. The hill lay naked. Across its side, a small dark figure was moving at a trot. I saw the paler flash of the face as he looked down. Then he was running again.

I went after him.

I went up the hill flat out. It was steep enough to make it necessary to use hands as well as feet. I used them. The fog came down again. I kept going until I had passed a small outcrop I had noticed. After that I bore right, across patches of scree now, towards where I had seen him last.

Wind was blowing on my face. The fog shifted again. I saw him a hundred yards away, below me, heading for a doorstep of rock that jutted out of the slope. He was looking the wrong way. I fell on my face in the deep heather. When he turned to look back he did not see me, but went on, towards the rocks.

The fog came down again. I ran forward and down, flat out. The dark loom of the rock came out of the grey soup. A heather-root caught my foot, and I went down, hard, on the edge of the outcrop, where the ledge of the doorstep jutted from the slope. My hand groped in front of me, touched a loose stone. The fingers closed.

Wind sighed in the rocks. There was silence. I took a deep breath, held it.

More silence.

Silence with breathing; the harsh breathing of a fit man who has been running uphill in terror of his life. Of more than his life.

I let out my own breath, quietly. I said, 'This is it, Prosper.'

A voice in the fog said, 'Ah.' It came from in front of me, on the ledge, towards the outside of the step. It was a little breathless, but otherwise it sounded as casual as if he had just lost a game of tennis inside the high white wall of his father's garden in Martinique, blazing with bougainvillea, scented with frangipani; while at the top of the terraces, the big white house looked down from its many windows across the bananas and the pineapples, and the irruptions of rain forest. The big white house. Mont Plaisir.

'Mount Pleasure,' I said.

The wind blew. The fog drifted away. He was sitting on a boulder in his black running tights, his eyebrows comical arches in his forehead, his teeth a big white crescent in his café-au-lait face, emptiness at his back. My old friend Prosper.

I said, 'Why the hell did you do it?'

'They can suck you in,' he said. 'Those Italian names.'

'You were smuggling cocaine into the States with Mancini while they were filming *Charlie Running*,' I said. 'He introduced you to Enzo Smith. You started a company, sold it a couple of old ships from your father's business. They got the waste. You repainted the drums and shipped it, and provided the local knowledge. Why did you do it?'

He ran his big brown hands through his hair, shrugged, the languid Creole shrug that used to drive the masters wild at school. He said, 'I had a little problem with a casino that belonged to some guys, cousins of Kurt's. I owed them some money. They said, start a freight agency, buy a ship. David Lundgren wanted supplies for his quarry. He kind of fell in love with Kurt, liked to have him around, you know. It all looked fine. I gave him a good freight rate, no problem. The rest was extras.'

'Twenty thousand pounds a week,' I said. 'And when the drums started to pop, everything dead all the way up to Skye.'

'It was going to be temporary,' he said. 'A temporary dump. I would have found those containers, you know. Dredged them up. Prosper the hero. And somebody else would have got rid of them.'

I said, 'Bullshit.'

His smile widened. 'Well, maybe,' he said. 'You know how it is. You have a thought, you change your mind. Maybe I would have left it there.'

'You can't change your mind about Jimmy Sullivan,' I said. 'Or Ewan.'

'Jimmy was a staff error,' he said. 'Pauwels did that. It was stupid.' He looked like a man deploring an administrative mistake. I thought about the Sullivan children. A surge of anger nearly choked me. I said, quietly, 'And you put a bomb under Ewan's shed after the regatta.'

The smile faded a little. Doggedly, I plugged on. 'Also, you gave me a dunking in the fish cage. Trying to warn me off. And you bribed Lisbeth to say you had been with her all the time.'

He looked hurt, pursed his lips. 'Typical lawyer's remark,' he said. 'I didn't have to bribe her. I just played her a little Beethoven, and showed her my double berth. Harry, I am getting depressed with you. Frankly, you have been bloody awkward. But because you are my old mate, I have been nice to you. Everyone else said, kill that guy Frazer. But I said, I used to be at school with him. No can do.'

It was too late for appeals to the old school spirit. 'When you thought I was getting too close, you went to Davina's little friend Giulio, and you found out about Eric, his tame doper. And then you introduced Eric to Vi, because you knew what Vi would do, and you knew I'd go running. You are a dirty little bastard, Prosper.'

He was frowning. He said, 'I know what it is. You've lost your edge, like I said. It's that bloody Fiona woman. Pity.' He put his hand in his pocket, took it out again. I heard a sharp click. Suddenly his right hand had grown a six-inch blade. 'But she's dead, and she can't tell anyone what you told her.'

I said, 'She's not dead.'

His eyes narrowed a fraction. 'Bullshit.'

'Nope,' I said. 'When you come down off this mountain, you are going to think you have walked into an aeroplane propeller. She knows the lot. Like I said, that's it, Prosper.'

He smiled, his big Martiniquais smile, the one he had used when we were ten, having tea in the Red Lion in Salisbury, and he had just swiped the last three cakes off the plate. He said, 'Sorry, old mate. When Prosper shoots, Prosper hits.'

There was a big silence under the croak of the raven in the swirl of the fog. I moved back. But the hill was steep. Too steep to climb. And Prosper and I had spent a month on a beach in the Grenadines, learning a lot about knives. We were both good with a knife.

'Come on,' said Prosper. 'You're going flying.'

I shook my head.

He shrugged, reversed the knife in his hand. I saw his brown fingers on the blade, like a circus knife-thrower's. The muscles in his face stiffened, the way they had stiffened before he served a tennis ball when we had been at school, playing for ice creams, my friend Prosper and me.

And I dropped flat in the heather.

Something went over my head and clattered on to a boulder. Prosper stood there, empty-handed.

I was not empty-handed.

I had my anger. And I had the stone my hand had closed on when I had tripped over the heather-root. I threw it at him. It hit him in the face with a dull, nasty thump. His hands went to his face. I hit him on the hands, hard. The blow smacked him upright. He staggered backwards, tripped on a rock, went down, and rolled. He rolled to the edge of the big stone step, and slid. His hand came away from his face, because he needed the fingers to claw at the stone edge of the step.

There were no holds.

He looked up at me, slowly; eyebrows up, the clown's look. There was a big smile on his face. Old Prosper. His fingers were sliding, now. Prosper, my old, old friend, was sliding over the edge.

I turned my back on him.

There was a nasty noise; a soft scraping. Then he spoke. He said, 'Ah, come *on*, Harry.'

Then there was a big scrape, and a gasp.

When I turned round, he was not there any more.

The step was a hundred feet high. He was at the bottom, among a jumble of boulders, face down, not moving. The fog drifted in and covered him.

Beyond him, the clouds were clearing, and Loch Linnhe was a wide highway of water heading through a map of plain and mountain to the sea. I slithered down the slope, and walked like an old man down the glen to Fort William. I called the police, and told them about the body on the mountain. Then, reluctantly, I went down to the quay.

Green Dolphin rode proudly at her anchor in the blue loch. At her masthead, in defiance of flag etiquette, fluttered the Red Ensign. I unhitched the tender from the steps, climbed aboard, and rowed away from the land and on to the clean water.

Sam Llewellyn

Blood Knot

Bill Tyrrell, sometime war correspondent and captain of the elderly cutter *Vixen*, has made it across the North Sea in a gale with a crew of eight unruly teenagers on probation. Now heading from the Thames estuary to historic Chatham docks for the Tall Ships celebrations, little can go wrong. But in the darkness, *Vixen* collides with the wreck of a small dinghy and something snags the propeller…a body. It seems that Bill's past is about to catch up with him.

Master storyteller Sam Llewellyn gives an expert twist to the sea story in this dramatic tale of political intrigue and violent death.

Blood Orange

'It was pitch black as I stumbled upon deck. There were no lights astern, where Ardmore should have been… Now, the comforting yellow glow was over to port, very close, and it was not comforting any more, but frightening.'

The racing trimaran *Street Express* is anchored in a gale off the coast of southern Ireland. Jimmy Dixon, widower, single father and timber-yard owner, and his long-time friend Ed Boniface are championship sailors. Tragedy strikes when the third crew member is washed overboard in the storm – or is he? The adrenalin pumps from the first pages of this taut ocean-racing drama: Dixon is caught up in a tale of intrigue and high finance, with the beautiful Agnès at his side.

SAM LLEWELLYN

CLAWHAMMER

Poet, explorer and expert on a very particular kind of duck, George Devis, has been visiting his sister and her Country-and-Western singer boyfriend in Ethiopia, where they work on an aid project. As he leaves with their two sons to return to England, armed bandits attack the settlement and the couple suffer a gruesome death. Determined to discover the truth about what happened, he teams up with a Boston journalist on the trail of the perpetrators. First off, a gruelling transatlantic race to publicise the cause – during which their boat is fired on and the journalist dies. And so George finds himself enmeshed in a deadly international conspiracy.

A brilliant, moving espionage novel by the acknowledged king of the sea-borne thriller.

DEAD RECKONING

Charlie Agutter is the popular designer of revolutionary ocean-going yachts. But when his brother is killed sailing one of his gleaming boats, everyone suspects the design is at fault – but Charlie knows better and sniffs sabotage. With so much money hanging on the forthcoming Captain's Cup race, it looks like someone has it in for Charlie. He must act fast to win back his good name and livelihood – not to mention the race.

Sam Llewellyn

The Iron Hotel

Hired to captain the rusty old *Glory of Saipan*, full of illegal immigrants bound for California, Jenkins finds that unless he obeys the rules of this Iron Hotel – violence OK, sex with the cargo OK, but no falling in love – he will end up with a dead daughter. But he determines to make his own rules, and on the trip across the Pacific hatches an ingenious way out.

Maelstrom

Seventy-eight-year-old Ernie Johnson, experienced yachtsman, dyed-in-the-wool leftie and pacifist, sails toward Ireland aboard *The Worker's Paradise*. When Customs Inspectors board the boat, they find a huge cache of arms and whisk Ernie away to face the music. Once in prison, Johnson is visited by his nephew, Fred Hope, who has his own reputation as a wild man. What follows is a compulsive tale of international treachery, Russian Mafiosi, stolen art treasures and political ghosts from the past – set against the freezing backdrop of the Norwegian Sea in winter.

OTHER TITLES BY SAM LLEWELLYN AVAILABLE DIRECT
FROM HOUSE OF STRATUS

Quantity	£	$(US)	$(CAN)	€
BLOOD KNOT	6.99	11.50	15.99	11.50
BLOOD ORANGE	6.99	11.50	15.99	11.50
CLAWHAMMER	6.99	11.50	15.99	11.50
DEAD RECKONING	6.99	11.50	15.99	11.50
DEATH ROLL	6.99	11.50	15.99	11.50
THE IRON HOTEL	6.99	11.50	15.99	11.50
MAELSTROM	6.99	11.50	15.99	11.50
PEGLEG (CHILDREN'S TITLE)	4.99	8.00	10.50	8.00
RIPTIDE	6.99	11.50	15.99	11.50

ALL HOUSE OF STRATUS BOOKS ARE AVAILABLE FROM GOOD BOOKSHOPS
OR DIRECT FROM THE PUBLISHER:

Internet: **www.houseofstratus.com** including author interviews, reviews, features.

Email: **sales@houseofstratus.com** please quote author, title and credit card details.

Hotline: UK ONLY: **0800 169 1780**, please quote author, title and credit card details.
INTERNATIONAL: **+44 (0) 20 7494 6400**, please quote author, title, and credit card details.

Send to: **House of Stratus**
24c Old Burlington Street
London
W1X 1RL
UK

Please allow following carriage costs per ORDER
(For goods up to free carriage limits shown)

	£(Sterling)	$(US)	$(CAN)	€(Euros)
UK	1.95	3.20	4.29	3.00
Europe	2.95	4.99	6.49	5.00
North America	2.95	4.99	6.49	5.00
Rest of World	2.95	5.99	7.75	6.00
Free carriage for goods value over:	50	75	100	75

PLEASE SEND CHEQUE, POSTAL ORDER (STERLING ONLY), EUROCHEQUE, OR
INTERNATIONAL MONEY ORDER (PLEASE CIRCLE METHOD OF PAYMENT YOU WISH TO USE)
MAKE PAYABLE TO: STRATUS HOLDINGS plc

Order total including postage:_____Please tick currency you wish to use and add total amount of order:

☐ £ (Sterling)　　☐ $ (US)　　☐ $ (CAN)　　☐ € (EUROS)

VISA, MASTERCARD, SWITCH, AMEX, SOLO, JCB:

☐☐☐☐☐☐☐☐☐☐☐☐☐☐☐☐☐☐☐☐☐☐

Issue number (Switch only):

☐☐☐

Start Date:　　　　　　　　**Expiry Date:**

☐☐/☐☐　　　　　　　☐☐/☐☐

Signature: _____

NAME: _____

ADDRESS: _____

_____

POSTCODE: _____

Please allow 28 days for delivery.

Prices subject to change without notice.
Please tick box if you do not wish to receive any additional information. ☐

House of Stratus publishes many other titles in this genre; please
check our website (**www.houseofstratus.com**) for more details